Shadows of Glory

ALSO BY OWEN PARRY

Faded Coat of Blue

Shadows of Glory

Owen Parry

William Morrow
An Imprint of HarperCollins*Publishers*

HarperCollins books may be purchased for educational, business, or sales promotional use. For information please write: Special Markets Department, HarperCollins Publishers Inc., 10 East 53rd Street, New York, NY 10022.

FIRST EDITION

Designed by Adam W. Cohen

Printed on acid-free paper

Library of Congress Cataloging-in-Publication Data has been applied for.

ISBN 0-380-97643-9

00 01 02 03 04 QW 10 9 8 7 6 5 4 3 2 1

To Maisie,

Who endured many a battlefield

GLENDOWER:
I can call spirits from the vasty deep.

HOTSPUR:
Why, so can I, or so can any man;
But will they come when you do call for them?

—SHAKESPEARE, *Henry IV, Part I*

I SAW HER FIRST AT THE BURYING, BEHIND THE WICKED CROWD. With the mob of them cursing and shaking their fists in the snow, twas her I saw. Still as if frozen she was, and only her eyes betrayed the fire devouring her. Aglow like embers in a winter hearth, those eyes would burn us all, and haunt me when she was gone.

Fanned by the wind, a lock of hair flamed from her shawl, scorching across her forehead. I would tell you that her hair was red as blood, to give you the vividness of her, but such would be untruthful. I know the look of blood, see. Her own would spot the snow before my eyes. Her hair was a darker thing than blood, though not so dark as her story.

I should have felt the queerness there at once, from the way the rest of the Irish kept off her. Careful they were with the lovely, though otherwise a bad pack. The men slurred and jostled. Drunk under noon, some of them were, and ragged. Bleezed with spite, their women put me in mind of white-faced crows, hard and deprived. Even the little ones come hating to the holy doors that day. For the Irish fear an informer more than the devil, and death excites them always. I worried that the coffin would not pass the gauntlet they made outside the poor boards of their church. As the representative of our Federal authority, I should have made order my business. And I meant to. Then the look of Nellie Kildare drew me from my duty, and I leaned—one fateful moment—on my cane.

But I must not go too quickly. There was blame in this death, and a bitter portion of it was mine. Had I not lain abed with General McClellan's own typhoid upon me, I might have come north a month the sooner, as Mr. Nicolay and Mr. Seward first intended. Our agent might have lived. Better it would have been for the widow and the little one, not to speak of the poor, blundering fellow himself.

They had tormented him before they killed him. I saw the marks of their work when I come fresh from the train that morning, fair running from the station, with ice on the streets of the town, and my leg bad in the cold, and the weakness still upon me from the fever. The coroner's assistant held the coffin open for my arrival, then disappeared. The Irish priest kept the widow away from the box. Kind doing that was. I ran into the church all snow-pestered and unready for the shock of it. How long I stared at the dead man I cannot tell you now. Long enough, though, to singe my eyes. Twas small of me to gobble so much time, for the widow was keening away in a locked room. But such matters bind us, and we forget consideration. My hands curled into fists beside the corpse, and not only to fight the cold there in that church. There is cruelty, I thought. Savagery. I had not seen so grim a sight since India and the inferno of the Mutiny.

I am a poor beast, as all men are, and would not question the Good Lord's grand design. Still, I wonder at that which He allows.

When I finally stepped away, two paddies nailed the box shut. Muttering and careless, they made it clear enough that they wanted no part of the business. But the priest fell hard upon them and soon they were jumping about and jabbering their sorries. Their voices took me back. I knew those accents from my old red regiment, the gurgling of that unextinguished tongue, harsh as lye-water in the mouth. Each fellow smelled of whisky.

The priest brought in the widow then, holding her up on her feet with one big arm. His other black sleeve held her babe. The little thing was bawling as if it knew all.

Beneath a statue of the sort the Irish idolize, the woman found her strength. She plunged forward, young and worn in her tattered dress, black shawl flying about her. Flinging herself upon the raw pine, she nearly upset the bier. Splinters soon bloodied her hands for the beating she gave the boards. Her wailing echoed in the empty church, raising a swell of laughter beyond the doors.

"The hoor's upon 'im now," a woman cried, triumphant. Her voice pierced the walls. "Oh, bring ye out the traitor's hoor. We'll give 'er what she's a-coming."

To calm the widow, the priest forced her babe into her arms. The woman's raw hands bled on the infant's face and wrappings. They prayed then, in the different way they do, all Latin and sorrow. The priest had eyebrows that met in a black knot and his shoulders were those of a navvy. Not young, not old, there was a worn solidity to him. He might have done for an elder soldier, had he not been a soldier of his faith. His name was McCorkle and he was no more born to America than I was.

I prayed my own prayers. Off to the side, and quiet like. I will not be small and think the Good Lord tends only to us chapel folk. For all the pagan coloration, there is a faith in your Irish Catholic that must call down pity from above. They do the best they can with what they know, and I would not damn them out of hand. But then I have found good among the Hindoo and the Musselman.

I prayed first for the dead man, then for his shattered family. Careful I was not to face their painted statues, but looked to the windows and Heaven beyond. Next, I gave my thanks. First for my Mary Myfanwy and our little John, and then for the passing of the old year. I believe I was as glad to see the back end of 1861 as was Mr. Lincoln himself.

I will not forget that awful year. First the coming of the war and the separation from my family, then the savaging of our Northern pride and the ruination of my leg at Bull Run. After that I fell into the Fowler matter—the needless, bitter death of that young man—and next come the typhoid that would have been the end of me in an army pest house had my friend Dr. Tyrone not taken affairs in hand. He was gone to the western armies now, called to Cairo, Illinois, and I missed him and waited on a letter. I prayed for Mick Tyrone. Not just in that cold church, but nightly. He was one of those stubborn, educated Irishmen who will not ask God's favor for themselves. And I wished a blessing on dear Mrs. Schutzengel, my Washington landlady, all girth and goodness, and then on that no-good Molloy, who doubtless would have been eyeing the communion silver had he been by my side. Finally, I prayed for the mob grumping and growling beyond the shut doors of the church, for such was my duty as a Christian.

The priest lifted the woman and child away from the coffin. He started in to barking, all sour, "Come ye now. Come here, ye."

I thought he was admonishing the Lord.

Twas the pallbearers he was addressing. Bent things they were. The two who had labored with hammer and nail scuttled forward again, followed by a pair of their butties. Each wore the dirt of a lifetime polished into his face, and they had not a full set of teeth between them. I could not understand a word they said. But they did not want to shoulder the load. That was clear from the way they glanced toward the noise beyond the doors.

They hoped in vain for rescue, for the priest, Father McCorkle, was a very Caesar with them.

"Out now, and into the wagon," he said against the widow's sobs. "And none o' your capering nonsense."

The priest arranged the procession with himself in the lead and the widow trailing closely, with her infant swaddled against her. By rights, the bereaved should have followed the coffin, but the priest knew his doings. He was no slave to ritual, I will say that for Father McCorkle. So the box bobbed behind the mourning wife and the little one as we started down the nave, with the pallbearers cowering at the thought of the mob.

I brought up the rear at a respectful distance, wondering if I could not have raised myself from my convalescence sooner. Had this poor fellow died because I lolled out a sick man's leave, reveling in Christmas by my own hearth while he did our nation's duty? I was not yet recovered to my full strength, but strong enough I would have been to come by rail. I should have sensed the urgency. But Mr. Nicolay himself told me to gather my health first, and didn't I grasp the excuse of it like a bad child? How easy it is to fall from our duties. And the results are as bitter as Peter's denials. I had only reached New York City when the coded telegram from Mr. Seward overtook me, instructing me to make all possible haste.

I well recall that foggy night in Washington when Mr. Nicolay, who was Mr. Lincoln's confidential secretary, recruited me with the warning, "They killed the last man we sent up there." And now "they" had killed another on the back roads of New York. Yet, we knew not who "they" were, but for a rumored Irishness. Mr. Seward, the fierce blaze of brains who had become our secretary of state, feared insurrection. New York was his state and he knew the war was not popular with all the souls left to the Union, least of all with the Irish lately come among us.

Mr. Lincoln himself had taken an interest in the matter, for much had begun to fray. As if the Confederates were not enough, rumor had the English on the edge of war with us, for their sympathies lay with Richmond. Canada, domain of eskimaux and the mighty bear, sheltered our enemies. To top it, some young fool of a naval officer of ours had boarded one of the Queen's ships to seize a pair of Rebels. My adopted country needed every honest man to stand to. And selfish Abel Jones had let better men down, enjoying his fever.

The priest threw open the doors. The stove inside the church had gone unlit and the nave stood dreary chill. Still, I was unprepared for the blast of wind and snow that swept in. Twas cold as death's own hand.

A gray world waited beyond those doors. The snow rushed against a near, gray sky. The gray-wrapped mob wore gray faces. They had tramped the earth to a gray muck. It was a prosperous little town, this Penn Yan. You saw that even on a skip from the railway station. But you would not have sensed it from this worst of buryings.

I expected a great howling to greet the opened doors, like the delight of Mr. Gibbon's Romans at their spectacles. Instead, the crowd fell silent. The mob parted before the priest, just wide enough for an unhindered passage, and our little procession descended into the slush. The pallbearers went slowly, careful of the ice on the steps and fearful of their neighbors. They crouched beneath their load like beaten dwarves. I followed apart and last, for I wanted the local Irish to see me proper. I had hit upon a strategy in the church, if I may dignify a moment's inspiration with such a mighty term, and wanted every man to mark my presence. But let that bide.

One voice—twas a woman's, for they are ever the boldest—cried, "Look at the traitor's slut, would ye? Look at the informer's hoor and 'er bastard. Bury 'em with 'im, says I . . ."

That set them going again. Loud as the sounds of battle. The gauntlet tightened around us. More than a hundred of them there were. A bandaged fist shook in my face, and then I realized it was not bound in bandages, but in rags to keep off the cold. None of them dared touch us yet. But our safety was fragile.

Twas only the power of the priest that held them back. I saw that. He was their own even when he stood against them.

But I could feel the devil's hand descending.

There is wicked, see. At that moment of danger, did I think of the poor widow and the infant in her arms? Oh, no, not Abel Jones. I thought of the fine new uniform I wore under my greatcoat, the grand blue frock with the oak leaves and the handsome striped trousers my Mary Myfanwy had presented me for my Christmas, an incitement for me to finish my cure and rise from the bed. So proud she was. When I told her it was too grand a cut for the likes of me, she reared right up and said that John Wesley himself wore silver buckles on his shoes, and silk, too, and a bit of braid was becoming to an officer newly risen to his majority. Ever proud of her I was, and heathen proud of my new soldier suit—though I had meant to leave such doings behind. I knew how she had saved and sewn to outfit me. So, too, we fall from duty. Selfish man that I was, I thought not of the unfortunates before me, but of the risk to my precious new uniform.

That, too, would be torn in time.

I bullied myself round to my task again and straightened my back. I am not one of these tall fellows, but I do show strong in the chest and shoulders. I kept my cane tight to my bad leg to brace my stride. A major of United States Volunteers shall not be daunted by a pack of hooligan Irish.

"Give way, you," I ordered one great lout.

"Why, ye little Welsh cod," he answered hard. But give way he did.

The priest led on in silence. A buckboard wagon waited in the street in a canyon of snow, the horses smoking. A shabby carriage lined up just behind.

I thought we were safe. Twas then I saw her, that woman who would reach into our souls. Well to the rear she stood, beyond the want of the wind-scraped faces—narrow as lies—and the pair of worried police fellows, their slouch hats wreathed with snow. It was as if she had called my name. As if a cry of "Abel Jones!" slashed through the mob. When I turned, I found those eyes upon me. Under that flame of hair.

Look you. There is a quality in some folk, though not in many, that commands us to see more fully than is our custom in the to and fro. They grant us a peek at the richness of life, and tantalize us with possibilities. The girl, God bless and forgive her, might have been the only one of the hundred of us who was fully alive on that day of death.

And so alive she was! Framed in the dour propriety of her garments—they were not rags—her skin had the whiteness of porcelain. The snow on her shawl showed filthy by compare. She was white as clean milk, as good paper. But for the burning spots on her cheeks. Her features were clear and definite, with a handsome angularity that scorned common beauty. Slender and tall, she stood encased in dignity. The sight of her stopped me cold.

And a snowball smacked the back of my head.

My hat tumbled, and with it the mob's hesitation fell away. They surged around us, stinking of sweat and whisky and homemade salves. Now I am an old bayonet, may the Good Lord forgive the follies of my youth, and my cane soon cleared a space about me. But I was not the object of their wrath. Twas the coffin they were after, and the widow.

The wooden box went down, pursued by screams. The priest set about him with his fists, cursing like a heedless sergeant, and none dared strike him back. He pulled the woman and child against himself and they disappeared as the crowd surged in again, with the snow twisting and screwing to confuse us all.

"Oh, feed the turncoat bastard to the dogs," a voice shouted. "Burying's too good."

"Judas!" a harridan shrieked. *"Judas!"*

I heard a wrenching and breaking, and wordless howls of rage.

Then the world changed. The crowd's pitch dropped of a sudden. Their motion slowed, then froze. One voice hushed another as a hard sobriety fell upon them. Slowly, one by one, they began to move again. Backing off, shunning their purpose. I heard gasps, and slivers of devout language from the women. The aura of children caught out settled over the crowd.

They had gotten their way, for all the good it did them. The box lay broken open in the muck, and the corpse had spilled onto its back. They all got a gander at the devil's handiwork then. I do not think they saw his cast-off suit, or even the broken skew of the fingers. No, they all saw what I had seen at first look, and no matter the rumors they might have heard, the brute doings shocked the hardest of them.

The top of the man's head—scalp and flesh—had been burned away, the skull charred and the eyes cooked out. Only the bottom of his face remained human, streaked here and there with pitch roasted into the skin. He had died with a grimace of agony. The coroner had taken the rope off him, of course, but the neck was still pinched small and scarred deep where the noose had gripped. The thought of death by hanging has always held a special dread for me, but I hoped for this man's sake the hanging had come before the other business.

"Whiteboys . . ." someone whispered behind me.

The priest had not been quick enough. Before he could shut his hands over the widow's eyes, she saw what they had made of her husband.

Her scream will never leave me.

The priest clutched her and the babe against him. For just a moment, he shut his own eyes, as if gathering strength. Then he gave it to the lot of them.

"Damned ye'll be for this. Damned all. *Damned.*"

Even the hard men made crosses on their chests and lowered their eyes. The women began to blubber, then to wail, and the children cowered behind skirts.

There is foolish, you will say, when I tell you what I did. I looked for the pale young woman with the flame of hair down her forehead. The girl who stood apart.

She was gone.

Her spell broke with her absence, and I turned to duty. The pallbearers had scuttled off to their holes, so I summoned a voice from drill fields past and ordered a few of the Irish lads to help me gather the body back into the coffin.

They were not so much unwilling as afraid. They are a superstitious people, the Irish. I could not get a one of them to move.

The police fellows come up then. They had been but two against the mob and knew better than to go into it. And one of them looked Irish himself. But now they sensed that the danger had passed. We got the body back into its place, though not before I saw enough to haunt me. The corpse still smelled of burned pitch and, queerly, of spent powder. We set the lid on the box again.

Commanding a raisin of a woman to hold the infant, the priest let the widow collapse in the snow and weep while he helped us lug the coffin to the buckboard. He had a workman's hands.

Twas I who come back first to help the widow to her feet. With the guilt in me. Her wet eyes were as dead as her husband's body, and she smelled of milk and misery.

We headed for the boneyard, with the police fellows riding behind. The crowd dispersed into the falling snow. The priest would not look at me, or at any man.

I did what I could for the widow. But four years passed before the government could be persuaded to grant her a pension for her husband's services. By then the child was dead. That, too, was bitter to me. But it does not bear on the tale I have to tell, so let that bide.

• • •

"Hell of a fellow, Seward. *He's* the one should have been president," Sheriff Underwood told me. He laid aside the bill of fare with the strong hand of a farmer—he had risen from the fields— and gave a tug to one of his mighty ears. "Don't order the pork. It's kept over from New Year's. Lamb's fresh killed, though."

He waved to a waiter. The serving fellow was as fancied up as the price of a meal was high. The Benham House was a topper of a hotel, with a piano going in the saloon bar and no spit on the floors. Plush chairs and dark wood set the tone in the dining room. Now there were fine hotels enough in Washington, and I had not come north for my pleasure, but glad I was of the warmth and the softness of my seat. The cemetery had been a cold, bleak spot of earth and my ride on the buckboard merciless.

"Tommy . . . I'll have that lamb I heard bleating out back," the sheriff said. The long tails of his mustache willowed as he spoke. "And you tell 'em I want it cooked good and dead."

"Yes, sir. And the major?" The waiter looked down at me. Twas no surprise he could read a rank. The hotel lobby had been speckled with military men, competing recruiters all, bursting with promises and bounties. Well quartered in Penn Yan's finest establishment, they seemed to have no regard for the terrible expense and deserved to be brought up on charges. There are always those who will find luxury at the back of a war.

"I will take the stew, if you please," I told him. There was an awkwardness to my mouth, for I was still thawing.

"One lamb plate, and a bowl of stew. Thank you, gentlemen."

"*Stew?*" Sheriff Underwood said as the waiter retreated. The afternoon had mellowed to amber in the dining room, and the tables had lonelied. Many of the guests who had congratulated my host upon his new position were gone already. "*Stew* won't keep a fellow going. You've got to eat for the weather. Red meat, man. Red *meat!* That's the thing. Feed yourself up."

The sheriff had a prosperous physique. You would have taken him for a politician, rather than a law man.

"I like a good stew," I said. For such men will not hear of economies. "It is healthful and warming on such a day. Sheriff Underwood, may I—"

"Call me John. And I'll call you Abel. If I'm able . . ." He laughed and gave one of his remarkable ears another scratch.

"John . . ." I tried the sound of it. First names do not come so quickly to me, see. I must become a better American that way. I looked at the sheriff, who was an imposing fellow in his very prime. Big, that one. He wore a bright neckcloth, well knotted and trailing, a bottle-green jacket and waistcoat of plaid. All looked of good quality, though a bit roguish by chapel standards. I would have given him the advantage of the fist over a criminal, though not of the chase, for his person did give evidence of a fondness for the table.

Before I could put my question, the sheriff rose to shake hands with yet another well-wisher—for he had been sheriff only since New Year's Day. A brief conversation ensued between the two of them, so I will take this time to tell you of those ears.

Now, we are not to speak unkindly of another fellow's peculiarities of person. Nor would I appear basely excitable. But the man had the ears of an elephant. Bristling with hair like a boar. They did not protrude bumpkinlike, but lay flat and fair shielded the side of his head with their length. Twas as if someone had hung red cutlets on the man, such great devices they were. He looked to have ten years advantage of me in the wisdom of age, which placed him square in his forties, and thus time had accustomed him to his awesome companions. But I had a ferocious time keeping my eyes from them. Powerful ears they were, and appropriate, see. For a man of the law must hear things others cannot.

Sitting again, and pleased with the world's respect, the sheriff told me, "Have to get you up to the farm. Show Washington what a New York welcome means. You can keep all that Secesh hospitality. Won't be served by no slaves up here. Just the wife and the house-girl." Smacking the prosperity of his physique with the flat of his hand, he laughed. "Wife's a devil of a cook. And sometimes she's just a devil. Don't I know it? Won't go near the jail, let alone hear tell of moving into it. Won't leave that farm even to visit the place. Would be a comedown, of course. Though the county built a nice enough set-up." His big fingers combed the bristles sprouting from an ear. "Turned it over to my deputy and his wife. Free livings. And aren't they glad of it? But that one can't cook to save her life, that Sarah Meeks. Couldn't very well invite you back there and feed you spittle and grease. So here we are." He gestured at our handsome surroundings. "Hotel don't put on a bad spread. Though it can't compare with good home cooking."

Now I am fond of my victuals, though I will not have extravagance, but it always seems to me a distraction to conduct business over food. The business is only half attended to, and a fine meal but half appreciated. It is how the better sort will have things done, yet I would as soon have met him at his jail and spared the cost.

"Sheriff Underwood?"

" 'John.' Got to call me 'John,' Abel."

"Well . . . John . . . I would like to know the details of the finding of our man's body. I must have the facts, see."

The sheriff frumped his chin, pulled an ear, and nodded. "Well, we aren't going to hold anything back from Bill Seward's personal agent. No, sir. That's fact number one right there. You'll have my personal support." But he sighed. "Don't you think we should save the grisly side of things for a glass in the club room?"

"I have taken the Pledge, sir."

A spark of light, perhaps of laughter, lit his eyes. But he mastered his demeanor. "Well, then . . . I guess there's no purpose in waiting, after all. Is there?" He deviled his ear again. "Look here, Abel. I want to get this business straightened out as badly as you do. Worse, I expect. I'm the sheriff, for crying in a bucket. Can't have folks running around like the old Iroquois, scalping and burning and hanging Federal men. Now can I?"

He slumped back, as though the cares of office had already overtaken him. "Bill Remer, now. Used to be sheriff. Gone off to Albany and bigger things. Worst doings he had to face up to was that serving girl drowned her little one in the outhouse last summer. Then that first fellow of yours got himself killed back in November. But Bill Remer knew how to bide his time. Don't I know it? Just packed up and handed it all on to me. He's off to the legislature, and it's all on my head now. And here I've got

Bill Seward sending his own special agent up to reckon with me, in case I can't tell a bull from a milk cow. What kind of sheriff is that going to make me look like in front of my voters?"

I almost told him that I was Mr. Lincoln's agent, not Mr. Seward's, but that would have been a needless display of pride. And, frankly, Mr. Seward seemed to have more play with the man.

"I have not been sent to chastise or bother," I declared. "I am prepared to work together, see, and would steal no man's credit."

He shook his head slowly. "If only old Thurlow wasn't off gallivanting in Europe . . ." Then he braced himself up. Stroking back hair and ear with a big hand, he said, "All right, Jones. I mean, Abel. Here's what I know. And I regret to say it isn't all that damned much . . ."

A farmer had found our fellow hanging from a tree beside the high road east of the lake. Our man, Reilly, had been recruited from among the local Irish by my predecessor—before his own death—and had not been a felicitous choice. Young Reilly had the curse of the drink upon him and talked grandly in his cups. His boasting of secret entrustments brought him low. His widow said they took him in the night, the masked and silent men who did the deed. She had gone to the priest, not the sheriff, and by the time Father McCorkle went to the authorities with his lean report, Gerald Reilly's head had been crowned with hot pitch, sprinkled with gunpowder, then set alight. They left him hanging in the winter winds.

"But . . ." I said, ". . . surely they hanged him first? Before this burning business?"

Sheriff Underwood looked at me with calculating eyes. Gray they were, like the weather. He petted the ends of his mustache where they hung below his chin. Then he reached for an ear. But this time he stopped himself and lowered his hand again.

"I couldn't say that. And, frankly, I didn't think to ask Alanson. That's the coroner. Alanson Potter. Related through the wife, by the way. Farm's the old Potter place. Grand old family, the Potters. They—" He caught himself drifting and shook his head. "Should have asked, I'll admit. But I didn't. Anyway, Potter's set off to the war himself. Go myself, if I was a younger man. Right thing to do. Essential, if a fellow expects to have a political career afterward. Of course, a sheriff does his part, too. Anyway, Potter's assistant might know something. We can ask him. Strikes me, though, that it probably went the other way around. With the burning business first. Somebody wanted to lay out a lesson. About the price a fellow has to pay for turning on his kind."

"But that's a torment like—"

"Like something out of a damned book of martyrs." The sheriff wrestled himself into a more comfortable position in his chair. "Don't I know it? Hardly the sort of thing the voters are going to tolerate in a law-abiding, progressive place like Yates County."

"At the church this morning—"

He snorted. A last patron, leaving, gave him a look.

"Know what had that crowd all riled?" the sheriff asked.

"Reilly had become known as an informer," I said. "He was prepared to compromise this matter of an Irish insurrection and—"

"No such thing!" Underwood said. He slapped down a big hand and the table settings jumped. "No such thing, friend. Insurrection, my backside. Couldn't get those micks out of the saloons long enough to stagger down for a hand-out of free hams. Know what had 'em riled? Somebody spread the word that Gerry Reilly's job was to put together a list of all able-bodied Irishmen in the county. So they could be rounded up for military service. And they're terrified of it. Don't I know it? Frightened as all get out that Old Abe's going to force them into a blue coat and put a gun in their paws and make 'em fight to free the Negro. That's what had 'em going this morning, Abel."

I sat back. For I had believed I had seen the stirrings of rebellion. When all I had seen was fear.

"But these . . . rumors of insurrection?"

The sheriff held up a hand to silence me. An instant later, the waiter appeared at my shoulder. My stew shone thick, and smelled handsomely of beef and pepper.

"You just wait right there, Tommy," the sheriff told the waiter after the lamb had been laid before him. My host then took up knife and fork and cut deeply into his meat. Twas done to a cinder, and a shame that, for the chop might have made a fine piece of eating. "Now that's what I like to see," the sheriff said happily. "A fellow who listens to what he's told." He nodded his dismissal to the waiter.

When the man had gone, Underwood leaned toward me. He had spent much of his life out of doors and the history of it was written on his skin. He brought his face so close I could read the veins in his eyes, and the trails of his neckcloth flirted with the gravy on his plate. I could not fathom this gesture of secrecy, for we were now the only diners left in the room. I had been long at the burying and our meal had been much delayed.

"Well, I've looked into it," the sheriff said. "All this Irish insurrection business. Don't know how the hell the rumor got started in the first place. Not a thing Bill Remer could find, or that I can find. Nor any of the men—deputies, constables or police. Not that the local police are worth much. They're taking on Irish fellows themselves. But goings-on? I'd hear about it, if anything was happening out in the hills. Farmers know me. I'm one of 'em, for crying in a bucket. They aren't going to hold anything back for the sake of the Irish—or anybody else. They don't want trouble coming around to spoil things. War's trouble enough, with so many of the boys gone. Ploughing and planting's going to go hard this year. And the drummers now. They hear things, if there's anything to hear. And they know to pass it on when they do. Likewise, your parsons and such. Even the mechanics and teamsters. The canal people. They all know enough to pass any word of trouble along to the sheriff, whether he's a new sheriff or old."

Elbow on the table, he made a great fist. Twas a sign of confidence, not anger. "I *know* what goes on in this county, Abel. And I haven't heard one squeak about an insurrection that hasn't come directly from Washington." He took time out for a chew and a swallow. "I'll take you down to the Irish boozers later. Down the way on lower Main. Then we'll go over to Jackson Street. Used to be all free Negroes back there. Now the Irish are crowding 'em out, and it's a change for the worse. Let you have yourself a look. And you can tell me if those sorry lumps of rags look ready to break out in armed revolt. Hell, they're just worrying about getting their next bowl of porridge—or their next drink—and staying out of the county jail." Speech done, he applied himself to his plate with masculine vigor.

I had been content to listen and eat my stew, for I would have it hot and healthful. Oh, I love to thrust a spoon into the hot, brown joy of a stew and to raise up the treasures the cook has concealed in its depths. But twas my turn to speak.

"Who, then, killed Reilly?"

The sheriff dropped his fork on the plate. It made a great clanking and spatter. "Criminals. Murderers." He grunted. "Don't you worry. I'll find 'em. You can be sure of that."

We both went at our eating for a bit, and lovely my stew was, though pricey and not to the standards of Mrs. Schutzengel, to say nothing of my Mary Myfanwy, or the wife of Hughes the Trains, or other famous cooks of my experience. Although I am told it is considered improper by some, I took a swipe of bread to the gravy leavings in my bowl, for waste is a sin. The sheriff did not seem to mind my habits, and I must tell you the fellow had failings of his own. All in all, I found these New York country folk a practical sort, and much to my liking. But let that bide.

"Have you ever," I asked, in my warmth and satisfaction, "heard anything of 'whiteboys'?"

I could see by his face he had not. He raised a lamb bone to his mouth, but paused long enough to say, "Never heard of such a thing."

Neither had I. Perhaps, I thought, I had misheard the voice in the mob. I let it go. For now I had a delicate subject to raise. But I would have an answer, for the truth of it is that I was cross. It had seemed to me a great oversight that only two timid police fellows had been present at the church that morning. And now that I realized Underwood had possessed reasons to fear trouble—based upon those rumors of draft lists and the hatred thus engendered—I was disturbed that he had not stood before the church himself, with the full weight of badge and law.

"I was surprised, John," I said, "that only two law officers were at St. Michael's this morning. There was a fuss."

He wiped his mouth, then his fingers, with his table linen. Rather than showing anger or resentment at my observation, he gave me a little smile of the sort gentlemen exchange in private.

"And you're sitting there wondering . . . if I know so damned much about what's going on . . . why the hell wasn't I out there with the militia called up and standing in ranks?" He nodded at the thought, amused, and squeezed the vast lobe of an ear. "Abel, my friend . . . did you and Bill Seward have a sit-down before he sent you up here? You two have a good talk?" He held out a leather case. "Cigar?"

"I do not take tobacco, sir."

He nodded. As if he had expected as much. "Mind if I have a smoke?"

Twas his business. I gave my head a little shake and said:

"Mr. Seward did honor me with an interview."

"He tell you anything about Yates County?" The sheriff applied a match to his filthy roll of weeds. Soon he was issuing smoke like the Lower Depths, filling the room with a noxious, wicked, unChristian stink. Twas vulgar and foul, and doubtless pleasing to Satan. But we must not judge the vices of others too severely, and I will say no more of it.

"We concentrated upon the matter of insurrection," I said.

"Oh, insurrection, my backside. I don't think Bill Seward knows a damned thing about insurrection. At least not up here in Yates County. Maybe down South there. And I'll tell you honestly—I'm not going to pretend I have all that close an acquaintance with our distinguished secretary of state. But I've met him a few times, one political fellow to another, little fish to a bigger one. I know old Thurlow Weed a sight better. He's the money man, he's got the reins. But I do know this much, Abel. Bill Seward knows how every county in this state operates. Every last one. Best governor we ever had, and a politician to talk the drawers off a vestal virgin. He could have told you that Yates is a fine county. Most folks up here walk straight ahead and work hard." His eyes shifted behind a veil of smoke. "But there's this other thing. I'd explain it to you . . . if I could explain it to myself."

He looked past me now, and took a fortifying draught of his tobacco. "These hills . . . they're kind of a place people run to. Oh, I don't mean criminals. No, sir. We keep a rein on that. But other sorts. Most of 'em just religious folks who didn't get along back home and don't want bothering. But some of 'em are full-moon crazy on a sunny afternoon." He stroked his ear gently, coaxing out thoughts. I feared the nub of cigar between his fingers would set his hair alight. "There's just something up there in those hills that don't make sense to the rest of us. Maybe it's that magnetism folks are always going on about. But we draw all kinds. Prophets—or so they call themselves. Queer sects and the like. Why, we even had two spiritualist conventions right here in Penn Yan! Don't that make you wonder?" He touched the ends of his mustache with thumb and forefinger. As if connecting the current in a scientific experiment. "Sometimes . . . I wonder if there isn't just some kind of madness up there above the lake. Something in the water or the wind. Ever hear of the Publick Universal Friend?"

"I have not."

"You will. Before you leave. She started it all. Old Jemima Wilkinson. Going to build the New Jerusalem in the wilderness. That was on to seventy years ago. Now we've got everything from shouting Methodists to these Elsasser Lutherans up my way in Potter—good folks, mind you, but they don't speak a word of English. I'm not sure they even know they're living in the nineteenth century. Hard to give a stump speech to folks who don't speak English, don't I know it?" For just a moment, he fell into the pit of electoral memories.

After clearing his throat of a cough, he called the glow back to the tip of his cigar. "Point is, things are changing. Progress, Abel. Has folks confused, cranky. Don't know what to make of all the newfangled goings-on. Can't reconcile themselves to the old ways going. So they start dreaming of some Garden of Eden that never was—at least not up this way. Desperate for something to turn to. And this war now. It draws things out in people. Not all of 'em good things. Most folks are for it, more or less. Yates is a solid Republican county, and Whig before that. But not all folks see things right. Not by a long ways. And people up here always had strong opinions, right or wrong. Your Presbyterians over in Branchport, for instance. Presby*ter*ians, mind you. Tighter with a penny than most men are with a twenty dollar gold piece. Few years back they went taking up collections to send Sharps rifles out to John Brown and those fellows in Kansas. And send 'em they did. 'Free men, free soil, and free the slaves.' Underground railway stations all over the county, both sides of the lake. But down county, toward Dundee, now that's a whole different story. Pennsylvania folk settled down that way. My own people were Rhode Islanders, so they were right-thinking. But those Pennsy fellows, they'd catch 'em a nigger running through and ship the poor bugger right back south for the reward money. Trussed like a hog." He paused to give me the fullness of the image while he enjoyed the last of his smoke.

"So," he resumed, "we've got wild-haired abolitionists, other folks who don't want anything to do with freeing any slaves, caterwauling Bible-whackers, mystic fellows and mesmerists, and now these Irish on top of everything." He gave me an intense look. "You realize more than one in ten residents of this town is Irish nowadays? And near every one of 'em turned up within the last fifteen years."

Yes. The Famine. My friend, Dr. Tyrone, had stories to tell. The blight on its praties had sent the Irish nation wandering. My regiment in India had teemed with the children of Erin.

The sheriff pushed his plate away, as if the sight of it suddenly offended him. "Now why am I telling you all this? What do you think? Well, first, you tell me something, Abel. How long have you been in this country yourself? And I mean no offense."

"I am four years an American."

"No offense intended now. The Welsh work hard, don't I know it, and they're always welcome. But what I want to get across is just this: The country—*our* country—runs on elections. No kings or queens, no dukes of this or that. Votes and voters, that's what we're all about. One man's right to choose, and another man's right to get himself elected. Now you just look at the scrambled-up mess of folks we have here in Yates County. And tell me a sheriff—or anybody else who stands for public office—doesn't have to think about how he plants his boots."

"And you believe Mr. Seward should have told me these things?"

"Hell, no. Not all of 'em, anyway. Don't expect he's got time for that. With this Mason and Slidell business and what not. But he should have told you about our Irish."

"What about the Irish? Specifically."

The waiter came to clear away our plates. The sheriff held back his words until we sat alone again.

"Well, think about it. More than one potential voter in ten here in Penn Yan's an Irishman. That's a lot of votes. And, of course, they're contrary, your Irish. Democrats to a man. And plenty of people—I'm speaking of the people who count now—they figure we can just ignore the boggies. But *I* say we have to think of the future. We have to do what's right for this country. And this country's changing. Why, we even have Italians on the county rolls. No, I say we can bring the Irish over to Mr. Lincoln. If we give 'em a fair shake. And turn the screws just enough, when we have to. But there's no need to antagonize 'em by sending the law down to their church. If you see what I mean." He sat back again. "The Irish just like to make a noise. Then it blows over. What harm was done this morning?"

I thought of the widow and child, and the coffin broken open.

"You'll see," Sheriff Underwood went on. "The Irish are all talk and temper. But there's no substance to 'em. They couldn't organize an insurrection to save their souls—and, anyway, what do they have to rebel against? They have it good. All that business about dark-of-the-night plots—that's nothing but spooks and haunts somebody in Albany dreamed up to put a scare into Bill Seward."

He lowered his voice and leaned toward me again. "But I will tell you this. We have two Federal men dead now. Or one Federal man, plus a half-breed, you might say. And, frankly, I lay it to nothing but outsider meddling. Leave the Irish alone, and they'll make no trouble that matters. They'll just beat the daylights out of one another, or take a strap to their wives and children. But poke a stick at 'em, and you'll find yourself in a nest of rattlesnakes."

Gray eyes hard upon me, he said, "Now you tell me something. How the hell do you expect to run a secret operation when the first thing you do when you get off the train is march over to Father McCorkle's den of thieves and let the whole world know what you're after?"

"I don't intend to run a secret operation," I said. "I want the killers to know who I am."

He looked at me in wonder. As if he could not decide whether any man could be the fool I seemed.

"Well . . ." he said, ". . . if you didn't come up to my county to run a secret operation and look for some fairy-story insurrection, what *did* you come for, Abel?"

"For the killers," I told him. "For when we have them, we'll have the truth of the rest of it."

He snorted and scratched a great ear. "Oh, and I suppose you expect the killers to just walk up to you and give themselves away?"

"Yes," I told him, "there is the trick of it. I know the Irish, see." The fellow had finished his cigar, so I saw no fault in giving him a stir. "And now I would like to see where they hanged poor Reilly."

Chapter 2

I HAD MISJUDGED THE SHERIFF. Set against the extravagance of the hotel, I feared the fellow had become a devotee of fine living and but a political creature—for I will tell you, though it shock, that the moral ingredients of political men are not always what they should be. But Underwood proved solid. He was as tough as the hills and glens that spawned him, and he proved it soon enough.

But I must not go too quickly.

The sheriff ordered a sleigh from the livery stable behind the hotel, and didn't they jump to it? Waiting on the rig, we stood in the horse spew and trodden snow of an alley. The passage brisked with boys on commercial errands and men shortening the distance to their destinations. Every one of them tipped his hat respectfully to the sheriff, casting a curious glance at me. Underwood greeted each citizen by name.

Now I must tell you a thing: I do not love the horse. It is a beast infernal as the juggernaut, and my discomfort with the four-legged leviathan was compounded by the memory of the great fire in those Washington stables that climaxed the Fowler affair. Twas a nightmare, nothing less. I see and hear the burning creatures still. Their agony will haunt me to the grave. Oh, I would not slight the work done by the horse—I understand we could not do without him—and the Good Lord did see fit to breathe life into the beast, after all. But how I dread the aspect of the creature! I would sooner box a Bengal tiger than sit upon the back of such a brute. And yet such worries must not be revealed, lest others think us weak. It is a sadness of our human kind that we will sooner mock another's fears than like his virtues.

I propped up manly on my cane, trying to ignore the slattering of hooves in the icy yard. I wished the sleigh well ready, and not only to confine said horse safely in harness. Twas blade cold in that alley, for all the steam of the droppings. The snow had stopped, but a freeze glassed the air. Greatcoat or no, I wanted myself under the travelling blanket.

"Fine town," Sheriff Underwood cried out, his breath a gush of steam. "Growing by leaps and bounds. Industry's the thing, Abel. Mills going up all along the outlet canal, and six trains through a day, two of 'em freights. It's a boom, that's what it is. *Good* afternoon, Donald, 'afternoon, George. Missus feeling better? And agriculture growing to beat the band. Orchards, timber. Sheepers up Italy Hill. Just got to keep folks patient and sensible, and no tomfoolery. 'Lo there, Jimmy. You tell your pa I said hello. So when they found your . . . predecessor . . . face down in the lake, and then that Reilly . . ."

He stood unbothered in that chapping cold, wearing naught but a light cape, hands bare of gloves and ears scarlet. Twas all I could do to keep from hopping about, for the winter come right up through my boots, despite the good greasing I had given them. But Underwood was a walrus at his polar revels.

"*Fine* town," he recited, louder than required for the ears of Abel Jones, "*fine* county. Plenty of future up here. *Plenty*. Future to spare, bushel and a peck of it." He turned his head of a sudden. "Bucky, what's keeping that damned sleigh?"

At that, a sleek, black cutter left the barn, led on by a Negro. Rigged for two horses it was, not the customary one.

I was not pleased. A cutter is an open rig. And I saw no blankets. Only a shovel tucked beneath the cushion fall, as if for arctic snows.

"About time," the sheriff said, catching the reins. "Let's go, Abel," he told me, "if you want to get there before dark."

I clambered up beside him, wary of the beast harnessed to my side of the cutter. The sheriff took up more than half the seat, but I am not excessive in size, so it mattered not. He snapped the whip in the air, and I half expected chips of ice to fall from the heavens. The horses pulled away as though they longed to run.

"Bucky knows better than to set me a weak team," the sheriff said. "And he knows I won't have bells." He steered the sleigh into a street ripe with business, then quickly turned us into an even more vivid thoroughfare.

"Main Street," he said.

A farmer's wagon crowded in between the snow banks, forcing us a-tilt to keep from worse. The sheriff let a curse I cannot set to paper, for profanity numbs the good as surely as cold numbs the flesh.

"Over there now," he said, settled again, with the horses stepping as if they, too, were proud of their environs, "you'll want to remember that shop there. Hamlin and Sons. Fellow trying to make a go of one of your 'temperance' stores. Won't sell alcohol nor tobacco. I predict bankruptcy."

We slid by handsome fronts with painted names: RAPLEE'S BANK; the FRANKLIN HOUSE HOTEL, of which I had heard critical report; GEORGE R. CORNWELL, BOOKSELLER AND STATIONER; ROBERTS AND CO., FANCY DRY GOODS. The snow-lined street harbored apothecaries, photographers and harness-dealers, dispatchers and brokers and readers in the law, barbers, a watchmaker and, up a flight of stairs, a school of music. The windows of an emporium of gaieties had been soaped with announcements of price reductions to greet the new year, and pink-cheeked women rushed in with their baskets. A little world of its own, this Penn Yan was.

Then we come to Egypt.

Saloons and glooming whisky bins clustered by the bridge.

Deviltry and shame, a curse upon the land. Forlorn figures hunched inside the doorwells.

The sheriff pointed his whip. "Those shabs there? Mick boozers. Stick your head in any one of 'em and you'll see familiar faces, that's a fact. Dirty as the glass they pour your poison in. I guarantee you half the crowd that was out howling at St. Mike's this morning are in there now. Glorying over their grand heroics and singing tearful laments about heroes and traitors and dying colleens. With their women home watering the last of the porridge and their brats dying like it's a cholera year."

A no-good in a hat with a chopped brim and a burlap scarf gave us the "go on, you" eyes. Fair daring the sheriff to stop. Underwood ignored the bravado, for he, too, understood the pride of broken men.

"On the other hand," he said, "you might not want to step in there just now. They do hold a grudge, your Irish." He laughed, get-upping the reins.

We skittered over a bridge dressed with ice and the sheriff insisted I look around. "Branch canal. Connects the lakes. You can go right up to the Erie Canal, all the way to Rochester, Buffalo—even New York City, way of the Hudson. Right from this spot. Miracle of modern engineering." He tugged an ear. "Oh, our canal may not be the biggest in the state. But we've got twelve dams and locks, with a three-hundred-foot fall. Every last lock built of solid stone. Puts the other canals to shame, if you're talking quality."

The white bed of the canal lay frozen over. A throng of boys skated, and joy they had of the day, although we might have wished them at their lessons.

"You wait," the sheriff told me. "Come March, she'll be going again. Soon as the ice breaks. 'Transporting our fair harvest to the sea,' as Staf Cleveland likes to say. Or to Albany, anyway."

"Deep, is it?" I asked, feigning an interest.

"Naw. Four foot most of the way. Got to deepen it. Hoping to. Everything has to be bigger and bigger nowadays. Bigger boats, heavier loads. Only way to make a venture pay is to think big. 'Course, it's going to take money. And Albany seems inclined to back the railroads nowadays. Then there's this war, top of everything else. Maybe you could put a word in Bill Seward's ear for us?"

He glanced at me, then did not press the matter. The horses trailed steam from their nostrils. Two gleeful boys ran after us.

"But your locks now," the sheriff continued. "That's a different story. They're deep enough. Gush like Niagara Falls when they're running. Power your mills, the way they set 'em in. That's where you get your drownings. In the locks. Fool kids. Terrible accidents. Have to take you out and show you the mills, though. Dozens of 'em. All the way down to Dresden. Grist and flour. Plaster. Flax. Two spoke factories and a wool carding manufactory. Industries of tomorrow. Oh, the future's going to be something up here, Abel."

"I do hear the railroads are hard on the canals," I offered. I had a personal interest there. "In Pennsylvania, where my wife and I—"

"Railroad's a fine thing, too! Nothing against 'em. All for 'em. We've got business enough for both up here in Yates."

We slid past the proofs of prosperity, from lesser houses set near the mills to fine gabled dwellings that climbed a slope. Turning right, we followed a main-travelled road.

"Lake's just over there," Underwood told me, pointing the whip across my chest. "Can't see it now with the weather. But you could throw a stone and hit it. If there's a lake more beautiful than Keuka on this continent, you'll have to show it to me."

I saw only gray, and a fall-off in the quality of the houses again, then open lots, and the lonesome look of gardens left till spring.

The road forked and we veered left up a hill. The sheriff touched the lead horse with the whip, just enough to keep him to his pace, and the sleigh rose into a crystaled fog. Black and shut, a farmhouse flanked the road. Twas a dark place of a sudden.

And cold. Now, I am not indulgent in my comforts, though I welcome a warm bed and ready meals. Nor am I unfamiliar with the winter, for the hills of Wales that bred me do not coddle. Yet this was cold to freeze forgotten parts. No Indus heat or sun of Punjab here. It was a very Russia of a place, if what I hear of Russia is half true. I sought to keep my shivering to myself, and sank into my greatcoat. For the truth is the typhoid had left me weakened.

I envied the sheriff's red hands, happy on the reins. My world felt hopeless drear.

There was melancholy, and I succumbed to it. Longing for wife and child and warmth I was, and wishing away my charge as a shirker will. What man would seem heroic, or virtuous, if we knew his private thoughts?

Sudden as a child's fear, a black form loomed before us. We had heard no sound. Yet there he was. Gathered like a ghost from shrouds of fog.

A horseman, coming on at a canter.

Perhaps I was too given to my dreaming, but the surprise of him made my heart jump. He pranced up beside us, great cape snapping out. His horse, if I may judge, was not so fine as his clothing wished itself. I saw a bearded smear of face set deep, shadowed by a broad hat of the sort artistics wear. His eyes were icy as the day itself.

Yet he was mortal, and seemed no menace, after all.

"A bracing afternoon, Sheriff," the rider called out.

I have an ear, see. It comes out of the Welshman's love of song. I can place a man by the music of his talk. And I picked out the rider as one of those Irishmen who strain to speak like an English gentleman. Worst of both worlds, you might say, if you were in a hard mood. He summed a lifetime's longing in four words.

The sheriff muttered half a greeting, and the lead horse gave his tail a be-gone flick. The rider faded toward the town and the hooves of our team crunched in steady rhythm. The horseman might as well have been a ghost.

"Fellow just went past?" Underwood said abruptly. "Calls himself 'the Great Kildare.' " He grunted. " 'Great Bamboozler' would be more like it. Professor of a dozen kinds of nonsense. So he claims. 'Science of Mesmerism, Egyptology, and Spiritualist Phenomena.' Figure that out."

He applied the whip to keep the team from slackening and scratched a crimson ear. Frost had formed on his mustache ends. "Took a rent on the Kyle place. Down toward the Steuben County line. Might as well be on the moon, it's so far to the back of nowhere. Worthless soil. All high and barren. But who knows what a fellow like that has in his head? Not here to plant corn, don't I know it? So we keep an eye on him. Though there's no warrant out on him in New York State. Bill Remer did tell me that much." He shifted and possessed a bit more of the seat. "I warned you about those damned-fool types that drift up here. All spooks and hobgoblins. And damn me if honest folk don't take 'em serious. Must be something in the air."

The only thing I felt in the air was cold.

And then grace struck. The road crested, and the fog and cloud fell behind us at the turn of a wheel. Twas as if we had pierced a wall.

There was beauty.

Now I have seen the Kush of the Hindoo, in all its brazen magnificence, and am no stranger to the ravishing Khyber. Not least have I seen the sweet valleys of Wales in the spring. But this . . . this was glory!

The horses welcomed the relief at the end of their climb, and we rushed between broad fields chaste with snow. A red sun fell. Stripped trees shone ruddy, glowing. The snow crimsoned between the shadows cast by black pines, and bracken lit gold.

Yet this was but a meager preparation.

Waves of ridges stretched westward, as far as Heaven, arrayed in lilac snow and dusky rose. The crests scorched scarlet, as if with winter burning. Words are too weak for such beauty! We might as well attempt to write of love.

As I watched, the sky formed into ribbons. Lavender bordered the purple of wine, and watery orange met lemon. Who could count the endless shades of red? I would tell you Heaven blazed like a heathen market in that hour, but all comparison is false. For the great bazaars are harsh, and hot, and sharp with calculation, but the Lord composes gently in His grandeur, and His generosity is endless. He fires the lily, and softens the flame.

In between the highlands, valleys dropped. Deep. Blue and purple declined to moody gray. Those gorges seemed all mystery to me. Oh, how I felt the yearning of that landscape!

Far below the high road that we followed, a crooked lake shone smooth with mending snow. Yet there, toward the center, yet unfrozen, a steely wet warned. Houses, tiny against majesty, smoked in the hollows. On a bluff, a lone horse stood, rimmed by the bloody sun.

I full forgot our purpose and the cold.

Now you will laugh and say, "This Abel Jones is a queer one, given to romantical blubbering like some poet fellow." And I will grant my fondness for the beautiful, and let you think it makes me less a man, if so you are determined. But when the Good Lord sends us such a prospect, you will not find ingratitude in me.

Oh, wonder of ravens atop a fence, feathers oiled against the flaming snow. Broken stalks stood gilded in the bracken, tangled as our lives. In a farmhouse window by the road, the first lamp of the day shone.

"There is beauty," I said, helplessly.

"What say?"

I blushed, for I had never meant to speak.

"A fine view, that," I told the sheriff. "You spoke well of your county. There is true."

He made a sound deep in his throat. "Got to get you out to see the mills, man. Industry's the thing."

So we rode, with the afternoon dying around us. We traveled some miles, though a shivering man cannot measure finely. Now I am hardy, as a rule, and a good healer. I showed the ones who said I'd lose my leg. But even the glory of all nature could not sustain me. I will not give excuses like a child, but the typhoid had blown me good, and I was not yet my old self. Cold it was, yet sweat come to my skin.

The landscape changed, although I could not say clearly when or where. Gone lonely, almost desolate, there was a wrongness about it now. Despite the blanket of snow, I sensed the poorness of the soil. The trees not cut for timber had a stunted look, and cattail fringes marked the moors and barrens. Twas the sort of place where the last-come farmer must work twice as hard for half the harvest. But beautiful still, I give the country that, though it lay a world removed from the prosperous town behind us.

"Should've told Bucky how long we'd be out," the sheriff said. "Could've mounted us a pair of lanterns. Won't be much moon."

"Is it far, then?" I asked. The muscles of my face were fair frozen, yet my back was slimed with sweat.

He shook his head. Melt sprayed from his eyebrows and his ears, and the trails of his mustache crackled. "Just shy of the tavern crossroads. Hop, skip and a jump."

The sleigh rushed through the spreading dark. Night swelled out of the ravines and copses, creeping up from the deep-set lake.

Without warning, the sheriff yanked back on the reins. As if we had come unexpectedly to the edge of a precipice.

We skated to a stop.

The lead horse saw whatever the sheriff had seen. He reared and fought the air. The mare beside him neighed and danced. I saw only empty road before us, and a sketch of blasted trees.

"Damn me to black blazes," the sheriff said, if you will forgive my frank report.

He jicked the reins, sending the horses forward again. Slowly. We hissed and scraped along ruts packed to ice. The sheriff stopped the team a length short of a great tree.

I saw it then.

Hanging by a rope from a black limb.

We both got down, my legs stiff as my cane.

There was little wind to feel, yet the figure swayed.

Too small to be a man.

Surely not a child?

Or . . . the poor widow?

I heard a queer rustling as we neared the figure.

Twas no man, but an effigy. A corn dolly of the kind the poor crafted for their children in the old country. Only this was bigger than any toy. And dressed in rags.

The sheriff struck a match.

The doll was garbed in blue, in a mockery of a uniform, with acorns fixed to the shoulders where an officer's rank would be. The top half of its head had been blackened with tar.

A signboard hung across its chest.

The match went out, and the sheriff struck another, holding it as high as he could. We struggled to read. Neither of us whispering a word.

LOOK HEER AND NO YUR FATE

The second match died and the sheriff made a clucking sound. He struck another light and turned to speak.

Twas then the shot rang out.

• • •

The panicked horses nearly knocked me down. My cane went rolling. But the sheriff moved with startling speed. He grabbed the lead horse by the bit. When it failed to calm, he punched it on the side of the head. Then he hurled the slackened reins at me. I caught them as if tossed a lighted bomb.

The sheriff grabbed the whip from its socket and leapt off through the snow, heading for the grove that held the gunman.

"Hold the damned horses," he shouted back over his shoulder. "I'm going to cut that bastard to the marrow. Shoot at me, will he . . ."

Now, I've been shot at with a better aim. No marksman that one, for no bullet hissed near by. Perhaps it was only a warning. But the monstrous pair of horses meant me ill, and no doubt there. I felt it. I did. I stood with a death grip on those reins, looking to my balance on the ice of the road, for without my cane I was as tethered to the team as they to me. Twas awful. I would have chased a band of assassins with naught but my knuckles, rather than mind those beasts.

I turned my face away from the brutes. So I would not have to see their hellish eyes. Still, I felt their breath morbid upon my ear. A gruesome snout come nudging at my back. A great Sindhi cobra would have held less terrors for me. Better a pack of Pushtoons with their jezails, or dacoits with their daggers, than the horror of a horse.

One of the monsters licked me.

But I forget my tale.

The sheriff jumped through the snow like a very deer. Perhaps it is a trick New York folk learn to get them to the privy in the winter. Spry as a lad in his courtship days, the big man raced toward the trees from which the muzzle had flashed. With no attempt to conceal himself. Bold as a drunken grenadier. Waving the whip and cursing to shame the devil.

"You bugger," he cried. "You dirty, sneaking bastard."

Such were by far the softest of his words.

I feared a closer shot would strike him down. But none came. He disappeared into the wood, a black shape melting into greater blackness, and I heard him thrash about. Five minutes more and he re-emerged farther down the treeline, a dark bulk motive on a field of snow.

Twas night.

He come back sweating and steaming, going at his ears as if to tear them off in his rage. "Won't be the end of *this* business," he barked. Oh, there was anger in the man. "Don't you think it will. I'll track that fellow to Canada, if I have to. All the way to Californy. Shoot at the damned sheriff . . ."

"I do not think, sir, that he was shooting at you."

We both glanced at the doll hung from the tree.

"Aw, call me John, would you? For cripes sake. You're stiff as a corpse, you know that, Abel? And you're here with me. Somebody takes a shot at you, they're as good as shooting at me." In a last burst of anger, he trudged to where the effigy dangled, gave a barely-successful leap—he was too solid a man to leave the earth for long—and yanked it by the leg. The dolly broke in twain and the bottom hushed to the ground, while the torso, sign and blackened head hung swaying.

"Oh, for crying in a bucket," he said, and kicked the fallen half of the doll.

"My cane," I said, pointing with my free hand. "Use my cane."

He took it up and knocked the dolly down. But for the head and neck caught by the noose. He tried and tried again, but could not reach the last of it.

Though not a quitting man, he finally stopped. He picked up the little signboard and tossed it in the sleigh, but left the rest of the figure.

"Well, you've seen the spot now," he said. "And seen it good. Reilly was hanging from the same damned limb." He patted at the lead horse and took the reins, offering me my cane. "Let's get on back to town. You're shaking like a man with the trots. Not used to the cold, I take it?"

I would not tell him of my bout with typhoid. For complaint makes us small.

We rode a while in silence, with the snowfields pale in the darkness. From a knoll, we saw lights in the distance, the town teasing us. A long, cold way remained.

The sheriff breathed hard long after his exercise, for such a body has great need of air. He puffed clouds. With an abiding fury upon him. Men of height and stature are not accustomed to challenge, though such is the lifelong lot of my slighter kind. Besides, he was a mighty man in his trim world, where all was subordinate. I knew the sort. The army makes them colonels, and they won't tolerate disorder or surprise.

I thought he had grown sullen. Then he laughed.

"Abel, my friend . . . you might be right about knowing the Irish. I'm not in a position to judge that. But it's sure starting to look like the Irish know you."

• • •

What is more welcoming than the glow of lighted windows, and the smell of woodsmoke, on a winter's night? The clouds were gone and starlight paled the streets. I longed for warmth, and the town seemed as welcome to me as home. Yet, behind its shutters and curtains, not all wished me well.

The villains knew I had come, whoever they were, and our match had begun. Now you will say, "What is this business of 'whoever'? Irish and guilty and done!" But the Fowler case had taught me to judge slowly. I would wait, and we would learn more of each other, like good enemies. The rascals would find I would not be discouraged by a doll or unskilled musketry. And I would find out what I could of them.

Still, I was glad I had packed the pistol given me by the boys in my old company to soothe our parting. It waited in my luggage. Now do not think me anxious to wield arms. I am a changed man from the hard days of my youth, when I thought a sergeant like unto a king, and I will not handle such tools but for necessity. Let us have amity, I say. But, sadly, not all men will have it so. So the thought of my Colt was a comfort.

Faint on the breathless air, I heard the sound of a harmonium playing "Annie Laurie." A maiden's voice joined in. Oh, music is a gift, and melody a blessing! Yet they are curses, too. For who can hear such sounds without recalling hearth and home? The ballad conjured my Mary Myfanwy and the nudging boy beside her, and soft hymns in the parlor of an evening. Her fair hands played the keys as brightly as she played upon my heart. How music gives us pain, yet we want more.

The sheriff snapped my revery.

"Set you down at the Benham House?"

Rich thoughts fled. After a moment, I told him, "That will be fine, sir."

" 'John.' You've got to call me John, Abel."

"That will be fine, then, John. For there is as good as anywhere."

He swerved to miss a man drunk on a weeknight. Fair tumbling out of a whisky shab. "Irish, I'll lay you five gold dollars. You . . . are staying at the Benham House?"

I was not. For I would not have such grand accommodations at government expense, any more than I would at my own.

"I've arranged to board with your Methodist pastor."

He seemed stunned for a moment, then gave a mighty laugh. It rang in the frozen canyon of the street. "Well, you'll see precious little meat on *that* table, I promise you. Which one of 'em?"

"Which one?"

"Of the preachers? Which of our Methodist shepherds is going to put you up?"

I had not known the town held more than one.

"The Reverend Mr. Morris."

He made a sound twixt groaning and delight.

"I had not realized," I continued, "that there were two Methodist congregations. Now a fine town it is, your Penn Yan, but hardly of a size to—"

He snorted. " 'Course, it's not. Your local Methodists went to feuding back in the forties. Scratching like cats. Half of 'em were pew-jumping abolitionists. 'Free the Negro,' and all that. Rest wanted to take things slower, not mix religion with politics. So they split. Breakaways built a new meetinghouse and parson's hole just up from the courthouse. That's where you'll be heading, if you've set your mind to starve with Rev' Morris."

"So the Reverend Mr. Morris . . . is of the abolitionist persuasion?" Though not of fanatical bent, I wished the Negro free, and would not have a chapel shut its eyes to bondage.

"Oh, he's an abolitionist, all right. And everything else under the sun." Underwood laughed again. "You're like to have a lively old time. Though the housekeeper's ornery. And sparing with wood for the stoves, so I hear. Oh, you'll have yourself a time." He chuckled, unable to master himself completely. "You'll have yourself a time, all right."

His mocking tone—and such it clearly was—disappointed me. A man of the cloth is owed unqualified respect, and the sheriff sounded little better than a heathen. I began to suspect he was an Episcopalian.

Well, modern Penn Yan may have been, but it did not have a gasworks. The streets were lit by kerosene lamps set on poles. They cast a paler, harsher light than gas. Twas not late, but the town looked tucked in. The snow lay heavy on the roofs. Almost with the heaviness of death.

We slid along Main Street. Beyond the shops, the houses of the gentry shone thriftless. Money enables. The finest of the homes had columned fronts, like the handsome courthouse farther along.

Just past the court, the sheriff drew back on the reins. We halted with a skid before a row of lighted windows.

"Looks like some sort of to-do at Rev' Morris's tonight," the sheriff told me. "Maybe they're having a welcoming party for you. God only knows . . ."

The man had degenerated into shameless mirth.

"Got your luggage and all?" he asked as I stepped down. He

pulled his ear hard, as if to hurt and keep himself from laughing. Yet he could not control himself.

"My bag was forwarded from the station, thank you."

He held out a big, red hand.

I could not but take it. If he was estranged from true religion, he had been brave and willing.

"Abel," he said, fair engulfing my hand, "I'm not sure whether trouble brought you to Yates County, or if you just brought more trouble to Yates. But I didn't like the looks of that nonsense back on the High Road."

"Indeed."

"Well, we'll get to the bottom of it." He seemed to mean it well. But even then he could not strap in his laughter. He let go of my hand and said, "You be sure to tell me how you like Rev' Morris's hospitality. And I'll make sure the Benham House has a room for you, if you need one. Don't you worry."

"A man of the cloth may live humbly, yet nobly," I assured him. "I will be content."

He grinned. His mustache spread, dripping beads of water and ice. "Well, we'll just see. 'Night now." He clicked his tongue at the horses to spare the whip and they stepped on.

A path had been cleared through the snow and I followed it up to the porch. The parsonage looked prim, but not falsely modest. Your Methodist works hard, and the results are to be seen in such provision.

A bell hung by the door. I rang it. Longing for warmth.

A conversation broke and footsteps come toward me. The door swung open and a clerical man stood before me where the light bordered the darkness. Lean and gray he was, with his hair combed up to a point and fixed with macassar.

"The Reverend Mr. Morris?" I asked.

He smiled as if in ecstasy. "The same, the same! And you're Brother Jones? Major Jones? You're Abel Jones? Of course you are, of course you are! She said you'd come in time." He fished a pocket watch from the billows of his waistcoat. "Right on the hour! See that? Right on the hour!"

The Reverend Mr. Morris seemed prone to enthusiasm.

"Come in, Brother Jones, come in!" he cried, clapping me on the shoulder in welcome. "You're just in time for our seance!"

Chapter 3

NOW, THAT WAS NOT IN THE ORDER OF THINGS.

The fashion for the seance was not unknown to me, you understand. Popular they were back in Pottsville, too. I even knew of one good chapel woman who had thus indulged, longing to contact her lost daughter. Of course, my wife and I never succumbed to such irregularities. We read of such, and heard things, but no more. Deviltry the business was, and worse.

The seance was the stuff of charlatans and impostors, its audience a harvest of old maids, widows, enthusiasts and improvident youth. The hard-learned answers were not good enough for them, and they sat around their rapping tables, summoning spooks. It churned me to ponder such seductions practiced upon the weak of mind and forlorn. I had no doubt that money changed hands.

I dismissed the public's appetite for spirit contact as nonsense and would not be enticed by the demonstrations advertised. For I had seen the fakirs of the East and knew the clever tricks such fellows play. Our "spiritualists," all rappings, claps and ghosties, were only shadows to that Hindoo dark. Still, the common mind wants gulling. It is the stuff of magic shows and politics. But seances were not what we expect within a pastor's home.

I determined to have no part of the wickedness. I would as soon have sat me down to cards. And drink, too.

That is how I felt. I will admit my temper was not of the best, for the strain of the day had left me peevish. When Mr. Morris showed me to my room, to spare me five minutes for my personals, I flared at the prospect of such folly lurking in a man of God's abode.

I held my tongue, though. For hasty speech brings long regrets.

My room was clean, I will say that. Methodism does not spare the broom. My Mary Myfanwy holds to a useful rule: The hand that ends the scrubbing of a floor before the last verse of a hymn is sung—and a hymn of Charles Wesley's, mind you—has not performed the duty of a housekeep.

"Hurry, now. Hurry back down, Brother Jones," the pastor had cried, eyes all aglow. Like our small John's lit up on Christmas morn, bedazzled by the German tree. "They're waiting for you. They're waiting, waiting. She said you'd come! She foretold it! They're waiting in the parlor."

My bag stood beside the bed, properly delivered. I put dry stockings on my feet, then sat. I would not be insulting to my host. But seances were infamous, and wrong. Theaters of the devil they were. As if the common theater did not hold sin enough. Resolved to tell the fellow that I had a great need of rest—which was truthful, see—I went back down the stairs. I wanted supper, but would forego it if I might thereby avoid the spirit nonsense.

Oh, Sheriff Underwood's warnings had a different ring now that I knew the doings that went on. I wondered if the Benham House had rooms that might not be as pricey as the rest, perhaps the sort tucked up beneath the eaves. With longing, I recalled my handsome stew.

Well, down I creaked, glad anyway of shelter for this night. For I was too worn and weary to depart again. Tomorrow would do. My hands and face remained cold as the tomb, my limbs were slow, and I felt light of head.

The Reverend Mr. Morris stood waiting for me in the down-stairs hall. Even the way his hair stuck up in a point annoyed me now. It seemed too gay and greased for his position, although his dress was dark and proper.

"Here he is!" he cried. "He's ready, he's ready! Here's Brother Jones!"

I heard a rush of whispers from the parlor.

The pastor seized my arm, as if to parade me down an aisle. I do not like such intimacy right off, but want a space around me until I know a fellow. Besides, I have my awkwardness of leg, and it is hard to keep step with another. I had to switch my cane to my left hand.

I had prepared a little speech that would allow me to retire politely—for rudeness is but a fist with no courage behind it. The words were on my lips as we went in.

Into that room that trapped me, heart and soul.

A red shawl wrapped the glass of the single lamp. The only other light come from the corner stove, its fire seething low behind the grate. The air felt as heavy as the parlor furniture. Hardly more than shadows, the other guests were seated at a table. Round it was, and large enough for six.

A vacant chair awaited me.

I saw too much too swiftly, despite the gloom, and must put it in order for you. As my eyes learned their way, I got a pair of shocks. Twas as if a boxing fellow had his one-two way with me.

Let me begin with the lesser astonishment.

Right there, between a pair of ladies in their prime, sat a great Negro fellow. Now do not misunderstand me. I have naught against the Negro. I wish him free and unsuffering, and hope he will again enjoy the pleasures of his African homeland. Nor do I think him less than other men in right, or soul, or even virtue. But surely you will understand my wonder that such a fellow, however finely dressed, had found a seat between two proper ladies.

And they were all holding hands!

Well, this was abolitionism sure.

That was the lesser matter. I saw it in a moment, for my eyes had no more time. Neither did I dwell upon the other man who sat there, although I recognized the horseman from the road. The one the sheriff called "the Great Kildare." His icy look meant nothing at the moment, for I had seen a sight that stopped my heart.

Twas the girl from the churchyard. The beauty whose beauty seemed wrong. She sat there in emerald velvet, red hair hanging free in waves of fire. The shadows adorned her, and her ivory complexion shone in the lamplight. Queer it was. Her features made no sense. All juts and angles, still they summed to beauty. But, above all, it was her eyes that called me. Brooding on such women, the Irish speak of spells, "come-hithers," put on boys and men.

Now, do not hear me wrongly. I do not hint at improprieties of deed or thought. For I was contented in my personal matters, and the blunders of my youth lay far behind me.

But she drew me! Those eyes burned. With the slow, deep fire of peat smoldering. There was no haste or drama in the girl. Or would you have me say "the woman"? For she seemed half of each. She gave no hint of pretense or imposture, but sat sedately. She might have been waiting for a coach.

And yet she ruled that room.

My mouth must have hung open like a boy's. I stood suspended. The tyrant Time had lost his grip.

She glanced up at me—only for a moment—and the spell abated. Perhaps she had decided to loosen her hold and let me go.

The party rose to its feet, as at a signal. One lank and bespectacled, the other merrily plump, the ladies fluffed their skirts free of their chairs. A great starched rustling they made as they fled the Negro's grip and ran to me. For his part, the black fellow straightened himself with a wonderful gravity of demeanor.

Noble he seemed, all tall and grand. The bearded horseman kept himself apart.

But I must say a few words more about the Negro. Hued though he was, the good darkie had a polish lacked by many a paler man. He wore a wealth of hair, touched with gray and shaped like Pharaoh's in a lithograph. His dress was matchless neat and somber. Intelligence sat on him, as though he were no African at all, but dark-skinned by some accident of birth. Stern of visage, his eyes mixed wariness with boundless sorrow. Now you will think me odd, but I will tell you: I looked at him and thought, "There is a man!"

For her part, the red-haired girl sat in peace. As if the world were no concern of hers.

Excepting the horseman and the girl, the pastor's guests seemed easy and familiar. You sensed their acquaintance had been a long one. Without the least breath of impropriety, I will say there was great warmth between them all.

"May I present," Mr. Morris began, "my dear, esteemed friends . . . esteemed friends . . . Mrs. Stanton and Miss Anthony?"

And didn't those two thrust out their hands like they were men? Startled, I could but shake their mild appendages, though with a little bow to soften the presumption.

Mrs. Stanton was the one that did things first. Round and vivacious, she rushed at you. She grasped my hand as if it were the handle of a pump and gave it a hearty up and down.

"An honor, sir," she said, "to shake the hand of a champion of our noble Union. But you have suffered wounds?" She glanced down at my leg.

"A minor matter, mum," I said, embarrassed.

"Oh, Susan," she said to her friend, "I do admire men in their regimentals! Would that we could fight beside them!" Before I could withdraw, she grasped one of my buttons to inspect it more closely.

"Lizzie!"

"Oh, don't be a buzzard, Susan. This is the uniform of emancipation, and it is only proper that we admire it. Isn't that right, Mr. Douglass?"

Miss Anthony, the stricter of the two, offered a crisp, official sort of handshake. She looked right into you, that one, though one eye seemed awry behind her spectacles. Deep waters there, I thought.

"And surely you have heard," Mr. Morris said, pulling me free and facing me toward the Negro fellow, "surely you've heard of that great philosopher of freedom . . . philosopher and publisher . . . the journalist and orator . . . the great orator, Mr. Frederick Douglass?"

I could not say I had. I murmured, as we do in such circumstances.

The African stood a giant in compare to me—although size is not all that makes a man. Regal he was, though—and I am measuring my words. Laugh if you will, but had you been beside me, you would have thought him more the president than dear Mr. Lincoln. Dignity attended each of the fellow's gestures, and he took my hand with a solemnity nearly morbid. I know not if the Africans had kings, but if they did he come of such descent.

"I am honored, Major," he said, voice deep as the wisdom of Solomon. "*Hon*ored. We stand informed of your heroic deeds on the field of Bull Run." Up close, his eyes seemed lonely as the grave, and twice as deep. "You are welcome among us, sir. Ah, could we but accord a hero's due . . ."

I turned in alarm to Mr. Morris, who read the question on my lips.

"Oh," he told me, "no need to hide your light under a bushel, Brother Jones. No need to hide your light. The Reverend Mr. Abernathy took the liberty . . . liberty of writing of your exploits. He wrote of your exploits, sir, upon the field of battle . . ." He looked around at his guests. "Achilles stands among us . . . an Achilles!"

I do not resemble Achilles. Anyway, I have read my Homer

and find all those Greeks a bad sort. Give me your Roman Cincinnatus, thank you. But I understood the fellow meant it kindly.

I will not tolerate exaggeration, though, much less error. I was no hero at Bull Run or elsewhere, but only did my duty, and that poorly. It is a wonder how these rumors start.

"You are mistaken, sir. I am no hero."

"Thus a hero speaks!" cried Mr. Douglass, raising an arm to hail me.

Kildare had crept up on us in the meantime.

"And here, Brother Jones," Mr. Morris said, "is our guest of honor . . . guest of honor. No. No, that's you, that's *you*." He reddened. "The 'captain of our endeavor,' let us say. Yes, the captain! Of our endeavor, our exploration!" He beamed respect upon the swarthy fellow. "The learned Professor Kildare, Master of Spiritualism, Mesmerism and Egyptology . . . of Egyptology, sir! Think of it, think of it! And Doctor of Ancient Languages, as well! Of languages! Oh, how I wish I had a little Greek!"

The Great Kildare bowed with a tight smile. "At your service, sir."

"And yours, sir," I said. Although I fear I did not mean the words. I am no friend to strangeness and was not at his service. Nor did I wish the man at mine. Yet social life demands these small dissemblings. We have fallen far from Eden.

Kildare stepped aside. As if parting a curtain. To reveal that pale vision of a girl.

"My daughter and apprentice," he said, "a vessel of the high arts of the ancients, of secrets lost for countless millennia— until recovered by myself from Arabia's sands." He flourished his hand like a common tout. "I give you . . . Miss Nellie Kildare."

The girl looked up. Her stare made me feel uncovered. I mean that in no vulgar sense, see. But twas as if she saw more than we are meant to.

I should have turned around and run away.

"Miss Kildare," I said, with a graver bow.

The girl made no reply. She sat divorced from her surroundings.

"Sit down, sit down," the Reverend Mr. Morris said. "How late it's become, how late! Everybody, please. Sit, sit!"

I meant to plead weariness. The Good Lord knows it is the truth. And yet I let them lead me to that table.

"Mr. Morris," I began, struggling with myself, "I really cannot . . ."

"Don't be shy! Don't be hesitant!" Of a sudden, he stopped and gave me an asking look. "Surely . . . surely, this is not a new experience, Brother Jones?"

"I dare not . . ."

"But here's your place! Just here. The place of honor. Of honor, Brother Jones!"

That vacant chair sat waiting by the girl.

I fought my fate, if weakly.

"Look you," I told them all, "I'm lately risen from a sickbed." Twas more than I had intended to reveal. "And there is tiredness in me . . ."

The pastor looked ruptured. "But Brother Jones? Brother Jones! We've been waiting . . . waiting. We cannot proceed without six. It must be six!"

Now I have been a keeper of accounts, and have sufficient skill to count to six. And they had six without me. Mr. Morris himself there was, and the two ladies. With that regal son of Nubia attending. Then Kildare and his daughter. Six. And no mistake.

"But I'm the seventh," I protested.

Mr. Morris wrapped his arm around me, as if I might flee. Twas a boney business, that arm, and made me think of meals too closely parsed.

"Not at all! Not at all! Professor Kildare cannot participate in the circle. Can*not* participate. It's the rule, the rule!" He gripped me in his skeletal embrace, all staleness and pomade. "We need you, Brother Jones, or all is wasted, all wasted!"

Lord forgive me, I sat down with them.

The girl. I smelled her. She wore lavender.

And then she closed her fine hand over mine. Mrs. Stanton took me by the other. But that second grip was bare of sensation to me.

"I want her to ask the spirits when we'll get the vote," Miss Anthony said.

So transposed was I that her words did not register. Until later. But let that bide.

The Great Kildare dropped himself into a chair by the stove. As if to leave the rest of us to our sport. Mr. Morris opened with a prayer, and nothing queer in it. Then each person nominated a spirit they desired to contact. Mr. Morris named Swedenborg, then Miss Anthony said, "George Washington." Mr. Douglass hoped to reach his mother, though he seemed somehow reluctant, and Mrs. Stanton asked for a visitation by Queen Elizabeth. Though goaded, I named none.

"Let the spirits find me," I said in jest.

Nellie closed her eyes—forgive me if I call her "Nellie" now. I think of her that way, see. Smooth as cat or snake, Kildare rose up again and come to her from the shadows. He took a stance behind her chair, so close I could smell the horse sweat on his trousers.

Her father waved his hands over her face and hair, then down over her shoulders. Modestly, of course. He repeated the motion again and again, each time bringing his palms and fingers closer to her, until it seemed certain he must touch her. His hands glided with unearthly smoothness, disturbing not a lock of hair or fold of fabric. The ritual went on long enough to make me drowsy.

The field of action of Kildare's hands narrowed until his fingertips circled just before her eyes. Smooth and constant as a gentle sea. Rocking like the waves. Watching brought back my lightheadedness. I had to force myself to look away. And even then the rhythms followed me. Kildare seemed to have taken possession of the room. I closed my eyes—I know not for how long.

When I looked again, Kildare was gone. Around the table, all other eyes were closed. Now I am not one to spoil a bit of fun, if it be decent. But there was something in the matter I still could not like. I had grown awfully tired, though, and found myself resigned to sit and let things pass to the flicker of the lamp. I would have preferred to lie abed, to sink into dreams. The whole weight of the day, of my long sickness, settled upon me.

I closed my eyes again, in case they looked. For none of us wants blame for disappointments. I felt something delicious now, almost a swoon. I seemed to be sinking, and watching myself as I sank.

Twas then I felt the cold. I thought Kildare had raised a window.

The cold flowed from the girl's hand.

Her grip strengthened, becoming as hard as a man's.

I had never felt a hand so chilled. I feared she was ill, or in a seizure. I thought I must cry out. And yet I only flowed along. As if we were all flowing together. But there was a restlessness, a struggle, somewhere under the calm.

Her soft voice stilled me.

"She comes . . ." the girl said, ". . . she . . . comes, the tawny one . . . fair as a princess . . ."

I popped my eyes open. Fearing some imposture by Kildare. But I saw nothing. Only earnest faces, dimly lit. And my eyes hated the least light. Darkness they wanted. Rest.

That cold hand.

". . . she's with us now . . . she's been waiting . . . waiting so long . . ."

Her grip grew so strong it hurt me.

". . . she brings a message . . . for the little man . . ."

Hand cold as a tomb. And the lush, falling darkness all around me.

The girl began to sing. Wordlessly. Softly. Beautifully. A whisper of a melody.

Twas a cradle song I knew. From old Lahore.

And so I learned fear. I do not like to think myself a coward. But I could not move. I could hardly breathe. I sensed danger, as a veteran soldier will at the edge of an ambush.

Then she crushed me.

The next voice that come out was not her own, but one I knew.

"Beloved . . . oh, Beloved of Allah . . . Beloved of Krishna and the White God pinched with nails . . ."

In battle, you will see a new recruit freeze upright. He wants to run, but waits there for his death. Standing till a bullet cuts him down. Twas thus I sat.

". . . a thousand mercies on you, heart of my heart . . . our son is with me here . . . we await our lord . . . here, in the turning wheels of time . . . the time that is so long . . . endless . . . a river . . . a river of blessings on the new wife you have taken . . . she is the rose of your heart now . . . the consolation of my love and master . . . your second son is strong . . ."

No bullet or blade could have pierced me like that voice.

". . . rejoice, oh Beloved . . . as I rejoice . . . for now I know our gods are the same . . . though yours be killed and eaten by his children . . . Oh, favored son of Allah and your Christ . . . love those who live, but clutch us in your memory . . . your first son is a spirit beautiful!"

"*Ameera!*" I shouted. I leapt to my feet, breaking the hold of that wintry hand, plunging upward through the darkness. I could not stop myself, nor did I try. A shame it is upon me, but I was set to clutch my lost love in my arms.

Nothing met my opened eyes.

I was a weak, disloyal, shattered man. I know we cannot love two such at once. It is not allowed, and cannot be right, and there's an end to it.

Yet, I loved her still. Though loving my dear wife no jot the less.

The girl who had caused my torment began to cough. And the cough worsened. She fell forward, twisting and contorting.

Kildare jumped up and tore the shawl from the lamp. In the shock of light, he flew to his daughter's side.

She coughed and gasped as though no air would fill her. Eyes huge, limbs shaking. She would have fallen from the chair, but Kildare caught her. He forced a handkerchief into her fingers, though she could barely hold it.

The others clustered round, but Kildare chased them back.

"She's caught between the worlds," he warned. "The spirits need room to leave us!"

She coughed up spots of blood, crimson on white linen. Twas then I realized what her pallor warned, and why those roses on her cheeks burned so. ·

Indeed, the girl was caught between two worlds, already halfway from ours to the other. She was dying of consumption.

• • •

I stood there, a helpless ass of a man. When the girl had partly settled, Kildare wrapped her in a cloak.

"Our horses!" he demanded.

Mr. Morris stood amazed. "But . . . the girl can't ride . . . can't ride . . . she . . ."

"She mustn't leave this house," Mrs. Stanton insisted. A fighter she was, that one. "She must be put to bed."

Mr. Morris looked at her doubtfully. "But the neighbors . . . neighbors . . ."

"I don't give a toot about your neighbors," Mrs. Stanton said. "Let 'em think what they want." She looked down at Kildare and his cringing daughter. "You'll kill that girl if you take her out on a night like this."

"Lizzie's right," Miss Anthony said. "Lizzie's always right about such things."

Mr. Douglass did not interfere. I expect he had seen worse.

Kildare swept his daughter into his arms and gave us all a look of scorn.

"The spirits will have her go," he fair shouted. "Do you think you can defy the spirits?" He turned his eyes and midnight beard to me. "*He* broke the circle . . . my daughter might have been lost in the darkness." I can't tell you the rage in him. "She *must* go home. I must consult my books."

He shoved past the pack of us, with the girl fainting in his arms. God forgive me, I did nothing to stop him. I had let myself be taken in by the hocus-pocus and stood stunned.

Kildare was strong enough to deal with daughter and door at once. That one had done more in his life than fuss over old books.

Then they were gone. Their horses must have been saddled in the back, in a shed or the like, for it was not long before we heard their hoofbeats. Two horses cracked the ice and crushed the snow.

I wanted to run after them. To save that girl from winter and her fate. But I lacked the force to move me from the spot.

All of their eyes were upon me. I had not even sensed it, so far gone I was.

"Why, Major Jones," Miss Anthony said at last, "you're weeping!"

• • •

The rest of the evening was a thing of shreds. Perhaps I, too, was caught between worlds. Not betwixt us and some foul sham of ghosties, but between now and India.

I was not even by them when they died, see. The regiment had moved to an encampment to get us from the fevered city. The cholera took them, and they were burned to dust with all the others, long before I could return. I was a sergeant then, and had my duties. And young enough I was to misapprehend which duties are more important. They died with only the old woman to tend them, and why the cholera took them and spared the crone I will never understand. By the time the heat broke and we marched back, the rooms where we had loved were occupied by strangers, and all her ornaments had long been stolen. I did not have a shred of cloth to hold.

But let that bide.

What mattered was the stench here of conspiracy. How had these Kildares found out my history, and what was their wicked purpose? The only one on these shores who knew about my ghosts was Jimmy Molloy. And Irish and a talker though he was, I knew him to be back in Washington. And for all the foolish deeds the scoundrel had done in his life, I did not think he would betray me. Unless he was deep in his cups.

The voice . . . how did she get the voice?

The party broke up. Mrs. Stanton and Miss Anthony were making a circuit of visits, allowing Mrs. Stanton to say farewell to her friends around the counties. She was moving to New York City, where her husband had been given a fine post. The two ladies, who appeared to hold some extravagant beliefs between them, were staying the night with other acquaintances, since they could hardly share a pastor's rooms. And respectable hotels would not admit women traveling without escort.

Mr. Douglass, for his part, remained at Mr. Morris's. Twas the first time I slept under the same roof as a Negro, and odd it seemed to me then. But no harm come of it.

Mr. Douglass had traveled down from Rochester, where he had a newspaper office, to mediate a dispute over the right to labor. Penn Yan had long employed its Negroes to clear the snow from the streets. When the Irish began to arrive, the work was shared out. Now the Irish wanted the privilege exclusively for themselves, and there had been threats. Twas nothing like the business with the Mollies that I would face in years to come. But it put things out of order in Penn Yan, for the citizens were settled in their ways.

The Irish leaders had declined to talk to Mr. Douglass, if I may put it gently. His only interlocutor on the Hibernian side had been Father McCorkle.

"He cannot see beyond his own countrymen," Mr. Douglass told us, with that boundless sorrow ever in his eyes, "though he doesn't seem a bad fellow, for all that."

"McCorkle, McCorkle," Mr. Morris said, "leading his flock to damnation . . . to damnation and no less. No light in that faith, no light . . . all mumbo-jumbo, superstition . . . worse, worse . . . darkness of Rome . . . darkness . . ."

I took my weariness up to my room without a supper. For I still had to write my nightly letter to my Mary Myfanwy, although I feared the words would not come easy. And I wanted to hide myself away. For I was mortified by my outburst during their parlor game, and at how I had been taken in. I feared they might have misunderstood. And, to tell you true, I feared they might have understood too much. I did not want to appear a rogue or a fool before them.

I know pride is a sin, but who has none? I would be thought well of, and think there is no wretchedness in that. For concern with the opinion of others keeps us upright.

My unmentionables were drenched, as though I had gone wading and fell in. My sweat reeked of sickness. I started to change, but went too slowly. When Mr. Morris burst in the door, he caught me in the very guise of Adam.

He hardly seemed to see, though.

"Brother Jones, Brother Jones!" he cried. "I almost forgot . . . almost forgot! You had a letter by the evening train. 'Urgent,' it says, 'Urgent'!" He held the missive in a shaking hand, as if the envelope enclosed a bomb. Even his peak of hair shivered. "A high government affair, no doubt, no doubt . . ."

I feared he would linger to read it with me. But the fellow was selective in his foolishness. Perhaps we are all fools one way or another. Anyway, he left me alone with the letter.

It was no urgent matter of the state. But welcome it was to me. Twas a letter from my dear friend Dr. Tyrone. It had arrived in Washington as soon as I departed, and my good landlady, Mrs. Schutzengel, fearing importance in the missive, had gone to the trouble of expediting it to me.

I smiled for the first time in hours. Picturing the mighty vastness of Hilda Schutzengel as she impressed her will upon the postal authorities, wartime or not. Once set upon a course, the woman was not one to be blocked, and the letter had raced me to my destination.

Now there is good, a letter from a friend. When we are crushed by life and left alone, how warm such papers feel held in our hands. Twas as if Mick Tyrone had been the seer, not those Kildares. As if he had known his friend, the blundering Abel, had need of comfort.

Despair, too, is a sin. And, though tempted, I have never given in to it, excepting that time in India.

I thought of Mick Tyrone and wept again, this time for the goodness that is in mankind.

Chapter 4

Cairo, Illinois
December 31, 1861

My Dear Friend,

I was delighted to receive your communication of the 22nd instant, not least for the hearthside circumstance of composition described therein. Perhaps next Christmas, with the cruel necessity of war behind us, I shall find myself able to accept your gracious offer of hospitality. I long to make the acquaintance of Mrs. Jones, and to admire the son who so fulfills your happiness. May the coming year bring health and contentment to all!

But now, cherished friend, an earnest warning! As a man of medicine, I find your intended departure for the wilds of New York disturbing in the extreme. You must rest, man! Typhoid undermines the constitution with great violence, and the subject may imagine himself recovered before his health is properly regained. You will do no good through haste. Had I remained at your bedside, I would have enforced a regimen of complete rest well into the new year. I must tell you, frankly, what I concealed from you some weeks ago, during the crisis of your fever. Your case was the most severe example of typhoid I have examined that did not end in mortality.

You are a lucky man, Abel. If I shared your superstitions, I would say a "blessed" man. But enough humbuggery.

I applaud your transfer to your own hearthside for convalescence—these American hospitals do not approach the lowest European establishments, and our military hospitals would embarrass the plague. But you must calm yourself. You write of "duty." A medical man knows the meaning of that word as well as does a soldier. The first requirement of duty is fitness for the task before us. Have patience, lest you cause lifelong impairment to your health.

Nor should you entertain the notion that you impress me with your nonsense about the "sturdiness of the Welsh." Firstly, my political philosophy does not allow me to share your belief in national characteristics—all men are brothers, Abel, and we must help them see it. Secondly, modern Science has defined the body as a machine of predictable and routine function, not unlike a mill or manufactory. The body's processes are all in common, until made eccentric by sickness, and its strengths and weaknesses are "democratic" when tabulated. Yes, some rare individuals may possess an innate robustness, but it is no matter of nationality, but, rather, of a peculiar heredity even now under investigation by Europe's most eminent doctors (I speak of the inheritance of physical advantage, not of the absurd charade of social rank through birth).

A few last riddles remain to Science, though we shall solve them in due course. Meanwhile, dear friend, do not succumb to some repugnant myth of national advantage over disease. You might as well believe in ghosts and witches!

For your own sake, man, rest!

Boundless thanks for your solicitude regarding my own slight misfortune. The wound was trivial, and free of subsequent infection. The bullet passed cleanly through the muscle and, though my shoulder retains an unaccustomed stiffness, I find I can saw through a femur as quickly as before. My dexterity in trying ligatures is not yet completely returned, but that will come.

I will admit a phase of alarm when I could not detect the formation of laudable pus during my healing period, but now conclude there was a subcutaneous manifestation of the substance which my body evacuated through healthy sweat. There is no other explanation. In short, I am well, and it is the height of absurdity for you to assume any blame in the matter. The fellows had to be stopped, and I am glad to have done my part in the face of such corruption. The risks you undertook were far greater.

Upon your return to Washington, please extend my compliments to Frau Schutzengel, our pie-baking evangelist of world revolution. I admire her, though I cannot share her enthusiasm for the Communist program. I have read her revered Mr. Marx and find him too heavy-spirited. He turns a strong phrase, but fails to allow for the temperament of our species. Communism is too thoroughly German for humanity at large—it will never expand beyond debating clubs and libraries. Marx is, however, not a bad journalist. I used to relish his dispatches in old Greeley's New York newspaper.

My greetings, also, to that acquaintance from your Indian service days, James Molloy. I believe you undervalue him. He is a perfect specimen of the individual of talent denied opportunity by an oppressive social hierarchy—and here I must lay down my pen and laugh. For I know you, Abel. Although our friendship has not yet been of long duration, I believe the bonds of mutual sympathy swiftly unveiled us one to the other. I see your eyebrows climbing up and your jaw twisting downward, as you tell yourself that my confidence in Molloy is but an example of one Irishman seeking to advance the other, no matter his flaws. I assure you, it is not so. Molloy has a gift. If, in the past, he has used it infamously upon occasion, let us hope that our fine, new country will enable him to rise above social obstacles—I believe this is the land where those "meek" of yours just might inherit the earth. And I will admit the fellow makes me laugh.

As to my present circumstances, I feel well rid of Washington intrigues and McClellan's indolence. Here, all is percolation. Although our military forays to date have been preliminary in condition, I believe major operations will soon commence. Once the mind becomes accustomed to the epidemic confusions of an army's endeavors, it begins to perceive the underlying thrust. It is not unlike diagnosis, in which the most obvious symptoms often mislead us. There are whispers of an advance up the Cumberland or Tennessee, into the enemy's heartland.

I must say that I like these Western men! At first, they seem rough—alternately drunken and taciturn—but they are honest fellows, and of good heart. When they say a thing, they will do it. I would not be surprised if they win this war while Little Mac dallies in the East like Marc Antony. Certainly, we, too, have our locust swarms of politicos in uniform, but there is no nonsense in General Grant's headquarters—and I have met a few fellows worth marking.

Firstly, I have made the acquaintance of a fellow surgeon for whom I have developed the greatest admiration. His name is John H. Brinton. As in "George Brinton McClellan." Initially, I thought him as pompous as his cousin. But that is only the Philadelphian sneer, as if they were all citizens of Athens gazing down at unlettered shepherds. He is a grand, hardworking fellow, and his accomplishments in organizing hospitals and setting up the rudiments of a field medical service have been splendid. General Grant admires him as much as I do. Brinton has made the going easier for all of us medicals.

Odd, too, that Brinton and I should only have met here, in this pestilential, rat-infested harbor—Cairo was chosen as headquarters solely for its command of the river junction (rivers are everything here, Abel, since the roads are nothing but quagmires). It appears that he and I missed intersecting time and again. Brinton studied in Vienna, at my old hospital, not a year after I fled to Budapest. We have numerous mutual friends and acquaintances, and he shares my curiosity about the theories of Dr. Semmelweis, whose personal demeanor has alienated so many—they say he is a madman, but I only found him a bother. Perhaps this war will bring us an opportunity to test his belief that a surgeon who washes his hands in chlorine solution between operations may reduce the rate of morbidity. I wish no wanton injuries upon our soldiers, but if make war we must, Science should profit.

Anyway, Brinton, who is near the top of the surgeon's roster (I'm near the bottom, of course), also served as president of the Medical Examining Board in Washington last year, departing just a week before my application was heard. But now we are met, and I find him an excellent fellow, of clear and scientific mind. I sense he was quite lonely upon his arrival here—a western river town is hardly Philadelphia—but he has made himself indispensable to the army and now, with my arrival, he can banter about the old days of his European studies and the like. A local apothecary of German origin even loans us the latest medical journals from Heidelberg and Berlin, where startling results have been obtained in the surgical theaters. Brinton is a sensitive man, for all his social position, and may be gotten to see the need for true equality in time.

Likely, you have not heard much of General Grant, unless you read of the engagement at Belmont in November (not Portia's Belmont, certainly). He is a brigadier, and my kind of soldier. I cannot predict his worth upon the battlefield, but I like him for his lack of pomp. He is, I am told, an old regular who served in the unjust war of conquest against Mexico, but failed in the peace. His detractors excoriate him as a bankrupt and a drunk, and I think he is watched by General Halleck's agents on the staff. Yet, I find him a quiet, good-humored man, of sound judgement and inexhaustible energies. His staff gets things done, and I have grown proud of my association with it. Grant is plain and short, and his russet hair goes unkempt. His uniform is proper, but Spartan and devoid of elaboration. He sits for hours over stacks of papers—that bane of war I never had expected—pipe in his mouth, calling occasionally for an adjutant. He reminds me, frankly, of a good surgeon—one who keeps the end in sight and will not be flustered by the radical measures necessary to a cure.

I have encountered a few other ranking officers of promise, although they are only in and out of headquarters, for Grant will not tolerate a lavish establishment. William T. Sherman, who visited, has the fire in his belly, and I would not want to get on his bad side. There is also one Lew Wallace, who writes. He has read his Gibbon and sees the tides at work in the affairs of men. But I fear he may think too much to make a good butcher. I do not like McClernand, who is proud.

You will note a large proportion of Scots among the highest officers, yet I have met no prejudice here against an Irishman such as myself. Well, these Scots are getting their own back on the English aristocrats transplanted to the South, I suppose. I will stand shoulder to shoulder with them, for if any war can be a good war, this is it.

Abel, you cannot imagine the plight of the Negro south of the Ohio! To read about slavery is one thing, and to see its tempered features in the streets of Washington yet another, but this is inhuman! The forlorn creatures run to us, following at the heels of our reconnaissance parties. We know not what to do with them all, and it is, of course, an issue of great sensitivity among the politicos. Grant and his staff wish the poor darkies away, since they become an impediment. But I, for one, am outraged by their suffering.

I must soon close, and apologize for my brevity. I have forgone the privileges of rank (a necessary evil in wartime) and volunteered for medical orderly duty this last eve of the year. It is my gift to those of stronger appetite bent upon celebrating the passing of the old and the coming of the new. There is much to do, for we have an outbreak of measles in the ranks. The men are tall and much to be regarded for their health upon arrival at the camps, but many are farm boys, who matured in isolation. They have not been exposed to those diseases that mark the passage from early childhood, and many die of illnesses an infant would cast off in a week. I study them as a man of Science, but feel their loss.

Tomorrow, Brinton has invited me to dinner to greet the new year, and I will go. He promises me "very good" wine, sent him by acquaintances back in his "civilized East." I know, my friend, you do not approve of any drink strong-brewed or fermented, but remember the pleasant story told of the Marriage at Cana. If I cannot share the theology of the event, I applaud the sentiment. You know I am no drinking man, yet a glass of wine is a gentle consolation.

Well, I am tame, I assure you. At night, I fall asleep clutching a book. Have you read the Darwin I lent you?

Again, my dearest friend, your first duty is complete recovery. This war can do without you for a few more weeks. Study patience!

Kindly greet Mrs. Jones, and kiss your little son for,

Yr Obt. Servt.
M. Tyrone
Surg. U.S.V.

• • •

Just such a man was my friend, Mick Tyrone. Blunt in his talk, but fine and eloquent with pen in hand. There is education for you.

I read the letter thrice. And then I knelt down in my nightshirt and prayed for all without stinting.

Chapter 5

I STOOD BESIDE THE PRIEST AS THEY RAISED THE BODY. The hooks they used to find her pierced her flesh and, as they drew her up, I imagined that those irons hurt her still. She rose between the blocks and shards of ice. Dripping deep water, her dress hung sodden down to her bare feet. She had left a second note in her shoes on the bank. Brogans they were, frozen hard. That last message said, "Give the shoes to Annie Slaney." She must have thought to write it in advance.

The first note, left in her shanty, said, "I am gone to the lock to see my Pat again. Pray care for my babes." The sheriff showed it to me. It was not spelled so well as I set it down now, but I will not mock her in her death.

I had gone, after a leaden sleep, to the priest's house that morning. I meant to query him about the affairs of his parishioners, but his housekeeper cackled, "Gone to the locks, 'e is, for the widder's drowned 'erself and they're drudging 'er up." I thought at first that she spoke of the widow of our agent, and I feared vicious murder. But it was not so. This was another widow, one Maire Haggerty.

The men tried to be gentle, for they were Irish, too, and she was theirs. But their hands suffered from working in the ice and the water, and they were ill clad, and they wanted to make an end of it. An awkward business it was, reaching poles through broken ice to find her.

The girl come up reluctant. As if mortified by our attentions, and shamed. Hauled up between two floats of ice, she bobbed and sank again, trailing a blue hand. Then a second hook snagged her and the workmen lifted her free.

She was frail. As though she had not eaten in a year. You felt her ribs limn through her soaking woolens. Water poured from her.

And her eyes were open. I know not why, but I had thought the drowned all had closed eyes. Somewhere I read it is a peaceful death. But her eyes bulged in shock, framed by undone hair.

She was not free of the water half a minute before a queer thing happened. The moisture froze upon her skin. In the bright, cold air. A veil of ice covered her face and arms, her fingers and raw feet. The high sun hit her and she shone, a golden fairy dancing on their hooks. Frost gilded her rag of a dress. Ice formed in her streaming hair. She rose encased and gleaming.

They dropped her on the bank.

Her blood was thick with death and the cold, and it made little roses when they worked their hooks away. She lay there staring at Heaven, a magical thing. The priest went down into the gorge to close her eyes—he slipped and when he righted himself snow covered the backside of his cloak—but he could not make them shut.

He gave up and began to strip off his own garment to cover her, but the workmen dragged a tarpaulin from a shed by the locksman's hut. The folds were as stiff as her body. The navvies edged the priest away, careful as with an angry dog, and shrouded her in the canvas. Then they removed their hats in expectation of a prayer.

But pray the priest did not. He turned his back on them and started up the slope again, struggling to keep his footing. He wore a poor man's shoes.

The sheriff had stepped up beside me. "Told you those locks were dangerous," he said. "Now you see it."

"I would have thought them well frozen," I remarked. A

smooth, white world surrounded the gorge, and I was mystified. Such a one as her could not have cracked her way down through thick ice.

"They break up the ice on the locks," Underwood told me. "Keeps the force of it from ruining the machinery and warping the sluice gates. Can't drain 'em, cause you have to keep pressure up on both sides, or you'd get even worse. And the current still runs down deep. Enough to keep a couple of the mills going. Top freezes up again, and they bust it open again. All winter long. It's good wages for the Irish."

The priest looked huge and black as he hauled himself up, grasping at vines and sedge with reddened hands. It was a steep, wild place, with the canal forty feet down. Toward the town, the gorge was deeper still.

Below, the Irish drew straws for who would touch the corpse. Death moves them powerfully, and this one was unhallowed.

"She would have known," the sheriff went on, "that one. About the breaking up of the ice. Husband was a day-tender on the locks. Before he went and joined up. Decent fellow, no trouble with the law. McCorkle says she got word yesterday they buried him down in Virginia."

"I hear my name sounded," Father McCorkle called. As though he would thrash the two of us for taking the liberty.

"Just telling the major here," Underwood said, "how all this came about. Her soldier fellow getting himself killed."

The priest steamed from the work of the climb. " 'Get himself killed' Pat Haggerty did not. The smallpox it was." He turned his black brows and blacker eyes on me. As if I were the spreader of that disease. "And there's the fine end to your bugling and drumming. Culling the best o' me boys with your rumors o' glory. Oh, there's a fine end to it, your lordship." He pulled the black cap from his head and feigned a bog-man's deference to my uniform. "Will I bow down to ye now, sir, and to your great guns and fine braids?"

"Father McCorkle," I said, "I'm sorry for this . . . misfortune. But there's no need—"

"Oh, is there none? Is there none, indeed?" He bore down upon me, and, if I may be honest, he looked more a brawler than a churchman. "An't it a worse mockery when the lot o' ye go making a war and turn to such poor, gullible lads as him to fight it for ye? Oh, off they went proud, to be sure. Marching like the boys o' Vinegar Hill. Pat Haggerty and Brian Brennan and the lot. To join up with the high likes o' Corcoran and Meagher, to prove the Irishman's worth! All 'green flag o' Erin' and moonshine. And not the ones we well could spare, no, but the best o' the boys run off, and husbands and steady workers among 'em." He bared yellow teeth. "Francie Kilgallen dead at your Bull Run . . ." He eyed the buttons on my greatcoat. ". . . when the rest o' ye went streaming off like hoors—"

I was shocked to hear such language from a priest, and fear my look betrayed it.

"—oh, like very hoors ye run. And Michael Duffy done o' the bloody flux, more glory to ye. And him with a family o' seven." His rage grew vast as the sky above us. "And what are the Irish to the lot o' ye, but white niggers and food for your guns? A feast for your black, murdering cannon." The fellow actually raised his fist at me. "You're bigger hoors than the Queen o' England!"

"Sir, you forget yourself," I said. "You have no cause to insult the Queen." My own fist tightened upon the ball of my cane. "And given her own recent loss . . ."

The Lord knows I do not love the English. But I will not have wanton insult heaped upon the good little Queen.

The priest spit on the snow. "That great hoor. The great hoor o' her. And what o' the Irish lost to buy her mounds o' jewels and satins? Starving by the million, with the grain pouring out to fatten the English purse. Driven here in the ships o' death by the little hoor, they were. And ye," he said to me, glaring, with maddened eyes, "ye are the worst o' the lot, ye runt taffies.

Naught but slaves o' the English, ye are, and selling your tiny souls for English gold."

I saw then he knew nothing of the Welsh, and settled, and let him rant on. Now you will say, "You did not stand up for your kind, and proud you should be of the land of your birth." But the loss that day was his, not mine, and I saw in that instant the desperate sorrow of the man, and how he only wanted to hurt the world that hurt him and his kind. I was my uniform, not a man, to him.

"And *her,*" the bull in the cassock cried, pointing down into the gorge. "Our lovely little Maire. Ye know well what ye've done to that one, don't ye? Oh, damned her is all. Even your black informer lies in consecrated ground. But not her, no. She'll sleep forever separate from her faith." And weren't there tears in the big fellow's eyes as he bellowed on? "Maire Haggerty was a soft one, she was. Not risen to the cruelties o' your world. Too soft and good for ye. And leaving two babes for to damn herself . . ."

The priest turned away. "Damn the lot o' ye," he barked. And he strode across the snow toward the town. Where the canal curved, a few chimneys smoked, marking hidden mills. The black plumes seemed to draw him.

We watched McCorkle go, John Underwood and I, until he was no more than a crow in the whiteness.

"I had hoped," I said wistfully, "to enlist his aid in my investigation."

Down below us, old-tongue voices rose. The navvies were hauling the dead girl up the slope.

"Wait until he calms down," the sheriff said, scratching one of his monumental ears. "He'll be sorry for taking on like that. That's just about the worst I've ever seen him." Then he clapped a hand upon my shoulder. "Come on, Abel. We'll leave it to the coroner's office now. Give you a ride back to town. Must've been some walk out here with that leg of yours."

We started for his cutter. But then he stopped again, looking out across the fields. Stubble quivered where the drifts had blown thin. The sheriff's eyes hunted for the priest.

"McCorkle's not really a bad sort," he said. "Just takes everything to heart, that's all. Irish are damned lucky to have him. He keeps 'em to the straight and narrow."

On the way back into town, with the horses kicking up a diamond dust of ice, Underwood glanced at me and said, "You walked all the way out here unarmed. Didn't you?"

I nodded. "Broad daylight it is. I saw no—"

"Have a pistol of your own?"

"I do. But—"

"Carry it."

• • •

I wanted that sewing machine. Not for me, mind you. But for my Mary Myfanwy. It sat there in the window, the very engine she had wished for her Christmas, only to be disappointed by the one who loved her most. Twas a Singer & Co. No. 1 Standard Shuttle Machine, and wasn't it lovely? All black and trimmed with gold, as if for the royal household. A very panther of a device it looked, as though it would do a wonderful damage to a yard of cloth. And the bitter thing was that it stood reduced for sale. Twas a brute amount still, yet I would have bought it in a minute for my darling, had I held cash money enough that was not come from government funds.

Now you will say, "There is poor economy, for Abel Jones was a well-paid clerk before he put on his blue coat, and now he is got up high to a major's income. Where is the money of it, and why did he not treat his beloved proper?" Well, I will tell you. I did a curious thing before I come up to New York. I had been planning it over on my sickbed, and I discussed it with my Mary Myfanwy. She was not without misgivings, and downcast she looked to break the heart, but she knew the man of the house must make the great decisions.

In short, I bought railroad stocks.

Now you will say, "There is wickedness. For the buying of shares is but gambling and speculation, and why not sit you down to a round of American poker, oh, hypocrite?" But I did not think it wrong. I was buying tickets to the future of my new country, see. For my family.

Evans the Bags from the Miner's Bank tried to dissuade me. Now he is a well-meaning Welshman, though no relation to my wife's uncle, Mr. Evan Evans, also of Pottsville, or to my buttie Evans the Telegraph. Well, Evans the Bags said the safety of our little savings was best left to the vaults of his bank. But I would not be put off. For in the course of the Fowler affair, I had met one Mr. Cawber of Philadelphia. A rich man he was, and got up there by himself. I come to admire the devil, for he was no more born to privilege than I was. So I made inquiries as to the railroads Matt Cawber was backing, and there I put our savings. In the end, Evans the Bags bought shares for himself, as well. For a Welshman can tell a cow from a calf.

I was resolved that we would not end poor. For there is no country for the penniless, not even sweet America. One day my love would have the finest of sewing machines, and we would not contest the price, unless it were unreasonable. But the joy of that throbbing needle must wait a little.

Oh, yes, I was resolved! I would scrape every penny into our investment! But now, in hard January, the sight of the Singer in that shop window broke my heart. For I would deny my dear wife nothing.

I turned on my cane, careful of the ice, when a beggar boy gave me a tug. Pulling on the flap-over of my coat, all timid like. Then he stood away. Irish he was, by the nose of him, and I do not mean the snot but the puckered shape. Yet, he was American in his speech.

"A penny, gen'rul, please?"

Now thrifty we must be, if we are to buy railroad certificates or grand sewing machines, and begging is not to be encouraged, for it harms the moral constitution.

Yet, I fished out a coin for the little one, and more than a penny.

"Hypocrite again!" you will say. But I could think only of our little John, and of the fragility of all human protections. I have known the hurts of children in my time.

Off he ran howling in triumph, with me wondering whether I had given him too much for his own good.

I had no more time for the admiration of mechanical progress. For time is money, too. I had an afternoon journey before me, with the sleigh already ordered up and waiting.

First, I had a purchase to make.

I went along the lovely street, considerate of the ladies when we passed between the snow piles narrowing the boardwalk. Across the way, I saw Mr. Douglass take himself into a bookseller's. For my part, I went into Munger's, an apothecary shop advertising ALL MEDICINES AND SUNDRIES.

The place smelled of bitters. A bald-headed counter fellow grinned a great toother to see me approach.

This was a matter of some delicacy. Fortunately, we were alone.

"Look you," I said. "I have an acquaintance who is troubled in the lungs."

"A temporary affliction?" he asked, quelled in manner. "Or do we speak of . . ."

"Consumption," I got the word out. "I fear it is the consumption."

His smile bloomed again. "Well, we have just the thing! A miracle of modern medicine. The very latest elixir. You've come to the right place, my friend."

He scooted around from the back of the counter, bending forward in his hurry, and searched along a row of well-dressed shelves.

"Your friend may be thankful," he said, "that we live in modern times. Here it is. Right down here. 'Winchester's Hydrophosphates.' Guaranteed infallible, if the patient is susceptible to cure." He held the lettered bottle out to me. "It's the very latest in tonics, recommended by the best physicians of New York City and Boston."

"How much is it, then?" I asked.

He looked at me soberly. "Well . . . it comes in different sizes. Seven-ounce bottle for one dollar, or six bottles for five dollars. Then there's a sixteen-ounce bottle for two dollars."

Medicine is an expensive thing. But I was determined. Both for the goodness of the deed and to buy me an excuse to see her.

I did the mathematics. Now, I can be chary of expenditure, and I considered buying only a dollar bottle. But the larger bottle was the bargain, clear. And I would not be mean of purse with a dying girl.

"I will have the two-dollar bottle," I said. Before he moved for his cash box, I held him with my eyes. "A cure is guaranteed, is it?"

He laughed, but kindly. "Not from a single bottle, no, sir. But it's a start. Your friend can try it out. If he or she doesn't see a wonderful improvement . . . well, then we'll try something else. But hundreds of documented cases claim that a full course of Winchester's will rid the body not only of consumption, but of asthma, chronic bronchitis and . . . female complaints."

"But she will see results? She'll feel them?"

He nodded gravely, then smiled again. "As long as she's susceptible to cure. Nobody can do a thing for those who won't be cured."

That made eminent sense, and I paid him.

As I was going out, a grand fellow stopped me. Upright, with a mighty beard and a fine Sunday topper on his head, I would have thought him president of the bank.

"Major Abel Jones?"

"I am he, sir. But you have the advantage—"

"Stafford Cleveland," he said. "Editor and publisher, *Yates County Chronicle*." He extended his hand. And then I saw he was a scribbler sure, for ink blackened his fingernails and the creases in his knuckles. As we shook, he continued, "We're the paper on the right side of the issues up here. Lincoln party, you know." He handed me his card.

I could not imagine what interest a newspaper fellow would have in me.

"I have not yet had the pleasure, sir, of reviewing your newspaper. But I am a regular reader of the *Evening Star,* Washington's finest—"

"Major Jones, how about an interview? My readers want the Federal view on these murders and this conspiracy business. And I'd also like to do a story on Washington's view of the British threats of war and—"

"Excuse me, sir," I said, pushing along. For I realized I had been ambushcadoed.

The fellow followed me, near knocking down a woman with her packages.

"Where're you going? Major Jones? The people have a right to know!"

I stopped and gave him a look. Now I like a good newspaper, but where would we be if lowly government officials such as myself, who cannot see the great design above them, went blathering to the press? Oh, that would be a sorry time. You might as well let the village idiot preach the sermon and Frenchmen set your morals. No, silence is a virtue. Let the great men talk, for they know what is to be said and not.

"Sir," I told him, "I cannot talk to a newspaper man. And I must not talk to a newspaper man. And I *will* not talk to a newspaper man. For it is not my place to talk to a newspaper man."

"The people have a right to know, Major Jones. When there's a danger of insurrection . . . atrocious murder on the roads . . ."

I lifted the head of my cane and fair shook it at him. For his presumption startled me. What if all newspaper fellows were so? Demanding answers of every decent sort going about his business?

I will admit my reaction was too fierce, for Stafford Cleveland turned out a good fellow in the end, and he wrote a fair page. But that is hindsight. And I was not myself, given the troubles inside of me and out.

"The people have a right to know," I said. "But *I* have no right to tell them. Even if I had a thing to tell, which I do not. Perhaps you should talk to your own Sheriff Underwood, and not go nattering after a Federal officer at his duties."

He looked nonplussed. "But Underwood sent me to *you*."

I saw the beauty of it then, for I am not always slow of mind. All at once, I understood how the game is played with these press fellows.

"You really need to talk to the coroner's assistant," I told him. "He's the fellow that knows, see."

I left him scribbling a note. Clutching the bottle of medicine, I hastened toward the livery stable. For I was late.

Nonetheless, I went a block out of my way to avoid the window with the Singer.

• • •

"I'm Reg'lar John," my driver told me, standing ready by the sleigh. His Ethiopian visage gleamed against the winter paleness. "Call me that cause I does everything reg'lar. Yes, sir. Reg'lar to church, reg'lar to work here, and reg'lar home to dinner, long as work ain't got me held fast."

I thrust out my hand. "A pleasure to meet you, sir."

He looked at me oddly. After glancing around us, he briefly took my hand.

"You know your way then?" I asked him.

He gave me a ready smile. "Know my way? Reg'lar John been up and down this county summer and winter." He soothed a spark of restiveness in the lead horse—from which I kept my distance. "You just name me a rabbit by name, I take you right up aside his hole."

"You know the Kyle place then?"

Of a sudden, the fine fellow changed. Shrinking against the flank of the stallion.

"I knows it," he said, voice lowered.

The alteration in the man was pronounced. As though I had raised my cane to threaten him.

"You seem hesitant, sir. Something wrong, is it?"

He shied his eyes toward the grit and snow of the livery yard. "No, sir. Nothing wrong. We going anyplace you wants to go. It's only . . ." He lifted his eyes back to me, examining me more closely than before. ". . . well, there's an unkindness in folks down that way. Don't like the Negro. Or any other color of outside people. They figures if they does right and stays up there in the hills, we all ought to stay down here and let 'em alone."

Now, I have seen something of the world. I know the disdain of the African is not a phenomenon that stops at the boundaries of Dixie. And I had no wish to endanger the good man.

"Perhaps, sir, it would be better if I took another driver? If the residents dislike—"

He waved his head at a greater horror. "No, sir. *No,* sir. I'm the reg'lar driver. And I does everything reg'lar."

"But I would not have you endangered, see."

He shook his head again. His woolen cap had a tassel atop it. The little ball swung from side to side. "No danger now. I just minds my own business while you does your business. I just minds my own business and takes care of my sleigh and my team. Anyways, only other fellow could go is Bucky, and he's blacker than a bucket of coal. Can't drive worth a bean, neither."

"Well then," I said, for time was running, "shall we go? You have the blankets?"

"Plenty of blankets, sir. Just like you said. They all tucked in back, you see? You going to be plenty warm, don't you worry."

He climbed up on his perch behind the horses, did Reg'lar John. Although the cost was greater, I had specified a larger vehicle, so that I might sit on the bench behind, farther from the monstrous brutes who must pull us. Mind you—I paid the difference from my own pocket and did not beleaguer our national treasury.

When I was seated and settled, with the blankets snug about me, the driver raised the whip. Then he hesitated.

"Folks say the Kyle farm haunted now," he told me. "All kinds of haunt doings up there. With that magic fellow."

"You believe in spirits, sir?" It was a topic newly of interest to me.

He shook his head and the little tassel swung. "Don't matter what I believes. It's what *is* that matters. See now. In the Bible, Jesus . . . He raised up folks from the dead. Got up Himself, too. So maybe some folks gets up ain't supposed to? Sneaky like? Though I'm not saying they will or they won't."

"Don't worry," I told the simple fellow, "we shall be safe." Although the truth was that I had my own fears in my heart. With the last sweat of my sickness down my back. And my pistol under my greatcoat.

We retraced the route the sheriff and I had taken the day before. I wondered if I had only been under a spell those lifelong hours ago, if those highland views would so affect me upon a second inspection. The splendor of the white-clad moors and glens, of that endless parade of ridges, had intoxicated me. But I had been fevered. And disappointment is the common reward of too much expectation. Much that we have seen is painted finer in the mind than in the fact.

I was not disappointed. We had not the glory of the setting sun, for it was high afternoon. But beauty has as many shapes as evil. Now, in the pure light, the trees seemed made of glass. Their iced limbs dazzled to hurt the eye. Weighted branches broke off, loud as shots, a skirmish in the groves. When big limbs fell, the horses shied, but my driver kept them under control handsomely. Where the road followed the ridgeline, you could see to China. Except for the teamster of a lumber sled, we did not pass another traveler.

Reg'lar John asked if he might sing, and I have never minded a pleasant melody. He had a warm, manly voice and, to his credit, the songs he chose were hymns and moral anthems. I joined him in a few, but did not assert the power of my lungs, for I did not want to shame the poor fellow. No one sings a hymn quite like a Welshman. And it was clear the horses were accustomed only to Reg'lar John's musicality, for they acted queer whenever I sang out.

We passed the tree where I had been hung in effigy. The corn-shuck head still dangled by the rope, but the driver did not notice and I did not wish to alarm him. A bit farther along, we approached a settlement and Reg'lar John gave the horses a taste of the whip. We passed between a pair of taverns and turned toward the heart of the highland plateau. The driver did not sing as we shushed through the hamlet. Twas cold, and few bodies stirred. But a fellow leaving a privy and another splitting wood paused to look us over.

When we had gotten a piece beyond—following a slighter road with fewer sleigh tracks—Reg'lar John called back to me:

"Two taverns back there? One called 'Bull Run,' other 'Manassas.' Union-minded folks goes to Bull Run, but them that got no liking for President Lincoln and this here war, they goes to Manassas. Terrible fights when everybody gets to drinking. Nothing else to do up here in the winter. Not much in summer, neither."

"I would not have thought," I called out over the rush of the runners and the clop of hooves, "that there would be so many people opposed to abolition this far north."

Reg'lar John shrugged his shoulders, then leaned back toward me. The tassel of his cap dangled. "Some folks just contrary," he told me. "Even in the Bible, there's folks inclined towards hating other folks. Way I looks at it, poor white folks lucky to have the black man to go opposing. Otherwise, they'd have to go opposing themselves, for all the spite they got to use up." He teased the whip in the air, alerting the horses without lashing them.

"There's just a meanness in this world," he told me. "Even Baby Jesus couldn't get it out of folks. So I just minds my ways and keeps reg'lar."

• • •

We passed through country poor as the Pushtoon hills. The tidy farmhouses near the town had long since given way to shacks. Instead of barns, there were sheds of gray boards, their roofs buckled under the weight of ice and snow. If not for the occasional trail of chimney smoke smudging the sky, you would have thought the landscape abandoned. The sleigh rode roughly.

"Not far now, that Kyle place," Reg'lar John told me. He had given up singing entirely.

To pass the time, I asked if he knew Frederick Douglass, the Negro fellow who was my fellow lodger.

"Oh, yes, sir. Yes, now. Everybody knows Fred Douglass."

"And you think him a good man?"

"He's a powerful, speechifying man. Brave man, even when there's no call for it." He gee-upped the team.

"You admire him then?"

"Much as I admires any unhappy man."

"You think him unhappy, sir?"

"Well . . . I'm not saying yes or no. But he does put me in mind of that priest fellow them Irish folks got. All raging against what the Lord set down here, and bent on fixing it all by himself."

"But surely . . . you would not accept injustice? I'm told Mr. Douglass is a great advocate for your people. A shining example . . ."

He glanced back at me with a rag of a smile. "Folks are different. Big folks like Fred Douglass and that priest fellow goes straight for the bull. That's their way. But Reg'lar John going to work his way around that pasture, 'cause he don't got no business with any bull and don't want none."

"But . . . you said you go to church regularly, sir? As Christians, we must all stand up to injustice!"

"Kyle place just down there." He pointed his whip toward a brown house behind a gnarl of trees. "Sir, I hopes to be a good Christian and to die in the Grace of the Lord. But there ain't no hurry about the dying part. See, I figure if folks nailed up Jesus for speaking His mind, I better just go quiet and reg'lar about things. That just works out best."

• • •

He knew I would come. For I had not been the first. Whatever else the Great Kildare was or was not, he was an experienced hunter of souls. And he knew the quarry would come for the bait he had set out.

He did not even make a game of it. He only looked me up and down as I stood atop the steps before his door. All of the previous night's anger had drained from his demeanor, leaving only a mocking smile behind his beard. He put things directly:

"You want to see my daughter, I expect?"

I did, indeed. No, "want" is too soft a word. I *had* to see her. For a night and a day, I had struggled against the thought of her and the message she had brought me from beyond. Throughout the long drive, I had jailed her at the very edge of my mind, in a place akin to a dream. But I had to see her. Had I glimpsed a thing forbidden, or only been a fool? I had to know.

I held the pathetic little bottle out toward him. He glanced at its jacket of brown paper, but swiftly raised his eyes to mine again. There was no kindness in those eyes, nor aught else that I could decipher.

"Medicine?" he asked, before I could explain. "Leave it, if you want."

"I *must* see her," I said. I stepped forward, as if to prevent him from shutting the door. Although he had not moved to do so.

"I know," he said. "But you can't."

I looked at him pleadingly. How do you force a man to grant you an interview with his daughter? I mustered up what little I knew of these types, these mesmerists and dark performers.

"I'll pay," I said. "To speak to her."

He nodded. Nothing I could do or say would surprise him. "Something can be arranged," he said in a dismissive tone. "But not now."

"Please, sir. I have . . . questions."

"Everyone has questions for Nellie. But let me save you further display, Major Jones. The reason you can't see her is that she isn't here."

"Where is she?" I demanded.

He smiled again. His lips did not part, but his beard bristled and spread, and the thin mouth curled.

The Great Kildare extended his arm toward the white horizon. "Out there," he told me. "Perhaps toward the lake. She communes with the spirits."

"I'll find her," I told him, desperate as a lover.

He kept his voice low and coldly polite. He did remind me of the Englishmen he aped. "I wish you luck. For all the good it will do you."

I took the shambles of my heart and my bad leg back toward the sleigh. In the yard of the place, two ugly men with trouble in their faces were giving hard looks to Reg'lar John. They had the Irishness upon them. My driver ignored the fellows, brushing the ice and slop from a horse's withers.

He was a good man, Reg'lar John, and he knew he had brought me down a bad road. But none of us knew it would lead to such a tragedy before the winter's end.

Chapter 6

I FOUND HER. We lost not an hour of the dying day. For all those rambling miles of whiteness, the horses pulled us toward her as if she had called them. A black slenderness glimpsed across the snow, she stood where the earth fell away from the moors. Standing at the end of the world. There was no face to the figure, but I knew it was her.

The horses would have left the track and rushed across the highlands, but the driver stopped them. There were marshes, he said, between the road and the girl, and ponds concealed by snow. The sleigh would surely go under.

He reined back the beasts and managed their stamping, while I climbed down and worked my way toward her. A withering wind come up, dusting old snow across the heights, and I drew my coat in tighter. My hat would not hold to my head, so I used it to shield my eyes against the blow. Keeping her in sight, I plunged along, cane sinking into the drifts. I feared she might vanish if I looked away for an instant.

In a grove nearby, the branches clashed like swords. Warning me away. Garbed all in black she was, black in a white world, the only color a flag of red hair snapping out from her shawl. She faced the far ridges and the falling sun, and I felt her clinging to the last ghost of warmth.

"Luck," you will say. "He found her by luck." But it was fate. I will believe that until the day I die. And perhaps beyond.

My boots crunched and squeaked as I hobbled across the snow. Suddenly, my bad leg sank down in a drift, and I will tell you: The fears of a man disturbed as I was are the terrors of a child. My cane found no bottom as I struggled. But then I broke loose again, for we are made tenacious. Only a bad knit of bone in my leg did not like the cold that returned with my freedom. The weaker of our parts would sleep forever, and only will and duty keep us well.

"Miss Kildare!" I called, but the wind took my words. I feared surprising the girl, for she stood at the edge of the promontory and I knew not what waited below.

Toward the end of the field the snow had swept thin over stalks and stubble. I heard a whinny and saw a black horse in the trees, head down. Now I am a man who notices things. But horse I had not seen.

Only her.

Her.

I called again, but still she did not turn. I wondered if I might not be mistaken, rushing to disturb a farmer's widow.

The wind stretched out her hair, longing to carry her away.

I stopped ten feet behind her. In a world silent but for the keening of the sky.

"Miss Kildare," I called.

She turned.

I had worried about the sick girl traipsing over the country-side in such weather. But now I understood.

Standing there, with the falling sun behind her, standing at the edge of the abyss of the lake, upright in that cold and matchless world, she belonged not to us but to Nature. She fitted it like the groves and bracken, like the lean fields and the sky. The rest of us were intruders on those high moors, but she had come home. For hers was no gossamer beauty, meant for parlors and linger-beds, but a sum of wildness.

And beautiful she was. Not of a cast as common as our desires, but possessed of a beauty invulnerable to our smallness.

Twas as if the wind were sculpting her before my eyes, defining her as I watched. That hair belonged as much to the sky as to her person. Her father had been right: Among us, the girl was caught between two worlds. But now she was where she belonged.

I had disturbed her. I felt as if I had touched her with coarse hands.

Yet she smiled. A meager smile to break the heart.

"I knew," she said. "I was waiting for you."

I stepped toward her, close enough to talk without raised voices. She seemed to have no fear or care of heights, but stood to dare the depths. The drop was not sheer, yet steep enough to kill, a long slide of ice. Far below, black trees pointed up from the lakeside. You would fall forever.

"Miss Kildare . . . I must talk to you."

A mask of hair covered her mouth. She swept it away.

"I cannot help you," she said.

All the miseries that I had held suspended since the night before, the devils I had fought down, the years of confined remembrance . . . of a love that scorched then died . . . all that swelled inside me.

I was not master of myself.

"*Please,*" I said. "I must know the trick of it. How you learned those things."

She shook her head in a sorrow I could not grasp. "I'm sorry, sir." Her speech was good, but when she said "sir" it come out "sor" and Irish.

The wind scoured the fields, sparkling the air between us, stinging.

"Miss Kildare . . . I *beg* you. The things you told me . . . about the woman and child . . . the matters described . . . her voice . . ."

"I cannot help you that way," she said, voice gentle. Pitying me from a distance. "I would, sir, but cannot."

"Was it a fraud? Please, Miss Kildare. Did someone put you

onto me? Now there is cruel. Was it a joke? *I must know.*" I looked at her through a veil of blown snow, adding, "I will not betray the secrets of your trade. I promise you."

She stared through me. With those peat-fire eyes. Behind the whips of hair, her forehead creased.

"Don't you understand?" she asked. "I thought you would be the one to understand . . ."

"Understand what, then?"

A crow rose from a thicket.

She closed her eyes and lowered her head. Her voice spoke from the depths of that storm of hair.

"That I don't *know*," she told me. "I don't *know* what I told you. In the trance . . . they come . . . the voices. But I can't remember! Don't *you* understand?"

"But surely, Miss Kildare . . ."

She parted a curtain of hair and the bones of her face re-emerged. In that moment, she looked mad.

"I see things . . . I see them now . . . spirits all around you . . . but so faint . . . I can't tell, can't make sense . . . how they follow you . . ." Twas her eyes pleaded now. "It's only the daytime things that I remember anymore . . ."

"You told me about a woman and a child. A woman . . . not my wife."

"I can't remember."

"Miss Kildare . . . I'll pay. If it's money, see."

That grieved her. "They all offer money."

"What do you want, then? For the love of God!"

"Peace," she said. "I want them to stop. I want them to leave me alone. I thought you'd be the one to understand. Spirits all around you . . . they told me you'd come."

She fell to her knees. At first, I thought she was in a faint and moved to catch her, fearing she would slip into the abyss. But she held herself straight-backed, mittens joined as if praying. Two tears fell, one from each eye. Their trails froze white.

"I just want them to *stop*," she said. "My . . . father . . .

doesn't understand. That I can't control them. Why I can do one thing and not another." She raised wet eyes to me. "He was in a rage last night. He wanted me to summon Queen Elizabeth . . . to pretend . . . for the Stanton woman. He thinks I lie about the trances. He thinks the Stanton woman hides her wealth, but he's wrong . . ."

Carefully, I moved toward her. Anxious to bring her back to her feet. On the edge of that precipice. "Miss Kildare, you must rise. You'll catch your death."

She looked up and laughed.

"I'm not afraid," she said.

"What . . . do you see now?" I asked in a coddling voice, inching closer. I knew not what to make of her or her confidences. "What spirits, then? Look you. I need to know. To keep the devil off me. Something. Anything. Tell what you can, I *beg* you."

She lowered her eyes to the snow.

"They're like gauze . . . so soft. They move when I try to look at them. As if they're playing with me . . . teasing me. They're all around you . . . an army of them . . . protecting you . . ."

A queen accepting aid, she let me lift her. For a moment, we stood so close I smelled her sickness.

Her smile twisted. As if she read my thoughts. "You doubt me. You of all men." She put on a hard, common look. "Will stage tricks be enough, then? To convince you? Do you want to see the things they line up to pay money for? Is that what you want?"

"Miss Kildare . . ."

She closed her eyes. "Beneath your coat . . . you carry a revolver . . . given to you . . . by younger men . . . given to ask forgiveness . . . they left you to die . . . there were horses . . . have a care, the second chamber will not fire, for you set a bad cap to it. And in your pocket . . . by your heart . . . a letter from a friend who saved your life . . ."

She opened her eyes and gave me a forlorn look. "More, sir? Or is that enough?"

"But how . . ."

She shook her head. The hair free of her shawl lashed her white face. "I can't explain. I've always had the gift." The pair of tears left trails upon her skin. "I thought you understood."

"But you claim to communicate with the dead? In your trances?"

Her smile turned wistful and blown snow narrowed our eyes. "The spirits say there is no death . . . but I don't know. I don't know what happens in the trances. Perhaps the spirits lie. Like men. I've told you . . . I know only that which comes to me . . . when I'm like this. The things I see by day. The rest is darkness." She canted her head and her hair streamed. Pulling her away. "Men have souls of glass. Their thoughts are all the same. I see them so clearly. But you're a hard one. They flee, but you come on. Even your wanting is different. When they stand in front of me, they're running away inside. And the Irish . . . they all believe I'm a witch. They'd burn me. Or worse, if they could. But you'll never run away. You understand. You're not like them." Slowly, a rising scale, her distress grew. "They'd push me under the ice." She glanced to the side. "Or over this edge . . ."

"Your father protects you, of course."

That fragile smile again. "The priest protects me."

"But surely your father . . ."

"Counts the money . . . it's always the money with him."

The light was quitting us. Instead of a grand-hued sunset, as on the day before, this twilight was soft, weak. A gloaming of lilac and gray.

"Miss Kildare," I began in a businesslike voice, for I had done my mental accounts in that instant, "I know not what you're about. Though wish you well, I do. Yet, there is something queer here, and you might begin by telling me . . . why you appear to reveal so much to me, a stranger? A stratagem is it? For it seems you've told me much, yet you've told me nothing at all. And this last confidence, regarding your father . . ." An inspired question struck me. One that would test her "visions" well enough. "Miss Kildare—would you just tell me this, then: Is there to be an insurrection among your Irish? Against our Union?"

My dullness crushed her.

"There is no insurrection," she said blandly. "No rebellion."

"Anything else, then? Any untoward doings of which you know? Anything you see in your visions?"

She shook her head. Slowly. "I cannot tell you such things."

The last of the sun filled with color: Twas red as blood again.

"Cannot? Or will not?"

"Will not."

"But why? After you've—"

She reached out and laid a mittened hand on my forearm. It quelled me instantly. As if a force had poured into my body.

"Don't you see?" she asked, near pleading. "It changes nothing. What comes, will come. I can only watch. None of us can change it."

"Then why . . . talk to me at all?"

She stood back, haloed by the sunset. Heels on the edge of oblivion. There was strange. Twas she who looked baffled now.

"But you're the *one*," she said. "Don't you know? Haven't the spirits told you?" She looked near despair. Clapping her hands to the side of her head, as if her thoughts pained her, she cried, "Please, help me . . . they play tricks . . . they won't stop. I can't tell what you know and what you don't. Only that you're the one . . ."

"The 'one' what, Miss Kildare? What am I, then?"

She looked at me, her beauty on fire, amazed at my ignorance.

"The one who came to kill my father."

• • •

Now what do you say to a mad thing like that? It shocked me. The very thought of such a thing. And that a daughter might say it so. I saw she was sadly touched, and not by mystic spirits.

She had jarred me with the parlor trick of describing my pistol and the letter in my blouse. But I had read enough of mesmerics in the newspapers to know that mountebanks had a knack for reading a fellow's eyes or getting their victim to suggest things with his expressions. I saw then that the seance of the night before had been a mere charade, its details but awaiting explanation. Naught but cruel mischief there. And I had been drawn in like a country lad by a recruiting sergeant. Weightier affairs wanted my attention, for I had a charge and a duty.

Yet, she drew me.

I sought to reason with her as the darkness gathered around us. But she was beyond the power of all but prayer, and only repeated that I was "the one." She said it in a voice that bore me no malice, but her words were all the madder for that. The air come colder over us, and I repeated my concern for her health. At that, she changed. Sudden as the tides of battle. She bid me *adoo* and fair leapt upon her horse. As if gone over to the spirits already.

I watched the beast carry her away, leaping drifts. She seemed a fearless horsewoman, but still I had no sense of her bravery. To me, she was only a lost girl, dying. Her cape and shawl streamed behind her, different shades of darkness. Then she disappeared into a swale. Twas a wild place, those high moors, and she as wild as any of it.

Reg'lar John awaited me along the farm track. "All reg'lar," as he said. Yet, he was relieved to see me.

"Ain't no good up here," he told me. "Nothing good never happens up this way."

The horses wanted to go, and we galloped along the ridge. Twas as if the beasts themselves were in haste to leave the place. They did not slacken until we had left behind the dueling taverns and the gibbet where the corn dolly's head still hung.

By the time the team had used up its spunk, we were back in the lowering of the ridge, where the farmhouses were larger and well tended, with proper barns. Yellow-lit windows cast their glow across the fields. Again, I saw the town in the distance.

Reg'lar John sang hymns as we descended. I felt the Colt hard against me and did not join in.

• • •

When I come into the parsonage, scraping the snow from my boots, the Reverend Mr. Morris and Mr. Douglass were already at table.

"We waited," Mr. Morris assured me, "waited as long as we could. Food getting cold, getting cold . . ."

"The major looks a bit chilled himself," Mr. Douglass said, rising from his chair to welcome me. As if I had become a valued friend. He really was a proper gentleman.

"Duty, duty," Mr. Morris said. "Brother Jones has his duties." He looked up from his plate, upon which a meager sadness of a meal lay sulking. "Are the killers discovered? Have you discovered the killers? Are we safe now?"

"The day," I answered, taking off my greatcoat, "went awry, see. But there is tomorrow."

"Dreadful about the Irish girl, dreadful," the pastor went on as he spooned up peas. "Weak creatures, so weak. Drawn to sin, the Hibernians . . ."

I sat me down, for the housekeeper had laid out a place for me, a paying lodger. "Sin," I said, tucking the napkin into my collar, "is in us all, is it not, sir? Did not the great Wesley—and I speak of John Wesley himself—did he not write in his *Christian Perfection* that no man can say 'I have no sin to be cleansed from'?"

"Surely, surely . . . Wesley, Wesley . . . but the Irish, Brother Jones . . . the Irish . . . magnitude . . . proclivities . . . proclivities, sir! And propensities!" His lacquered peak of hair shook at the ceiling.

I looked at Mr. Douglass, wondering what a Negro might make of such a judgement, for such a one must know what it is like to be convicted by his brother's fall. But the African only smiled a bit and applied himself to his plate.

"Mr. Douglass?" I said, wishing to change the subject. For I had Irish behind me and Irish before me, and would not have them with my supper, as well.

That solemn Nubian turned his eyes upon me.

"I have met one of your fellows this day," I continued. "A certain 'Reg'lar John.' He claims you are not unacquainted."

Mr. Douglass chewed, nodded and swallowed. "That would be John Brent." Suddenly, he grinned, with strong teeth. Now Mr. Douglass was not a smiling man by nature, but mirth he saw in something I had said. "Tell me, Major Jones, how did this 'Reg'lar John' fellow strike you?"

"John Brent, our John Brent," Mr. Morris added in support.

I swallowed a mash of peas. "Why, a good enough fellow. Simple." I thought over the day. "Likes a good hymn," I said, with a glance at Mr. Morris.

Now there were any number of looks shooting about that table: Mr. Douglass at the pastor, the pastor at me then at Douglass, Douglass at me, and me looking at both of them in turn.

At last, Mr. Douglass laughed out loud, collecting a chuckle from Mr. Morris.

"Do you," Mr. Douglass asked when he had settled again, "hold acquaintance with many of the sons and daughters of Africa, sir?"

Well, I had lived some months in Washington, where the poor creatures were still enslaved under the law, if quietly. And freed men there were, too. But my contact with them had not been close.

"I have observed such, sir, but regret I cannot count them my intimates."

Douglass let a smaller laugh. "Well, regret it or not, I'll let you in on a little secret, Major Jones. The simpler a Negro appears, the more he conceals. It is . . . a hard-learned trait. Born of suffering." He smiled with unanticipated warmth.

"Suffering," Mr. Morris repeated, "terrible suffering . . . human bondage . . ."

"Now you take John Brent," Mr. Douglass went on. "Employed in a livery stable, yes. Although few people know that he is also half owner of the establishment. Some achievements are best enjoyed quietly, and a man must reckon his circumstances. But I will confide in you, as an agent of Mr. Lincoln's government: John Brent has been one of the great heroes of the underground railroad. Surely, Major Jones, you have heard of that desperate path to freedom?"

I nodded, for I had. My Mary Myfanwy had long been a great one for the emancipation of the Negro, and had tugged me to not a few lectures upon the subject back in Pottsville.

"Well, the underground railroad ran heavily along Keuka Lake here. Fortunately, we have ever less necessity of it now. But even in recent years, there was great danger," Douglass said. "Greater danger than you might credit. Slave-catchers, rewards, nightriders, the kidnapping of Negroes born free . . . none of it frightened John Brent. He would walk from here to Bath to lead our people to freedom. Why, he must know these hills better than any man alive. And a tireless man. Fearless. Yet careful, for bravado is the enemy of such enterprises. Still," that son of the equator concluded, "I understand he barely escaped the mob and a noose during the Dundee troubles, and remains unwelcome in some corners."

"Dundee, Dundee! Elder of the church, as well," Mr. Morris exclaimed. "An elder! You'll hear him in the choir this very night, at evening meeting! Evening meeting, Brother Jones!" His hair seemed to rise higher with his excitement.

Look you. I would have enjoyed an evening of prayer and community, for such is ever a comfort. But I had not yet done my full day's work. I had one last call to pay.

"I would come, sir," I told Mr. Morris, "and most rapturous. But government business intrudes, see."

"But where will you go, where will you go?" the pastor asked, in Christian disappointment. "It's night, night!"

"I believe the Catholic evening worship finishes soon?" I drew out my pocket watch to verify the time.

"Yes, yes. Gone to their drinking, gone to their drinking. Not like honest—"

"Well, then," I said, already done with my starve of a supper, "I will call upon Father McCorkle, for we parted upon a break that must be repaired."

"McCorkle? McCorkle? Surely, *he* could wait . . . evening meeting . . . congregation . . . meet the congregation . . . honored guest . . . honored . . ."

"I fear," Mr. Douglass interjected, with his deep eyes upon me, "that we are both disappointments to Mr. Morris. For though we share a commitment to abolition, I cannot share his . . . beliefs. I have moved onward."

Disappointment there. For such a grand fellow as he should have been a paragon of faith.

I am a plain man, and Mr. Douglass read my thoughts more clearly than the girl had done.

He smiled. Twas a request for understanding, that little twist of the lips. "I have no wish to offend . . ." He nodded to Mr. Morris. ". . . our gracious host." He turned his prophet's eyes back to me. "Or you, sir. Good men may have differences, yet work toward noble goals they hold in common. But I will not dissemble in the matter of religion."

I pitied the great fellow then, and not for his sable skin. For he was a handsome creature. But can you imagine the loneliness of men without faith? I thought, of course, of dear old Mick Tyrone. And now I recognized the sorrow that followed Mr. Douglass like an echo. They bent over books in their longing, and failed to lift up their eyes to the light. Now I like a good book, mind you, but would not trade my faith for all the libraries of London. Even if their science proved me wrong, I would believe. For there is no other lasting comfort, and kingdoms are nothing.

We all stood up to part. Mr. Douglass reached into his vest and drew out a card.

"I'm off to Rochester early in the morning," he told me. "So we may not have an opportunity to say farewell." He looked down at me, for he was a tall one. "I hope you have more good out of old McCorkle than I did, sir. No progress at all. Nothing to show for the time and effort. He's so pigheaded about his beloved Irish. And I've got a paper to publish." He offered me the calling card, then his strong hand. "If your duties ever bring you to Rochester, I would consider it an honor to be your host, sir. The world is short of heroes nowadays."

"I'm not—"

"No demurrals! No demurrals!" Mr. Morris insisted. "A hero, a hero!"

Douglass released my grasp. I had no inkling of the greatness of the man at that time, for I can be near of sight in some things. Nor did I have any notion of the disappointments that awaited him. But let that bide.

"I'll stop by the stable on my way to the train in the morning," he added, "and have a talk with 'Reg'lar John.' I'll tell him he can stop that good-darkie nonsense with you. He and I . . ." Here the great fellow's eyes clouded. "We both began our lives on the Eastern Shore of Maryland. Under circumstances foreign to human decency. We understand each other, John Brent and I." Then he snapped himself out of the past and repeated, "If you're ever in Rochester, Major Jones . . ."

"Time for chapel! Time for meeting!"

The truth was that I would have preferred to follow the Reverend Mr. Morris into the meeting hall, where my fellow Methodists were already gathering. For I had need of succor. And I will tell you: Selfish Abel had no wish to trudge off through the cold and dark. It is a weakness, how we love our comforts. But a Welshman is a dutiful fellow, most terrible in his determinations, and twas time to take matters in hand.

• • •

Father McCorkle answered the door himself. The pleasure on his face was sublime.

"An't it the good Major Jones himself? Sure, and a blessing it is that ye've come to me door. For wasn't I thinking upon ye but now, and shaming meself for me doings and carryings-on? And here ye are, man. Made flesh, upon me word!"

Well, that was a change.

The fellow invited me in. Lean it was in his shiver of a house. Seizing my coat, he set me a chair by his own, close to the hearth. He poked up a blaze with a quivering hand and his shadow grew gigantic on the back wall. "And don't the winters seem longer with the years, boyo? But the years themselves grow shorter . . ." The firelight hunted over the crags of his face and the dark cliff of his brows. "Now Mayo's a hard place, ye know. But her winters are naught, held up to those of New York." He sighed. "When I was young I took meself to Rome, by the Grace of Our Lady, and wasn't that lovely and warm? Tis a joy in the memory."

We sat down. "Will ye have tea?" Then he gave me a wink. "Or there's not a bad poteen I can offer, for they bring it along to soothe me."

"I have taken the pledge, sir."

He raised his chin and lowered it again in approval. The firelight left half his face in shadow. The stern man of the burying and the titan of the morning were gone, leaving a worn old fellow behind.

"Oh, and a grand thing that is, the Temperance! I give poor Morris that, for all his follies. He does keep his flock off the bottle. Tis a curse on the Irish, the drink. But then so little they have . . . will it be tea, then?"

"I would join you, sir. If you're having a cup yourself, see."

He set a kettle over the flames, then parsed out leaves that had been used and dried. His furnishings were but sticks, dusty even in the dark. Twas a poor place set beside our Methodist comforts.

He drew his chair closer to mine. Until our knees all but touched.

"Oh, I'm a proud one," he said. "Tis my besetting sin. And so I delay. But there's no avoiding the act o' contrition. Sorry I am for my cursing o' ye. For the language. And for the sentiment, as well. Wrong it was, and wrong I was. Though disagree we will o'er Victoria Regina. No, ye just got in the way o' the storm and it blew on ye." He looked at me, but his eyes were lost in canyons of shadow. You saw but a gleam. "Am I to have forgiveness, then, Major Jones? What shall be penance enough?"

"Sir . . . we are all sinners . . . I'm hardly in a position . . ."

A slender log broke crisp and sparks rained upward, lighting a volume of Tacitus the priest had set aside.

He smiled and bent to turn the kettle on the irons. "Oh, ye Protestants. Couldn't I weep for ye, though? For ye do not understand the glories and gentlings o' forgiveness. It is a thing the True Faith has, if naught else . . . but are we mended then? Can ye overlook the madness that come upon me?"

It had been a great day for madness.

"It is behind us, sir."

"I thank ye for the kindness o' that! As I thank the Lord and his archangels." A veil of sorrow settled over his features. "The girl, it was. Our little Maire." He shook his head. Slowly. "The Lord has His wisdom, sure, and it is not upon the likes o' us to question it. But times there are when tis hard. For He calls the good wine to Him, and leaves the dregs behind." He searched my face, my eyes. "She was good, and wronged by this life."

"A tragedy," I said.

He mused on that. "Too small for a tragedy. But a sorrow . . ."

The kettle called. He lifted it barehanded from the irons and set it by while he dusted the tea leaves into a chipped pot. He poured the water slowly, with the steam rising about his hand.

Twas as if all things in his life had to be measured. The careful-
ness of Mr. Morris's table was luxury to this.

"Sugar there's none," he said.

"There is good," I lied. "For I do not like sweetenings."

He raised one end of that line of brows. "And I thought the
Welsh were great ones for their sugaring?"

"I have known such," I said. "But would have mine hot and
clean."

"Hot it will be, then." He did not steep it long, but poured the
pot empty, straining the beverage through cheesecloth to collect
straying leaves. He handed me the better of his cups. The tea
smelled sour, but the cup was lovely warm in my hands.

"Now ye'll be asking me," he said, seated again, "about all
the bad doings amongst us. The lad bedeviled and hung, and
your Federal man took up before him. And rumors o' rebellions
and risings. Will ye not?"

I nodded.

"Tis to be expected," he said. "For ye have your duties, as I
have mine. But there's sad little I can tell ye. Even was I to parley the secrets o' the confessional, which I am not like to do. But
there's this much sure: Neither rebellion nor insurrection against
the government. For what's to be gained by the likes o' that? No
risings nor revolutions, Major Jones. But if it's unhappiness of
which ye talk, you'll find a plenty. For the poor are always with
us, and injustice. The hatred of Cain is upon the land."

The man looked even older now.

"But . . . if there's no plan of rebellion . . . if there's nothing,"
I said, "then why kill a Federal officer? And an employed agent?"

"A 'spy,' ye mean. For let us be plain. Oh, ye do not understand the Irish a jot, if ye fail to see the terrors an informer holds
for them. Tis the bane of our nation's story, the informer." He
leaned closer, lowering his teacup. "And what did ye hope to
gain by such recruitments? Surely ye see that the silver of Judas
only buys lies when the truth will not do? Tall tales he will tell
ye, all smothered in a cream o' fine words. No, I will tell ye the

truth of it—informers will be rooted out and done with. That is the way of it, and not even I could stop them. Though I will not excuse murder. No, there's no taming the wildness in them when they smell the stink o' the spy among them. Tis the way o' things, and a lesson taught by Britannia."

"And the Federal agent? Captain Michaels?"

"Sorry I am for the loss o' him. But there's nothing I can tell ye there. Mayhaps he crossed the wrong man, or the wrong line. They say he was a drinker himself, your Captain Michaels."

"Father McCorkle"—I called him "father," for that is how these people would be addressed, and meant it only as politeness—"surely you see that the government must pursue the matter. Look you. Two men dead. And killed ugly. The law will have its way."

He weighed an empty palm. "I cannot help ye. For I know nothing."

"But will you keep your ears open? Surely, you see the danger to your flock. I speak of prejudice, sir. America has been a ready refuge to the Irish, but murder will not be condoned and what will good citizens think—"

He closed a big hand over my knee. Twas my bad leg, but no matter.

"Speak ye o' America? And of a ready refuge? When men are paid starvation wages, and their women less than that? Do ye know, man, that I've so many cannot afford to marry that there's less being born than dying amongst us? They go talking o' Irish immorality, the fine ones. But let them look close and honest, and a sad crop o' spinsters they'll see, withering away. And young men all longings and rags. No, I'll never put the joys o' Temperance in their heads, though I shout meself blue in the face. For the lot o' them are naught but looking for a way to numb the pain till they're called." He sat back in his comfortless chair. "Maire Haggerty now. Who's to say she wouldn't have been better for the comfort o' drink than damning her immortal soul with her doings?"

"This country," I said, "is man's hope and pride. Now, in its hour of peril—"

He stood up. For he was past listening, though his mood fell short of anger. "Will ye come with me this half hour?" he asked. "For as ye lay claim to being a Christian man, there's a thing I would show ye."

"I am at your service, sir," I said. For I meant to indulge him. He was a compelling sort, and I wished to mend our relations. I recalled the drowned girl, frozen and shining, and the priest's rage above the canal. Twas all Heaven had been the object of his anger, and not small Abel Jones.

He tamped down the fire to ward off a conflagration, then pulled on the black cloak that served him for a winter overgarment.

"Come with me," he said, "and I'll show ye a thing."

We went along the darkened street, past little houses closed against the cold. He led me toward the canal. The houses became shanties, and the shanties grew smaller. Off to the left rose the black wall of a mill. In low barns, mules complained. Along the outlet, the barges were moored in ice. Kerosene lamps glowed behind the shutters and oiled-cloth windows of the cabins on the decks.

"The poor devils live on the boats year round," the priest told me, turning us right toward the lake itself. "For the canal's all a world o' its own, and a poor one for those that take their living from it. And the railroads go making it harder. For your locomotive needn't wait for spring and the thaw."

He near made me feel guilty about my investment. But progress is ever hard. I had seen that in the wretched streets of Merthyr, where I come into my young manhood.

"I had an encounter last night," I said, tapping along on my cane, "with a fellow who calls himself 'the Great Kildare.' He is of your country and faith, I believe?"

I felt the priest go darker than the darkness. "Perhaps o' me country, but not o' me faith, that one. Not with those doings o' his, and naught to it but eternal damnation. Tis Satan's business, and no less—and your Mr. Morris entertains the fellow! Wickedness and damnation!"

Now I had expected as much from him, for the Catholic faith is stern down deep, while ours is stern on the surface. But I did not expect the change that next come over his voice. For it softened.

"And yet I don't truly know the man," he said. "And there may be good stirred in with the evil. For the world is not so clear as you people would have it."

"Perhaps . . . there is good in the daughter?" I was testing him. For she had claimed the priest as her protector.

"I hardly know her but to see," he said. "Though I keep the worst of them off her. They'd kill her for a witch, if not for her beauty alone. She sets a fear in men, that Nellie. And worries them with wanting, besides." He sighed, and a fog of breath preceded his next step. "She'll be damned as sure as her father, if she doesn't turn back to the church before the cough takes her."

"She's very ill," I said. "She—"

But then I heard the music. It come jigging through the darkness. A dollar fiddle and a squeezebox, played to the pulse of a flat drum. Faint it was, but fevered. Growing louder with our steps. The path turned by a boathouse. Across a waste of snow, a barn bled light. Or perhaps it was a warehouse. For it was set by the water. Ramshackle, anyway, and overflowing with humankind. Those who could not get inside danced by a rubbish fire. Wild as the Pushtoon, they were, when that murderous savage capers to his war drums.

I expected the priest to put a halt to the business.

But I was wrong. He kept his silence, and the great dark shape of him hardly disturbed the revelers. A few cast wary looks upon our approach, but soon went back to their joys. Twas as if the priest had left his own dominion and entered another where his law did not prevail. We seemed but half visible.

Spirits, see.

A fighter-faced fellow leaned by the door, collecting the penny admission. He let the priest by unmolested, but had his cent of me. I did not like his eyes. Or the hammered look of his flesh, or the twist of his nose.

But in we went. A few of the young girls calmed their reeling at Father McCorkle's entry, lowering their skirts again to cover their petticoats. Even then, they swirled on, no more demure than the famed Spanish dancers of Gibraltar, whom I had seen when my India-bound ship put in—I was a foolish fellow then, and young.

But these girls flew! And not the girls alone, but the men, by whom the fairer sex was well outnumbered. Fellows danced with fellows, grinning silly. Couples past their best years trotted, too. There was but a small stove set in the corner of the vasty place, but the air was tropic hot and wet. The entertainment stank of sweat and whisky.

We stood at the back, the priest and I, amid the old men with their pipes. I watched the turning faces. Is anything more hopeful than a young girl at her dancing? With all her dreads suspended, and the moment a cloud of thoughtless beauty? Now there are those who would condemn such pastimes, and right they are that we must beware lasciviousness, for temptation is like any danger and finds us stronger on one day than another. Yet I would not forbid the dance, so long as things are done proper. For there is joy in the stepping, to be sure, and joy is a thing of sufficient rarity. I will even admit to tapping along with my cane, although I made no vulgar display.

Their faces careened before us, and soon the priest was forgot. The girls picked up their long skirts again, and, proof of the devil, I caught myself looking once. For I am not invulnerable to beauty, though a married man and content.

But their faces! If the priest had no dominion here, neither did misery, or poverty. For an hour these gay carousers reeled free of care. They whirled and laughed the darkness down, some aspects fair, others gray and toothless. Wart noses and cleft lips, or soft cheeks pinked by exertion, from handsome to haggard went the run of their features, from moony, pudding faces or chins as sharp as blades to the colleen splendor of young darlings. Some were clean, while others staunched the cold with layers of dirty woolens, but all had succumbed to the joy of the music, and the hoopla wildness, and the freedom of brief forgetting.

The priest said naught, but let me watch unbothered. And then, with the fiddler and squeezer and pounder gone off for a moment to fuel themselves up, a young man took the stage, led on by a baldheaded banty. Blind the boy was, but pretty as an angel, with a lick of hair falling over his forehead and the purity of his misfortune on his face. The young girls watched him, mired in regret, for such a one as he was not for marrying.

He sang. And I believe the night wind stopped to listen, and the stars come down closer to hear. He sang of a lost love, away in Killarney, her eyes soft as dew, and her lips like a rose. They were to be wedded, but winter come o'er her, and laid his love down 'neath a blanket of snow.

They all wept like children. And then he sang of lonesome Connemara.

They do have tenors, the Irish. I will give them that. But they will never have the power and unity of a Welsh chorus, for, though clannish, they cannot hold together in the clinch, but each will bully his own way. They are a folk for solos. I think it is the way the English beat them down the years, see. For one Englishman will set aside his differences and pull beside another until the dirty work is done, but the Irish would settle their differences first.

But let that bide. The blind boy moved me.

I drew out my handkerchief—for my Mary Myfanwy had accustomed me to the device, and I no longer believed it an affectation—and touched my own eyes.

Then I saw them. Watching me.

Across the big room, lolling about by a trestle where whisky was traded. Chewing little cigars.

Twas the two men I had seen in Kildare's yard. Night had not improved them.

I raised myself up on my toes to catch the priest's ear without a needless raising of my voice. He gave me a startled look, as if he had forgotten me completely.

"Those two. By the liquor seller. The big one and the lesser. Who might they be, then?"

He saw them at once. For they were not shy about their staring and did not stop.

"The O'Hara brothers," Father McCorkle told me. "Napper and Bull. A wise man would cross the street to keep shut o' them."

The fiddle called, and broken hairs flew from the bow. The fiddler stamped and sawed his little instrument, and the clapping began. Then the squeezebox joined in, and the round drum fixed the time. In moments, the company set to rollicking again, the sum of their joy beyond the mathematics of Mr. Newton. I lost sight of the brothers O'Hara in the confusion, and did not mind. For I will tell you true: The joy of that music reached me, although it was a raw thing and the makeshift dancehall no fit place for the respectable.

The priest bent down toward me, keeping his eyes on his people.

"This is what I wanted ye to see, Major. Look at them. A Christian man, are ye? Then look ye well. For there before ye are the people He came among." The priest's voice twined dreams and anger. "The Magdalene herself, I could point out to ye. And at least a pair o' thieves. Luke and John that take a poor living from the water. Mary and Martha, unmarried and waiting. And ye've had your Judas, haven't ye? And your innocents slaughtered? Oh, those are the ones He came down to. Not your fine bankers and senators. These are the ones who flocked to Him, who came to hear the Sermon on the Mount. Crawling, they were. Crawling on their bellies, when their weak limbs failed them. To hear the blessed music o' His words. Craving in their souls for one sight o' Him. The scorned and despised o' the world. *There* are your children o' Israel."

He turned his eyes to me then.

"Now tell me, Major Jones. Is this to be their promised land? Or did they trade one bondage for another?"

Chapter 7

I MADE NO PROGRESS. A month I stayed, or nearly. Twas time enough to make nodding acquaintance of the citizens who displayed themselves on Main Street, and to ride the county up and down in Reg'lar John Brent's sleigh. Sheriff Underwood was an honest man, ready to support me when I had need, yet I came to see that he wished no trouble upon his county and would not go looking for it uninvited. He did send a pair of constables to chop down the tree where Reilly then my effigy had hung. I got to know the place, and my sense of danger lessened with familiarity. I loved the land. Yet the winter was dreary, the days short, and the diet poor.

Although I found their range of interests a marvel and concern, I took comfort amid the Reverend Mr. Morris's congregation. For their faith was strong, despite the odd notions that crept in among them. And they liked their sacred music, as did I.

Now, I go at the singing of a hymn with a wonderful bellicosity, and blessed are the Welsh in their voices. My vocal expenditures astonished all. Good, humble folk, they could not even meet my eye when I sang out, but only smiled at each other in their delight.

A miracle it was, too, how the pulpit transfigured Mr. Morris. He shed his repetitions to reveal an orator all sharp and clear and true. He preached with a tongue of fire. That greased point of hair quivered, but his eyes steadied upon eternity. He opened the hand of salvation to all, and spoke of light where other men saw darkness. There was much love in the man, and it was revealed in his little chapel.

We are small and foolish creatures. I had all but dismissed Mr. Morris as a silly whack of a fellow before I heard him preach. Thus I learned for the hundredth time that our rash judgements will be rued.

Oh, I learned the back roads and the front pews, the passing faces and the names of farms, the shops and beggar boys. All this I did, but could not crack the Irish.

They have a way of talking grand and saying nothing, those Hibernians. Some look you in the eye but shut their souls. Others will not face you at all, but crab off muttering. I tried politeness and cajolery, appeals to patriotism for their new-gained land, and even threats. I visited their sick with Father McCorkle. I even tried to excite the charity of my fellow Wesleyans on their behalf, but truth be told they found it easier to love a distant slave than a day laborer down in a shanty. Armored in the rectitude of duty, I went into the whisky shabs to see what might be gleaned amid damnation. When that failed, I appealed to those who had climbed up a step—for some of the Irish had painted houses and clothes that asked no mending. But they feared the loss of the little they had gotten, and such were ever glad to see the back of me. The Irish remained as closed to me as the book with seven seals.

I tried to open back doors. At Hammondsport, at the bottom of the lake, I accepted the hospitality of a family of co-religionists while I nosed about, for the hotels were notorious. Now that was a sad little settlement, come near to ruin with the success of Penn Yan across the water. The population had no outlet canal nor railroad of their own, only a troublesome waterfront bunch and a demon scheme of growing grapes for wine. A shame it was, for I have never seen a prettier frame for a village—but, then, I have known many a place poor and beautiful at once. I believe that only prayer kept it from collapse, for the place was wonderful with Methodists.

Northward, in Geneva, I found high society and learning, but no plots. To the south, in Bath—a pretty place—commerce lifted all and even the Irish seemed contented. Elmira was a blue-clad town, with late-recruited soldiers in the streets and bunting on the saloons. Everywhere, I listened in vain for the whispers that would lead me to Irish plots or to the perpetrators of the murders.

The situation dragged my thoughts back to John Company and India. I do not speak of personal matters now. Twas the feeling of exclusion that was the same. We were as shut out from the world of the Irish as we had been from the schemes of the Hindoo or the Musselman. I found no least hint of rebellion, but well I remembered the Mutiny, and the signs we failed to see then, and the suddenness and slaughter that nearly finished us.

I sensed a darkness in the hills, though I could not find its source.

Look you. I would not pretend to Nellie Kildare's visions. Yet, there was trouble lurking just under the snows, and I knew it. My forebodings grew as January passed into February without event. For an old soldier knows that spring brings death, not life.

I knew not what to do, and felt a failure. But for a pair of queries, Washington trusted me, with confidence misplaced. Of course, the attentions of the great were elsewhere. Although Mason and Slidell, the Confederates our navy had seized from a British deck, had been handed back, the newspapers warned of London's surging truculence. The Rebels sought to parley Manchester's hunger for cotton into an alliance of war. Even the French were sniffing opportunity in Mexico like low mongrels. Meanwhile, we could not fight the war we had. Congress deviled Mr. Lincoln for results, with Mr. Seward damned in a new gazette each week. Twas a dark winter.

"He is not telling all," you will say. "For he was not quits with the spirit girl, that Nellie." But there is sad little to report. I went again to visit the Kyle place, where they abided. I took money along. For she had said her father had a hunger for it.

The Great Kildare allowed a *conversazione,* as he called it. We sat around a little table, the three of us this time, with the curtains drawn against the afternoon. But nothing come of it. The girl remained withdrawn in her father's presence, and the trance brought not the least hint of spookery. I felt she was resisting. In recompense to me, her father made her do tricks, like calling out a number upon which I concentrated. She brightened long enough to promise I would be happy, but I might have had that of a gypsy at a fair. At last, she fell to coughing. There was a new leanness to her, the sickness hewing her down, and her father quickly led her from the room.

Kildare returned for his money and explained that the spirits would not be moved that day. He pressed upon me a tract he had written on phrenology, along with a little pamphlet on "Swedenborg's Doctrine of Correspondences."

I left, with those O'Hara brothers watching from the barn door. As the sleigh pulled off, I heard Kildare's voice shouting at the girl.

When I went back again they were gone. Mr. Morris, whose admiration for Kildare had not faltered, explained that father and daughter had embarked upon a lyceum tour of a few weeks' duration. He showed me a handbill. The Kildares would go first to Elmira and Ithaca, then west as far as Erie and Buffalo, finishing with a "spiritualist gala" in Rochester. Young men and women would have their matrimonials predicted by the spirit world, and visions from beyond would startle all.

"He has to do that sort of thing," the pastor explained, "*has* to do it. Money for his research, money for his work."

At the end of January, we had a brilliant thaw. Patches of brown appeared in the fields, and there were birds in the air. If you went abroad at night, you heard the groaning of the ice on the waters. But all was false. With the start of February, winter bullied back. The wind screamed down, and the snows resumed in earnest.

One bitter day, when it was almost too cold for the horses to be out, John Brent drove me down to Himrod's Corners, where I wished to ask a few questions. In the course of our rides, I learned more from that man than from any other in the county. He had a handsome, even bookish speech when we were alone. If we neared other white people, though, he returned to the jolly dialect of the minstrel, for which he asked my indulgence. Twas the reverse of an Irishman, who will speak his best in your presence, then curse you in his brogue when you go off. But the Negro occupies a peculiar spot in our society, and I think it will take a generation before he is valued as equal to a white man.

Himrod's Corners was a barren, hardheaded place, a cluster of shacks excused by a meeting of roads. The sole tavern was low, its only patrons farmers going bad. I found no Irish. Still, my queries met silence or diversion, for these were closed-off folk from the glens. We soon began the ride home to Penn Yan.

The team trotted along a ridgeline and I watched a train cross the fallow land, peeling back the snow from the rails before it. Of a sudden, I saw that I had to leave. To return to Washington and make a report. And, perhaps, to recruit my own informer, though the matter lay heavy in my breast.

I will tell you: I was not unselfish in my plans. I would set my departure so that I might have a Saturday night at home, in Pennsylvania, along my way. For I had left a thing undone these last years that wanted doing.

I had tamed the spirits called up by Nellie Kildare, and saw the business clear for a fraud, if still an inexplicable one. The girl's sickness of body had unbalanced her mind, and her father, the mesmerist, had put things in her thoughts that he had learned on the quiet. How or why I knew not. But answers there would be in time to come, and no spooks or goblins would be found. Meanwhile, an earthly duty lay before me. Painful it would be. But that is the price of duty delayed.

I left Penn Yan in a snowfall.

• • •

The railroad makes us thoughtful. It brings us to one another with remarkable speed, and that is a welcome thing. But along the way it lifts us out of our familiar order. Old notions rise unbidden, and the journey—so eagerly begun—fills with a sense of loss. We feel uprooted, and we are. It is the times. For we live in an age of confusions, unlike the long and simple days of our grandfathers. Our world is a mighty locomotive, hurtling onward, regardless. And war worsens all. What man would not be glad of a little peace?

The train outraced the storm, and when I left the Tenth Avenue depot, all New York City was out in its finery along the avenues. There was bustle. Cheering sparked in the streets at the sight of blue uniforms—which I must say I found a grand and welcome surprise—and I was pressed to avoid the to-do spilling off the curb at each next public house. Fellows tried to fit great schooners of beer into my hand, congratulating me blindly, for too many are the men who associate patriotism with drink. I had to wave my cane to open my path.

With hours to spend before the Pennsylvania train, I walked across town to the district headquarters. Twas staffed by a plump, bewhiskered lot, all merry. They were drinking French champagne. In the middle of the afternoon.

"Haven't you heard?" a rotund colonel asked in response to my bewilderment. Waving his glass, he surveyed his fellow sybarites in uniform. "The fellow hasn't heard! Of all things!"

Fort Henry had fallen the day before. Our gunboats beat down its walls even as our army marched upon it. The fortress lay upon a Western river, such as those of which Mick Tyrone had written, and I prayed that my friend was safe. The officers said it was the start of a grand campaign and the beginning of a death blow to the Confederacy.

I found a sober clerk and sent a supplemental telegraphic to Mr. Nicolay, assuring him of my arrival in Washington on Monday. Then I wandered out the time until my train.

A bit too far I wandered. For not all was wealth and patriotic fervor in New York City. I come to slums that made me turn around. Irish, they were. And bitter. The inhabitants cursed me and my uniform by daylight, and on a wall I read a sloven script:

> NO IRISH BLOD FOR THER BATTALS!
>
> NO NIGUR KINGS!
>
> FAIRE WAGES!

And a bummer spit on my boots. If insurrection broke out, it would be here. Not in the somnolence of Yates County.

Then there was a block of boys for sale, cheeky and got up fancy.

I fled.

I had to travel by way of Philadelphia, a city with harsh memories for me. From there, I found a space in a mail car going to Reading in the night, and, thanks to my uniform and rank, a bunk was granted me on a coaler returning to Pottsville with empty cars.

Twas dark as we clipped the last miles, but I could not sleep. I felt my newfound home rise up around me. The towns and farms of Little Germany slipped behind, and we curved into the water gap, where the Schuylkill washed the valley. Our own canal lay there, and the disordered settlements that had grown up at the landings. All sleeping now. We slowed but did not stop in Schuylkill Haven, home to well-fed Dutchmen, and chugged into Pottsville under a hint of light.

Twas a vigorous place, our Pottsville, built upon anthracite.

The yards were quick with shouts when we come in. Our locked wheels squealed on the rails. Switchmen strained over levers. All smelled of ash, but the familiarity was sweet to me.

Despite the hard duty before me, I longed to see my love. For she was my joy. Twas not five weeks since last I had held her to me, yet it seemed a year. My young son drew me, too, but I will tell you truly, not like her.

I feared what was to come.

I had to speak to Hughes the Trains, to insure a place for a Sunday leaving. Meanwhile, I sent a boy along to warn my wife of my arrival. For enough surprises she would have, and to spare.

• • •

I told her all. We sent Young John to Mrs. Roberts, next house but one, and let that good woman think what she would. Then we sat in the parlor, for this was a serious matter, and I began straight out. No breakfast I allowed myself, nor pretension that all was well. She wanted but to hold me, my beloved, but I could deceive her no longer, and made her take a place on her proud cushions. I should have made a clean breast of it years back, before we married, when first I come back from India and found her in the garden. But men are weak, and I had been at my weakest then. Now I would be paid back with hard interest for my dishonesty and cowardice.

I told her of my dead love and the babe, and she learned at last why my letters had stopped for so long.

"I will not be false now," I told her downcast head. Her hair was pinned back sleek, her gray dress prim. "I loved Ameera. And the little one. Without benefit of clergy, we were. But a family none the less. For all the devils of India, I loved her. As I love you now and forever." Her head sank toward her knees and her small shoulders quivered. "As I love our little John."

I let her cry, and cry she did. Sobbing hard. She was a woman of great reserve in her parlor ways, but privately she kept no walls between us. She was better than I deserved, and I knew it and had taken the gift in silence. And never think that silence is no lie. It lulls the decent heart until it kills.

"I'm sorry," I said. "I'm so sorry, Mary. But you had to know the truth of it. Wrong it was of me to keep it from you. Wrong and cowardly."

"You . . . would not have left her, then?" my love begged. "Had she lived? You would not have . . . returned to marry me?"

The words come so heavy. But I would not lie to her now.

"I would not have left her. Or the child."

She wept from the depths of her, face in her hands. Tears ran down her wrists and into her sleeves.

I wished to be strong. But I could restrain myself no longer. I cast myself upon my knees before her.

"I'm so sorry. I've broken your heart . . ."

She cringed as if afraid that I would touch her, so I did not. Though I longed to gather her to me. I felt my fine life dissolving, and wondered if it would not have been better had I not risen from my fever bed.

"I've broken all your faith in me," I whispered, and I was weeping, too. "And brought you only disappointment . . ."

Suddenly, she straightened. Face fierce as the Black Mountains. She grasped my wrists with her little hands. Strong from the scrubbing, they were.

"Don't you understand?" she cried. "Oh, don't you?"

"I do," I assured her. "I'm so sorry, my love."

She shook her head. Denying that I could ever understand. Then, all unexpected, she flew from the chair and clutched me. Holding me hard.

"I'm such a wicked woman," she told me, sobbing. "It's me who's the wicked one, don't you see?" I felt the rise and fall of her breast against me. "I'd feared so much the worse of you, my darling."

• • •

Twas night, and our little John slept. We had already put certain things behind us, my sweetie and I. Too vivid in our love, we could not sleep.

"I don't know what to make of it all," I told her. For I valued her advice above that of all others. "Mr. Seward insists there's to be an insurrection. Yet I can find no clear sign of it. I feel myself a failure, see. And the business with the girl and her visions and sickness fair took my balance off." I sighed, turning to hold her the better. I loved the scent of her hair. "Well, I will go to Washington. And tell them what is and what is not. Then we will see."

"Then all agree there is no insurrection?" my love asked.

"Just so."

"Yet there is murder?"

"That, too."

"But Mr. Seward thinks there will be trouble?"

"He does."

"And so do you?"

"I do."

She got up on an elbow, hair cascading in the lamplight. "Then you are right," she said.

I gave her a look. For she must explain.

"There is simple," she went on. "There is murder, and trouble afoot, but no rebellion."

"And?"

"No 'and.' And you keep your mittens down, until we've done our talking."

I ceased my molestations.

"I do not see where you have gotten to," I admitted. For she was ever quicker.

"Look you, Abel. There is murder, and trouble, but no insurrection against the government. Well, that is it. No insurrection, no rebellion. But something else. You are looking for a goat because they sent you to look for a goat. And so you do not see the sheep."

"What sheep, then, my little shepherdess?"

She gave me a slap. "You will behave, Mr. Jones. Until we have gotten to the end of this. Or you'll get none of what you want, and plenty of what you don't."

She was ever a hard one, when she set her mind on a thing.

"And how many questions did you ask up in New York?" She tried a new approach to make me see.

"Questions, my little one? I asked a thousand. And every answer come back the same."

"That is because you did not ask a thousand questions, but one question a thousand times. Will you not see that there's no Irish rebellion there? Although there may be something else entirely, and Irishmen aplenty in the doings. Do you not see it, then? You will not have the right answer until you put the right question. Oh, I swear—"

"Mary!"

"Well, I do. Though only to you. And upon this one occasion. I tell you that I've never known a man so clever and foolish at once. You have the saddle ready before you've caught the horse."

"I would saddle no horse, girl."

"Look you," my love commanded. "If they will send you back, forget rebellions. Begin again. You've been working backward from what this Seward has decided. Without a true knowing. Instead of starting with the facts and going forward."

I saw it. I did. She was as right as I was slow of conception. It is my sense of duty, see. I would do what my superiors ask of me. Even when I should know better.

"Well, there is clever," I said.

"Clever there's none. You'll use the brains the Lord bestowed upon you. And come home safely."

When I looked at her lovely outline by the lamp, then thought of the mind that worked within my darling, I almost could agree with Mrs. Stanton and Miss Anthony as to Woman's possibilities. Although I know that is a foolish business, and trouble.

"Well, then," I said. "I have my orders. From General Jones herself. And but one question left to close the matter."

She looked at me all fierce, my little lioness. "What, then?"

"Would you turn down the lamp and come closer?"

"No. For we are not done."

"More, then?"

"More. The girl. This Nellie."

"Oh, Mary! There is naught between us. I never—"

She smiled at that and gave me a gandy look. "Oh, Abel, I know. I can see you're taken with her, but not in a way to trouble me. For I know that I will keep you, and fight I would, besides. But fight I will not have to, for you would fight yourself first."

"She's dying."

"We're all dying," my wife said. "That's what we do. She's only dying faster. Does it not seem queer to you, Abel, that we should all put in our claims for Heaven, but fear the going so?"

"The body fears what the soul would have. But there is strange. I do not think the girl fears dying. It's the living that frights her."

"Well, I meant not to be hard. That was not my meaning. Only that I think she knows more than she has told you, and I do not speak of spirits. You will need to talk to her again. And help her if you can, for that is Christian. But pity with a clear head. And that business with her father. There is a mystery. Perhaps he is like your rebellion."

"How, my little one?"

"Something other than he seems. I do not like the sound of him."

"Nor would you like his look. Different from the girl, he is. I wish that they were parted."

She rose still higher above me. "Do you? Do you wish that, Abel Jones? Without knowing the history of them, and what that girl needs when the doors are shut?"

"She's burning away," I said.

My love softened. "Oh, I know it. You've said. And though I have no fear, I will give you jealousy. When I hear you speak of her beauty. And know I will never be such."

I moved to hold her, full of words of praise and adoration. But she set her free hand to my chest and kept me back.

"Be careful," she said. "Only be careful, Abel. For I know how it is with these consumptives. When they're going, they crave the life of all around them. There is passion in them then, and heat. So much it is unholy. I know, for I have nursed them. And the girl's mad. Though not so mad as you think her."

"But, surely you don't believe in—"

"I believe," she said, looking down at her pillow, "in what I can hold. And in what the Gospels tell me. I'm a simple woman, Major Jones." She reached for the lamp. "And now I would hold my husband."

• • •

Rising from my Juliet, I did not hear the lark of Mr. Shake-speare, but woke to early church bells up the hill. I took the nightpot outside, then washed in the cold under the pump, and lit the stove. I started to make the breakfast, then realized it was a kindness that would wound her. For she would want to break the eggs and spill the pancakes on the griddle for me. I only put the kettle on for coffee, that joy of good Americans.

My footsteps up the stairs woke little John, and he woke her. There was not enough time. A better man would have counted himself lucky to be home for even an hour, when vast armies were condemned to winter quarters and unbroken loneliness. But the torment of another does not lessen the hurt of our hang-nail, and we are selfish creatures to the core.

I ate mightily, making up for a month at Mr. Morris's table.

We went to chapel as a family, but I had to leave before the final hymn. I heard them singing "O Thou who camest from above," as I flew down the street with my bag. My eyes were so bothered I was nearly run over by one of Mr. Yuengling's brew-ery wagons, off to water some profane gathering up in the patches. That would have been a hard end for a Methodist.

Chapter 8

"OOOOCH, MAJOR JONES! You are coming again!" Mrs. Schutzengel, my Washington landlady, waved her mixing spoon like a saber. Filling her doorway, she seemed a bulwark of all that is good and homely. "We beat them slavekeepers *gut und hart, nicht wahr?* Now pie I am making!"

Even as she said the word "pie," her rapture withered and her broad face sprouted worry. *"Ein Apfelkuchen ist schon gemacht,"* she continued, but the beauteous passion with which she customarily spoke of food deserted her. She looked me up and down, as if appraising a youth set under her charge who had ranged delinquent. *"Mein Gott,"* she declared, "he *ist* only the bones and all starfed! They have taken half of him away! Where *ist* you gone, Major Jones? And why *ist* you knocking and not coming in? *Sind Sie nicht hier zuhause?"*

Of a sudden, the woman puckered with tears.

"My dear Mrs. Schutzengel," I began, "there is good to see you again. I only thought that, since I'm no longer a boarder, I had best knock. I was hoping, see, that you might have an open room for a night or two, perhaps in the attic and—"

Now, I know that a bull is not a female creature, yet Mrs. Schutzengel was a bull of a woman. And that is nicely meant. It is her strength I would convey to you. And, yes, her presence of body evidenced a good table. Yet, delicate in her feelings she was. Tears fair poured from her, even as her great red face exploded with anger. She brandished the mixing spoon above her head again.

"*Herrgott erbarme,*" she wailed, with her Communist eyes raised to Heaven, "*dass der gute Mann so wenig von der Schutzengel hält! Meint er, dass ich nur ein böser Kapitalist bin?*"

And then she began to scold. Still waving that spoon.

"Ooooch, now my heart *ist* all broken in *Stücken*. That you are thinking I am only after the money!" Oh, she wept. "*So geldgierig ist die Schutzengel nicht!* You will have a room in the attic? *Nein! Nein, bis zur Ewigkeit!* And what is wrong with the room you are already having? Is it not all *sauber und* waiting for you?

"But . . . my good lady . . . I gave up my room when I went to New York . . ."

Didn't she give me the fierce then?

"You gived up your room. *Jawohl!* But your room is not giving up you! Even if them Rebels are coming, Hilda Schutzengel is guarding your room *wie ein alter Grenadier!*"

"But . . . I explained . . . that I cannot pay for two—"

She near slashed me dead with the mixing spoon. A hard end that would have been. Though not worse than mortality under a beer wagon.

"Pay? Who *ist* saying to pay? How else will Hilda Schutzengel fight for the Union *und die Freiheit*? For the freedom of the peoples, I give you the room when you are gone." Great choring muscles rippled beneath the cloth of her workadays. "Ooooch, if I am being a man, I make worse for them Rebels than Fort Henry! Over the head, I will hit them!"

A woman of passions she was. Of fire and mood. Again, she drooped into sorrow.

"But only the bones you are! *Nichts als Knochen!* Like the prisoner! Come inside. *Komm! Marsch, marsch!* Eat!"

The truth is that we would have liked to hug each other. But such things are not done in proper society. Even by Communists.

When my dear landlady shifted to allow me inside, I saw Annie Fitzgerald, the housemaid, standing behind her in the hallway. The stalk of a girl had been rendered invisible until then by the capacity of Mrs. Schutzengel's mortal coil. I had done Annie a small good turn once, but hardly expected to be remembered for it. Yet she cried to greet me, too. Now I would not have women weep for me, for I have never been the kind who takes joy in the suffering of the poor creatures—though some men do. But who does not like a nice welcome?

"Oh, Major Jones," Miss Fitzgerald said to me, "I dreamed you were gone into danger, and prayed to Our Lady til dawn."

Mrs. Schutzengel grunted. With a tad of jealousy in it. As if she had been trumped in her devotions.

"Major Jones must eat now," she admonished the girl. "And there *ist* plenty you are cleaning."

Humbled, Annie Fitzgerald curtsied and said, "Yes, Madame."

But Hilda Schutzengel truly did believe in the Brotherhood of Man, and her good woolen sense always conquered the high silk of her temper in the end. She softened and laid a mighty arm around the girl.

"*Doch*, first we are all having pie."

• • •

With my belt loosened a notch, I tapped along toward the President's House. The streets were mires. Even where cobbled, they had been muddied over by countless wagon wheels and the leavings of horses. Rain spit. Smoke and the smell of slaughtered cattle thickened the air. Twas past the visiting hour, so the fine carriages were put up, and nobody strolled for the joy of it. Only those without choices walked the streets, and the drabs kept to the doorways.

A regiment of pale recruits, not yet issued waterproofs, marched soddenly from one camp to another. They had the faces of long-punished children, and the sergeants failed to keep the step. Army supply wagons grumbled along behind delivery carts, the teamsters huddled low beneath broad hats and turned-up collars. The drivers lacked the spark to curse, which, though a blessing, tells you of the dreariness. Rats slicked about, unafraid. A miserable day it was, a winter Monday, bare as bones. It put me in mind of Britannia's damp, and of coughing children.

Yet, there was something in the town I liked. Perhaps it had only grown familiar. But I had spent a barren night in Philadelphia, delayed by trains diverted, and would not have traded the ferment of our capital for all the elegance of Rittenhouse Square. Although I might have wished for better sewerage.

The President's mansion was a shambles. The public hall was filled up dense as a barroom when oysters are set out free, and the look of the guests was no better. Shabbiness of dress vied with shoddy ostentation. Nor was every man sober. Now, I am told there is such a thing as a good cigar, but I smelled nothing of the kind that day. A cannonade does not leave smoke so thick. Twas a wonder the President's family could bear the stench.

The horde of men waited sullenly, for Mr. Lincoln would see all who waited upon him, but never soon enough to suit their vanity. Office-seekers and favor-beggars spoke loudly to one another, as if the volume justified their claims.

"Old Abe's forgot the likes of them put him in," a fellow with tobacco juice in his beard told his neighbor.

"Gone all high and awmighty," the next man agreed, "and thar's a fact."

Another visitor cut a souvenir from the draperies with his clasp knife.

As I went up to Mr. Nicolay's office, the supplicants lining the stairs complained about the military pushing good men out of the way and damned West Pointers—though I am far from such. I passed a bald man with the shakes and he called out, "Lookee there. It's a pegleg puss-in-boots." But when men speak to hurt, their own wounds show.

Mr. Nicolay himself answered my knock. He got me inside through the crush and complaints, then closed the door and locked it. The smoke seeped through.

The President's private secretary looked as though he had not slept in weeks. He bid me sit and took a chair himself.

"These people," Nicolay said, with just a trace of German heaviness, "I tell Mr. Lincoln they must go. But he lets them come. I tell him he must say they are to join the army, if they wish to serve the government. But he laughs and says that the best thing he can do for the army is to keep men like these out of it. What are we to do?"

Germans. Where the Englishman is only clever, the German is intelligent and earnest. And when he is not wanted, he keeps to his beer and cabbage. Loyal, too, your German, and he does not fear work. If only others made so little trouble.

"I fear," I told him, "I do not have a head for political matters."

He did not smile, for your German is a somber fellow at his workplace. But I sensed he was amused.

"The paradox of democracy, Major Jones. The bad man is born for politics, but governing requires the good man."

"Mr. Lincoln is a good man, it seems to me."

He sat up straight. Mustering all his Teutonic intensity.

"Mr. Lincoln is a *great* man. A very great man," he said. "They will see."

"Look you . . . I'm afraid my purpose has been frustrated in New York, Mr. Nicolay. I have done naught of value."

He half rose from his chair. "No, Jones, no. Your reports have been read, sir. You are a valued man."

"But I have found nothing."

"To the relief of all. Yet . . . your last telegraph message . . . implies doubts. You yourself continue to believe in insurrection, I think? Perhaps among the Irish? As Seward fears?"

I shook my head. "No, sir, I do not. Although Abel Jones has been wrong more than once in his life. I do not think the Irish are plotting rebellion. Nor will others rise against our government. Yet, there is something afoot. But there is strange. I cannot say what that something may be."

"You will continue to examine the matter?"

My shoulders shrugged before my voice could speak. "That's up to you, sir. And to the President and Mr. Seward. But I fear the expense to the government of my activities. When I come to you without result."

He did smile this time. Twas a rare expression on that man's face.

"Oh, we will bear the expense, I think." He chuckled. "General McClellan insists it takes a hundred thousand men to empty a slop pail. So I think one man is not too many for the peace of all New York."

"I wish I had more to tell," I said honestly. "But twas all in the cables and scribblings. I would not disappoint Mr. Lincoln, see."

Nicolay glummed at the mention of the President's name. Out in the hall, a round of laughter ended in coughs and phlegm.

"The President wanted to see you himself," he said. Downcast and sorrowing now, as if he had recalled a heavy burden. "But he's overcome. I can't even get him to sleep."

"The news from Fort Henry cheered him, I hope?"

His mouth twisted. "Oh. Yes. Fort Henry. The generals are already arguing about who should have the credit. The only thing they agree on is that none of the praise should go to any of the men in the field. To listen, you would think the war is fought in the headquarters alone." He sighed. "Well, that fellow Grant is marching on Fort Donelson. While the others talk. Perhaps we will not squander this chance entirely."

Now, you will think it disrespectful, but I will tell you: I never met a man I sooner would have employed as a clerk than John Nicolay, and that is high praise from one who has kept accounts. He had the soul of one who keeps good books.

The little German met my eyes again. "And . . . there's something else. The President's sons are ill. Perhaps you've heard the rumors? Well, they're true. Willie and Tad both. The doctors say it is a bilious fever. But I fear the typhoid. It is very bad, I think. And Mrs. Lincoln is not . . . always sensible. The President spends hours by their bedsides. It is hard to make him leave them. Even for the greatest matters. That is why he does not meet you."

"That is only sensible, sir. For his sons must come first."

Now you will say: "This Abel Jones does not understand the importance of great matters of state. Lincoln should have sacrificed his personal concerns, for he was President." But I will tell you: Even a war must wait for a sick son. It is a lesson I learned hard in India. And I had not even the excuse of battle.

"Seward wants to talk to you, though," Mr. Nicolay continued. "He said to send you over to his office this afternoon."

"Yes, sir."

"And Major Jones? Before you go?"

"Sir?"

"I had a message . . . from the clerk who manages the secret service fund. He . . . complains of irregularities. In your claims and account."

I do not think I ever leapt to my feet so fast.

"Irregularities? About money is it?"

"Now, now. It is a minor matter, I have no doubt."

"Irregularities?"

"Well, yes. He insists your claims are too low. You are not spending half of what the other agents do. He wondered if your receipts might not be incomplete . . . if you might not wish to revise them?"

"Revise them?"

"Well, he thinks you should be spending more."

"He . . . wants me to spend more? Of the government's money, then? He wishes me to make false claims? Waste and steal is it? I'd sooner—"

"I'm not sure I would say it in such a way, I think. But he fears it looks improper when your field expenses are so low and the other accounts are so much higher. A Congressional auditor looking into the secret service fund might wonder why those other claims are—"

"Well, let him wonder, see," I interrupted. For I was in a dudgeon. "I will not have waste and wanton expenditures! Oh, there is wicked, when men in service load themselves with luxuries, Mr. Nicolay. Our government is not a milk cow. So let this auditor wonder, and Abel Jones will tell him what is proper, if he comes asking."

Nicolay gave me his second smile of the day. This one showed teeth below his mustache.

"I see you are right, Major Jones," he said. "You have no head for political matters." He sighed. "Neither do I, I am afraid."

He moved to usher me out, for he had work in plenty. But I had to ask him, "Mr. Nicolay . . . think you that there are no good politicals, then? Besides Mr. Lincoln?"

He began to reply, then caught himself, as men must in Washington. And yet, he had spoken truly when he said that he, too, lacked a head for politics. After a pause, he answered me squarely, which is not the Washington manner.

"There's Seward," he said. "All thought he and the President would be enemies, since Seward was to have the nomination. They knew Seward's pride and expected jealousy. They would have enjoyed that, I think. But Seward is a bigger man than they believed. I think he has become the President's only friend in Washington, the only one to be trusted."

"But you, sir, are Mr. Lincoln's friend, and can be trusted."

A wistful look crossed his face as he laid his hand on the doorlatch. "I do not signify. I am a small man, meant for doing the little work. When God allows, I think I do it well. But Seward rises to greatness. He has kept us out of war with Britain. So far."

As if speaking to himself, Nicolay added, "I think of him as Saul become Paul."

• • •

"Sonofabitch," Mr. Seward barked.

Twas a hard greeting.

"Son-of-a-goddamned-bitch," he expanded. Chewing his cigar as if to eat it.

I knew my results had been poor, but I had been dutiful. I will admit disappointment at my reception by our Secretary of State.

"Son-of-a-goddamned-worthless-bitch," Mr. Seward continued, as if declining Latin. The paper in his hand quivered. In a room thick with smoke. All Cuba's tobacco might have burned there in a day.

"Sir," I said, "I have done my best, and if—"

"What the hell? Oh, Jones. Not you. Goddamn it. *Fred!*"

A moment later, a handsome fellow of perhaps thirty popped his head through the door.

"Yes, father?"

"Goddamned Canadians let two blockade runners into Halifax harbor again."

"Father, in the interests of accuracy," he said, with a glance at me, "I must remind you that Halifax is not part of the Canadas for diplomatic purposes, although it's administered by—"

Seward yanked the cigar from his mouth. It looked tormented. "Just get that bugger Lyons down here."

Fred Seward blushed royally. Or should we Americans say "blushed democratically?" Anyway, he slipped inside and closed the door behind him. His poise had deserted him.

"Lord Lyons is already here, Father. He's just outside."

Seward rammed the cigar back into his mouth then pulled it out again. "Well, let him wait, goddamn it. Can't have him thinking he has the run of the place. And get that goddamned picture of the Prince of Wales back out and put it on the mantel."

"Yes, Father. Would you like to review the latest correspondence from Ambassador Adams before you speak to the British ambassador?"

Seward grunted. I believe it passed for a yes. He was a small, bowlegged, bignosed, scrawny giant of a man. The sort who, despite his size, makes you think he could heave the world and have a hand to spare. A born scrapper, that one. Like the little pea-pod of a recruit who proves a demon in battle when the brawny waver. I do not excuse his lamentable excesses of language, of course, and would not report them were it not our duty to record the utterances of great men.

"Know Charlie Adams, Jones?"

I reviewed my acquaintances. "There was a Charles Adams in my regiment, sir. Died of too much gin in the Punjab."

"Not the same one. Hell. If Charles Francis Adams dies of any excess, it'll be an overdose of propriety. Damned fine ambassador to send to London, though. One of our own goddamned 'aristocrats.' Best kind to deal with old buggers like Palmerston. And that Russell. Buggers every one. Way they bring 'em up." He caught himself. "Not English, are you?"

"I am American, sir. Although born and bred in Wales."

"Don't have their proclivities, then. Good for you. Now tell me about this Fenian rebellion of ours. Cigar?"

"No, sir. Thank you, sir. There is no rebellion, sir."

"Sure of that?"

"I see no indication of such doings."

"You goddamned sure, though?"

"There is only so much certainty to be had in such matters, sir. But I see no insurrection against our Union."

He stood there before me, hardly taller than I was myself, with his neckcloth awry and ashes on his lapels. But his eyes, ladies and gentlemen! Fine writers tell of "piercing eyes." Well, Seward's went through you like roundshot. Looking back, I think he was too intelligent—certainly too well read, for he loved books—for the rough world of local politics through which he had risen. He had learned early to disguise his brains and learning, and now the rough disguise had become as comfortable as an old waistcoat.

"Well," he said, "my sources back home in Auburn *still* insist there's an Irish uprising in the works up there. Of course, the same thickheaded sonsabitches told me I'd be President." He gobbled smoke from his cigar. Augmenting the fog in his office, he continued, "All right, then, Jones. Tell me what *is* going on."

"I do not know, sir."

"But your dispatches, man. According to them, you think *some*thing's going on. Even if it's not an insurrection. Well, what is it, man?"

"I don't know, sir. But I will try to find out."

He began to pace. "Hell and damnation. Anybody giving you trouble up there? Getting in your way?"

"No, sir."

"They do, you let me know, goddamn it."

"Yes, sir."

"Well, what do you think, though? Man to man. One banty bird to another."

"Sir . . . I believe there is trouble coming . . . and it may well be Irish trouble. But I do not see insurrection. They are too few for a rising." The smoke was thick enough to hide in. "They know their weakness, see. And to what end would they do such a thing? There is no sense in it. The best of them are gone to the army, anyway."

He snorted. "First thing you learn in politics, Jones, is not to expect sense out of people. Just assume every last fellow's born crazy, but doesn't want anybody else to know. That's how this society works. Hell, *all* societies. Nothing but lunatics on their best behavior. Call it 'civilization.' Each last man and woman convinced they're the only one who's crazy and afraid to let it show. But give 'em an excuse and they'll be dancing naked as jaybirds in front of the county courthouse. And singing to beat the band."

That did not accord with my vision of mankind.

"Damn it, Jones. Keep on the matter. Would you? *Some*thing's wrong up there. We both agree on that. And this nation can't afford any more trouble now, internal or external. This Mason and Slidell business isn't quite as solidly behind us as the newspapers think. Damned British aristocrats *want* this country to fail. It's an example they don't like. An embarrassment. Afraid their own goddamned working classes are going to rise up and kick 'em in the pants. And their moneybags want Southern cotton for their mills. London bankers hate the damn blockade. Crown sent eight thousand more troops to Canada. Which doesn't strike yours truly, Billy Seward, as a friendly action. Goddamned 'Royal Artillery' and the like." He looked me up and down. "You served in Her Majesty's forces as I recall?"

"In John Company's ranks, sir. An East India regiment. But the Mutiny changed—"

"They any good? Can the Brits fight?"

"The men can fight, sir. And will fight. For the sheer delight of it. For they are not all good Christians. And the officers, begging your pardon, are too stupid to know when they have been beaten. It is a devil's combination, see, and they win even when they should lose."

He grunted. "Damnation. President's right, you know. He sees it. Don't underestimate that man. Did it myself. And how, I underestimated him. But he damned well knows his business. Fool the hell out of you, Lincoln. 'One war at a time,' he says. And he's right. Can't afford a war with Britain now." He dropped the ragged bits of his cigar into a brass bowl.

Twas good to hear him speak so. For I am loyal to our America, and no question there. But I do not long to fight another Welshman, nor any who had served beside me once. No, Abel Jones did not want a war with Britain and her armies and fleets.

"Anyway, Jones. Get to the bottom of things up there. Do whatever you have to. Money help?"

"I am adequately supplied, sir."

He grunted. "Well, don't be stingy with bribes. Especially with the Irish. And hire all the turncoats you want. Take some of these new green dollars. Federal-backed paper money. That'll make 'em think. You just box 'em in. Don't want any trouble up in New York, with Canada full of redcoats and bayonets just across the river and 'Merry Old England' spoiling for a fight. Can't have any appearance that New York's disloyal to the Union, either. John Bull needs to understand that we mean to hold together. Insurrection or whatever, you keep your thumb on it."

He briefly sorted through the chaos of his desk. Or perhaps it was only a private order others could not decipher, for he found what he was seeking soon enough.

He held out a sealed envelope.

"Here, Jones. Special orders. In an emergency, you're authorized to call up the militia on Federal authority. And to assume command of any U.S. troops or volunteers in the area. Rank immaterial." Those stabbing eyes cut through me yet again. "Don't hesitate. Least sign of trouble, crush the bastards. We need peace up there, and I'll pay in blood to get it."

"Sir . . . I . . ."

"Be *hard,* Jones. Don't look into their faces. Don't think of them as men. Just stop them. As if they were mad dogs. Make an example at the least sign of trouble. The Union's more important than any thousand of us."

I was just thinking that, were he not our Secretary of State, he would have made a splendid sergeant, when he turned back to the great business of his office.

"Goddamn it to hell. Now I've got to see that pompous bugger Lyons. 'Her majesty wishes to inform . . .' More excuses than an old whore caught filching. Succoring damned blockade runners and privateers . . ."

The door to the office opened. I feared it was Lord Lyons barging in, for Britannia is proud and impatient.

Twas Mr. Lincoln.

Stooping under the lintel, he was. All the great tallness of him. Tears covered his face.

Now I am small and undistinguished, and I do not think Mr. Lincoln saw me at all that day. His ravaged eyes looked only at my host.

"Seward," he said, "my boy's gone."

• • •

In those days, our Department of State was allotted a building hardly the size of a middling gentleman's country house. We were a nation that looked inward and not out, Westward and not East, though that would change. I left those cluttered offices and copy clerks for the lamplit world outside.

Rain spotted my coat.

I expressed no condolences to Mr. Lincoln, for we must know when we are not to speak. But it was not for lack of sympathy. Mr. Lincoln, see, looked a sad one on the sunniest of days, and think of the weight on him. Then this. I would say he was a very Job, but Job was no president faced with civil war. No, old Job faced the lesser trial. I slipped away, quiet like.

Twas clear that I must go back to New York in the morning, which left me with a list of things to do. I had meant to visit my friend Evans the Telegraph, and he would be wounded by my neglect, but time for such indulgence there was none. I would see Fine Jim, though, for but a moment. There was smallpox in the city, as well as the typhoid, and I feared to find him missing from his corner.

There he stood. An apprentice rooster, ragged and shivering by his pile of papers. When he saw me, Fine Jim fair lit like a rocket, running to meet me halfway across the street.

"Captain Jones!" he cried, smile wonderful. Then he corrected himself, "*Ma*jor Jones! Why, yer going fit as a racehorse! Ya all back then? Ya back to stay, sir? Ain't that leg looking good as new? Ain't it good as new?"

"Better," I told him.

"And yer back to stay?"

I shook my head and crushed the joy of his evening. And little enough joy the newsboy had. I recalled the misfortune he had suffered because of the overcoat I tried to provide him. He paid a high price for nothing, as the poor so often do. But let that bide.

"I only come by for my paper, see. A little visit it is. But I would know that you are well."

His smile returned. Oh, he was resilient. As children of privilege never will be.

"I'm tops, Major Jones. Just tops. Want yer paper, do ya?"

I looked at him. At the small, dirt-streaked face that found such joy in the moment. Twas a face born to sweat for great men who would never know his name, and to fight their wars and die for their speeches and pride. He stood shivering and wet through beside his stack of gazettes. A wrap of oiled canvas protected the merchandise, but not him. Perhaps Mick Tyrone and Mrs. Schutzengel are right about the injustice of the world and the need for changes in society, although I do not approve of uproar and attacks upon authority.

Fine Jim held out a copy of the *Evening Star*. He was little more than a matchstick shadow under the gaslight.

What do you see in a child's face? When life turns their way for just a matter of seconds? It may be the slightest transaction, a father's glance or the sale of a newspaper, yet they greet it with such delight. There is no gift so pure as a child's eyes. Now I speak of purity, not innocence. Too much is made of innocence, and we grow hard and unpardoning. Innocence perishes—too often through no fault of our own—yet purity may endure. I knew Fine Jim had seen things many a grown man has been spared. No, twas not innocence in his face, but a wonderful, gleaming purity. And faith. The faith that good will come, despite all. Is that not the soul of all religion?

"I must have not one, but three-and-thirty copies," I told him. For at three cents each, that made ninety-nine cents, and I might spare him the final penny without shaming him. "Here is the dollar." I held out the coin.

He looked at me, doing his own figuring. "But Major Jones," he said, "ya can't read but one."

"They are not for me," I lied. Yes, lied. "I have friends in New York who would each have their own copy when I return. I must not disappoint them, see."

He counted out the papers. I had reduced the stack by half. Perhaps he could escape the weather early.

Our business done, he could not meet my eyes. But only said, "We miss ya, Major Jones."

"You will see me again, boy," I told him. "For I am a bad penny, and will turn up. Keep well now."

I left him in his wet rags. Once, I looked back, and saw him watching me. Now I would not question the Gospels, for in them lies our salvation. But sorry I am of the warning that "the poor will always be with us." It isn't fair, see. And I would rather give a boy a chance than a dollar.

• • •

I waited until I had walked well out of sight, then laid down all of the papers but one. I tapped along as quickly as I could, for I had business to transact before the shops closed and more to do thereafter.

Slipped early from their duties, staff officers paired along the sidewalks, jovial and headed for Willard's Hotel or lesser establishments. Not a few would seek out Murder Bay, with its women of sorrow and liquor to blind. Provost riders clopped along, swollen lumps under India rubber capes, and clerks scurried across the mucky streets. A serving maid hastened on a late errand, basket clutched against her.

The shop was well lit and clean, as always. M. FEINBERG AND SONS. I needed a second major's get-up, see, for the lovely uniform made by my Mary Myfanwy was already wearing a bit and

I would preserve it for ceremonies and Sundays. And Mr. Feinberg had treated me fairly in the past.

Now you will say, "That Abel Jones is so tight in the purse he buys Jew shoddy." But you will only make me angry. For I will tell you: When I clerked in the War Department, it was the great lot of uniforms from Brooks Brothers that we had to condemn, not the honest cloth of Moses Feinberg.

When I come in, the old fellow saw me at once. And didn't he drop the very business he was doing with a customer, throw his hands up in the air and rush toward me?

"A miracle!" he cried. "A miracle!"

Now I am glad of a welcome, but this seemed excessive.

He stopped before me, all beard and deep brown eyes, hands still upraised.

"A miracle!" he repeated. "Major Jones, your coming is a miracle!"

"I was looking for trousers and a frock coat, see."

But he had turned again, calling to his younger son behind the counter, "Levi, see to the customer, like a good boy. *Viel kaufen will er.* Where's your brother?" And then, to me again, "A miracle, a miracle!"

"Solly's in back, Pop. Like always. Where else is he going to be?"

The lad sounded as flinty and American as the old man sounded foreign.

"Come, Major Jones," the old man begged. "Come. Save my boy."

He led me to the room where they cut and sewed. Twas windowless, and heavy with the smells of flannel and digestion. The elder boy sat doing fine-work by a kerosene lamp. He was a handsome fellow, like the young men in those Bible prints, but lean as a diet of hardtack. Spectacles pinched his nose and he had the fingers of a lacemaker.

"Solly, you remember Major Jones? 'Not a penny more!' Remember?"

The young man put aside his work and laid his glasses on the cloth. He stood up respectfully. If there was a hundred pounds of him, I am Achilles, after all.

" 'Evening, sir," he said, accent as purely American as his brother's. I noticed a volume of Walter Scott tucked behind the tailoring.

"Solly, Major Jones wants to talk to you. He wants to talk sense to you."

Well, this was news to me. But the old man explained:

"A terrible thing! Terrible! The army he joins. To go and fight for the *Schwartze*." He pointed at his son. "Does he look like a soldier? I ask you. Tell him, Major Jones. Tell him what a fool he is. And ungrateful! Look at these hands, worked to the bone to put food on the table! He's breaking his mother's heart, and mine, too!"

I looked at the two of them. The father had naught but love and worry in his eyes, while the son burned with the determination of youth.

"I will talk to him, Mr. Feinberg," I said. Although I was not certain what I would say. For though the boy did not look like the material of a soldier, many is the man that would have said the same of me. And it was not my duty to discourage those who would serve our Union. But the weight of a father's love and loss had been impressed upon me that very afternoon. "Perhaps . . . you could leave us for a few minutes, sir?"

The old man went, muttering about miracles.

"Sit down, boy," I said.

He sat.

"Going for a soldier, is it?"

He nodded.

"It is a hard life. Blood and boredom. Only the fool finds joy in it. And not for long."

"You don't think I'd make a good soldier," he said, with gentle accusation in his voice. For he was alert to the world.

I waved my hand. "David may do as well as Goliath. Or better. I would only tell you that it is not all flags and trumpets. Or strolls with the ladies on Pennsylvania Avenue, with you in a fine uniform. There is death and misery, and the surgeon with his saw."

"I'm going to join up."

I nodded and fingered the head of my cane. "That is your affair, boy." I pointed at the novel that lay half-hidden. "I would only have you know that there is more of Cain and Abel in the business than there is of Mr. Scott and his stories. It goes hard, see. And there is always sickness, and the cold."

"I *have* to join," he said.

"And why is that, boy?"

He looked at me fiercely. "Because I'm a Jew."

I did not understand him.

"Because they all say we're cowards," he went on. "And thieves. 'Greedy Jews.' You know what they call us."

Yes, I knew.

He leaned toward me, a soul on fire. "If I don't go . . . when all the others are going . . . maybe they have a right to think that way. Why shouldn't I fight, too? Isn't this my country? Will it ever really be my country, if I don't join up like everybody else?" He looked at me in a transport of devotion to his vision. "By George, I'm going to show them, Major Jones. A Jew can fight as well as the next man. Better, too."

"Little is proved in war," I told him, though the words verged on a lie. For though we like it not, war is taken as a proof of too many things upon this earth.

Then he beat me completely.

"Don't you think this country's worth fighting for?" he asked.

Youth is cruel.

I took some time to answer. For the boy was right. Yet I feared for him. There was too much conviction in him, and too little fear. A certain fear preserves us, while conviction kills the saint.

"Yes," I said. "There is true. It is worth the fight, our Union.

Still, not every man is carved for battle. Think on it, boy. Do nothing rash. Perhaps you should wait until you are a little older. . . ."

The skinny little fellow jumped to his feet like a lion. "I'm twenty-one years old, and I'm going to join up." Then he looked at me with his father's lovely brown eyes. "It's our fight, too," he told me, softer-voiced. "If not here, where, Major Jones? If not now, when?"

"Only think on it," I said lamely.

Mr. Feinberg tried to give me too great a discount in gratitude, for he assumed I had succeeded.

I would not take any reduction.

"I do not know if the boy will listen," I said. "I do not even think he heard me."

The old man's face was sculpted by a lifetime's work, by joys and sorrows. Twas a good face, that.

"A man tries to do good," he said. "When a man tries, he should be rewarded."

"The price is fair," I said, "and I will pay it all."

The boy did not listen, of course. He joined up. I did what I could to ease his way. Working through Mrs. Schutzengel's acquaintances, I arranged for his transfer to a German-speaking regiment, for the Germans have less prejudice against the Jew than the rest of us. I hoped it would protect him, but he fell the next year at Chancellorsville. They told me he stood to his post while others ran, but that meant nothing to his father. The old man was inconsolable.

Chapter 9

ANNIE FITZGERALD, THE HOUSEMAID, HAD MORE SPUNK THAN I KNEW. I thought the poor child a mouse, all drabness and devotions, running to mass whenever a moment come free. For there is a difference between worship and hiding, see. The Lord would have us pray, but live, as well. We must not run from life, but face it. We are enjoined to "fear not." And I thought Annie weak with fear of living.

How we misjudge.

Twas she who got me through to Jimmy Molloy.

But first, I must tell of the pot roast.

You will recall this was a Monday night. And beef was reserved for Sunday afternoons or payday Saturdays. Nonetheless, dear Mrs. Schutzengel covered the table with meat. You would have thought she'd coaxed a stray cow into her kitchen. Oh, lovely it was. Sliced thick and bathed in gravy, with carrots and potatoes, onions and turnips simmered in the gravy of it. It made me want to shout a hymn of praise, though I did not.

The steam itself was thick enough for spooning. The sauce gleamed. If beef could speak, that roast would have cried out, "Devour me!" No gray and withered cheapness on that platter, but fine brown slabs. Tender to a falling into bits.

Oh, glory!

The other boarders marveled at the splendor, and I think they were pleased to see me then. All but one. *Herr* Mager, a closeboweled compatriot of Mrs. Schutzengel's, could not like any matter concerning me. For he and I had fallen out over a matter of sausages some months before—twas but a misunderstanding on my part—and the German, for all his virtues, does not forget. Though I wonder if Mager was truly German, for he had the Frenchman's acid and his bile.

He scowled, but ate his share.

Well, let Mager bide. The chewing was glorious, and wasn't there pie and cake to help the beef home? Now I do not mind a sweet, and do not think the eating of such unmanly. Is there more robustness in whisky and the gutter than in a golden pie, thick with the apples of Eden? And your German can bake a cake, too. I used to think chocolate a queer thing. But one does grow accustomed to the way it paints up a fine, three-layered cake. And who does not admire the gentle springing back of a fine cake under the fork, and the delight of it in the mouth, and the last lick of frosting on the lips? I would say that a well-wrought cake makes children of us all, but my own youth was never as sweet as this. Yet, I must not favor the cake unfairly. That pie would not be slighted, with its apples soft as clotted cream in the mouth and a crackling crust to tame the wanton sugar. I had two pieces of each to show my appreciation. All washed down with coffee hot and black.

When the other fellows went outside to have a smoke and line up for the privy, I spoke to Annie, who was clearing plates. For she and Jimmy Molloy had made acquaintance during the Fowler case.

"Miss Fitzgerald?" I began.

She looked up from her gathering of the tinware.

"Would you . . . by any chance . . . know the present where-abouts of James Molloy?"

"Jimmy Molloy? Sure, and that one's never been hard to find, sir."

"You know where I might locate him then?"

She lowered her bouquet of utensils. "Oh, and will you look

in on him, sir? Isn't that a kindness? For that one can always do with a bit of regulating."

I did not tell her that it was selfishness, not kindness, that drove me to seek out Jimmy Molloy, the regimental silver thief. Who should have been jailed in Delhi still. For all his wickedness, the man had talents, too. The Good Lord, in his mercy, is a spendthrift. And I had need of the fellow and his skills.

"I would look in on him, yes. If you can point me to him."

Mrs. Schutzengel came in, face huffed at Annie's slowness. When she saw I had engaged the girl, she calmed.

"Begging your pardon, sir, I can't do that," Annie said.

"So you *don't* know where he is?"

"Begging your pardon, I do, sir."

"Then . . . what is the difficulty, Miss Fitzgerald?"

"There's no describing the place," she said. "For it's over to Swampoodle. I'd have to be showing you meself, sir."

"*Was denn?*" Mrs. Schutzengel asked. "*Was ist mit dem Swampoodle?*" She had a curiosity, that woman. And all her heavy books could not appease it.

"I need to find Molloy," I told her. "You remember him, I believe."

"Molloy? *Der nette?* That sweet boy?"

Molloy was ever one for fooling the ladies. And the colonels. And even a sergeant, now and then.

"Yes, Molloy," I said. "Mrs. Schutzengel . . . if you wouldn't mind . . . if you'd do me the kindness . . . of allowing Miss Fitzgerald to guide me to Molloy's address?" Here I will tell you that I feared the worst, for Molloy was the sort who could fall while lying down. "That is, if Miss Fitzgerald has no objections? And if she judges there to be no danger, of course."

"Oh, none, sir. None at all." The girl seemed positively eager to be going. What poor housemaid will not escape her drudgery for an hour?

"But," Mrs. Schutzengel said, with heartrending disappointment on her face, "there is still cake for eating."

"Mrs. Schutzengel . . . my dear lady . . . I could not eat another bite."

"*Ooooch, ja,*" she sighed at the ingratitude of the world and its unfathomable lack of appetite. Then she looked at Annie. "*Geh mal mit, Kind.* Go with the major now. And clean your shoes before you come back in." Suddenly, she brightened. "Take the poor boy pie. And cake. I will make a package." She looked at me. "He has the great commitment to the world revolution, *der Junge.*"

Molloy had nothing of the kind, and I knew it. Twas all blarney. The only thing to which he was committed was roguery. And sloth, as well. Still, I said nothing. For I would not speak ill of a man whom I would shortly ask to risk his life.

• • •

I knew the streets that led to Swampoodle. But no outsider knew the alleys within. The provost marshal's men went there only by daylight, and the Washington police did naught but collect the bodies floating in Tiber Creek. Irish, the place was, in the lowest sense. I'd taken a beating there once, in the course of the Fowler affair, and entered on my guard.

Before we plunged too deeply into that swamp of sorrow and poverty, I brought us to a halt.

"Miss Fitzgerald," I said, "I really cannot allow you to go any farther. For the place is a danger to all."

"Oh," she said blithely, "they'd not harm one of their own, sir."

"Really, Miss Fitzgerald, if you would only direct me from here, I'd—"

"Sure, and you'd never find the place, sir. Tucked away, it is. Where the landlord's own hounds would run circles."

"I cannot—"

"Come, sir. For I owe you more than ever I could pay. For you kindness."

"Twas nothing, Miss—"

On she went, carrying Mrs. Schutzengel's bag of treats for that unworthy Molloy, and what could I do but follow?

Soot and sorrow marked our way. Lost women who no longer had the looks or health for even Murder Bay haunted the darkness. Hard boys and drunkards patrolled their domain or huddled about dust fires. The gas lamps ran out and only the occasional torch of pitch and pine lit the muddy alleys.

Annie fit her arm through mine and pulled me close. As though we were . . . intimates.

"Miss Fitzgerald," I said, recoiling, "I will not take liberties . . ."

But she would not let me go. She had pulled her hood well over her brow, and her voice come from the darkness.

"Hush, sir. They must think I'm . . . one of those women. And that you're my gatherings of the evening."

"Miss Fitzgerald!"

"Please to hush, sir. For there is danger for you, if not for me. They're hard after them that goes about in Union blue these days, and they take officers for the worst. And a Welshie officer would be a terrible bait to them. It's the rumors of grafting them into the army, sir. They'll have none of it, the ones what are left." She pulled me closer still. So close I could feel the hungry childhood that trailed her through life. "You'll be fine, if you're quiet now and come along, sir. For the boys would not take the bread from the mouth of the lowest of women. We're not so cruel as your Protestants, begging your pardon, sir."

Such are the braveries we must remember when dark nights come upon us. The girl had known what she was doing from the start, and meant to protect me with the only armor she possessed: her honor.

We wound past shanties too poor for kerosene, lit by wicks afloat in bowls of fat, then trudged by hovels with no lights at all. Yet, you felt the life in them. Cradled babes cried out that life goes on. We were troubled by no more than a scattering of curses and surprises of filth beneath our feet.

She brought me to an alley brighter than the others, lit with enough torches for a small parade. Roistering, it was. On a Monday night. She pulled her hood lower and clutched the bag of food against her like a shield.

There was music now, in competition. A piano jangled against the weep of a fiddle across the way. Women painted and got up like a mockery of society ladies laughed at little Annie in her cloak, calling to me, "Ye'll have no fun with that one, bucko. She'll go weeping all the while."

A saddled mule stood tethered to a post.

"Here," Annie said, pulling me into a doorway.

A heathen hole it was. Although unexpected in its cleanliness, I will admit. I speak in local comparison, of course. And twas all lit proper inside, with no dark corners for skullduggery in the little room. There was a bar cobbled up, and tables made of planks and sawhorses. A trio in their cups sang to a squeezebox. Other patrons looked well past the singing. But there was a certain order to the wickedness, reminiscent of a garrison canteen. The sawdust on the floor was fresh.

The greatest surprise, though, was the busier of the two barkeeps. Molloy himself it was. With a clean shirt and garters on his sleeves, a new and sleek mustache all Irish red, and . . . an aspect of sobriety. But the fellow was born a dissembler, a master of falsehood and disguise.

"Jaysus, Mary and Joseph," he cried when he saw me. Fair shouting, he was. "By all the saints in Ireland and the sinners in London town! By the skirts of the blessed Magdalene! Tis little Sergeant Jones come up to see us!"

I would not have chosen to be the center of attention.

Molloy did all but leap upon the bar. "Hold your fire, boys," he called to the clientele, "for the man what lifts a finger at the good sergeant, and him a great major now, will have to fight his way through Jimmy Molloy."

He looked at the figure beside me and ran his hand over his hair. Hastening out from behind that counter of Satan, he grinned and said, "Sure, Annie, and we'll not tell Father Patrick that we've seen ye here tonight."

"Go on with you," the girl said. She still kept under the shelter of her hood. But her voice had a fresh warmth. Almost as if she were pleased at the attention from the low devil. "Here is a gift you don't deserve, and from a good lady."

Molloy seized the parcel and peered inside with the shamelessness of a savage. Then he remembered himself and set down the victuals.

"Will ye not go back into the lady's saloon?" Molloy asked my escort, with a glance around the room. "For tis safe and clean, ye know, and I'll keep out the ruinations till ye go again. But ye can't stay out here, Annie, for I cannot have such beauty distracting the boys."

Artfully, almost gracefully, he guided her into a back room. The Irish can charm, when they have a mind to. For a moment, I feared for the girl's welfare. But such thoughts were unfair. The Irish have their rules among themselves. And for all his wickedness, I never knew Molloy to harm woman or child. On the contrary, the fellow was afflicted with that profligate generosity you find only among the poor. The thief's hand is open when the banker's is closed. I offer this but as an observation, not in approval. Although I will admit thinking of Father McCorkle in that moment, suspecting that the fellow would have said that Jesus Himself got more respect from a thief than from a king. But look you. At times, the wisdom of the Gospels lies beyond us. Read without the filter of morality, we might mistake them for texts of revolution to make pale the doctrines of Mrs. Schutzengel or Dr. Tyrone. For it is a fact that society folk only made time for our Savior when they needed their water turned into wine in a hurry. Of course, the world has changed since then, and order is virtue, and too much thought breeds indolence and error. So let that bide.

Molloy come back out with respectable promptness, shutting the door behind him.

"She'll be in there telling her beads all the while, that one," he said. "Born for marriage, not sporting." Then he fair sang out. "Oh, Sergeant Jones, ye great major, ye. Just look at ye. Ye'll be a high general next. Like Wellington himself. 'Up Guards and at 'em!' I'd buy ye a drink and a dozen more, and kiss ye like me own mother or worse, but for I know ye'd call out an army o' constables after me."

He thrust out his hand and I took it.

"A round for all on the house," he cried.

That took care of the Irish.

• • •

We sat over a trestle of planks by the rear wall. Pipe smoke mixed with the whiff of kerosene and the stink of sweat and liquors. I had expected to find Molloy as I had found him before, a beggar in rags. But here he was, shaven, employed and sober. Even if his employment was that of the devil, this was progress.

"I would not interrupt you at your work," I said, "but have only this night to speak to you. And speak to you I must. I hope it will not trouble the proprietor?"

He lowered a great slice of pie from his mouth and swallowed. Twas like watching a snake gulp down a rodent. Then he gave me the old Molloy smile that had got past many a sentry hours after the barracks was shut.

"Oh, the proprietor will give me the liberty, I'm sure of it." He waved a hand at the interior, as if surveying the lobby of a fine hotel. "For who do ye think his ownership is, if not James Molloy, Esquire, himself? Oh, Amerikee's a grand place for a fellow with ambitions."

"But . . . Molloy . . . when last we met, you were destitute."

He looked at me with that childish affection the Irish develop. "And who do I have to thank for me entry into the ranks o' the capitalists? If not himself, the good major? Though he was only got up to a captaincy then. And an't he looking grandiose under them shoulderboards? Ye'll recall the money ye give me that first

night for old time's sake and for me services in the fray thereafter. Well, didn't I invest it? Oh, a terrible rooster he was, the
gamecock of all Amerikee, with spurs like a *sirdar*'s saber. And
didn't I win me a pile? And didn't old Dorsey go under, drinking
both profits and debts? And then wasn't this fine place to be let?
Why, the widow didn't wait til they'd waked him proper before
she went hawking his substance. A sin and a shame, it was. But
Jimmy Molloy was ever a friend to opportunity. Oh, tis a lovely
thing to become a man o' substance, Sergeant Jones."

"Please, Molloy. It's 'Major' Jones. Sergeant Jones is dead and
gone."

"And sorry I am for it. For wasn't he a lovely, tyrannical fellow? Why, I recall that day above Attock Fort, with the plague
behind us and a thousand raging Pushtoons in front of us, and
the poor captain dead as a rat got by a terrier, and the leftenant
collapsed with the sun. And wasn't ye grand, the way ye took
over the shreds o' the comp'ny, bayonet all bubbling with gore?
I remember ye all a-thrusting, just sticking and clubbing away.
Screaming the while, ye were. 'Who'll stand by me, boys? Who'll
stand by me, men?' And the heathen buggers all around us, with
their knives hungry for white meat. Who stood by ye then and
brung ye back bloody when ye toppled down? Oh, didn't we
have lovely murdering that day, Sergeant Jones? Weren't that a
beautiful slaughter?"

"Twas long ago," I said. "And you were valiant, Molloy. I
will credit that. Although you were undisciplined and a thief."

" 'Let bygones be bygones,' says I. For I forgive ye the thousand cruelties I suffered under ye. I know ye meant 'em all for
me own good. And sorry I am to this day about the regimental
silver."

"Your own regiment, too," I said. "When the highlanders
were but a low wall away."

"The shame o' the doings haunts me still," he said, smiling.
"Oh, tis grand to remmynis, tis a loveliness worth the treasur-
ing."

"Yes, Molloy. Under the proper circumstances, of course. And when events are recalled with proper decorum. But let us return to the present."

I regarded the man life had sculpted. He should have looked a ruin, but remained youthful in aspect. And handsome, in a low, unsavory way. Having devoured the pie, and the cake before that, he addressed himself to a shingle of beef. He did not seal his lips while chewing, but shared his pleasure with the wide world.

"I . . . offer my congratulations on your success," I continued. "Although I wish it were in another field of endeavor."

"Oh, Major Jones," he lisped through a great chew of carcass, "tis Amerikee, and a man o' business must give the public what it wants. Tis the way o' democracy and the path to profit."

I did not want to argue with the fellow. How can you convince the devil that hellfire is undesirable? Twas no time for lectures, in any case.

"Molloy, I . . . need your help."

He set down the beef. "Again? And didn't we just have wickedness enough with those Philadelphy fellows?"

"Yes. Again. For though you were a disgrace to your regiment, and your morals are weak, you have talents needed by your country."

" 'Me country,' says he? Oh, mother, hide the jewels and hold your purse! For when they come down the lane crying about 'your country,' ye know they mean to pluck your feathers good."

"Look here, Molloy. You said yourself America's been good to you."

"And an't I good to Amerikee, then? Working like a beaten dog to set up me own business, struggling day and night, and giving out jobs right and left? An't I building the country up with me own two hands?"

"Please, Molloy. I need to talk to you. Seriously."

"An't me ears wide open to me old friend? An't I listening this very minute?"

"I need you to come to New York State with me."

"Are they fighting there, then?"

"Not yet. And I hope not ever. Look you. Ever a sly one, you were. With your mimicry and disguises and such like. This time you'd hardly need to pretend. For I'd only want you to be an Irishman, see."

"Sure, and you'll be explaining that, Major Jones?"

"In good time. You see, Molloy, our Union is threatened on many fronts. And there are rumors. Of risings and insurrections on the part of the Irish."

"Oh, and an't we great ones for the risings? There's none can rebel like the Irish. Though beat us down in the end the buggers do."

"I do not think it is a rising, see. There is something else. Trouble. And I cannot find the thread of it. So I need you to go among the Irish and find out what they are up to."

He looked at me darkly then. Serious at last. The mouth that was ever so quick turned still. When he spoke, twas in a voice reduced:

"An informer? You want me to go an informer?"

"I want you to serve as an agent of the government. You would not be betraying anyone you know or to whom you are bound in any way."

"Still, an informer. . . ."

"An enrolled agent of the United States government."

"Oh, Major Jones," he shook his head, "and wouldn't I love to help ye? For hard, wicked devil that ever ye were, ye were square to me and sweet as me own mother with the honey o' understanding. If not for ye, the black English buggers would of give me twenty years in Delhi jail and not ten—although I was obliged to leave those premises early anyway, for the quality o' the accomodations was lowly and not to be endured, and thanks be to the black cholera for me blessed deliverance. Oh, don't I love ye for the justice that is in ye and the charity all reluctant?

But I'm a great businessman now. Sure, and ye can see that for yourself. I can't go traipsing off to the wilderness and carrying on like a lad o' twenty. I'm a gentleman o' substance, with high responsibilities . . ."

He bent back to his eating.

"You won't do it then?"

"Oh, ye know I would if I could. But I can't, so I won't. And there it is. An informer . . ." He puffed his cheek and blew the idea to nothing, spitting shreds of beef upon the boards.

He had been my last hope. For the Irish were as shut to me as the thoughts of the Grand Chinee.

Molloy must have marked the disappointment on my face. As soon as he was finished with his meal, he wiped his snout and paws on the cloth that had wrapped it and said, "Oh, Major Jones, me lovely, darling man. Sure, and ye don't need the likes o' me, anyways. Nor are ye wanting such likes. For trouble I am, and always was. Me own mother, who was a great, pop'lar beauty back in Dublin, and every one o' me fathers in turn said I was trouble. And right they were. No, ye'll not be wanting the likes o' me for your delicate doings . . ."

I put my head down in my hand, searching my brain for ideas. "I wish Dr. Tyrone were here. Perhaps he could help."

Molloy perked up. "Help ye? With the Irish? That Orangeman? That black Protestant? Now, I'd not offend ye, Major Jones, and I've naught against the person o' the man, but ye'd be a fool to trust a low souper Protestant like that one."

"I'm Protestant myself, Molloy."

He waved that away. "Ye are but a Welshman, and not counted by the Holy Mother Church. For the Virgin knows that such are born benighted, and she'll intercede for ye and lessen your sufferings. But an Orangeman's damned to the blackest pit o' Hell."

"Dr. Tyrone is actually quite fond of you, you know."

"And don't I love the fellow meself? For he's sweet and full o' learning, and I'll not hear a word said against him. But he's damned for all that, and not to be trusted. Like every Orange-man ever born. Why, he'd not last an hour as an informer, that one. Sure, and the Whiteboys would set the pitch cap on him and hang him so high—"

I caught him by the wrist. "What did you say, Molloy? 'Whiteboys?' What are 'Whiteboys'?"

He did not lose his jocularity, but rolled on. "Sure, and nothing but thieves, the most o' them. For times are hard, and men are brought low. But long ago, in the days o' Black Oliver and down to the '98, they was the hardest o' patriot secret societies. 'All for Ireland!' 'Liberty or Death.' 'Erin go brach.' Oh, they weren't all high and fine like Tone and Tandy. But they made the Uniteds look like dolly-girls when deeds were to be done. Cutting the tendons on the landlord's cattle, they were. And sometimes on the landlord himself. Quick hands with a torch, that lot, though not so quick with their heads. It took the likes o' Father Murphy to manage 'em. And whenever they found an Irishman who grew too close to the English and betrayed his own, they'd set the pitch cap on him. Although I heard the cap was first thought up by a sergeant o' German George."

"The pitch cap," I said. "That would be pitch poured over the head? And gunpowder rubbed in it? Then set alight? And the poor man left to hang thereafter?"

He grinned in delighted agreement. "There ye have it! Just so. Ye've seen it yourself! Oh, sometimes they let the devil's hands free and he'll go tearing the flaming hair from his own skull and—"

Molloy stopped.

His face changed utterly. He looked at me with a greater sobriety than ever I had seen upon his features.

"Ye've seen it yourself," he repeated, in a flattened voice.

"I have."

"In these New York doings?"

"Yes."

He reached across the table to grasp hold of me, but thought better of it and only leaned in close. I saw the clots of wax on his mustache.

"I'm begging ye," he whispered. "If that's what ye found in New York, go elsewhere. For the likes o' them will kill ye horrible. They're worse than dacoits. Crueler than the Pushtoon."

"I will do my duty," I told the dark-eyed urgency the man had become. "At least I understand your reluctance to aid your new country now."

"Oh, bugger me country." His voice went up. "And every other country, too. For the truth is, they've done naught for the likes o' us. Your landlady's right about that, though smitten she is with Amerikee. And lucky we are, the two o' us, that we've still got our heads on our shoulders, and the use o' our arms and legs . . ."

He glanced down then. As if he could see through the planks of the table. To where my bad leg rested.

"Sure, and ye've done your share for two countries," he told me. "One after the other." Something like fondness colored his voice. "Leave Whiteboys and such be. For the sweet love o' Mary."

For the love of two Marys. The one he meant, and my Mary Myfanwy. How little such a fellow understood of duty and obligation. Molloy had been a brave soldier in his day, but courage is no more constant than the temperature, and physical valor is not tied to virtue. Perhaps he thought I relished the sordid business. Imagining that I had lost my senses since they made me an officer. The truth is that I only wanted to be home again, clerking in Mr. Evans's coal company office and lying in my nightshirt by my love, with my son in the next room. But we are not put upon this earth for our selfish pleasures alone.

"Thank you, Molloy," I said, rising. "Your information has

been of value to me. Now I know what I am facing, see. I wish you luck in your endeavors." I looked down at that long-familiar face. "Abide by the law and avoid depravity."

The Irish are great ones for making every room into a theater. Such a despairing expression the fellow put on then!

"Oh, me darling man," he said, shaking his head as gently as a willow and smacking his greased lips, "your wife won't even see ye in your coffin. For they'll have to nail it shut to hide your ruin."

• • •

"And won't he be helping you then, sir?" Annie Fitzgerald asked me, when we were almost free of the valley of the shadow that was Swampoodle.

"Helping me?"

The hood that covered her face turned toward me. "Sure, sir, and you weren't come all this way only to visit the likes of that one for your pleasures? But did he refuse you, sir?"

"Mr. Molloy . . . is engaged in other occupations."

She made a sound as if scorning all of England. "Always putting on airs, he is. And shows no respect to his betters."

"Now, now, Miss Fitzgerald. We'll have no talk of 'betters.' For this is America, see."

"And was it the Garden of Eden," she said, "there would still be better and worse." I had never known the girl to speak so freshly. "And what kind of husband would that one make, I ask you, sir, to some poor woman? When he won't do a bit for a friend? And one who was like a father to him?"

The girl was spanking angry. I would not have recognized the forlorn creature I had met three months before.

"I was no father to him, Miss Fitzgerald. For I was hard on him in ways a father is not. Besides, we were of an age, or near it."

"That one! He'll never be more than a boy. And a bad one, too."

We passed by a line of unfortunate women, each figure withered with the evening's failures. Annie Fitzgerald was so stoked up that I do not think she saw them. Or, perhaps, she had seen them too often.

"And I asked him to do more than 'a bit' for me," I continued. "His response was only reasonable."

"I'll give that one 'reasonable.' Letting down our kindly Major Jones. And won't he make a fine tale of your visit, though? Bragging how the world comes to his door!"

"Each man . . . must find his own way, Miss Fitzgerald."

She made a *hooomph* of a sound, fierce for the size of her lungs.

"That one couldn't find the pot beneath the bed."

We had come free of that vale of misery. A hack clattered by, and a constable leaned on a streetlamp.

Annie Fitzgerald stopped cold.

"Mother Mary!" she cried, laying her hand—delicately—upon my arm. "Oh, Major Jones! And didn't I forget the doings I promised Mother Flaherty? And me with only this single chance to go by? You know your way to the house from here, don't you, sir?"

"Miss Fitzgerald . . ."

"I won't be the hour," she said, already turning back toward Swampoodle. "Won't you make my excuses to Mrs. Schutzengel, sir? For she's good of heart and worries."

"I can't possibly allow you to go back into that . . . morass . . . alone."

She laughed gaily. "Oh, and you were always the gentleman, sir! A girl can tell you were raised by a steady hand. But you're not to worry. For we're not like your highborns, and the boys won't bother a girl who keeps herself proper."

She would not hear of my accompanying her. Then, slowly—for I am not quick in such matters—I saw that she was likely borrowing the opportunity to pass a moment with some fellow who had her affections. As Mr. Shakespeare put it, we must not "admit impediments" to such efforts, but wish young lovers well.

"Go you, then," I said, a touch embarrassed at my dullness. Yet, I felt some guardianship for the girl. She had been orphaned like myself. And life is hard even for those with two honest parents. So I called after her, "Beware false promises, now. And know your worth, Miss Fitzgerald."

She laughed like a plain little angel.

• • •

I went to the depot early, heavy in heart and soul. My bag was heavier, too, with the new uniform and all the aromatic provisions Mrs. Schutzengel had thrust upon me. With a tear in her generous eye. Those baked delights and ransoms of cold beef should have boosted my spirits. But I felt so alone I just stood under the roof of the platform, one step shy of the sleet coming down. I had not even had an opportunity to thank Annie Fitzgerald for her kindness, for she had not returned and must have stayed the night with Mother Flaherty.

An empty man, I was. Waiting for a train to failure.

I watched them loading cars of convalescents. The lines were quiet here, but sickness fired volleys in the camps. The shirkers transferring the weak from the ambulance wagons went roughly about their work, careless of the comfort of their charges, and heedless of the weather. For no one feels true gratitude to soldiers.

A pair of bearers dropped a boy in the slush and mud. The lad foundered, too weak to right himself, and the devils found it amusing.

I was just stepping off to interfere—and would have done so sooner any other day—when I heard my name shouted. By a long-familiar voice.

Twas Molloy. Dragging a bright carpet bag. The trouser legs below his soaking overcoat would have blinded a circus barker. On his head, one of those new Derby hats collected the sleet.

Glad to see him, I was. But I made him wait until I had given the ambulance crews a fine piece of Welsh temper and saw our boys properly berthed.

"I did not expect your coming this morning, Molloy." I kept my voice level, though it was a struggle. I made a great to-do of brushing the melt from my greatcoat.

He put on a face that rued his own folly, then shot me that smile I first saw in old Lahore. "Oh, and me conscience deviled me up and down so's I didn't know which end the porridge went in and which end it come out. Wicked, how the weight o' me obligations crushed down upon me. For conscience is crueler than famine." His grin stretched up to his ears. "And didn't I jump up then and say to meself, 'Our little Sergeant Jones—who's come up a major—is terrible in need. And how will Jimmy Molloy live with himself if the Whiteboys take him?' And here I am. Though how I'm delivered beside ye, I'm hardly awake to tell."

"I'm pleased, Molloy, that you have risen to your duty to our country." Twas all that I could say, see. Though I knew he come for me and not a flag. There are some things a man cannot bear in the morning. And I would not have such a fellow think me a servant of my emotions.

Now you will say: "We knew that he would come. For there are bonds that soldiers never lose." But I did not expect him, see. For hope does not make sound policy. And we must ever prepare for the worst in this lovely world.

We rode and talked and planned all the way to Philadelphia, sharing the food from my landlady's kitchen. He was a sharp one, I will give Molloy that. And he knew his people. His scheme to go inside them was ingenious. And brave. It even put me to worrying that I had, indeed, asked too much of him. For I would be just and not expect more of another than of myself.

But by then Molloy was in fine fettle, enjoying himself like a child, and insisting that it was just like old times, only better.

As we drew into the Pennsylvania yards, he said but one thing that was out of place.

"Women," he muttered, "will get a man in trouble every time."

Chapter 10

THERE WAS TROUBLE, BUT NO WOMAN
IN IT. Unless you count the jailer's frightened wife. Men with guns and torches met
my train. The police fellows had carbines,
while most of the other men carried sporting pieces. A brace of
hounds yearned after scent, tugging a plump man with a
revolver along the platform. Outside the station door, a commercial traveler waited with his trunk and valise, doubtless
recounting a lifetime's dishonesties as he watched the forces of
law surround the train.

John Underwood stood beside a railroad man. The sheriff's
hand lay on his holstered pistol.

As I stepped down, I caught the sense of things. The lawmen
were not there to search the train, but to prevent a boarding.
They surrounded the locomotive and the string of cars, while
horsemen galloped ahead along the line. When the train began
to move again, with the drummer safe in his coach and praying
thanks, riders paralleled the wagons until the train surpassed
their speed.

The sheriff come up to me right off, for I had telegraphed him
from New York regarding my return.

"Don't you worry," he told me. "He won't get away."

"Who, then?" I hoped he would lead me inside the depot
building to continue the discussion, for the wind was ripping.

"Nolan," he said. "That damned Nolan." He scratched a

mighty ear. "Oh, for crying in a bucket. I knew they shouldn't have hired an Irishman onto the police."

"And what," I asked, for all was new to me, "did Mr. Nolan do?"

Underwood looked down at me, face boiling with chagrin.

"He killed the fellow who was set to answer all your questions."

• • •

The sheriff drove me to Liberty Street, to a Greek Revival house done up in stucco. Twas the jail. Passing by, you would have judged it a fine place for a family, for you could not see the harder portion from the front.

No sooner had we entered than the jailer's wife went wild. Wailing in a voice to chase cats. Mr. Meeks, the jailer and sheriff's deputy, sat in a corner chair, head down and hands clutched between his thighs. But his wife was up and going like a dervish.

"It wunt his fault," she cried. "He couldn't help it. Don't put us out in the street. It wunt his—"

"Nobody's putting anybody out in the street," Sheriff Underwood told her. But you know how it is when a woman has had too much time to think on a matter. Mrs. Meeks was set to speak, not listen.

"That dirty Irishman," she cried. "That Nolan. That's who it was. That Nolan." She looked at her broken husband. "I told him you can't trust no Irishman. I told him. But would he listen? Would he listen to me?"

"Theo?" Underwood said.

The jailer looked up. His face was gray.

"Theo, could you and the missus give us a little privacy for business?"

The man nodded. "Anything you say, sheriff." But he did not move.

The woman threw herself onto her knees. With a sideward glance at me. "I'm begging you. I'm *plead*ing, John Underwood.

My husband's an honest man, and he don't deserve to be put out into the street."

Small towns, see. They have their shames, but not the hardness of the city. Everyone knows everyone else, and must live with them. So John Underwood did not raise his voice, or scold, or threaten. No, he lowered his voice still further.

"Now, now, Sarah. Don't you worry. I know it wasn't Theo's fault. But I'd be grateful if you'd cook up some coffee. And you take Theo out and let him gather up his wits. It's been a hard day for everybody. You just cook us up some coffee, all right?"

Give a woman a task for her hands, see, and she will rest her mind.

Out she went, meek as a mouse and husband in tow, shutting the door behind her.

The sheriff shook his head. "Shock to 'em. Don't I know it? Never had such doings around here." He cocked an eye at me. As if a part of him still suspected that I myself had brought on all this trouble. "Found O'Connor with his throat cut. Right there in his cell. Back of his calves sliced through, for good measure. And what do you think of that? You kill a man, what's the sense of cutting his tendons? Sure isn't going to run off on you."

I said nothing.

"This morning, that's when it was. Sarah was off buying her groceries. And gossiping, no doubt. Well, some fellow Theo's never laid eyes on before comes running in yelling that I need him—that *I* need him—over at the number five lock. That we got another drowning. Irish fellow, the one who run in hollering. And who's here in the jail office just then? Just by sheer chance? Nolan. Our grand Irish policeman. And Theo leaves him here with the keys and everything else."

The sheriff sighed, investigating an ear with a sausage finger. "Damned lie, and nothing but. There wasn't any drowning. I was still up at the farm, just getting a late start, that's all. There's days like that." He looked at me, a truant child. "Wife's been ailing, you know." A flush of anger colored his brow. "They knew damned well where I was. Damned well." He grunted. "Then Theo gets out to the lock. And there's no sign of a drowning. Not even a crow to pass the time of day with. Everything's just all froze up and waiting for the work gang to come around again. Well, he realizes something's fishy. So he rushes on back. And there sure isn't any Nolan, no sirree. Office here is empty as the tomb on the third day."

He looked around at the walls. With their legal notices and likenesses of criminals. "So now Theo's fretting. He goes and gets out his old dragoon pistol—Nolan didn't steal anything, at least—and he goes on back to check the cells. And what does he find but old Chauncey O'Connor lying there, every inch of him covered in blood. And the missus sitting by him and rocking and crying how I'm going to boot them out of the house for letting a thing like that happen. Well, first thing Theo thought was that the missus did it. She's got a temper, that Sarah. And Theo figures maybe O'Connor got smart-mouthed about the food. But soon as he came to his senses, he saw he'd been made a fool of. Letting Nolan alone in the jail like that." He sighed. "Theo did his duty, once he saw it. Say that for him. Ready to take his medicine like a man. Sent Jonah Clarke up after me. Met me coming down the Potter road. Told me about the killing and Nolan disappearing. First thing I did was to call everybody out—constables, police, for what they're worth, and all the fellows we keep on the rolls as reserve deputies. That's always been an honor kind of thing. Never had to call 'em up before. Well, I got 'em out on the roads fast as they could scoot. On *all* the roads. And you saw how we're handling the trains."

"This Nolan," I said. "Perhaps he's already gone. With a good horse. Surely, he wouldn't just wait to be taken."

Underwood twisted up his mouth until it seemed his lips would touch his ear. "There's the thing. Nolan's Irish. No horse of his own. And nobody's missing a horse. Morning train was long gone. Lake's froze, and the canal. So he must've gone off on foot. Or he's hiding."

I nodded, but meant nothing by it. "Tell me about Nolan, then. If you would, John."

He snorted. "Damned disappointment. Treachery, and nothing but. Must've been a spy for the Irish all along."

"What was he like? Young? Old? I would like to know, see."

"A murderer. That's what he's like. A damned murderer." He looked at me, baffled by his thoughts. Twas clear he was shaken, too. "Here I was figuring there was hope for the Irish. Seemed like young Nolan was the best fellow of all the local police—not that I have much use for any of 'em. But he kept himself sober. No funny business. Supporting his mother and sisters. And saving up to be married, so he always said. Seemed determined to be as respectable as normal people. Hardly seemed Irish—that's how they fool you." He shifted a clot of unpleasantness higher in his throat. "That Nolan fooled everybody. And more fool me."

Mrs. Meeks delivered coffee in tin cups. I suspect they were those used for the inmates, but no matter. The beverage smelled harsh and looked thin. She smiled and cooed, and you could feel her straining to hold her tongue.

"Thanks, Sarah," the sheriff said. "You go back out and sit with Theo now. He's had a hard day."

And out she went, trailing doubt and apron strings.

"Now, John," I said, "you made a certain claim at the station."

"Claim?"

"That . . . the murdered fellow, this O'Connor . . ."

"Chauncey O'Connor. Dead as a throat-cut hog."

"That he had been about to answer all my questions."

"That's right." Then he considered. "Or a lot of them, anyways."

"And who is—was—Mr. O'Connor?"

The sheriff shrugged. Whenever he did so, the lower half of

his ears—those magnificent appendages—flared outward. "Irish. Old fellow. Well, maybe not so old. You know how they seem. Older for the drink. Although O'Connor wasn't the worst of 'em by a long stretch. Just liked his poteen. Every so often we'd bring him in to quiet him down and let him sleep it off. Then he'd behave for a couple of months. No, he wasn't the worst of 'em."

"He came to you? As an informer?"

"Oh, no. No. We just brought him in drunk. He was down on Main Street, shouting his lungs out. How we were all going to see, how the Irish were going to show us, and how the Irish nation was going to rise up under the green flag of Erin. Any other time, I would've figured it was just more of their hooting and hollering. Nolan brought him in for disturbing the peace."

"Nolan?"

"Yep. Then he killed him. Because of what O'Connor said to Theo."

"And what was that?"

He smiled, the cat who ate the canary. "That 'President' Kildare was going to make the Irish a country of their own. And he didn't just say it to Theo Meeks. He was yelling it in the street when Nolan brought him in. With a pack of the saloon Irish trailing behind. Hollering that every Irishman was going to have his own home and land. That President Kildare was going to give it to them. That the mighty would be cast down."

He was pleased with his revelations. And clearly expected me to be pleased, too. When I did not reply, he continued:

"So, there you are, plain as day. Hate to say it, but I was wrong. Irish are up to their tricks, after all. It's a rebellion, all right. But now the cat's out of the bag." He gave a laugh that come close to a spit. " 'President' Kildare. Fellow ever shows his face down this way again, I'll give him 'president.' We're going to nip this insurrection nonsense in the bud. You and me, Abel. Think we should send Bill Seward a telegram about all this?"

"There is no insurrection," I said.

He sat up. "What?"

"No insurrection. No rebellion." For I had thought hard during my journey, and found myself thinking even harder now.

"The hell you say. Why, the evidence is right in front of your face, man! *You're* the one who was making all the fuss about it!" He yanked a mustache end as though he would pull it off his face. "Now, with bloody murder right here in my own jail, and as good as an admission from one of the Irish, suddenly you don't . . . you don't . . ." His face went red as cured ham.

I put down my cup of coffee. Twas still near full, for the coffee was only fit for a jail, and then as a punishment.

"John . . . you've done good work. You've helped me. But I must ask you to trust me now. There is trouble, see. But no insurrection. For we have read the signs wrong, and must begin again. And do not annoy Kildare. Please. Let him go about his business. Until we see what that business is."

"If he even comes back. Once he hears about this."

"He will come back."

"Well, you sound pretty damned sure of yourself."

"He will come back. Because he is clever, see. If he would run, he would give himself away. And there is no good evidence against him. We do not even know what he's about. He will see as much."

"I bet he runs."

"We will see." The truth was that I was not completely certain. I could not think of Kildare without thinking of Nellie. And that clouded things. Perhaps it was only that I wanted them to return. Because I was not finished with either of them.

"Well, we damned well *will* know what he's up to," Underwood said. "Once we find that damned Nolan."

"You will find Nolan, that is sure."

"Don't I know it? And then we'll find out just what's going on. Rebellion and Kildare and the whole business."

"You will find Nolan," I said, but my voice was grim now. "But he will tell you nothing."

Piqued, the sheriff turned his head and gave me a side look. As if I were too full of myself. But I was only full of troubled thoughts. For the clearer one thing became, the foggier ten others appeared.

"Once I get my hands on Nolan," the sheriff said, "you can bet your bottom dollar he's going to talk. And that's a promise."

"John," I said, in a gentling voice, "you will not find him alive."

• • •

Now you will say, "Well, where is that Molloy? He was not on the train with Abel Jones. And is he to be trusted, after all?" But you must wait for answers, for these things happen slowly.

Molloy and I parted in Philadelphia—for people always see what they shouldn't—and he went off to make his way alone. We had arranged the methods of our meetings. I tried to give him money from my funds, but he was wiser and saw that too much money always wants explanation. So off he went, with his Derby hat on his head.

I hoped that head would remain upon his shoulders. Without a pitch cap. For he would be on my conscience now. As for trusting him, look you. In some regards, he was more to be trusted than myself. For he had come to aid a friend in need, and there is goodness. While I was still not free of Nellie Kildare. And although I meant no baseness, Molloy was right. A woman will get you in trouble.

But let that bide.

Twas late when I left the jail, and whipping snow, but I went to see Father McCorkle. For I had thought on him, too, during my journey. And I had more cause to think on him now.

He made a fuss, all "Look what the wind blew in," and "How are ye, man, how are ye?" Yet he did not seem surprised to see me. With that knotting together of his black brows and his workman's shoulders.

His rooms smelled of a cabbage supper.

We sat by his fire again, but this time I declined his tea.

"Ah, Major Jones," he said, with the fire dancing on his face, "I see ye come back with heavy matters on your mind."

I inched closer to the hearth, for I had forgotten too quickly how cold it was in old New York.

"There is true," I said. "Heavy matters. And not unlike those weighing upon your own mind, sir."

He rocked back on his chair, a big man. "Is that so? And will we be welcoming ye into the Holy Mother Church? Or what do ye mean?"

"Nolan."

Oh, yes. I caught the fleeting darkness in his eyes. "I hear the boy's gone missing, Major Jones. And accused of a terrible thing, he is."

"A thing he did not do."

"And is that so? Sure, and I'm glad to hear it. For he was always regular to Mass, at least on Sundays. And cared for his mother, and kept his sisters decent. Won't they be pleased to know the boy's innocent?"

"They won't be pleased to know he's dead."

"Is he now?" He shook his head and sighed. "I had not heard that. Oh, the times are hard we're living in."

The fire snapped and flared, then calmed again. The brief rush of warmth was a lovely thing. I watched the flames and changed my line of talk.

"And how are the Latin lessons going?" I asked him.

"Oh, they get on well enough. But boys have little interest in such matters."

"I have heard, sir, that your Latin is excellent."

He allowed himself a little smile. "It was not bad in years gone by."

"I am told that boys who are not Catholics pay for lessons. To prepare them for their examinations, or even to go on to college."

"Tis a poor parish, and the little fees lessen the burden on my flock. Sure, and you don't begrudge me . . ."

"Not at all, sir. It is not the fees that interest me, see, but the skill."

"'Tis not so fine. But have ye need of Latin, then?"

"Father McCorkle . . . do you know much about the Negro?"

"The sons of Ham," he said. "Are ye sure ye'll not take a drop o' tea, major? 'Twill clear your head of Latin and Negroes and what not."

I shook my head. "Thank you, sir. But it is the Negro I am interested in now."

He cocked a bushy brow. "Here, and I thought it was me lovely Irish ye come about. Will ye make an abolitionist of me, then?"

"I am told," I said, "that his sufferings have taught the Negro to dissemble. That, often, a Negro who can write a fine hand and read a sound book will nonetheless play the fool. For his safety, and to ease his way among those who prefer him unlettered and a fool."

He understood me.

"It occurred to me," I went on, for I would have things said aloud, "that a man who has better Latin than the schoolmasters at the Academy would not be limited to the speech of bog farmers and the vocabulary of the saloon."

He smiled. But it was different this time. "Ye'd have me spout like an English lord, Major? Taking on airs? When I'm only speaking to be understood by me own, who have not been to your fine academies?"

"A man may speak as he pleases. For this is America. But I think you are an intelligent man, see. A very intelligent man. Who plays the potato digger. To keep off trouble. But now I think trouble has come. And you know more about it than you will say. You put us off with homely speeches. And trap us in our prejudices."

"I've told ye, Jones, there is no rebellion."

"I said naught of rebellion."

"Oh, I've heard about O'Connor's carryings-on. The 'President Kildare' business. But the man was a famous drunkard. Addled. Pickled by drink. And as little as I like Kildare and his damnable doings, I'd not jump to the conclusion that the man's about to lead an insurrection."

"I said naught of insurrection."

"As for the Latin, every priest has the language. Some just remember it the better. It's no more than a trick of the mind, man. A few scraps of Latin do not bespeak a great intelligence." He smiled wistfully, as if remembering. "I'm only a poor fool, like most men, and a priest with a poor parish. 'I am fortune's fool . . .' "

"And that is Mr. Shakespeare, not the Bible."

"What do you want, Jones?"

I took up the poker and teased the fire. To spare the man the rising. For he looked weary. I believe he went through every day a weary man. For much lay upon those shoulders. And muscles have no strength over matters of the soul.

"I believe I want the same thing as you, see. In the end. The welfare of your parish." I stirred the fire and glanced at him. But I did not stare. For there are times when a man must be left to himself. "I believe you know who killed O'Connor and Nolan. Oh, maybe not the individuals. But you know the cause. And the crowd behind the matter."

"I would never condone . . ." He near jumped from his chair.

I poked the stingy flames with the iron. "I did not say you liked the matters. Or had a hand in them. Only that you know. For I believe you are the one man who knows everything. Or nearly so. But you will not go to the law because you will not betray your own kind."

"A priest tainted with murder would be damned."

I nodded. "I cannot speak for your theology. Only for common sense. And common sense tells me that you know these things. Not every man can hold his tongue on his pillow or in his cups. And if the men do not come to you, the women do. They tell you things they do not rightly understand. But you understand them." I looked at him then. "What's Kildare about, sir? You can stop this business now."

He had put on a mask. A smiling mask. "Sure, and Major Jones, I've always heard tell that a Welshman's too clever by half and will tie himself up in knots. And I see that there's truth in the stories. For ye've gone off fantastical on me."

I would not smile with him. "You're making a mistake. Look you. You are not helping your people. You're hurting them. For they will only suffer in the end." I fear I waved the poker, as if it were the cane left by my chair. "Whatever the matter that's underway, it will not succeed. Whatever they have built up will crash down upon them. And then you will see hatred. And prejudice. And death."

He kept up that smile. But twas hollow. And brutal. "Are ye a prophet now, Jones? Or are ye only seeing things? Perhaps ye see Kildare's banshees and devils and haunts? Are they dancing around ye now? Have ye looked too long in the fire?"

"I've looked into hotter fires than this," I told him. For we are all vain and foolish. Then I edged toward him. "For God's sake, man! Protect your own people. Put a stop to all this killing, this . . . this madness. Don't let it go any further. For the love of God."

There was no living face before me.

"And what," he said, "would ye know about the love of God?"

• • •

They found Nolan in the morning, hanging from a tree where the road turned into the sheriff's farm. The pitch cap had been set upon him.

Underwood wanted to call up the militia. He raved about rebellion and elections and lack of respect. I think he was ready to hang the Irish by the dozen. And that would be just what the dark men wanted.

I talked sense into him at last. By warning of the impression of panic. Still, he raged back and forth in the parlor of his splendid home—twas no common farmhouse he lived in, and John Underwood was not a man who needed the job of sheriff to earn his daily bread.

"This is war," he insisted. "Nothing but a goddamned war."

I did not let him know. But he was right.

$Chapter$ 11

 WELL, THERE IS WAR AND WAR. At the end of the week, I had a letter from Mick Tyrone. Some of the pages were smudged a dark brown. Twas the look of blood. My friend had seen the kind of war I knew.

Headquarters, along the Tennessee
February 7, 1862

My Dear Friend,

I have seen the elephant. I had imagined that I knew something of war from street mêlées in Vienna and the skirmishes I attended in Hungary. Brutal as those affairs were, this was a different matter. I believe you understand me.

You have heard by now of our conquest of Fort Henry, but you will know to distrust the newspaper accounts. Certainly, it was a victory, welcome and worthy. But the ease of accomplishment reported by the journalists—few of whom were on the field—slighted the facts.

Perhaps you would excuse our initial confusion as attendant to the mounting of any grand campaign, but I must say that we boarded the steamboats with only the vaguest intuition of a plan. No doubt Grant, Foote and Rawlins

knew our intent full well. We medicos, however, simply
followed, like the rest of the army. I recall sudden orders,
long waits, eternal lines, and blank faces.

I must say the spectacle was grand, though, when a fellow stood back. Dozens of steamboats and barges banked
to the levee in the odd river light, as an endless flow of
blue-clad regiments trudged up the planks to board. Odd,
to see horses upon a deck. Toward the far shore, our gunboats gnashed at the water, snapping turtles of wood and
iron, bristling with cannon and trailing smoke as they
patrolled against enemy encroachments. I was startled at
the number of women who attempted to board the transports, only to be turned back by the officers. Children and
dogs ran about the embankments, while men with queasy
stomachs broke from the ranks to perform the basest of
duties squatting in full sight of a thousand of their fellows.
As a medical man, I am accustomed to the body's mechanical functions, yet it was a sorry sight. The artist does not
depict the full range of the hero's activities.

We made a grand procession sailing up the river. From
each bend, a long succession of transports chugged along
in the high, brown waters. It seemed to me an invincible
display of might. May I say, at the risk of your mockery,
that all felt a great exhilaration to be underway at last.

I did not see Grant until we disembarked. And that scene
was but a greater chaos to me. It is the impedimenta of an
army that the novice least expects. A mule becomes contrary in the mud, braking the progress of a hundred others.
Soldiers made stevedores unload supplies without end,
yet who can find that for which he seeks? Cooking fires
appear, only to be scotched by officers wary of their
smoke, and nervous boys finger muskets. Regiments form
and sergeants bray, while quartermasters lay out bivouacs
in conflict one with the other and disappointing to all.
Grant stood watching from the deck of his vessel, uncon-

cerned, a cigar in his mouth where his old pipe was wont to be. I thought that, should the Rebels strike our unloading, we would be beaten shamefully. But nothing transpired.

The plan, I now know, anticipated a coordination of forces, with our regiments of infantry advancing overland to take Fort Henry in the rear, while the gunboats steamed ahead and engaged in a duel with the fortification's cannon. I expected a grand panorama of battle and took the opportunity, while the orderlies established our field surgery, of joining a party of cavalry upon the west and unoccupied bank of the river. I went at the invitation of their adjutant, whom I had treated for a fistula. He should not have been astride a horse. But all wanted to partake of events.

We blundered through scrub trees and wallows for a time, until a scout led us to a promontory across the river from the fort. Dismounting, we took up positions amid abandoned gun emplacements. From our vantage point, no telescope was required to see the enemy's battle flag and the scurrying of cannoneers upon the ramparts. We also saw columns of men in gray, brown, blue—seemingly every color—departing the fort overland. We thought, then, that they would challenge our regiments in the field. In fact, they were fleeing. Only a brave rear guard remained to hold the fort.

Our gunboats closed toward the works and both sides opened with long-range guns. I will tell you that the Confederates, despite the wickedness of their cause, showed valor. They stood to their guns, despite the falling shot and spectacular losses. The gunboats paddled forward, engines groaning to drive those irresistible machines of war. The adjutant pointed out to me that the Rebel engineers had planned and built badly, and that the high water put our war machines level with the enemy's gunports. It seemed, indeed, as though our vessels might float right up to the walls and fire point-blank into la fortressa.

But where was the army? No sound of field engagements reached our ears, nor did we see the expected lines of blue break from the trees. The gunboats fired remorselessly. We watched their dark shells hurtle through the air, each impact followed by a great splash of debris from the earthworks. The slaughter was indescribable. Now that I have seen the human body disintegrated by shell, I better understand your loathing of war.

The defenders appeared as small as monkeys from our perch, yet we knew they were men. We held a firm allegiance to our own side, of course, yet one could not help admiring the bold rushing to and fro of men under fire, and the hasty serving of the guns by dwindling crews. Then a shell from one of our guns struck a magazine. The blast seemed to stun the very earth, and the smoke increased severalfold. When we could begin to see again, the interior of the fort had been cratered, the walls smashed, and guns lay bored into the earth, their carriages shattered. We knew then that we had won the day. Still, the Confederates would not yet yield. Toward the end, an officer discarded his sword and served one of the remaining guns himself. I know I shall never possess such valor.

For our part, the enemy's shot seemed to bounce from the armored sides of our vessels. The worst damage appeared to be to smoke stacks. I thought it a perfect example of the supremacy of the machine age.

Under a last, furious bombardment, the Rebel fire failed. Although I had imagined a relentless progress for our vessels, Captain Foote had kept them at a careful range, where few of the Rebel cannon could reach them. The Confederates could only suffer, with slight chance of retaliation.

Loaned a spyglass, I viewed ruptured bodies everywhere along the Southron ramparts, and gutted mules behind the batteries, and blood so thick it discolored the mud.

The enemy raised the white banner, and the field fell silent. We still could not see our army.

I made my excuses to my mounted colleagues, for I felt I must return to the landing. Although it appeared that little harm had been done to our naval arm, a surgeon, too, has his duties. Incidental injuries could not be ruled out. Further, I expected we would extend treatment to the vanquished defenders who must face not only the pain of their wounds but the ignominy of capture.

After blundering about on my willful horse, I returned to the point of disembarkation and was ferried to the east bank. The first gunboats were just putting in. Grant, by the way, was in a lather, although those who have not observed him regularly failed to notice. The infantry, it seems, had become mired in the low country, all mud and creeks risen over their banks. The mass of the enemy, far from intending to engage, had fled toward Fort Donelson, twenty miles to the east and the principal Confederate fortification in the region. Overlooking the Cumberland River where it parallels the Tennessee, the citadel of Donelson intends to hold the forces of Justice at bay. But now that the Rebel designs have failed in part, I am confident they soon will fail entirely. As I write, Grant is preparing to move across the isthmus to lay siege to their works.

But now I must tell you what I truly learned of war. Fortuitous inspiration led me to make swift my return to the field surgery, for my untutored eyes had misjudged the loss to our own side. Even before the gunboats reached the bank, we heard the screaming above the shudder of their engines and splash of their wheels. Sailors and soldiers pressed into a waterborne role leaned out of hatches, or stood upon the walks, waving and shouting. All, even those miraculously unwounded, were splashed over with blood.

I leapt aboard the first vessel to approach the shore and entered hell. The armor had not repelled all of the Confederate shells, and others had entered through the opened ports. The darkened gundeck was a vision of slaughter. I could barely keep my balance for the slickness of the blood. I have heard that, in Nelson's day, the Royal Navy painted the decks and inner walls of its ships red to keep down the appearance of gore in battle. The practice wants revival.

I stood for a shameful moment, riveted. The lull of the great engines made the deck throb beneath my feet, and the screams seemed oddly far away. Boys flailed, untended, made freakish by the loss of limb and queer thrust of bone. All was shattered. Beams smoldered where fires had been imperfectly quenched. Wreckage, material and human, jumbled together. Some of their comrades tried to ease the suffering of the wounded, but most survivors had fled the cauldron of that ship. Speaking of cauldrons, a boiler exploded on another vessel, scalding men to death.

Somehow, I righted my will and went to work. Immediately, a fellow's artery exploded in my face—the poor man had turned to beg for help and a sharpness of bone cut him. I was nearly blinded and could only thrust my hand into the squash of his thigh until I found the source of the blood. Then I was helpless—I shall never go anywhere without my medical kit again—fixed to a man who would die should I release him. I called to a sailor to help me—the fellow was sitting there droll-eyed and useless—only to realize the man was dead and his stare vacant. Eventually, another sailor responded to my cries and I got him to hold his fellow's artery—a slippery business, that—while I tried to devise a tourniquet. But leather belts were too gross, nor would they hold in the slop, and rope was worse. The fellow convulsed and died as I struggled to help him.

Timidly, the boy who had crawled over to help asked me to look at his own impairment. In the gloom and slop and din, it was hard to make out exactly what had happened to him. Embarrassedly, and more dazed than pained, he let down the scraps of his trousers. There was a bedazzled expression on his face, I shall never forget it. The boy was nothing but shreds. I remember a ghostly voice, in that flat speech of the Westerner, asking me, "What kin ya see, doc? What kin ya see?" The truth was that I could see nothing but a hopeless stew of gore. And he was a fair young lad, though mere countenance should not move a man of science.

More help arrived, and we began clearing the men to the shore. One old fellow with a broken back babbled on as though he were being jollied home from a drunken evening. An army captain, seconded to the fleet, clutched the arm that had been torn from him, refusing to surrender it, cooing to it as though it were a baby. Those who had lost fingers or hands manning the guns were the lucky members of the crew, and half a dozen men had lost their sight.

When lanterns were brought aboard, I saw that I was in the cave of the man-eating Cyclops. Vital organs were strewn everywhere—one poor devil whose life should have fled instantly, lay stuffing intestines back into the cavity of his stomach. The queerest thing was that they were not his own guts, but those of a mate who had been blown in two beside him. Bones stuck out of the walls like arrows, and brains fell bit by bit from the wood above my head, like water dripping in a cavern. When I emerged to hasten to the surgery, those who saw me thought I was myself a casualty. I tasted other men's blood upon my lips.

We did our best, though paltry it was. The carnage I witnessed in Hungary, during the revolution there, had not moved the youth I then was to the degree this bloodletting moved the mature man. What was I thinking then, old friend, in life's April? How hard of heart is youth! I romped through suffering, regarding all as a clinical matter and a benefit to my studies. In truth, I had seen nothing to compare to this horrid day on the river, nothing of such bodily distortions, but never believe those who claim a man's hide thickens with the years. Wars are fought by young men because only they can bear it.

I am a man of science. But the heart will have its due. How hard it is to tell the orderlies, "Bring that one to the table," thus leaving the next fellow to die. One tries to choose wisely, to assist hope and avoid squandering effort on those who will not be rescued. But it is too much an imitation of the gods for me. I confess I prefer standing at my surgeon's table, allowing others to choose who will lie beneath my knife. I find I am a coward when I look into those faces blank with injuries yet unreal, or into eyes vast with the freshness of pain.

Last night, I longed for hospitals and order, for time above all. The skills I worked these long years to perfect declined to a fevered hacking and sawing, with a black-fingered assistant left to sew up what could be sewn and irons to cauterize the rest. At first, I tried to rinse my utensils in a bucket. But soon the bucket held nothing but crimson slime. I did my butchering through the night and into the dawn. They tell me I worked upon our enemies, as well, but I could not tell the difference.

What does it mean to the soul of which you speak, Abel, when a man finds himself in the midst of taking off a man's leg just because it is the easier course? What penalty that a boy will go legless because I was out of temper and grown impatient? Not all the universities in the world prepare a man for this.

An old fellow who served in the war with Mexico tells me that this was nothing but a skirmish and the casualties light. It makes me wish I enjoyed your faith, for I do not know where I will find the strength for a real battle.

I will close soon, for I crave sleep. Tomorrow we will move with the army, and Brinton generously offered to have a letter of mine taken along with the military dispatches back to Washington, so I must seal this. I find, dear friend, that you are not only my most cherished correspondent, but forced to endure my confessions. How odd the needs of a man!

I fear I am jealous of your decency and disposition.

But I am selfish, and have not answered the queries from your welcome letter! Let me offer but a sketch, to be followed by an in-depth report when duty permits.

This "Doctor" Kildare sounds as though he is typical of the skilled mesmerist. Although I will not accord the art the merit of a science, there is something to it. The mind is unexplored, and surprises us. Most of the business is a nonsense, no more than a parlor trick. But I myself have been impressed by some demonstrations conducted under the strictest of conditions, first in Dublin, then in Vienna.

But I have seen the mesmerist's horrid failures, as well. My own "unexplored mind" read your missive and recalled a tragic circumstance I witnessed during my first years of study. It involved a fellow who sounds like a younger version of your Kildare—the name in the case was actually Kilraine, as I recall, and he was, indeed, a doctor. He had all the passion and conviction of youth, and declared that he could mesmerize a patient about to undergo surgery, eliminating all sensation. This was in poor, old Dublin, in '46, I believe. Chloroform and ether had not come into common use, and the restraint of a patient during surgery was a challenge. This Dr. Kilraine— a deep-eyed fellow, dark and handsome—finally gained the acquiescence of Dr. Joyce, the head of surgical instruction, to put under a trance a woman who would undergo the removal of a cancered bosom. We students watched avidly from the galleries, some skeptical, others hopeful of all that was newfangled. And Kilraine, who had only left his own student days a year or two behind him, enchanted us with the ease with which he robbed the patient of all sensation. She went into the deepest of sleeps. Here, it seemed, was a great possibility!

But tragedy followed. Thoughtlessly, the sleeper was not subjected to the usual restraint of straps and bindings. Midway through the operation, she awoke, screaming horribly, and sat up into the blade of the surgeon's knife. It pierced her heart. Dr. Joyce's reputation was, of course, secure. But Kilraine was forever discredited and dropped from sight. Of course, there is no relation to the fellow you encountered, I am but reminiscing. For you speak of a daughter of twenty, and Kilraine was yet unmarried not sixteen years ago. Thus it could not be the same man, even if the odds allowed.

I remember poor Kilraine, though. His humiliation, and subsequent degradation, was formidable. He was ruined. Yet, looking back, I believe he had the best of intentions.

As to the daughter of whom you write with such feeling, I am sorry. If your descriptions of her symptoms are correct, I see no hope. It is only a question of the speed of her decline. And do not waste your money upon shop remedies. They are useless. Tuberculosis is fatal. The only reported successes—and they are rare—come from the German-speaking lands, where the ailment is now treated by long residence in alpine retreats. Some claim the effect of the mountains is magic, but I don't suppose Miss Kildare is in a position to retire to Switzerland.

Lastly, I must confess that even science still has a few limits—I cannot explain the tricks performed by the girl. Yet, I have no doubt that explanations will be forthcoming with the years. We press ever forward!

With that as prelude, my views may surprise you, dear friend. I suspect there is more to such matters than we presently understand. I speak not of the supernatural, but of a few remaining natural phenomena that still resist our understanding (though understanding will come, inevitably). Although most "mediums" and "spiritualists" have been exposed as frauds, a few resist all debunking. I do not think it a matter of spirits, although those afflicted with these "gifts" interpret it as such in their ignorance. Rather, I believe some individuals may possess still-unmeasured talents—not unlike an "ear" for music. Perhaps they "hear" more acutely than others.

I have been struck by the ability of a hound to read its master's mood—why should not some beings of higher evolution find themselves able to "read" the book of our faces, or to sense more about us than a clod may discover? Even a man of medicine must diagnose matters his eye cannot penetrate—and not all correct judgments are explained by reason. Let us but survive this war, dear friend, and science will unmask all riddles in the next decades. Your Miss Kildare may prove to be but a girl born with a form of "perfect pitch." Or she may prove devious, after all, and party to a foul hoax, deserving of our scorn. Or simply mad.

But I forget myself, and plead tiredness. For the poor young woman will not prove anything in years to come. She will be gone from us before that. Do I wound you? I would not. For your care comes through the pages of your letter and the fine voice of your lines. I wish I could offer hope for the girl, but you will never hear a lie from

Yr. Obt. Servt.
M. Tyrone
Surg. U.S.V.

• • •

At times I am like the Irish priest, confusing the words of our Lord with those of Mr. Shakespeare. I think of the Prince of Denmark in the graveyard, forlorn at the knowledge that his intelligence will never fathom the mysteries of the world. This life goes hard, and we are feeble creatures. I ponder mortality and injustice, when I should be thankful for the eternal promise. But let that bide.

Chapter 12

THAT WINTER WAS THE HARDEST YOUNG MEN COULD REMEMBER, AL-THOUGH OLD MEN INSISTED THE WIN-TERS OF THEIR YOUTHS HAD BEEN COLDER STILL, AND THE SNOWS DEEPER, AND THE CEL-LARS LESS ABUNDANTLY PROVISIONED. Whatever the truth of those memories, Penn Yan reached for an extra blanket, and woodcutters found generous reward for their labors. Signs that creaked in the wind froze to a stop, and the snow shoveled up higher than the shop windows.

You could walk across the lake, although none would do it by dark, for then you heard the groans of giants from the deep. When the women braved errands, they looked like Pushtoon brides, faces swathed and only eyes exposed. The wind cut. The toughest boys did not last half an hour at play, and when they buried Nolan, the policeman, the gravediggers had to light fires to soften the earth beneath.

A granite angel cracked in two as the navvies were shoveling the grave, and they ran. Old women said a darkness had come upon the land. They did not mean the war, but their own hills. Fort Donelson fell, but that was far away. Our celebrations were pale and brief, and Mick Tyrone had most of my concern, for war is hard on the good. The light lasted a bit longer each day, but the world felt heavy and old. The days grew too bitter for the horses to draw the sleigh over the hills, and I could only sit in my room and read, and think, or meet John Underwood at the jail to calm his fears.

And fears the good man had. He wished to please his people, and to keep them sure and safe. The death of a Federal man had been alarming, but finally the fellow was an outsider. The same went for poor Reilly, the informer, whose Irishness set him apart from the honorable citizenry. The last two had been Irish, as well. But their deaths were different, with one a policeman hung up by the gate of the sheriff's own property and the other murdered within the walls of the county jail.

Rumors flew of secret societies preparing to slaughter respectable folk in their beds, and the complaints began, and the letters to the newspapers, and the political scheming. When the Irish went door-to-door looking for work, they saw shadows moving behind the frosted glass, but got no answers to their knocks. Ladies glanced down nervously at their Galway seamstresses, and housemaids from Sligo found themselves locked in their rooms at night. Twas all I could do to keep Sheriff Underwood from arresting every Irishman who failed to tip his hat.

The priest, though, was the one who would not see the damage done and pending. I did not badger him, but saw him often in the streets, a black bulk bent against the wind as he rushed off to the shanty of a dying infant or descended upon a grocer to settle a fuss about a widow's debts. He pretended that nothing had changed. But there was a new hatred blowing down the valleys, and fear.

I heard of a rift between the priest and the Irish families that had got up to painted shutters and lace curtains, for such folk worried about the loss of the little respectability their efforts had earned them. What they asked of him I could not learn. But Father McCorkle scorched them. The priest lived to his reading of the Gospels, I will say that for him. For the poor were his, and I believe he would have carried them all in his arms like babes if he could have done so. On Main Street, his ravaged eyes looked past me without seeing. He was a true man of his faith, but should have spared his kind the coming ignominy.

Let that bide.

The winter slowed all things, excepting homeward footsteps. Jimmy Molloy did not contact me. We had agreed he would give his signal only when matters wanted reporting. But I followed him from a distance. The *Steuben Courier,* a paper from the county south of the lake, reported an epidemic of Irish misbehavior in the village of Bath. The outbreak centered on a transient fellow, one Seamus O'Bannon, whose excesses culminated in a saloon brawl that cracked the heads of two policemen and caused a constable to decline further employment. O'Bannon then enlivened the local jail with songs about Irish liberty, as well as with other tunes inappropriate for the ears of ladies and children, and the effect of his musical gifts upon his keepers was such that they arranged for an expeditious hearing. O'Bannon was offered the choice of enlisting in a Union regiment about to depart from Elmira or being remanded to state custody for grave crimes to be specified. The prisoner gave a brief patriotic declamation, swore he would put the military skills he learned under Her Majesty's yoke to work for Mr. Lincoln, then promptly slipped away from the two lawmen accompanying him to his muster. The authorities were seeking him in local Irishtowns and offered a small reward.

Jimmy Molloy had made his debut before his Irish brethren.

All I could do was to wait and hope. And I read, which is a lovely thing. I finished a most edifying history, *The Rise of the Dutch Republic,* in which the author proves that honesty and hard work decide the fate of nations. I also read those pamphlets given me by Kildare. The treatise on Swedenborg was a broth of sense and senselessness, the other sheets worthless. And I read the local weeklies, for I like a newspaper. Mr. Cleveland, the editor who had alarmed me in his quest for an interview, wrote a noble line and did not lack imagination—which, I suppose, is the essence of journalism. He published a piece speculating that

America and Britain would go to war, that America would raze Liverpool and occupy London, and that our little Washington would become the greatest capital in the world. Imagine. I fear he does not grasp Britannia's might and majesty. Though it be rued, London's glory will last as long as Rome's.

And the Kildares, father and daughter, were ever on my mind. They were still off on their spiritualist tour, and the brown house in the hills slept dark and smokeless when I had John Brent steer our sleigh past it. Sheriff Underwood sent queries, of course, following the double murder. But Kildare was firmly fixed in Buffalo that day, displaying his daughter to rowdies at twenty-five cents a head.

I thought of her, and of how she had wounded me, only to see the good that she had done by it. For a lie had lain between my wife and me, an abyss of things untold, and long had I dreaded revelation. How great our secret fears become! Yet, my confession had only brought my wife and me closer, a thing I would not have believed possible, and the curve of my Mary Myfanwy's hand inked love into each word she wrote to me.

My days emptied. I had been everywhere, asking every blockhead the same dull questions, and I burdened Mr. Morris with my moping about the parsonage. I knew not what to do, while the fear of what might come swelled up in me. Twas fear of failure, too, for I would do my duty properly, like those good Dutchmen in the book.

Then one morning, reading the Gospels by a window, with sunlight pouring in to warm my shoulders and the first beads of melt from the roof making great plops on the front steps, I knew I had to stir. For I had let the winter mesmerize me as deeply as the Great Kildare himself might have done. Twas time to shake my bones and lift my feet.

A minute later I was in my bedroom, with a flyer in my hand. I had to think a moment to remember the date that morning, for the February days had grown identical.

If Kildare would not come to me, I would go to him. To the

last grand performance of their tour, in the famed metropolis of Rochester. The show was still a night away, and the trains were steady.

I would observe Kildare from a safe distance and examine his tricks. This time, I would be the one in command, the scientist observer. I knew the course was right the instant I decided upon it. Suddenly, I was as confident as I had been despondent not a quarter hour before. Oh, a Welshman is a tenacious thing when you spin him up. I was ready to take on the world.

And I would see Nellie.

• • •

Magnificent Rochester! What does it lack? Canals and railroads converge upon its fine harbor, while across the lake lies the Canadian shore of Britain's trading empire. Great mills adorn the falls of the Genesee, where a host of chimneys strive Heavenward. The city is even the center of telegraphic communication, with its Western Union company. Here the wealth of America's East embraces the harvests of its West in fruitful marriage. Arcades of multiple stories, shielded from nature's moods by vasty skylights, hold shops that would not disgrace old London town. There are more paved streets by thrice than in poor Washington, and the handsome boulevards and avenues are regularly cleansed of snow. A regiment of steeples and cupolas stands guard above the town's good Northern bricks, and Greek columns set a high tone, as though Ulysses had founded his final kingdom on the strand of Lake Ontario. Gaslamps brighten all.

I am told a man must see Venice before he dies—but I say let him see Rochester while he lives! With my first steps from the New York Central station, I felt invigorated—although one young rascal did try, unsuccessfully, to pick my pocket, for we are a race to despoil Eden.

I predict that Rochester will be among the greatest of America's cities in days to come, surpassing weary Philadelphia and even New York City in its glory. It is a very confluence of blessings.

Mr. Douglass lived at the edge of the city, where the farms retreated before the advance of progress. The native-born American is a curious fellow in his willingness to travel great distances to and from his work so that he may have his space and greenery about him in his hours of rest. It took me over an hour to make the walk.

The noble moor welcomed me, and I do believe his pleasure was heartfelt in that first instant. Yet, more than the usual sadness come up in his eyes then. Some uncertainty, some untold embarrassment marred the air. I could not figure the contradiction, for I saw no cause for shame. His house was decent, if not grand. Though not an abode of mirth, it was clean as a barracks just before the colonel's inspection, and who would not choose cleanliness and order over sloven levity? But as he introduced his wife to me, hesitation made him stumble. I did not understand that at all, for the woman appeared devoted and an enviable housekeep. I wondered if they had been fussing before my arrival.

Twas only over dinner that I grasped it.

His poor wife was, indeed, the cause of his dismay. She was a woman of sound domesticity, but not of intellect or cultivation. Her speech wanted correction, and even her gentleness could not disguise the coarseness of her manners. Her husband had risen beyond her. She could not keep the pace his life had set, and was no partner to the great man's soul.

And a great man Douglass was. Alarmed by my ignorance, my Mary Myfanwy had given me a fine scolding for my lack of respect in his presence, although I had done naught to give offense. I simply had not known of his achievements. Now that towering figure sat embarrassed by his mate's simplicity. For he was proud. And proud men see only what is lacking.

If it is better to marry than to burn, I am not convinced it is better to marry with too much youth. Look you. Who has not seen couples age out of symmetry, and passionate attachment wane to disappointment? I am blessed to have my wife a friend, and would wish such a blessing on all others. But there is no speaking to the young, for energy is their gift, not judgement. Too often, the beauty of form that sears the novice heart leaves naught but ashes in the aging breast.

I slept well, for mashed potatoes always make me settle. Following a morning tour of Mr. Douglass's printing office—a humble source of great affairs—I set myself to see Rochester properly. For we never know what knowledge may prove useful, and diligence is rewarded.

Of fine hotels there was a plenty, led by the Blossom and the Waverly. The latter establishment was grander than Willard's in Washington. I looked in to get the beauty of it, but took my midday meal at a farmer's hotel, where the portions were sound and the prices sensible. I would have liked to sit warm in the common room all afternoon, for it was cold outside, with a fierce wind off the lake, and my leg was a bother. But the fever, at least, was long behind me, and time must not be squandered. I roused myself and scouted all I could, from the great aqueduct to the last boatyard.

"There is prosperity," I thought. Even the Irish seemed busily employed, and sober at their ropes and saws and lifting.

I ended the afternoon at the farmhouse where Miss Anthony lived with her family. The land had been sold off as lots for new dwellings, but a residue of country charm remained. Apple trees held birds awaiting spring, and the air tasted lovely after the city's smoke. Too, my visitor's task was a happy one. My beloved wished Miss Anthony's signature to paste in our album. It seemed Miss Anthony was a figure of some fame, as well.

There is, I must say, a great deal of famousness in America. Mr. Douglass had presented me with a signed copy of his own life story—such printed confessions have become a national habit of late, arousing fear for our modesty. Why should we tell our secrets to the world? There is foolishness enough without addition. Of course, Mr. Douglass's reminiscences are meant to edify.

It makes a fellow think, though, to find a Negro has authored a book. How can we not regard such like as welcome among us? Reg'lar John Brent, master of horse and sleigh, might have said that the more books the African authored, the less of a welcome he would find. For he sees in us all a greater desire to look down than to look up. But I will believe better of my fellow man. We only need familiarity, see. Then brotherhood will come.

Miss Anthony was everybody's maiden aunt, stern of visage behind those tin spectacle frames, but soft in her doings. Her family kept a proper Christian household—Quakers, though we never talked devotions. Twas a home where there is enough for all, but never extra for any—though a portion will be found for one in need. That makes a goodly life. For Satan loves waste, while the Lord would have us value every morsel.

I set down my cup of coffee, into which I had introduced one sugar, though I wanted two.

"Miss Anthony," I said, "there is a thing I do not understand."

Her eyes rose behind the glass ovals.

"Mr. Douglass engaged in a seance with Kildare in Penn Yan," I continued, "but will not go to see his show in Rochester. I thought that he might join us. Embarrassment is it? At being associated with such matters in the public eye?"

She moved to pour more coffee, but I held up my hand to decline. For I had marked the thinning of the stream when last she poured, and would not shame her with an empty pot.

"Yes," she said, "Mr. Douglass is embarrassed. That he is. Although it has nothing to do with Spiritualism." She settled the pot on stained lace. "We have made progress, Major Jones. And we shall make far more. But progress is . . . uneven by its nature."

Her eyes glinted, but her voice avoided anger. She had the patience born of lengthy struggles.

"You see, Mr. Douglass is welcome upon the speaker's platform. But he's not . . . a colored man is not yet so welcome in the
audience. Except at abolitionist meetings, of course. Certain
rules still pertain in our dear Rochester. And they are ignorant,
silly rules, when not repulsive. If he went with us tonight, he
would be expected to sit at the back of the hall, where the
benches are set high. 'Nigger heaven,' it's called. And even such
seating becomes unavailable when sufficient white men purchase
tickets." She sighed. "He takes such things to heart. If only he
saw more clearly what women must endure."

I thought of proud Douglass, of his lovely cadences and lordly
voice, of his newspaper and book. And of his needless shame
over his wife. Reg'lar John Brent had called him "unhappy." Let
us settle on that mild word. For we will never understand such
wounds as his.

• • •

Miss Anthony drove us into town in a pony cart, which a boy
minded for a nickel. A fog had risen from the lake, muting the
gaslamps. You heard footsteps, but saw nothing. Until a human
shape appeared a step away, only to vanish with another step.
The wind was down and the night clung to the skin. A stranger
never would have found his way. But Miss Anthony's course
was sure.

From down the street, the Corinthian Hall was but a glow in
the murk. We heard the hubbub of the crowd before we could
reckon the edifice. Then, as we hurried across Exchange Place
between the crush of carriages, the great building emerged. Tiers
of windows shone golden through the fog and Roman symme-
tries made the hall appear grand as an opera house. Although I
would not ascribe the wickedness of the French to the honest citizens of Rochester, this was how we might imagine Paris!

Now you will say, "Hypocrite yet again! This Jones would
claim to be an honest Methodist, but here he goes frequenting
a theater to gawk at a young woman." But I will tell you:

Corinthian Hall was home to edifying programs and noble sentiments, and not the sad domain of scrambling players. And my concerns for Nellie were chaste. My visit to the hall was first a duty.

A rough crowd marred the entrance, composed of the penniless sort who hope for trouble.

Miss Anthony pulled her shawl tighter and leaned forward, a soldier on the march. I had to work my cane hard to keep pace with her.

As we approached the slot for paying customers, the hooting began. A fellow who had tied his cap to his head with a scarf hallooed, "There's the one wants to set women up on top of men. With the little soldier feller."

A second voice answered, "Well, *I* sure wouldn't get on top of *her*."

They laughed. Calling Miss Anthony names as unjustified as they were miserable. For she was moral as a martyr, if extreme in her expectations.

"Just thinka them two going at it," a boy with half his teeth gone lisped. "Just thinka it."

Such was not to be tolerated. I turned on them, wielding my cane. But Miss Anthony seized my arm and drew me along.

"It's worse when we meet for women's rights," she said. "Or for the Negro."

"Bet that little feller fits right up under her skirts," a last voice yelled. "Pee*yoo!*"

Inside, the hall was brilliant as a summer noon. I paid for seats toward the front. Twas not an extravagance, for I felt I had to see what could be seen. And I will tell you, the audience was a revelation to me! If ruffians lurked without, the cream of Rochester's society had gathered within. I even saw a lady wearing diamonds! And plenty of parson's collars there were, with parson's necks behind them. On winter leave, officers glittered, their ladies graceful swans upon their arms. Bewhiskered husbands in their prime napped beside matrons whose hair had been gathered back tightly with ribbons and lace and splendid ornament. The younger members of the feminine division wore ringlets in rows or gleaming hair put up in the Roman fashion. Zouave jackets and garibaldis were the rage among the unmarried girls, and the new magenta satins shone between Genoa velvets of emerald green or havannah. My Mary Myfanwy, a born mistress of needle and cloth, could have sewn no finer garments. The dress put Washington society to shame, although I am not certain shame is felt in our poor capital.

Miss Anthony was welcomed by a few and known to many, but she made short work of social frivolities and remained a sturdy Quaker in her dress. As soon as we sat down, she nudged up her spectacles and readied pencil and paper.

The evening began with a lecture on Assyrian mysteries and the hierarchies of Babylon by a famous doctor of whom I had not heard. He claimed affiliation with a university in France, though his accent was flinty American. Now I take an interest in self-improvement and appreciate an elevated speech or sermon, but that fellow was dull enough to put a man into a snoring trance before the evening's mesmeric show began. Silly he was, too. But the crowd devoured every dusty word.

I snapped to life at the sight of Nellie. She did not come out with her father at first, but stood waiting back of the curtains. I could just see her.

Standing there, she looked pale unto death. Slender to disappearing. Yet she wore a greater beauty on her brow than all the splendid ladies in that hall. I thought that the man who married her might do naught but stare for a lifetime. Then I recalled she was not like to marry.

I do not understand why the Good Lord would create such beauty only to treat it so. But faith is our lot, not understanding.

Kildare himself seemed darker than ever, his midnight beard a veil to hide the man. He hypnotized a pair of fellows from the audience, chosen from the less expensive seats. He made them quack like ducks and waddle about the stage. Then the lankier lad stretched out between two chairs. Stiff as death, he was, with only his heels on one chair and the back of his head on the other. The stockier fellow sat upon his middle, feet in the air, without lessening the rigidity of the human plank. Next, Kildare convinced the bulkier subject that the other was his beloved. The poor oaf knelt and blubbered for the favors of his mustachioed companion.

Twas nothing to the least fakir of India. Naught but shabby circus doings. It played well with the rear rows, though. Kildare knew that he had to please them all.

He called for the dimming of the lamps. The flames flickered down in the chandeliers and sconces. Gloom settled in where the gas pipes ended and shadows quivered at the back of the hall. The stage alone remained a realm of gold.

Deepening his voice again, Kildare spoke of distant Arabia, of lost cities and secrets whose possession meant death to the uninitiated. His speech had a slow rhythm that put me in mind of tides. I don't know how he did it, but he kept deacon and dowager on the edge of their seats.

Soon the hall was his.

And then he brought out Nellie, leading her by a white hand held high. She was already in her other world. The bell of her sleeve hung down between her and her father.

She stood facing the audience, red hair free over satin. It was the very opposite of fashion to appear with hair undone, yet many a female heart must have filled with jealousy at the sight of her. In the odd light, I could not tell if her dress was gray or lavender, but no matter. She might have come in rags and looked a queen. A fairy queen, who needed no adornment. I read no hint of madness on her now. She cast a spell of peace and boundless distance.

Gently, as if he feared waking her, her father placed a chair behind her skirts then bid her sit.

The audience hushed. Breathless.

Kildare looked out upon them with those eyes.

"Who is in love?" he asked. "Who waits and longs? Who yearns?"

He paused, staring into the rear of the hall, as if he could not see the rising hands.

"Who would know the secrets of the future?" he called.

A hundred hands went high. Young men cried out, their voices half a plea and half demand. The fairer sex demurely volunteered.

Kildare stepped up to the lip of the stage, scanning the turbulent rows. Tormenting them with his hesitation. Letting them ache for attention, for a glimpse into eternity. He might have played the devil in a drawing room.

At last he called on two men of the cloth.

"Reverend gentlemen, I beg your assistance. To maintain the highest level of morality and decorum, as well as to confirm the veracity of the experiment, your humble servant requests that you select our volunteers. They must total ten, chosen alike from those formed after Eve and from the sons of Adam. If any be known to you and of good character, choose them first, so that the world may see there is no fraud."

Shameless, I call it still. Two white-haired vicars jumping at Kildare's bidding. Amid squeals of delight and groans of disappointment, they shepherded six young men and four young ladies to the stage.

A handy fellow produced a stool of the sort that does not interfere with a lady's crinolines, if I may be so blunt. Kildare adjusted it before Nellie, then turned to the audience again. Across the stage, three of the girls looked as though they already regretted their participation, while the fourth was flirting with the boys who had come up.

"Ladies and gentlemen," Kildare declaimed, "in the interests of delicacy, the conversations between my daughter and this young nobility of feminine beauty must remain private. But after each conference, I will ask the affected party to report to you the accuracy of our mystic intelligences." He folded his arms, flashing teeth amid his wilderness of beard. "The gentlemen . . . may expect no such mercies."

The audience laughed, but softly. With the grace of a Maharajee's servant, Kildare led a fretful missy to the stool. He whispered a last assurance to her and the young lady sat down facing Nellie, arranging her skirts about her. Back to us, the girl was a very hourglass, waist tiny and posture prim. Rows of brown ringlets flanked the pedestal of her neck.

Nellie leaned toward her. Curtains of red hair closed around the girl, until I could see but a sliver of her cheek. She began to fall, slowly, toward the prophetess, as if drawn by invisible ribbons. Then her chin rose and she paused in her swoon. She might have been offering her throat for a kiss.

Nellie's head began to sway, queerly, as I have seen the cobra do in rising from its basket. Slowing time to never-ending moments.

The girl jerked back. As if bitten. We all heard her gasp. Raising her hand to her mouth.

The audience jumped with the girl. We had become a single creature.

The lights lowered yet again, deepening the shadows. Nellie bid the girl come back to her. We could not hear, but understood the message on her lips. The girl leaned forward, sinking into the spell. Nellie brought her face, her lips, to the girl's ear. Auburn hair brushed the girl's cheek, cascading down her neck and breast like blood.

I had a sense that Nellie was draining the girl. Not of her blood, God forgive me, but of her soul.

Miss Anthony's pencil lay forgotten.

Nellie's lips brushed the girl's ear again, then glided down her neck and pulled away. She sat back like some legendary queen, her look triumphant.

No. Sated. She looked sated.

Kildare offered his arm to the girl and led her, shaking, toward the audience. Her face wore a lattice of tears. But she was smiling.

"Tell them," he commanded, extending a hand toward the audience.

"*It's true,*" the girl burst out. "It's true. It's all *true.*" Then she broke down, sobbing and smiling as I have only known women to do in the deepest privacy. One of the reverend gentlemen helped her from the stage. He treated her like a sacred relic.

The second girl's interview ended wistfully, but with another confession that all had been accurately revealed. The third rose in a fit of joy, a child granted its wish. When her turn came, the flirt jumped up before her time was done, shouting, "I'll *never* have the beast, not in a hundred lifetimes!"

There was strange. We all knew she was wrong.

"Miss Kildare's a marvel," Miss Anthony whispered.

The first of the fellows sat down and leaned toward Nellie, anxious for those lips to find his ear. But Nellie kept her distance from the gentlemen, and spoke aloud. The great hall was so quiet her voice reached the rafters. Twas a deeper voice than the one I had heard on the hill. Fit to marshal the spirit world. The doubting girl was gone, at least this night.

Some of the maidens mentioned by name were in the audience, and swoons were not infrequent. The last boy fled the stage, fearing exposure.

But all this was prologue. When the game of hearts was done, Kildare led Nellie forward. She seemed to float toward us. Then he began that gliding passage of the hands over her, ending again by circling her eyes in a long, slow rhythm.

I felt my own eyes fighting a drowse.

When Kildare was done, Nellie stood with her eyes closed, hands extended from her billowing sleeves. Welcoming an invisible guest.

"In return for their gracious assistance . . . in maintaining the Christian virtue of this hall," Kildare announced, "our two reverend gentlemen may take the liberty of asking my daughter one question each. Any question, gentlemen . . ."

The first man, chiseled for a High Church parish, asked when the terrible war would end.

Her answer shocked, and might be marked the first failure of the evening. For it seemed unbelievable. With hardly a moment's hesitation, she said:

"Full three years more must pass. Three years of blood and sorrow. Then hate dies in the spring."

The hall broke into turmoil.

"But . . . but . . ." the minister stammered, ". . . the Union will win, of course . . . the . . ."

"Only one question, sir," Kildare said. "One question each. The strain is too great."

As the clamor subsided, the other preacher stepped forward. With a smug look. He was shorter than his colleague, and had the stoutness of the Lutheran.

"When," he asked in a mighty pulpit voice, "will our Savior return?"

The audience exclaimed at his boldness. But the man was undeterred. Even pleased at his effect, I thought.

"When will we again know the peaceable kingdom?" he continued. "When will the lion lie down with the lamb? When shall we look upon our Savior's face?"

I watched the rise and fall of Nellie's bosom. Expecting her to break down in a fit of coughing under the weight of such a test. But her disease seemed to have left her for the evening. In the course of the interviews, she had even gained a flush to vanquish her paleness.

"Never," she said.

You may imagine the shock in that hall. But she continued, voice rising to pierce us. "Never . . . until the day He is welcome again. He is not wanted now. Men's hearts are hard and cold . . . their hands hold fresh nails ready . . ."

"*Blasphemy!*" someone cried behind me. But the charge

found little echo. Instead, the audience passed from its confusion into mourning. As if each man and woman knew the girl was right.

Kildare leapt to the rescue, face alarmed. He held up his hands for silence, calling out, "*Gen*tlemen . . . *la*dies . . . please . . ."

When he had them broken to a murmur, he turned to Nellie a last time and called, "Princess of the Ancient Mysteries . . . these good souls beg a response to the first reverend gentleman's unanswered question. What *is* to be the future of our beloved Union? Will it endure? What shall we see? What fate awaits this country?"

She lifted her face and said:

"Glory."

• • •

I offered to accompany Miss Anthony home, but she would have none of it.

"Women must learn to fend for themselves," she said, get-upping her pony. The cart rolled into the fog.

Twas a relief, I will admit. For though I would behave as a gentleman ought, I hoped to intercept the Kildares as they departed. Dodging lamplit cabs, I hurried back toward the hall and met the last of the audience issuing from its doors. Slow they were, with somber faces. Clinging to the evening, or perhaps only to the false gaiety of the gaslamps. This was no night to pace through lonely rooms.

Hooks of conversation caught my ear.

"Nonsense, the war will be over by . . . Did you see the look on . . . They say she's . . . Oh, where the blazes did I . . . If you were Jesus, would you . . . felt it hovering, I *did* . . . My, what a lovely . . . haven't seen you in . . . I distinctly told . . . nothing but a diseased Irish slut . . ."

The last come from a woman's voice. For men will wound, but women speak to kill.

Just as I approached, Kildare swept out, leading Nellie along.

She wore a velvet traveling cloak, with a hood that shadowed her face. The rowdies on the fringe of the crowd hollered about the "ghost girl," and damnation, but the respectable folk made way. You felt a mix of fear and yearning in them, an aching to reach out restrained by a peppery urge to run. A bit of it touched me. For we sensed we had approached a strange frontier, and the safety of what we knew checked the promise of that beyond. A coach waited. Kildare hustled the girl inside.

Neither gave a sign that they had seen me. There are blessings in a certain compactness of physique.

I thought that I had missed my chance—and had, regarding Nellie. But Kildare did not follow his daughter into the vehicle. He shut the door on her and tapped the driver's bench with his walking stick.

The coach pulled off.

A covey of ladies approached Kildare, holding out autograph books. He signed a pair of them, then announced, "I am called, I am called," in that actor-fellow's voice of his. And off he swept, cape trailing.

Now, you will forgive me if I admit I longed to speak to Nellie. I had thought much about her, about her words and doings, and had my bit to say and more to ask. But I count it a good thing that her father packed her off, for it left me no choice but to do my duty. And my duty was to follow Kildare.

I had not inquired for him at the hotels, nor at the police offices. For I did not want him to learn I had come to Rochester. Perhaps the girl knew. I know not what she sensed and what she missed, whether the future was clear as a painted picture to her, or but a boiling up of this and that. But I did not believe she would tell Kildare if she saw me in her visions. For there was more to that situation than the two let on. But let that bide. For now.

I hastened after Kildare, pursuing him into the fog. Away from the lighted front of the hall, the air was thick as guncotton, and the lamps but will-o'-the-wisps, teasing a fellow on. I dared not trail him too closely, and could not see much beyond the length of an arm. So I concentrated on his footsteps, the way we tracked the assassin to his lair in old Lahore. And I will tell you: Not a few British throats were cut in that distant darkness.

Kildare marched along with a purpose, fair slapping the pavement with his walking stick and careless of the ice. Twas hard to keep up with him. I could not use my cane, see. For it makes a wicked racket as I go, and sounds swell in the fog, and he would know it was more than the tapping of a gentleman's stick. So I scurried along, bad leg a bother. Yet, I would not make too much of the discomfort, for I was grateful to have the leg at all. Bull Run had almost won it of me.

We walked a quarter mile, I judge, down streets tucked up and others roiling sin. Where saloons sent out their lighted invitations, I had to slow and let him stretch his lead. Then the sad women called to me, for they imagined—hoped—I had slackened my pace for them.

Now, I would have none of them, as you would not, yet I will not judge the Magdalenes too harshly. For their Hell is here and now, and I had seen more than I wished of their lot in the Fowler case. Only think on it. To stand abroad on an icy night, counting on the Providence you have rejected to guide half a dollar to your bed, is to be damned before you shed your mortal husk. Tis fine to look out from your carriage, with your husband by your side and furs to warm you, madame. But it is a harder thing to look upon that carriage from without. And, if you will pardon me the honesty, not all husbands keep to their carriages when their wives are not by. The heart and flesh meander, and good fortune is not always born of justice.

The girls shivered in their cast-off gowns, while drunken hands played "Camptown Races" loud. Now I am a sufficient man, but know I am not grand or nobly handsome. So I must leave a bit of sympathy even with the wicked when a girl is disappointed by my passing.

I feared that I had lost Kildare's track. After the light of the bars and bawdiness, the fog seemed heavier still. More lost voices called their invitations. Perhaps they marked the queerness of my gait, and thought that I was drunk and fallen, too. Then, in the heavy dark, the voices changed to those of children.

There is sorrow.

I caught Kildare's footsteps again. Distinct and bold they were. Like the slap of his cane. He began to whistle. Shameless.

I shuddered at our surroundings. For I am an old bayonet and know full well the wantonness of men, but do not like to think upon such things as the purchase of a child. My heart hardens at those who would take such advantage. Christian charity deserts me.

"Lo, Kilraine!" a voice called. English as a fox chase.

And yes. He said, "Kilraine," and not "Kildare."

Kildare's footsteps ceased. As did the whistling.

"You're *late*," the Englishman accused. "And I'm *bored.* However *can* one amuse oneself in this . . . *vil*lage? It's duller than Scotland."

"I'm sorry, sir," Kildare said. Oh, twas his voice, and no mistaking. But stripped of pride and power of a sudden. "The performance . . . the first speaker rambled on . . ."

"All right, Kilraine. Done is done. Walk with me, old man. Tell me where we stand."

In that fog, all character was sound. Although I dared not follow closely enough to hear their speech—they lowered their voices as they got on to their business—the contrast of their footfalls and the tapping of their sticks told who was who. Kildare adjusted his pace to his companion, and his cane went out of rhythm. The other fellow strolled, easy as if promenading on Pall Mall, stick touching down lightly. The English gentleman has a way of capturing the world's attention by ignoring it.

I come along behind, trying to be quiet. With my rough stick unused, though it was wanted.

They walked and talked for a fair half hour, the Englishman's voice pitched high but imperious, while Kildare—Kilraine—

remained subservient in tone, a debtor who has been told his loan cannot be extended. I ached to hear their words, but feared discovery.

Still, I had gained much. *Kilraine.* Oh, yes, I recalled the name from Mick Tyrone's letter. And isn't the world small for the wicked? But what on earth did the fellow have to do with a high English gentleman who fussed about in alleys where children were bartered? What should he have to do with an Englishman at all, him Irish and mixed up with rumors of Fenian risings, and murder, and mysteries?

One mystery more, that was.

We slipped back into a well-lit world. I recognized a street of better shops and fine hotels. Dull with the cold, a policeman shuffled between the gaslamps.

I yearned to rush forward and have a good look at the Englishman. But more light demanded more distance between us. Still, I saw his outline, slender even dressed for winter and as rigid in his posture as he was rumpled in his associations. I knew the type. They went to schools where there was time for sport, then made each other's sisters unhappy in marriage. The very best of Britannia's officers come of that stock, and the very worst.

They turned into the Waverly Hotel, Rochester's grandest. And that was a blessing, for I was able to watch them through a window as they talked amid plush and palms.

Graceful as a captain at a regimental ball, the Englishman turned toward me.

I *knew* that face. I could not put a name to it, and held it not in personal account. But I *knew* the man. Perhaps through the illustrated papers or the like.

He was pale, though not like Nellie. His complexion spoke of wealth and not of illness. A mustache grassed below a pointed nose. Slim and fair-haired, he was not handsome, but looked as though he expected the world to think him so. He slipped off his coat—twas fashioned with a quarter cape over the shoulders—

and his finery set him off from every other fellow in that lobby.
When a stout guest bumped him and erupted with apologies, the
Englishman merely glanced down as he might at an errant dog.

Oh, the English. They disdain the world until it submits. It is
their genius.

He gave Kildare a tap on the chest with the noggin of his stick,
then smiled and turned away. As he strolled toward the stair-
case, the staff cleared a path for him, bobbing up and down like
Chinamen.

Kildare stood in a slump. He wore the look of a man who had
been taken where he did not want to go then abandoned.

Snapping into motion, he fled. Trailing fear like a stink. He
burst out of the doors before I could get well away, but still he
failed to spot me. For all his yapping about visions, he seemed to
see nothing at all now. He rushed into the fog and disappeared.

I let him go this time. For I had other matters to attend.

Inside the hotel I went, licensed by my uniform. I gave myself
marching orders, since I had to overcome a certain reluctance to
take the first step. I was entering upon a matter painful to me,
see. Good money might be lost.

The Englishman was up the steps and gone. I picked out the
steward who most resembled a quartermaster's sergeant.

"Look you," I said. "A fellow dressed up to the nines dropped
this outside." I opened my palm to reveal a five-dollar gold
piece. "An English fellow, see."

The steward reached for the money. "I'll give it to him."

I shut my palm. "I would know the man I'm doing proper.
Does he have a name, then?"

The fellow looked me over. At first his face was pinched and
cold, for he knew I was not a guest of the hotel. And his livery
was finer than my uniform. Then he glanced about the lobby.
Seeing the other guests were not attentive, he put on a street-
corner face and said, "Whatever you're up to, it won't work,
Jacko. That soldier get-up of yours won't fool nobody, let alone
the likes of him. He's wise to all the tricks, the bastard. That's

the Earl of Thretford, the richest man in England, and he don't need no five bucks." The steward held out his hand. "But I'll take it for not putting the coppers onto you."

He had the eye of one born to small triumphs.

I gave the fellow the gold piece without a fuss. For I was stunned like a recruit surrounded in his first engagement.

I shuttled off, leaning upon my cane again. The fog outside seemed welcoming, for my thoughts were dark and unclear.

The Earl of Thretford was not the richest man in England. He was, though, one of the richest, and among the most famous. At a time when the aristocracy despised industry and trade, his father had made investments scorned by his peers. The matter was a scandal in my youth. Now the son owned half of Manchester, a quarter of Sheffield, and at least an eighth of Glasgow. He even had holdings in sad Merthyr, where my father was broken and the Reverend Mr. Griffiths took me in. Arthur Langley, Earl of Thretford, was a great figure in politics, as well, an associate of Palmerston and Russell, and a favored shooting companion of Prince Albert, until that gentleman's tragic demise. To find such a fellow in Rochester, New York, consorting with the likes of Kildare or Kilraine or name him as you will . . .

I had so much to think on that I forgot to regret the gold piece.

Chapter 13

"WELL, I HAVE BEEN A FOOL," I SAID TO SHERIFF UNDERWOOD. "And not for the first time, John."

His mighty ears sagged. "Guess that makes two of us, Abel." Consoling himself with a sip of jailhouse coffee, he confided, "Never thought this darned job would be so much trouble. Of course, it's different for you, being a detective and all."

Detective?

I put down my tin cup. The jailer had not lost his job over the murder fuss and his scold of a wife retained charge of the cookery. Her coffee was a monstrous, cruel thing, and I pitied the prisoners. But the sheriff had shone a queer light on my doings, and my thoughts turned to myself.

Detective?

My mouth must have hung wide. For I had not considered matters in such a light. I was a military officer, doing my country's duty, and, temporarily, a confidential agent. Detectives were characters in the lowest of the weeklies, intemperate of garment, with little black cigars stuffed in their mouths. The wicked pursuing the wickeder. Had I not been a middle-aged man of thirty-three, I might have thrashed the fellow who called me such.

I let it go. For Underwood and I had other matters before us. And I think he meant it well.

"There is folly," I told him. "That I would fail to see the need of the thing. With even the least suspicion of Kildare, I should have tracked his journeyings. I should have got the authorities to report his meetings and the like. I let the man run wild."

Underwood nodded. "Funny, ain't it? How a thing seems so clear once you're behind it?"

I tapped the floor with my cane, a bad habit I was developing. "If he *is* involved in organizing the Irish for some scheme, then these Mesmerism tours give him the excuse to meet the local leaders." I gave the floorboards a sudden punch with my stick. "It's *worse* than a fool, I am. For even a fool would have seen it."

"What I don't get, though, is this Englishman." Underwood smoothed his mustache. "Rich fella like that. Now what's he up to? I thought the English didn't like the Irish?"

"They like them on their knees, well enough."

He sat back and crossed his arms. "Well . . . what do you make of it, Abel? What do you figure? About this duke fella, or whatever he is?"

The connection between Kildare and the Earl of Thretford made as little sense to me as to Underwood.

"What if he's just another of these spiritualist loonies?" the sheriff continued. "All crazy after seances and funny business like that?"

Now, sanity is not the first virtue of the English aristocracy, but I did not think the earl had come to Rochester in winter to embrace the occult. I shook my head, dismissing the notion.

The sheriff knocked his empty mug on the table. Between me going on with my cane, and him tapping like that, we made a fine racket. We might have been mistaken for seance rappers ourselves.

Underwood had the look of a puzzled child. On his great, red face. "Think he might be after the girl? Cougher or not, the look of her sticks to a fellow."

Given where Kildare—or Kilraine—had met the Earl of Thretford, I did not think the nobleman's interest lay in Nellie.

"It makes no sense to me," I said. "Yet, twas not their first meeting. No, John, they knew each other well, those two. Master and man, they were. Kildare is on some business for the Englishman, that's sure. And I look for it to be a dark business. But what it is I cannot say."

He placed his paws on the swell of his thighs. "Oh, for crying in a bucket. Why did this Kildare have to pick Yates County? I ask you now. As if we don't have trouble enough with the war." He looked at me with a face that trusted, and I hoped I would not let him down. "Just this morning . . . old Howie Bates was running after me, hollering bloody murder. Wanted me to arrest his oldest boy so's he couldn't join up with the volunteers." Underwood glanced out through a window that wanted a cleaning. "This darned snow gets around to melting, the planting's going to go shy of hands. Houck boys just went off, too. And folks think I should stop 'em somehow."

"That would be wrong," I said. "And unpatriotic."

Underwood grunted. "Well, you try to tell folks that. Then stand for re-election." He looked at me. "War's a terrible thing, Abel. Don't I know it?"

The good man did not know it. For he had never served beneath the colors. Yet, he was right. For there is nothing good to say of war.

The sheriff looked out through the window again, chewing unspoken words.

"Blizzard weather," he said finally. "Look how close that sky is. Every day it holds off, worse it's going to be. Meanest winter I ever saw."

I rose to go. For I had a visit to make. Twas two days since the Rochester performance. I had come back a day late, by coach, so that Kildare would not encounter me on the train and no one might associate my journey with his affairs. The roads had been difficult, and the inns in decline where the railroad did not stop. The coaches were shabby. You felt loss, and change. From Canandaigua south, only sleighs could manage the roads. Where the rails crossed your course, you waited in the cold and watched a locomotive charge the future.

As I was doing up my greatcoat, I said, "Do not worry, John. We will get to the bottom of this." Poor Underwood looked as though the weight of the hills lay upon him. "For good men will put things right in the end." I looked about for my gauntlets, but could not find them. I fear I was distracted.

"Almost forgot to tell you," the sheriff said of a sudden. "Make of *this* what you can. Know who went running up after Kildare soon as he got back?"

"The priest," I said. "McCorkle."

Underwood stared at me, bewildered.

"The Great Kildare," I explained, "has great need of salvation."

Twas more than that, yet I withheld my suspicions from good John Underwood. For I would not accuse any man unjustly, and least of all a man of the cloth. Nor did I want the priest arrested too soon.

• • •

"And Mr. Douglass sends his regards," I said, standing well back.

Reg'lar John Brent nodded, readying a hideous beast for the harness. "Poor old Fred."

Yes. Poor old Fred.

"Well, then, Mr. Brent . . . what news in Penn Yan?" I was struggling to maintain my composure in that stable, for I found the place more loathsome than a snake pit. "Any fusses in my absence?"

He soothed the horse and buckled down the leathers. "I believe the citizens have had excitement enough, sir. The rumors are worrisome, though." He straightened his back for a moment and looked at me. "Major Jones, people are afraid. I'm glad I'm a Negro, and not Irish." He turned to the animal again, testing straps as a good sergeant will check a private's haversack before the march. "The talk of violence and insurrection is getting worse. It's supposed to transpire as soon as the weather breaks. The well-to-do are to be slaughtered in their beds."

"There will be no insurrection, Mr. Brent."

"Yes, sir. We agree on that. The Irish aren't as senseless as all that. But I'm beginning to wonder if there won't be a massacre."

I put my hand on the fellow's shoulder.

"A massacre?"

"Of the Irish," he said, looking at me now. "Fear leads to madness. And madness rides the stallion of violence." He patted the horse, which answered with a little neigh. "Some of the hot-heads may get a mind to do unto the Irish before the Irish can do unto them."

I had not thought of things in that light. And felt the fool again.

Douglass had been right. John Brent was a clever man, and well-spoken, when we two were alone. He read relentlessly. That appetite for learning had cost him lashes before he ran north, and had cost him many a penny candle since.

"There will be no massacre of the Irish," I assured him. As if to reassure myself. "Sheriff Underwood will see to that. But . . . you agree with me, then? There's no Irish rebellion in the wind? It's all nonsense?"

You see, I had begun to doubt myself.

He lifted a second harness from the hooks on the wall, lugging it toward a great black snorter.

"Major Jones, have you ever visited our Southern states?"

I had seen the camps of northern Virginia, and served in one ill-starred battle on Dixie's soil. But that was not what the good fellow meant.

"No, sir, I have not."

He stroked and soothed the horse, then deftly slipped the straps and bridling over it. "Well, the citizens of our Southland live in constant fear of slave rebellions. It's a madness with them. A curse upon them, I would say." He bent to cinch the belly strap. "It doesn't matter that slave rebellions have been few, and small, and every one a failure. Or that the cost to the black man has ever been immeasurably greater than to his white master." I caught the corner of a smile on his turned-away face. Twas a bitter thing, although he was no bitter man. "Even old Nat Turner killed less of those folks than they kill of themselves every year, with their dueling and drinking and horse racing. And now this war. Yet, they live in constant fear of the man they hold in bondage."

The brittle smile changed. I could see but a fraction of his face, for he worked as he talked, yet his expression was as complex as any I have seen on a man. "You might even say there's a measure of justice in it," he continued. "In that fear of theirs. They've created their own nightmare. Surrounded themselves with it. Oh, they're fanatical about the notion of male bravery. The frightened are always obsessed with courage, Major Jones. But I suspect you know that, from your military endeavors." He wiped his brow with a coatsleeve, sweating in the cold. "I promise you, sir, this war will not be short. The Southron would rather die than admit his fears. Or face up to the error of his ways."

He turned his head and I could not see his face at all. He spoke to an invisible audience. "Whenever the fear becomes too great, these paragons of manhood take a stiff drink of whisky and hang a black man, or two—or ten—from a tree. Nor is hanging enough. Their victims are abused, sir. With abuses worse than those credited to our Irish." He managed a faint laugh. "They say it is done to teach my kind a lesson. But we know it is evidence of their fears. They live in terror of the world they've wrought."

I longed to leave that stew of horsestink and grunting and the banging of stalls behind me. But I wanted the wisdom of John Brent even more than I wanted to escape. Once upon the road, there were limits to the depths of a conversation. I stepped next to him, hungry to know more.

"But . . . you don't believe there will be a slave rising, Mr. Brent? Even now? With our forces marching to the succor of the black man?"

He looked at me. For an instant, derision commanded his features. It soon dissolved into sorrow.

"Major Jones," he said, "I believe you're an honest man and a good Christian. So I'll honor you with a frank answer. No. There will be no slave rebellion. Firstly, because the armies of our Union aren't marching much of anywhere, at the moment. Unless that squabbling out west amounts to something. Secondly, when they do march, they will march for their own advantage, not to free the black man. Our freedom, should it come, will be incidental. Until we, too, are allowed to serve in uniform, many will see such freedoms as may be granted us as unearned and undeserved."

His head fell as he turned to finish with the second horse. "The condition of the Negro resembles that of the Irishman, Major Jones. Although the latter is not held in chains. Neither will rebel, for each is too downtrodden. Consider our American Revolution. Was it made by the wretched? No, sir. It was made by gentlemen. Even Mr. Paine, whom I admire, did not write for the slave. He aimed his volleys upward, sir." He paused in his labors and looked at me. "Even the subsequent events in France, the Reign of Terror, must be blamed on the educated—sometimes I fear my own books. But then I turn again unto the Gospels." He shook his head in sorrow. "It's the well-fed who rise up. In hopes of being better-fed still."

He led the black, tugging on its bridle. I gave the creature plenty of space. "It's never the poor who make the revolutions," he said. "They swell the crowd, but do not rise until aroused by men who otherwise despise them, men who use them for their own ends. No, sir. The poor do not spend their time thinking about high ideals, but about bread and the avoidance of the lash . . . about gaining a bit of shelter for their families, if such they are allowed to have . . . and about living through each day.

Easy, boy, easy now. That's just our friend, the major. No, the Irish will not rise. Not without a leader from another class. Even then, they'll need convincing. They know they have it better than they might. Why, I'd even wager that—"

Other footsteps trod upon the planks, and a sharp voice called for service. Twas a gentleman of the town, whom I had passed a time or two.

"Yassuh," John Brent answered, crimping down his shoulders and shuffling as he guided the horse toward the light. "Yassuh, Mistuh Farnum. Reg'lar John's a-coming. Ooooh, I be coming like I'se bee-stung. *Ya*ssuh."

•   •   •

I asked John Brent to take me to the highlands, to the heath that Nellie loved.

I knew she would be there.

The clouds hung plump and low, with a dirty look. As though the coming snow would fall unclean. The horizon closed, and the snow-clad earth showed lighter than the sky. I knew John Brent did not want to go up there, but go the good man did.

I had no fear of Nellie. But she was not alone in that half-forgotten world of moors and glens. I carried my Colt, belted beneath my greatcoat.

Twas cold. But now it was only discomfort and not misery that I felt, for I had my health again. At least, my health of body. My soul remained a vexed and troubled thing.

No singing now, not from John Brent nor me. No hymns or sprightly tunes to pass the miles. Those black-bellied clouds would not have it. And the road had thawed and frozen again. Reg'lar John had to pay attention, to keep the horses from breaking their legs. The sleigh skittered from side to side, threatening to plunge into a ditch.

We passed the taverns, Bull Run and Manassas, shut against the cold but plumed with smoke. The quiet was not of slumber, but of a world holding its breath.

No living creature showed itself. Even the birds were in hiding.

He knew his way, John Brent. He followed trails I had forgotten, where no sleigh or wagon had passed for weeks. Often, there was no track at all. He found his way by judging lines of trees and marking the shanties in the hollows.

Then we saw the hoofmarks. Plunging down the lane beyond our team.

Twas her. I knew it. Out riding. As if she could outrace death.

The heavens sat so low she seemed enfolded: A black wraith at the border of the world. There were no grand perspectives now, no endless ridges or burning twilights. Only the gunpowder gray of the sky, and the old-bandage color of the snow. As if a battle had been fought and lost. With only the girl left standing.

I got down from the sleigh. Recalling the wind from the time before, and my own desperation. Now the world held still. No flags of hair, no blowing capes. Only the smallness of her form across the heath.

"Careful, sir," John Brent said in a hushed voice. "Step clear of the places where the snow's sunken down. The ponds don't freeze properly up here."

I left him blanketing his horses.

She had been waiting for me. The Lord only knew how long she had been waiting. In that cold.

For me.

I trudged toward her, with the snow crusted hard. In the troughs between the drifts, my boots squeaked. I did not sink this time. I walked above the earth.

Like her.

Only I went like an old man, hands buried in my pockets. For I never had found my gauntlets.

She turned before I reached her. Perhaps at the sound of my boots. Or at the bidding of her spirits.

The snow had iced over where the earth fell away. I wondered how she kept her balance. So fearsomely close to the edge.

A new fur cap warmed her. Twas a dark, rich thing. Her hair fell from it.

"I thought you'd come to me in Rochester," she said. "After the performance."

"Miss Kildare—"

"Then I realized you had to follow my father. I understood."

"You saw me, then?"

"I knew you were there. I always know when you're there."

"But you didn't tell Kildare. Did you?"

She shook her head. "We cannot change the—"

"You didn't tell him," I said, "because you *want* me to kill him."

She gasped. Struck in the heart by a bullet of words.

"I . . . never . . . my father . . . I . . ."

"Stop it. He's not your father. He's no more your father than I am."

She bent over. I thought a fit had seized her, and feared she would tumble backward into the abyss. But twas only sorrow.

"I never wanted . . . I . . ."

I moved toward her. Carefully. And took her by the arm. Drawing her away from the ledge.

"I never wanted . . ."

"I know, girl, I know. I spoke too hard. We do not always see the thing we want." I smelled her sickness and her sweetness. The ends of her hair brushed the hand I had fixed upon her. Beneath the heavy sleeves I felt a wasting.

She wept.

"Does he . . . abuse you?" I asked her.

She shook her head. "It was worse in the madhouse. Please, don't let them take me back there."

Now you will say, "He must have been amazed at such an utterance." But I was not. For I had been thinking long on the matter. Look you. We label "madness" all that asks too much. For we want peace, and not cruel revelation. We have less patience with the seer than the sinner, and shun the least discomfort of the mind. When the parlor games are done, we'll have no spirits.

"Don't let them take me back there," she repeated. "Promise me."

"I promise," I said. And I meant it, Lord help me. "I will not let them take you to such a place again. For you don't belong there."

I was holding her like a child by then, though I know not how we come to it. She wept against the rough nap of my coat. Head upon my shoulder.

"I only want them to leave me alone," she whispered. "But they never will."

"It's all right," I said, though it was not.

"I can't explain it. Sure, and I'd tell it all to you, if I could."

"I know."

"She came to me again. By day. She told me all. She had a message for you."

I laid a finger across her lips. Her flesh was fever hot, her temples wet.

"I'll have no message, girl," I said gently. "For we must let the dead go. Twas me you heard, not her. I was the one who kept her from her rest."

I did not know if such a thing was true. I do not know if any of it was true, or if it was only Mesmerism and dreams. Let philosophers and men of science argue about such like. I only know the dying girl believed. And for that moment, I believed with her. Thereafter, I was free of it. But let that bide.

"It's all that I can give you," she said. "My visions."

"You have given me what I need, see. And there's an end to it."

"I've tried to find out for you. About his doings. With the Irish. But he tells me nothing. He locks me in my room. The way they did in the madhouse. Only now . . . he's the only one who comes to me. Who comes to me that way. It's better so. He's the only one. And he isn't cruel. He's not a cruel man. He doesn't hurt me. But he doesn't tell me the things you want to know. He says he'll put me back in the madhouse, if I don't do what he wants. I'd rather die than go back . . ."

"No one will—"

"*You can't know what it's like.* No one can know. The screaming. They never stop screaming. I'm not like them. I hurt no one, sir. Even when they let me be, I never can sleep for the screaming."

Twas then I understood her love of those highlands. And of their silence.

"Nellie, I must ask you—"

"I know," she said, shutting her eyes and squeezing more tears free.

"I *must* ask you about these matters. It is my duty, see. You say he tells you nothing. But when last we stood here . . . you insisted there'd be no insurrection, no rebellion. You seemed certain."

"I know there's none, sir."

"Do the spirits tell you that?" I was struggling to sort reality from madness. "Please, girl. Try to think clearly. How do you know such a thing?"

The clouds had lowered around us. We stood alone in the world.

"From the men he keeps about the yard. The O'Haras." I felt her body tense as if frighted. By one of her thousand ghosts. "They . . . came to me once. To my room. When he was away. They . . . only did it that once . . . they were drunk . . ."

I held her close and shut my own eyes, too. We might have been falling down over the edge of the heath, over the edge of the world.

". . . they laughed afterwards . . . they . . . asked me if I'd be a princess . . . when Kildare was King of the French. You see? There's nothing like rebellion in the air. It's all a lark. For he'll never be king of the French. He's mad, too."

"You're not mad," I said. I knew not what she was, but would not shame her with a curse of "madness." Was she less sound than those who made this war? Or those who excused bondage from their pulpits?

I let her weep for a bit, then broke her hold. "You must come with me now. It's over, all this 'Great Kildare' business. We'll take good—"

She tore away from me. Face repelled, eyes gone to great horizons. She shook her head with the abandon of a child, whipping her hair from side to side.

"No," she said. "They'll put me in the madhouse, sure. You don't understand."

"I won't let them. I promise you."

The shaking of her head slowed, and the sweep of her hair with it. "You won't be able to stop them. I know you want to help me. The spirits told me long ago. Your spirit's tall and strong. But you won't be able to stop them."

"You can't go on like this . . . Nellie . . . *please* . . . let me see you safe and cared for."

"I can't go with you," she said.

"Why?" Twas I who was the stubborn child now.

"Because you have your life. And I'm no part of it. Because you do not know the thing you want yourself. For men are blind, where women see."

"Why won't you come with me, girl? I'll see that you're looked after. There are good people in the world. They're not all like Kildare."

She laughed. "He's far from the worst."

"Come with me."

"No."

"Why, then?"

She mustered the saddest smile in the world. "Because I'm dying. Tis no secret, sir. And I won't die inside their walls." She looked around at the snow-clad world. "I'd rather freeze than die where they'd put me."

"My church could organize something for you. There are so many good people. Why, I could even take you to my own—"

She laid her fingers over my lips this time, for twas her turn to do the hushing. She wore no gloves herself, and her fingers were as cold as her lips had been fiery. "You can't ask as much of others as you do of yourself. Take your happiness. Have joy of it. Don't bring in temptation."

"Miss Kildare, I assure you—"

The smile turned wistful now. "We're twined, you and I. Two castaways. I've become her, don't you see? She's so warm. And I've felt only cold for so long." She wiped a reddened hand across her eyes. "Now go. And leave me what I have."

"I can't just go."

She closed her eyes and breathed so deeply it lifted the bosom of her coat. "It's so wonderful up here. The smell. The clean smell. For years, I smelled only the madhouse." She breathed again, glutting herself on the frozen air.

"I can't just leave you," I said.

The deep breaths had calmed her. She laid her hand upon the sleeve of my coat.

"I'm not afraid of the dying," she told me. "I'm only afraid of dying their way."

"Please . . . you mustn't give up . . ."

She laughed. Lightly. Amused. But when she spoke, the laughter lay a thousand years behind her.

"I just want to die where it's clean."

And then the great gulps she had taken of the sky turned against her. She began to cough, naught but a sick girl now. Coughing and coughing. I moved to help her, but she thrust out a hand to keep me back. Staggering off into the field.

"Nellie!"

She bent as if retching. Gagging and gasping. Spitting upon the snow.

I went after her, but she had passed beyond me. She used the last of her will to straighten and warn me off.

"Leave me now."

"Come *with* me. For the love of God."

She shook her head and silenced me one last time. You could not paint such sorrow in a face.

"We'll never meet again," she said.

Twas final. I cannot tell you why, but I obeyed her. I watched until she was but a shadow in the gray. Then she was nothing at all. Hoofbeats galloped into eternity. They had naught to do with a living girl.

I looked down, and saw her blood upon the snow.

Chapter *14*

 "A MYSTERY!" THE REVEREND MR. MORRIS CRIED. "A mystery, Major Jones! I found it there, just there." He pointed at the barren kitchen table. "A note, a note! For you!" He extended a filthy paper, folded up square.

to majur jones

"Spies and stratagems!" the good preacher continued. "Sneaking about, sneaking about! It was lying right there."

The fellow did not seem the least bit alarmed by the intrusion into his parsonage. Instead, he was excited. But think you of a country parson's life. He is a witness to sorrows repetitive, which he must share, but he is seldom called when joys are divvied out. And Morris had no wife. We spoke about the Bible in the evenings, and he wished to hear more about India than I could bear to tell him, and he brought me hard-wrought sermons to review. He wanted a friend, and I was all he got.

I unfolded the missive, with my greatcoat still upon me. And read:

atuk fart

Well, twas a wonder Molloy could write at all. If he could not spell "Attock Fort," he knew how to have a note delivered cleanly, and how to see a dirty day's work well done.

We had agreed he would contact me when he had news worth the telling. Our two-word code—wrought of our shared past—meant I would meet him in Hammondsport, at the other end of the lake, the day after I received his communication. I hoped eyes might be less watchful in another county.

"Is it a great secret?" Mr. Morris asked, with the eager face of a child. "Is it a secret?"

"Yes," I told him. "It is a very great secret, see. Now you are party to a high government matter, and lives depend upon your silence."

Oh, wasn't the poor fellow delighted. "I'll never tell," he said. "Not a word, sir, not one word. I'll go to the grave with the knowledge locked in my breast . . ."

I only meant to give him what he longed for, and no harm done. For who would not have a feeling of importance added to his life? Still, the fellow needed calming.

"There will be no great hurry," I told him, "about anybody going to the grave. We'll keep our secret quiet, you and I."

The fellow kept his silence. I wish I had been right about the grave.

• • •

In the morning, before I left for Hammondsport, I went to see Father McCorkle. To make a last plea.

"He's over ta church," the housekeep told me. "Praying for all ye sinners, and ta take off the snows."

Well, he was in the church, but not at prayer. I entered as quietly as I could, with no wish to disturb his talk with the Lord, but found him sitting below the altar, humming and polishing a communion cup. He did not raise his eyes, but went on with his doings, scrubbing the shining chalice with a fury.

I cleared my throat.

He remained bent over the cup. "Tis late enough ye come," he said. "The boards want a proper scrubbing today, not just a sweep o' the broom."

"Father McCorkle?"

He lifted those black brows. With a look first of surprise, then of wariness.

"Sorry to disturb, sir," I told him.

He set the chalice down, but held onto the cloth. "Ye've been a disturbance to me since the day ye arrived. Will there be no end to this nonsense, Major Jones?"

I stepped down the aisle. Into the cold depths of the place.

"There will be an end. And soon enough."

"Are ye leaving us then?"

He did not bid me sit, so I stood before him. "I will go. When my duty is done."

"And when might that be, pray tell?"

Now a man of the cloth must be an actor in our Lord's theater, if you will forgive such comparison, for his despair must not show, and he must impart hope where none belongs, and he must hear things decent ears would shun, and listen without meanness. McCorkle was a master of his roles. I sensed the return of the hostility he had shown me when they fished up the drowned girl. But it lay in the air, and not upon his features.

"I will go," I said, "when Kildare has been stopped. From whatever it is he is doing. I admit I know not what he's up to. But there is trouble. And I will stop it, see. And I will stop you, too." I did not falter under those fierce eyes. "I know you are a party to the business."

He put on his Irishness, and gave me the face they give the tax collector. "I don't know what you're talking about, Jones. And look at ye. All raging in here like a madman, and bursting with accusations. Have ye no sense o' decency, man?"

But I was not raging. My voice was calm. And I was decent and not mad.

"I suspect," I continued, "that it is some scheme to advance your Irish. And that there is great wrong in it. I do not know what has moved you to go along. Although I know you would favor the poor. But the business will end badly. And, if there is violence, it will end badly, indeed." I leaned forward, hands closed over the ball of my cane. As if I might weigh down upon the priest. "Consider the fears you're rousing. And all that might come of it. If the people of this county turn upon your flock. Then there will be blood. And an end to advancement. Is that what you want for your Irish?"

He looked at me like a cocky private, not a priest.

"Are ye threatening me then, Major?"

Twas the last thing I intended. "Look you, Father McCorkle. I'm doing my best to help. Lay aside these schemes, whatever they may be. They'll do no good, see. Turn from the business and help me."

He called up a smile. Twas meant to look jovial. But it was mean.

"Sure, and don't your people like to say that God helps those who help themselves? And don't they think it's fine to free the nigger, that pious lot o' yours? While letting the Irishman rot?" He sighed, with a sound more like a snore. "Here ye've gotten me talking all theoretical. And I'm patient with ye out o' pity. For it appears that poor Morris's silliness has gotten to ye. All his talking spirits and queer doings. Why, ye've been talking mad enough to want locking up."

"It is not Abel Jones who will see the other side of the lock."

His smile withered to a twisted thing. Still a smile. But merciless as famine.

"No," he said, "it may not be. But tell me, major. What do ye think o' the girl? Our Nellie?"

I did not see how she came into this.

"And what should I think of her?"

"Well . . . I'm hearing evidences that she's naught but a madwoman herself. I even hear she was locked away in the past, and for more than a fortnight. To keep her off o' decent folk, it was. And for her own protection. I wonder . . . if twould not be better to see her safely shut away again?"

There was wicked.

I smiled. Twas grim as any smile I ever wore. Over the nakedness of his doings. But I could not find one word to fit to this.

Of course, Kildare knew all, and would have shared the knowledge. My experiences during the seance come because the fellow had hypnotized me along with Nellie. Worried, I had asked poor Morris to recount all that had transpired that evening. The man knew nothing of a spirit from far India, though he had been sitting just across the table. The business had been all inside my head. Or twixt Nellie and me.

And now I saw the full extent of my blindness. Twas plain as day, and so obvious you have doubtless figured it before me. Kildare knew *all* that passed between me and the girl. And the poor child did not even know what she told him. For he had only to hypnotize her and have her recite, then order her to forget the recitation. She was his human tool. He knew my fears as well as he knew hers.

And he knew that I cared for her. Not in the way I cared for my wife, mind you. Or for my lost love of India. Nothing improper. But in a way for which we have no words. Kildare knew that I would not want her harmed. And he forewarned the priest.

I was not laboring against a world of gossamer spirits, but against the viciousness of men. Sharpened to a point.

"You'll leave the girl alone," I cried. But well I sensed my weakness.

No doubt, the priest did, too. Twas his vocation. He raised one eyebrow, and held up a weathered hand. "Oh, twould only be for the girl's own good, the confinement. For we cannot have her doing herself harm. Tis against the Church and true religion. To say nothing o' the meanness in neglecting the helpless likes o' herself. Letting her gallivant about in the cold, when everyone knows it only does her an injury."

Unbidden or not, I sat down. You see, I was unprepared for such cruelty, no matter all that I had seen in life.

Now you will say, "That priest was evil, and no true man of

God." But I do not think it so. He did an evil thing that day. I will not excuse it. Yet, even then, I saw what it cost him. He hoped that he might do a greater good. McCorkle was, in truth, a saintly man, and such are ever prone to cruelty.

"I . . . will not permit it," I told him.

He raised both eyebrows now, and gave a laugh. "Oh, ye won't? And are ye her father then? Or family elsewise? What rights will ye call upon, and what laws?" His smile worsened. "For all the commotion, wicked minds might start to think ye'd taken advantage o' the poor child. Given such deep concerns, and ye no relation to her."

I ignored the worst of it, for twas meant to provoke. I only said, "Kildare is not her father."

"Oh, and is he not? Would legal papers lie? Why, ye'd have the devil's own time proving such a thing. I'd have to pity ye the shameless attempt."

"And his name's not Kildare. It's Kilraine."

Oh, yes. I saw a flicker in his eyes at that. But, fool me, I did not pursue it. For my mind was not a clear thing at the moment.

"It matters not a bit," the priest said, "whatever his name is."

"You'll kill her if you lock her up."

He shrugged. "An't the poor child dying already? Oh, tis a torment to see her." He held out a hand that was not meant to help. "Would it not be better . . . to see the poor thing warm and comforted as she goes?"

"I won't let you do it," I said again. "And I won't be alone. I'll have Mr. Morris on my side. And all the others who know her. Powerful people . . ."

This time he laughed out loud, bending down and shaking his head. "Oh, ye little Welsh fool," he said. With tears of laughter starting from his eyes. "Sure, and I can see ye've never been a priest or such like, for ye know not the first bit about your fellows. Do ye really think, then, that the good citizens will rally to the girl, when they learn they've all been made into laughing-stocks? Taken in by a mad girl, fresh from the asylum? With her ramblings o' spirits and the like? And them all reverent and believing and open o' purse? How do ye really think such folk will be, when they learn they've been made into asses?"

I sat there in my greatcoat. Smaller than any man should be.

"What do you want?" I asked, after a long time had passed.

He became the practical man again. In outward form, at least.

"Oh, tis little enough, Major Jones. I'd only have ye cease your pestering. Let my flock go its way. And Kildare, too. For I promise ye, as I've done a dozen times, that there'll be no harm to your cherished Union, nor to the good people o' this town. Or to the bad ones, for that matter." His deep eyes stared into me. "Just mind your business. And we'll all leave Nellie to her foolishness."

I stood up.

"There's a good fellow now," McCorkle went on. "Don't go bothering where ye don't belong, and we'll none o' us see any harm. As you're a Christian man, will ye only agree to that?"

• • •

Reg'lar John Brent had known me long enough to sense I was not in a sociable mood. He guided the horses and left me to my grump. Oh, I was in a stew. For you will think me a simpleton in the ways of the world, but I will not accept injustice. To think of what they would do to a dying girl to further their purposes covered the world in ugliness deeper than any snow.

And still I did not know the purposes they meant to further. I hoped Jimmy Molloy would have my answers, and not just blarney spent to warm the air.

We traveled down the west side of the lake, by a low, straight road that ran through tidy villages. Those whose work brought them out of doors took time to wave as we passed. It was a different world from those highlands east of the lake, where death and cruelty hid behind the beauty. The harness creaked and jingled as we slid along. The clouds drooped down, covering the hills and ridges, and the cold come off the lake to hurt your bones. Yet, this side of the lake felt all at peace, the houses built by men of sound decision.

With a snap of the whip, we passed a farmer's wagon.

"Major Jones?" John Brent leaned back toward me. "May I ask you, sir, if you plan a lengthy visit in Hammondsport?"

There was a note of concern in his voice. I wondered if there was danger for the fellow in the village, as well as in the high country.

"We will see, Mr. Brent. A problem is it?"

He nodded at the lowering sky. "I do believe we'll have a heavy snowfall. I was surprised it didn't begin yesterday. Feels like a big one coming."

"I will do my best to waste no time, then."

I hoped Molloy would be there. Waiting. Though he had been a thief and given to drink, I trusted his skills and his promise.

I pondered over Nellie as we drove. Trying to imagine the terrors and devils that beset her, and all of her own mind's making. No, that was not true. For her terror of the asylum was no fantasy, nor was the danger Kildare would betray her. I wished that I might see things through her eyes. But we are ever separate from each other, and she more so than most.

Sometimes, when my spirits weaken, I see our Savior's cross as naught but lonely.

I thought of her, so vivid in the snow, telling me we would not meet again.

Again, I wondered what she truly knew. Longing to rescue her from both her worlds. There was sadness. For I knew even then that I would fail her.

I pulled the travel rug tighter.

The south end of the lake drew in like a string bag. We saw the frozen boats and shoreline buildings. Hammondsport slept out the winter's day under a gray blanket. Ramshackle, the shops and low hotels looked too dull for serious vice. I knew there were pleasant houses higher up the hill, with a fine little army of Methodists to give the village mettle. I recalled that the townspeople—not the Methodists, mind you—had a scheme of growing rich by raising grapes for wine. I thought them just as likely to strike gold. For Temperance will put an end to drink in our lifetimes. Then where will such ambitions find themselves?

There was no masking my arrival, for small towns have eyes for things they should not see. I told John Brent to drive right up past the shops on the square, to lay aside suspicion. Then I had him stop before the Rhys home—abode of a fine Welsh family, whose welcome I had enjoyed on a previous visit. Methodists, too. Twas a sober, pleasant house, set on the hillside, not far from where a high stone mill stood derelict.

The path was clear of ice and snow, for the Welsh are conscientious. I gave the door a rap.

Mrs. Rhys appeared in her apron, cleaning her hands from her kitchen business. She was surprised, of course.

"Why, Major Jones! A visit is it? There is good. Inside with you, then, for the heat will go out and the cold come in."

Now I am a proud American, and if you find a prouder let me know. But there is lovely to hear the lilt of the homeland in a voice.

And a fine visit it might have been, for the Welsh will cook you up proper, and not let you rise until your belly is so full of good things that you fear you cannot rise at all. But I had my duty.

"Mrs. Rhys . . . I was but passing, see. And wished to say hello. Is Mr. Rhys at home, then?"

"Missed him by a whisker, you did. He's back to the shop with his dinner in him."

"It's greetings I would leave him."

"But, surely, we'll have you for supper, Major Jones?"

"I cannot stay, mum. For there is duty to our government."

She shook her head in warm, Welsh sympathy—there is none finer or more sincere, I will tell you. For we are not like the English, who only have you in to get you gone. Twas cruel to come and not stay on to eat.

"Ah," she sighed, "isn't duty a terrible thing?"

"Mrs. Rhys . . . I have a thing to ask."

"Well, ask you, then."

"I would . . . like to visit your privy."

She shivered at the very thought. "You'll freeze to the marrow. And need there's none. For there's a pot in the cellar."

"I would . . . if you don't mind . . . rather use the outhouse."

She made a face. "Shy now, is he? And doesn't he know what it's like when you're ten to the house and no secrets?"

"I beg you, mum. Let me use your outhouse."

She rolled her eyes and slapped her hands on her apron. Miffed. "Won't stay to eat, he won't. But he'll go off traipsing through the snows on us. Is that the duty you're after doing? Well, go you, then. You know where the door lies."

I hurried through the house and out the back. Shutting myself in the frigid cabin, I peeked through the air hole until I saw that Mrs. Rhys was well away from her windows. And then I was out the door and into the trees.

I made my way through drifts and thickets, testing my way with my cane and thrashing down brush. Twas good it was not summer. For I was alone, unbothered by child or dog. Or prying eyes. I crossed a steep road cut into a hollow, then turned downward. The mill loomed, its knocked-out windows blackened eyes. You could see the man who built it had grand hopes, though they were dashed. Not old, the mill stood abandoned but for a part of the ground floor locked up for storage.

I did not see Molloy. I worked my way up to the wall facing the steep of the hillside and scanned about me. Cold stone, snow and trees. I did not want to walk around the building, for the opposite side faced a street, with houses on the other side. I hoped Molloy was not so foolish as to put himself on display for all to see.

Twas cold, and I fear I did a bit of Quaker dancing to keep me warm. The clouds crawled down the hills, and I well remembered John Brent's fear of snow. I could not afford to be trapped here while great events transpired without me.

Shivering, I leaned against a window sill. To ease the moment's pressure on my leg.

A hand grabbed me.

Molloy it was. Putting the fear of dacoits and assassins into me. He crawled out of the building. In which he had no right to be. For that was private property.

"I didn't know ye was a gandy dancer," he said, with that mile-wide grin on his mug. "Oh, me darling man, ye'll set me to admiring the Welsh yet."

I resumed my usual dignity. "Are you all right, then? No harm's come to you, Molloy?"

"Oh, a rare day that'll be, when the likes o' them troubles Jimmy Molloy. Major Jones, ye've no idea the great fools they are. They're touched in the head every one. Ye'd get to thinking there's something in the air up here."

Molloy was one of those odd fellows who appear dapper even in threadbare clothes. In a low manner, of course. He looked a sight, in his battered derby and overcoat.

And a welcome sight, if I am to be honest. For I felt more affection for the fellow than I like to say. I will not have you think me too soft-hearted, or the dupe of a confidence man. But he was brave, see. Irish though he was, he had his qualities.

"Tell me," I demanded. "Tell me what you've learned, man."

"Oh, an't it an embarrassment for the glorious Irish race? Tis the silliest thing I've heard tell in me life. Kildare leading 'em round by the snouts, and them following at his heels like the dumbest o' sepoys, all faith and nary a question. And the O'Hara boys, trading in government rifles and—"

"What's that? Government rifles?"

He looked at me. Amazed. "Well, blind me with a stick if I didn't think ye knew that much, at least? Ye didn't know about the guns they're after buying? And with gold, too? Direct from the arsenal, and sold by your fine Federal officers." He made a face of absolute disgust. "Oh, I've never trusted an officer in me life, and there ye see why." He glanced at me, then added, "Present company excepted, o' course. But then ye was a sergeant in your prime . . ."

"*Why* are they buying the guns, Molloy? How many? Where are they keeping them? What are—"

"Oh, Katie bar the door, for the man thinks he's a rushing racehorse. Would ye hold onto your drawers, Sergeant Jones?"

" 'Major' Jones, thank you."

"Well, Major, sir, just let me get me answers out, so's we can look at 'em teeth to tail in the light o' day. Now first off, I can't say all what they've bought in the past, but I know they just bought fifty Enfield rifles. Fine and handy they are, too."

"How do you know that?"

"How do I know? Didn't I just unload 'em meself, and me with the pain in me back where that Seekh fellow put his boot till ye shot his face off. Why, do ye remember that day—"

"Where did you unload them?"

"Oh, up to the barn. On the farm where Kildare hangs his hat. With that quare, blazing daughter o' his, and an't that a shame the decay o' her?"

"Kildare has government rifles in his barn?"

"Well, government rifles they were. But now they're his."

"Is there anything else in the barn?"

He thought for a moment. "Only the uniforms. And a cow and a couple o' horses."

"Uniforms?"

"For the Fenian army. And handsome green, they are. Like the sacred flag o' Erin." He stopped and gave me another baffled look. "Ye didn't know that, either?"

"What's the army for? How big is it? What are they planning to do? And . . . how did you get them to trust you to such an extent?"

Molloy looked many things—he had a knack for disguises, that one—but I do not think he ever looked trustworthy. Of course, the Irish probably judge differently.

"Trust me? Sure, and don't they all love me? If it wan't all such a lunacy, I'd be tempted to join 'em meself. Treat me proper, they do. As befits a former sergeant o' Her Britannic Majesty, who can teach 'em how to stand-to proper, and to march and fix a bayonet."

"You were never a sergeant, Molloy. And your corporalcy didn't last six months."

Exasperation twisted that rubber face. "Sure, and didn't I have to tell 'em something? To convince 'em I'm worth the trusting?"

Yes. Of course. But I did not like his pretense to a sergeancy. For rank was hard-earned under the sun of India.

"I hope you're not teaching them too much," I said. "Or too well."

"And what would it matter, me darling man? For all their doings are no more than hoopla." He looked up the hillside as if looking into the future, and his face saddened. For he, too, was capable of sincere emotion. "Don't I hate the thought o' the boys dying by the dozen and marching off into captivity? For excepting Kildare and that Napper and Bull O'Hara, they're naught but poor bogtrotters all tricked into throwing their lives away. As if they'd ever teach the Queen a lesson. No matter how many hundred Kildare says he's raised in the cities. They won't make it through their first battle."

I grasped him by the arm. To force an answer. "For God's sake, man. What are you talking about? With your 'teaching the Queen a lesson,' and battles and hundreds of men?"

He shrugged. "The invasion o' Canada. What else?"

Well, that made me skip a breath. I watched a gray bird hop across the snow. And back again. Twas Molloy broke the silence, not me.

"Now an't that the craziest thing what ye've heard, Major Jones? An invasion o' the Queen's American dominions! And the Frenchies supposed to rise up in Kewbeck, as if a Frenchman could ever be trusted to raise a hand before the battle was won.

And them going to set up an Irish kingdom, with the Frenchies in it, too, and all with a mob o' Mayo boys what an't got the alphabet between 'em."

"Canada," I said. To the frozen air.

"An't that the craziest thing ye've heard?" Molloy went on. "Twould never come off in a thousand years. So have no fears. There's no rebellion against the Union or such. Naught but a crazy scheme that will never work."

"It's not supposed to work," I said softly. For I saw it all now. Every bit.

Molloy looked at me oddly. I never knew him at a loss for words, but he took a moment to find his way back to speech this time. He re-set the hat upon his head and his eyes hunted over me.

"Now . . . Major Jones. Would ye only be telling me the riddle o' that? Here's great preparations, and men all incited to die to avenge dear, old Ireland, with lovely, oiled guns, and all set to go as soon as the ice melts so's they can get across the river into Canada. And a priest to bless them on their bloody way. And . . . ye say it's not supposed to work? Now where would be the sense in that?"

"Molloy," I said, bucking up my spine, "if you were still in uniform, I'd see you decorated. You've done your country a noteworthy service. And now I need you to do another." I looked into that long-familiar face, into the eyes that were never serious even in a regimental lockup, at the mouth born to smile at life. The risk to him was greater than he realized. Or perhaps he did realize it. For Jimmy Molloy was never a coward, I must give him that.

"Ye'll be wanting me to keep watch over them still," he said.

"Yes. And you must let me know the instant they're about to move. The very instant, Molloy."

"But couldn't ye just go out and arrest 'em? With what I've told ye already?"

I shook my head. "It's best to take them in the deed. If only at the beginning. With weapons in hand, and all the men identified."

The skin tightened around his eyes. A troubled look, that. "Sure, Major Jones, sir. The boys don't know what they're about, and I'd hate to see 'em come to needless harm. Without Kildare they'd do nothing. For he's only talked 'em all into the doings, and they have no sense o' the foolishness."

"No man will come to harm unnecessarily. But we must make a thorough cleaning. Or the business will be tried again. And next time, your countrymen will bleed."

He tipped his hat forward and gave his hair a scratch. Lice, probably. "Well, I'll do it for ye. As ye know I will. And I'll move heaven and earth to let ye know the minute they're set to move. But I pity them, I do."

"There's a good soldier, Molloy."

He smiled wistfully. "I'm not a soldier anymore, Major Jones."

"No. Of course not. I forgot."

"Sure, and it's nothing. It's only old times ye were thinking on. But I would have one thing o' ye. For curious I ever was, and ye know it."

"What's that?"

"Just what I asked ye. What did ye mean that this invasion scheme's not intended to succeed? For what could be the sense in the likes o' that?"

"If I tell you, your life might be in even greater danger."

He shrugged. And smiled. "If they get wind o' me doings, my life won't be worth a turd. So I'd thank ye not to let me die in ignorance."

"I do not expect you to die, Molloy."

"And I'm not expecting it, neither. For twould spoil me plans. But what did ye mean that the Canada go is meant to fail?"

"Molloy . . . have you ever heard of the Earl of Thretford?"

"Can't say as I have. Though he sounds like a low, high-born Englishman."

"That he is. And a very rich Englishman. A man of power."

"Is he in Canada, then? Or what do ye mean?"

"He may be in Canada by now. When last I saw him, he was in Rochester. Talking with Kildare. Whose name, by the way, is Kilraine."

Twas his turn for bafflement. "Is an Englishman backing the Irish, then?"

"No. The Irish are backing the English. Had I not seen him, I never would have figured it out. And we would have been at war with England, and us wondering what happened."

"War with England?" To his credit, Molloy looked aghast. He knew what stood behind that thin red line.

"The Earl of Thretford . . . and his kind . . . represent industry . . . the mills of Manchester and such like. They want Southern cotton. And they'd gladly spend the lives it takes to get it. They want England to come in on the Confederate side. But they can't get the government to move. For Palmerston is cautious behind the bluster." I thought back on the land that had shaped my sorrows. "Kildare's the paid agent of Thretford and his party. He's to lead your invasion of Canada from American soil. With U.S. government rifles. And Lord Russell and Palmerston and the rest of them will have no choice but to respond as befits the dignity of Her Majesty. The rich will have their war. And we will see the Union broken. It's clear as day," I told Molloy, although this day was hardly clear.

"So . . ." Molloy said slowly, ". . . the Irish think they're striking a blow against the English. But they're really fighting *for* the English. So the English have an excuse to fight us."

"Exactly, Molloy."

He looked down, with a slow and solemn shake of the head. "Oh, Sergeant Jones, I tell ye. I don't know whether to pee or go blind."

Now that ungentlemanly comment reminded me that I had places to be, and a pretense to maintain. I hoped that Mrs. Rhys had not gone out to the privy to see if I was still alive.

"We'll stop them, Molloy. And we'll keep little fools from becoming great ones. You've done your new country proud."

But he was in no mood for praise that day. He stood there as sober as ever I had seen him.

"Bastards," he said. With unmistakable hatred in his voice. "The day will come when Ireland will be shut o' the dirty, pasty-faced English bastards."

"For now," I said, "let's just keep this country free of them."

I left him muttering. For my part, I went running. With the first snowflakes floating through the trees. Back of the Rhys's yard, I prowled about the outhouse for a moment. When I did not see Mrs. Rhys behind her windows, I made my way down to the back door.

When I come in, she had a washbasin waiting. And coffee and pie on the table. She shook her head maternally, as all good Welsh housewives do.

"You must be frozen to the heart of you," she said.

Chapter 15

NOW THERE IS PIE, AND THERE IS PIE, AND I MUST PAUSE TO TELL YOU. My mind was all on invasions of Canada and streaming snows when I come back into the house, but when Mrs. Rhys placed that bounteous slice in front of me, with its crust golden as the dreams of Midas and the filling red as rubies, I could do naught but sit me down and eat. For hungry I was, and there was courtesy to take into account, too. The good lady had baked it for their evening meal, twas clear, but cut it fresh for me. The oven's warmth was still in it, and cream spooned thick from the jug covered it over, and the flavor packed a wallop. Twas made of cherries she had put up, that pie, with black walnuts to take the sweet off, and oh, such a puckering beauty you will rarely hold in your mouth. That pie demanded more than I could give, for savoring was owed it, and second helpings, and a plush chair thereafter in which to glow and drowse. But time there was none.

The poor woman was baffled and amazed by my goings-on, but she bore it like a Christian and sent a lovely piece of pie along for John Brent as I dashed out into the snow again.

Now you will say, "Oh, this Jones is an eternal hypocrite. For he fair trumpets his respect for this Reg'lar John, along with his swelling regard for the Negro race, then leaves the poor fellow to freeze while he gluts himself sick in the warm with his own kind." But I will tell you: Firstly, Mrs. Rhys would have had him at her table and wondered only that he did not help himself to a bigger portion. And secondly, I would have had him inside, too. But he knew his world, John Brent. He never went needlessly into a white man's house, and never would he put himself alone with a white woman. For he grasped that innocence is ever weaker than suspicion, and tongues will tell more than they know. John Brent was regular, all right. And cautious, too. But let that bide.

He put up the horse blankets and off we went into the blow, with the flesh of cherries clinging to my gums. The storm had come out of the north, and the wind was up. The driving snow cut into the eyes of the horses, making them shy. Big flakes fell fast, and all of John Brent's skill was wanted to keep the sleigh on the road. Not halfway up the lake, we come upon a spilled-over log sled, and a mule down broken-legged and braying. Its jittered fellows fought the harness and worsened the beast's sufferings. A mile farther on, I had to get down and lead our team by the bridle, with the horse fear in me all the while and John Brent steadying their path. The snow grew so deep I could not lead the pair properly, and my friend had to turn to the whip— of which he was ever sparing—to carry us into the gale.

All the way I worried. For though we would do best to wait and catch Kildare deeper in his deeds and all uncovered, I had to get off a coded telegraphic to Washington warning Seward of what was afoot. Next, I must share my intelligences with Sheriff Underwood, then make a plan to bring up soldiers from Elmira to see the business of arresting these fellows done orderly. For where fifty rifles had gone, five hundred might have preceded them. We needed to find every store of arms, and break every conspiracy. It would not do to lock up Kildare—or Kilraine— only to learn that his plot would go on without him. A crushing was needed. Not cruel, but thorough. War with England would ruin us all.

We made it back into Penn Yan after dark, with the snow scraping the belly of the sleigh. John Brent dropped me before the parsonage, remarking, "I've got to get these horses into the barn. They're blown, sir." His strong features showed no self-concern, despite the cold, but only alarm for his animals. For he loved all that the Good Lord had created.

The truth is we were as blown as the beasts. There is a special weariness comes of the cold, and it slows a man's thoughts as surely as it does his limbs. Oh, I was born to be a fool that day.

I intended to thaw my fingers then set to work with my code book. After sending off the message to Seward, I would go by the jail to see if Sheriff Underwood was still there—although I suspected he would be gone home to his farm with such a storm upon us. For we would see no rebellion, nor invasion, nor common crime in such a snow as this.

Still, I was anxious to take matters in hand. For duty delayed is duty betrayed, and the man who begins by putting off a chore ends by putting off his salvation.

I did not even get inside Mr. Morris's front door before a boy ploughed up to me and gave my coat a tug. Snow cascaded from my shoulders.

"Major Jones!" he cried. "Major Jones!"

I had seen him somewhere before, but could not fix him. Then he wiped his nose with the back of his mitten and I remembered. He had begged a penny of me in the street a month before, and I had given him ten cents. He was the boy with the Irish face and American voice.

"What is it, lad?" He should not have been out on such a day, but inside, fed and warm. I pitied the lad and thought of my own son.

"Sheriff Underwood sent me to ya. He needs ya right now."

Oh, how I longed to go inside and thaw.

"Where is he, boy? The jail is it?"

The little fellow shook his head. "No, sir. He's gone home to his farm. Had to go real quick. Says to tell ya, 'Bloody murder,' and that yer to come to him quick, no matter what."

"More, then?"

He shook his head and shivered. "Kin I go now, sir? It's awful cold."

I gave him another ten-cent piece and sent him off.

There was hard. For I was cold and weary, and wanted my rest. I felt near sickness again and, despite the dark, my eyes were all bedazzled. But Underwood would not have sent for me on such a night had the matter not been urgent.

Murder was it? Again? And the constables and deputies no doubt out in the storm themselves, with a shivering boy sent to fetch me.

But what was I to do? John Brent could not take me, for his horses were spent. Besides, the sleigh would not cut through the depths of the snowfall any longer.

Now I am human like you, see. For a moment, I wondered if I could not plead the weather and stay in until the morning. And such I might have done, had a lesser man called for me.

I shook as much of the snow as I could from my coat and boots, and went inside.

Mr. Morris come running.

"I was afraid, afraid!" he cried, with his peaked hair aquiver. "A terrible storm! I prayed for you and our John Brent. I prayed! And now my prayers are answered! Isn't the storm terrible, terrible? A judgement, a judgement . . ."

"Mr. Morris . . . I must ask a favor, sir."

"A favor? A favor? Anything, anything!"

"I would like to borrow your horse."

"My horse?"

Yes, his horse. Twas a sad, decrepit animal, fit only for a preacher's gentle rounds. Yet, it was little less of a terror to me, for all that. I would as soon have mounted a dragon. But I saw no other way to reach Underwood's farm. For it was too far to walk, and my good leg was as frozen as the bad one, and the drifts were half as high as me and growing.

"The sheriff has called for me," I told him. "It is an urgent matter, see."

"Urgent? But the storm, the storm . . ."

"Your prayers will see us along, Mr. Morris."

The poor fellow looked at me in fear. He faced eternity boldly, but had his qualms about the day-to-day. And truth be told, the horse was precious to him. I have never understood the bond between the human and the equine.

"Prayer? Surely, surely. Yes, prayer. An urgent matter? You said it was urgent?"

"Murder," I said. Forgive me, but I knew the fellow liked a bit of excitement.

"Murder?"

"Murder."

He looked about himself, at tables and at chairs, as if a tool to prevent my foolishness might be found lying around like a book or a pair of misplaced spectacles.

"Then you must go," he said, despairingly. "Go, go. I'll saddle Priscilla. But you're all wet, all cold . . ."

"I will change my socks, and that will do." You will note that, selfishly, I did not try to dissuade him from saddling the mount himself. For I would endure horrors enough upon its back without attempting to girdle the creature with leathers.

"You know the way?" Morris pleaded. "You . . ."

I nodded firmly. For I had traveled the road past the sheriff's farm many a time, if in better weather, and I had visited him at his homestead twice.

"So cold," the preacher said, "awfully cold, the storm . . . the storm . . ." And off he went to help me all he could.

I changed my socks in haste and pulled on another length of unmentionables beneath my trousers. It made for a snug waist and seat. But the warmth was worth the squeeze. I repositioned the pistol for what little comfort I might have, then chose my greatcoat over my India rubber cape. For I wanted the warmth without the sweat of it. I should have taken the time to write a note, detailing all that I had learned. But my brain was as frozen as my fingers.

We think too little, and learn too late.

Morris led the horse around to the front, stepping high to make his way through the snow. I had a problem with the placement of my cane and fiddled about. Sitting a horse is an awkward business. And my shivering come not from the cold alone. For that sunk-backed beast seemed a viper to me. At last, I handed my cane down to the pastor.

"I will not need it to ride," I told him, "and Underwood will loan me a walking stick."

"Yes, ride, ride," poor Morris said. "Oh, what a dreadful night! It makes me fear the Apocalypse!"

I snapped the reins and rode off after murder.

I never lost my way. It was a trial, but I had not soldiered all those years for naught. If a man can find his way through the killing deserts of the Pushtoon and come out with all his parts still on him, he will not go astray in New York State.

Still, I often had to trust the horse and my instincts, for there was little enough to see. With the snow blowing against us and the dark down, my eyes found no more than a shroud of earth, and that close as the walls of a coffin. Only the trees by the roadside, white to windward and black on the lee, gave reassurance that we had not suffered a second Flood, and this time a frozen one.

Twas hard going for the horse. I hate the creatures, yet I will be fair. She did good service, though after some miles of plunging through the drifts she could do no more than plod. I sang hymns to help us both along, and the animal did perk up all startled at the handsome sound of my voice. Even a beast will take comfort in a nice hymn.

I sang out "Old One Hundred," for that one pleases me ever, with its feel of marching Heavenward. Then I gave the night "Rock of Ages," which, though newfangled, has meat on its bones. On I went through Watts and Wesley, with snowflakes darting into my mouth and the wind like the breath of the devil.

I prayed between melodies, asking for safe deliverance from

the perils of the night. I know we are not meant to pray selfishly, asking the Lord for favors and comforts. But the horse was going feebly now, and the drifts looked as high as my shoulders, and I will tell you without shame that I was afraid. For men may be faced down, but nature is implacable.

Well, there are ever those worse off than us, and sometimes we are guided to their aid. Passing through a grove, under branches clacking in torment, I heard a human cry.

It made me jump, I will tell you. For the dark seemed full of devils, though I am not one for spooks.

I heard it plain.

A human voice, weakened and calling for help.

I saw the figure then. Plunged into the snow beside the road. Pleading with a desperate, upraised hand.

"Help me," a man's voice called, all broken. "Please . . . help me . . ."

I pulled up closer to the dark lump in the snow and, holding the reins tightly in my hand, let myself down from the saddle.

I dropped into snow up to my hips.

". . . help . . . me . . ."

The poor fellow sounded Irish of a sudden. It occurred to me that he was likely drunk, and lost, and would have died had I not happened by. I felt a lilt of pride at the prospect of rescuing my fellow man.

I bent toward him, thinking of the Good Samaritan.

• • •

The light shocked me. The world was naught but a blaze. Pain pushed outward from my head, greater than my skull, and the world wore a killing glare.

I shut my eyes again and went back under.

I do not recall any dreams, and my sleep had not been notched by day and night. I would tell you that I knew only a long darkness, but that is looking back. Then I did not know if my sleep was long or short, or if it was a sleep at all. Twas a nothingness.

On dark days, when my devils come upon me, I fear eternity will be so. But then I turn again to my Redeemer.

I woke a second time. Moments later? Hours? Days? I was too wrecked to wonder. All was a jumble, and so that day remains. I have but scraps, stuffed in the pocket of memory.

A ceiling of unfinished boards, gray and uneven.

The smell of rough soap used in quantity. Prickly as briars in the nose.

Wind. Before I found the strength to turn my head and look around me, I heard the wind screaming to come inside. It strained the walls and smacked against the windows. A vandal of a wind, it was, with a sharp keen to it.

My face was cold. My body lay cocooned, but coldness pressed down on my eyes, my cheeks, my nose.

I did not try to move at first. I did not even think of it. Something in me knew I could not yet take on so great a task.

My eyes would not stay open. The light hurt too much. I hid behind my eyelids, letting myself sink again. Yet, something braked me before I lost consciousness, and I lay between the worlds. Perhaps I had a glimpse of Nellie's days. Thoughts rose vivid and out of rhyme, without the comfort of order. Images sought to lure me from all decency, and darkness seeped out of my corners.

I was visited by my Mary Myfanwy and our little John, by President Lincoln sitting in a coach, by flaunting girls that I had long forgotten and a drunken quartermaster recalled from India. The cholera dead rose, too, not least my mother. Countless phantoms robbed me of my peace, and those who should have comforted did not.

Do you believe we ever know ourselves? What hides within us, waiting to emerge?

Not sense, that's certain. If I speak of myself. I had forgotten the invasion of Canada and government arms and the Irish. I had no recall of my night ride through the snow. Twas as if my brain were going carefully with me, testing me with pictures from the past before bullying me back to present duty.

I remember turning my head as if called. The room was spare as a country chapel. There was a single window.

Beyond the glass, the sky was so blue that I want a better word to tell the color. I felt that I had never seen a sky so blue.

The wind howled and the panes shook.

Only then did I wonder where I was. For nothing was familiar. My sense of time and place had slipped askew. I did not know the room. Or the smells, at once familiar and foreign. I floated under my blankets, chill air on my cheeks.

Thinking was too hard and soon I slept.

I awoke to find a woman standing over me. She jumped when I opened my eyes.

"Du lieber Gott!" she said, laying her hand over her mouth in alarm. But then she lowered the hand. And smiled. *"Verzeih'mir. Hab's nit erwartet."*

She had a face just wearing beyond youth, with brown hair gathered back. All kindness she looked. Handsome, in a sound and solid manner.

Her eyes, though, were treasures. They poured over you like honey.

"You are . . . waking?" she asked, in my tongue. But I could not respond. I could only look up at her, an angel hovering over me. And then I could not do that much.

When next I woke it was dark. I felt a need to carry out a personal matter. Quickly.

Fortunately, my limbs had come back to me. With needles in them. Great complainers they had become, my arms and legs. And there was a business that wanted hasty attention.

I got up on an elbow.

Too fast.

The room swirled and hurt and pushed me back toward the pillow.

All I could think of was my need. I wanted to cry out. With no sense of past or future. I dreaded the embarrassment of soiling the bed. A strange bed, at that. A bed between worlds.

I bullied my way out from under the blankets, unsteady as if I were drunk. Which I was not, you understand.

My bare feet found the floor. The sharp cold of it. And I toppled over.

Then it was day and I was sitting up. The angel spooned broth into me. I could not remember waking, but suddenly the world seemed clear. Twas not, to tell the truth. But I thought it was. My head held a mighty hurt.

I had a sense of something gone wrong.

Of something gone terribly wrong.

"... day ... is it?"

"*Was?*"

"... day ..."

Her face was oval and full, with life's cares just beginning to mark it.

"*Montag.*" She tipped the broth into my mouth. "Monday is today."

I tried to shake my head. I don't know if I managed it. "Date ... *the date?*"

The question seemed to confuse her. "*Weiss nit. Muss mal gucken.*"

She took away the empty bowl. And left me with a child's sense of loss.

The sky was gray that day, but the wind was down. For the first time, I heard an infant's cries. It occurred to me that the poor woman had two infants to feed now.

Bits and pieces, pieces and bits. Molloy kept popping into my head, but I did not get the sense of it. Then I slept and dreamed I was confined in a madhouse—a place of horrors it was—and could not convince anyone that I did not belong there. I woke sweating, leaping up only to collapse back into dizziness, with the great ache ever in my head.

Isn't it queer how one little drop of thought can unleash a flood of memories? As when your life's love kisses you a certain way and erases the years? Well, I had no kiss, but, of all things, the pistol that the boys in my old company had given me come suddenly into my mind.

Where was it? For though I have no love of such instruments in general, that Colt was holstered in sentiment. I distinctly remembered having it with me that night.

The rest of the night returned in a blink.

And more come back to me, too.

My head throbbed. Too small a jug for so many thoughts. Fair clobbered I was by remembering.

I had to go. Had to warn Seward. Had to raise Underwood. Call up the regulars . . .

How many days had I lain there?

The room was ever cold, but now I fair froze at the thought that Kildare might already have launched his invasion, that our beloved country might be rushing toward an ocean-spanning war, and that it might be my fault.

The woman stepped in, just as I attempted to rise. I was got up in somebody else's unmentionables, far too large for me. Of course, I covered myself again. Unwilling to think of all that she had seen while I slept, or of the shames I doubtless had committed.

"Uniform?" I asked her. "Do you . . . have my uniform?"

She looked at me, unable to understand at first. But her confusion lasted only a moment, for the word is nearly the same in the German tongue, though they will speak it peculiar.

"*Ja,* we have."

"Please," I said. "Bring it to me. Please."

I know not what I intended, but she saw clearly that it was beyond my capabilities. "*Morgen.* Tomorrow, I bring."

I did not argue with her. For all my strength had gone into the request. I lay back.

"How . . . how did I come here?"

"To here?"

"Yes. What happened to me?"

She chewed her lip for a moment. Thinking. She had an openness that was her greatest charm, and gave all without calculation.

"Weiss nit genau was passiert ist. Mein Mann . . . my husband finds you. In much snow. You are dead, he thinks." A look of frustration come over her. *"Ach, wie sagt man? Sie waren grausam mit Blut geschmiert.* All blood is on you. He comes late from the wood-selling, *mein Mann. Dann hat er dieses komische Mägdlein gesehen. Schockiert, war der Gute. Es war nit richtig bekleidet, das Mägdlein.* The girl he sees. Her clothings are not enough. *Doch, es hat dich gerettet. Es hat ihn die Stelle gezeigt.* Alone, he is never finding you, she is showing him. *Dann ist es weg.* Without the girl to help, he never finds you. *Und* you die, I think." She sighed. *"Der Herrgott hat dich lieb."*

Now I was not in my clarities, see. I let the remarks about the girl pass, thinking it a reference to a daughter I had not seen.

That evening, the woman brought me a dinner to fill a right belly. Twas no rich man's fare, but honest. She sat beside the candle, watching long enough to be sure I could eat by myself.

When she come back for the plate, her husband followed her in. Twas the first time I had seen him.

Tall, with shoulders broad as a yoke, he wore a full beard. But you only saw the true man when he stepped in close and the flame of the candle caught his eyes. Now husband and wife they were, and different in hue and stature. But didn't they have the same warm eyes? The two of them looked as if life were a constant gift they longed to share with the rest of the world. Overflowing, they seemed to me. *Overflowing.* Though not with worldly treasures. You would have known them for kindly sorts if you had met them in a prison or a battle.

"Guten Abend," the fellow said.

Now I knew that much from dear Mrs. Schutzengel.

"Goodenbend to you, sir," I answered in my finest Dutch.

The woman took up the utensils. "My husband . . . helps you. If you want to sit by the fire and become warm. You are so strong?"

Of a sudden, the room's cold bit me. Few things in life have sounded as lovely to me as a place by a hearth did then.

Standing remained a trial, and walking was worse. Twas the dizziness that comes with a great crack over the head. I had a great scab on the back of my skull, where my assailants had, no doubt, expected my brains to spill out. But a Welshman is hard to knock down, and harder still to keep there.

The husband smelled of work and winter barns, of hay freshened with a pitchfork and sweat on leather. He helped me into a set of his own clothes, which were twice too big but served for modesty. Then he guided me out of that poor little room as though I were a child taking its first steps.

He placed me in a rocking chair, surprisingly gentle in his doings, then laid a quilt over me. Oh, that fire was a glory. The flames smiled, I tell you. I was close enough to feel the heat on my face. Only the dizziness would not settle at first.

When I come to myself proper, the couple were just done with their after-dinner chores. The woman lifted an infant from a low cradle and soothed it in her arms, sitting down in a chair across from me. Twas not so good a chair as mine, for they had given me the place of honor. The husband brought a kitchen chair and placed it close to the flames, then he fetched a big Bible—*Die Bibel,* they call it—with metal clasps. He sat down and opened the book.

He read to us by the firelight, tracing the lines with his finger. *"Selig sind, die um Gerechtigkeit willen verfolgt werden; denn das Himmelreich ist ihr . . ."*

Even the infant seemed to listen. I knew not their tongue, but got the spirit. What better tonic for the wounded flesh than that tonic of the soul? The fellow could have read those words in Hindoo and would have reached me still.

When it come time to get down and pray, I struggled to join

them on their knees. But I was too wobbly and only interrupted their devotions. Together, they tucked me back into the chair.

Then they spoke the Our Father, and no mistaking it. I did not know the words their way, but mumbled along. When they bowed their heads in silence—with the firelight coloring their faces—I said my own prayers, too.

They stayed a long time on their knees, with the woman clutching the infant. And what better attitude of prayer might there be, than a mother holding her child?

Even prayer was not enough to hold me. My mind drifted and I began to doze, only to wake again to a stabbing clarity. For the first time, I noticed the bed of bundled hay. Made up on the floor, behind the cradle. And I understood. The bed they had given me was their own. Twas all the bed they had, and they gave it to me to soil.

Would I have done a thing as fine as that?

Our selfishness resounds in our small lives.

I sat and watched them, husband, wife and child, praying on the splinters. Perhaps such folk will wait for us, on the day we are most in need, to help us limp across the River Jordan.

• • •

In the morning, the husband helped me down to breakfast at their table. The woman had my uniform—the one from Mr. Feinberg's shop—stitched up and cleaned. She handled it as if it were dangerous.

"How long was I . . . how long did I sleep? How many days?"

They looked at one another, then spoke in quick German. The woman began to count up on her fingers.

She stopped when she reached seven.

I sat up, spoon halfway to my mouth.

"I must go," I said.

The woman shook her head and looked at the man.

German again.

"Es geht nur bis zur Scheune," he said. *"So ein tiefer Schnee hab' ich nie gesehen."*

"He says the snow is too deep. Only to go to the barn is possible. He has not seen such a snow."

"The road . . . how far is it to the road?"

She translated. She knew the distance well, but wanted counsel.

"Die Strasse ist nit zu befahren," the man said. *"Geht nit. Keineswegs."*

"My husband says it is not possible to go. The road is under the snow, too."

But which road? A main road? Were other roads open? If the snow was still so deep . . . then likely Kildare had not made his move. But I had to be sure. I could not loll about, shying from my duty. I had to be on my way.

I had the senselessness that follows a great, jellying whack on the noggin, see. They tried to reason with me, but I got on my greatcoat. A madman, I lurched into the yard.

Beyond the barn lay a white sea. We needed a Moses now, to part the snows.

I plunged ahead.

Stubbornness has its place in this life, and it has won not a few battles that rightfully should have been lost, but I fear I went to an extreme that morning. I charged the drifts where the house faced front and a road should have waited.

At first, I thought I would make a go of it, for the snow was crusted hard. I climbed up on the bank and limped along, careful of a slip. But not six paces out I broke through the surface. And found myself engulfed up to my chest.

The husband dug me out and carried me in. At the edge of a swoon, I asked him to put me on the bed of straw and to take his own bedroom to himself again, but he ignored me. Undressed, I slept the day out and the night.

Now the only thing duller than a convalescence is listening to a report of a convalescence. So I will spare you more of such matters for the moment, and let you take a breath.

Later, when I returned to the world of common days, I found a letter waiting from Mick Tyrone. Although I like things kept in proper order, I will share that letter with you now, to lift you from the boredom of my bed. And you will see my little woes were nothing.

Chapter 16

Dover, Tennessee
February 26, 1862

My Dear Friend,

I hope my scrawl is legible. My hands shake. They have done too much these last weeks, and little well. I thought I was a man of Science. I'm nothing but a threepenny butcher. I wear more blood on my hands than old Macbeth and his wife together. Far more. My "medicine" is no more than a hacking at flesh and bone. What Rebel bullets left unfinished, my fingers completed. I have bathed in a river of gore and cannot sleep. Man is a beast, and I am but a jackal.

I will tell you of the struggle for Fort Donelson to purge myself of it. But first allow me to venture an answer to the query contained in your last communication. Given what I have seen of Mesmerism over the years, I believe you are correct in assuming that this Kildare may have lulled you and the others present into a trance while pretending to work his will solely upon his daughter. Once he had you in that waking sleep, it would have been an easy thing to suggest to you the presence of a soul dearly remembered and lost—you would have made your own choice of visions, requiring no previous knowledge on the mesmerist's part.

I do not credit your notions of a life beyond the grave—
we are naught but food for worms—but, in the caverns of
the mind, we do keep others "alive" in some sense. Kildare
asked you to "see" a thing you longed to see, to believe
what you wished to believe. It is how the confidence man
succeeds, whether he is a mesmerist or not.

As for the girl, I advise you to break all bonds with her.
You cannot save her. Nor is she yours to save. Your kindness and attachment leave you vulnerable. Turn away.
Such people drain our strength. No doubt, her sort gave
rise to the legend of the vampire. It is only a question of
whether her sickness or her madness will first overtake her.
Turn away!

Doubtless, my counsel seems cruel to you. But a doctor
learns some things. Even on the battlefield, we must turn
from the cries of the wounded who cannot be rescued in
order to save those who retain a chance at survival. You,
too, must concentrate upon those who have a chance, and
leave the doomed behind. It is life's stern rule.

Far from heartless, my friend, I find I bear too much
emotion to do my job as well as it might be done.

Molloy's remarks opened an old wound, although your
innocent discussion with him had no such intent. It sad-
dens me to read of the old, hard words spoken in a new
and hopeful country. Yes, I am an Irish Protestant by birth,
though I have left both the religion and the land behind.
What of my birth? Why should it mean I cannot like Molloy, nor he old Mick Tyrone? These swift, unreasoned
hatreds will forever be the downfall of the Irishman.

Molloy would have me and my forebears no more than
tools of the English. Yet, my grandfather died fighting
against the English at Ballynahinch, in the rising of 1798.
He fought for Ireland's freedom. His thanks were death
and the confiscation of our lands by the Crown. The English hanged his brother, too, although the man was inno-

cent of any involvement with the rebels. The family tie was enough.

My own father, born to wealth, matured in penury. He made himself a doctor through sacrifice and will, determined that our family would rise again. He died in the early years of the Famine, of typhus, while treating the starving and diseased of his county. Yes, he was an "Orangeman." Indeed—a Protestant who went into dens of affliction a priest would not enter. He died serving those who despised him, and brought home the typhus that killed my sister.

Do you understand now why I will have nothing of their nationalism? Why I believe that universal brotherhood is the only sensible path for mankind? These hatreds must be laid aside forever!

Hatred! It seems I cannot escape it. We exult in slaughter, Abel. Even Darwin cannot explain the extent of our thirst for blood.

I must tell you of the battle.

After the swiftness of Fort Henry's fall, the soldiers thought they were off on a lark. Even the weather smiled upon our ranks, warming until you would have mistaken February for May. Marching across the neck of land from Henry to Donelson, the troops cast off their blankets and overcoats, as well as not a few haversacks and other impedimenta. When I made the journey myself after concluding my duty at the old field hospital, the countryside looked like a battlefield without bodies. All the litter of war lay beside the roads and trails.

Yet, fate plays hardest with those who take her for granted! No sooner had we invested the lines about Fort Donelson than winter returned with icy ferocity. The Confederates, though besieged, slept snug in their cabins and tents, while our men lay upon the ground, squirming together like worms in a jar as they attempted to gain some warmth from one another. It is a wonder the entire army did not freeze. The human body is, truly, a wonderful mechanism, and full of contradiction. A mass of men will survive freezing nights, and a boy will pull through the amputation of his every limb, yet a light tap on the head will kill the giant. This war makes me feel as though I am constantly learning, yet I can never quite say what it is that I have learned.

We expected a siege and, eventually, a surrender. Our gunboats made a run at Fort Donelson, too, but had not recovered sufficiently from the duel for Fort Henry. Our boats were run off, at a high cost. Yet, Grant appeared untroubled. When I visited our headquarters, which had been established in a country cabin, he seemed the calmest of men, confident that his course was right. All believed we had the Confederates trapped.

Of course, I am learning that warfare is largely the art of dealing with the unexpected. With the snow thick over the earth and the roads coated with ice, the Rebels broke from their entrenchments and attacked. I recall the moment I heard the cannon's roar and the first snap of the rifles. I was seeing to a boy paved over with boils. He could not sit or lie or even bear the weight of his woolens upon him. The eruptions needed lancing, and such would be painful. He stood there with fear and sadness in his eyes, a child got up as a soldier, and I was just about to call to an orderly to assist me when the ground shook and the lantern swayed from the pole of my tent.

It might have been our own forces attacking, yet, inexplicably, I knew it was the reverse. The sounds arose well forward and to the south, carrying easily through the cold air. After a moment, it became clear that this was more than another skirmish. I shouted to the men to prepare for casualties and to have the ambulance mules put in harness. The fellows went ploddingly about their business, especially the hostlers. Our ambulances had not yet been needed, the few casualties we had suffered being easily managed by those vehicles assigned within the brigades of foot. But the human mind fascinates me endlessly—I do believe I will make the brain the object of my study when this war is over. Somehow, I knew that we had a hard day's work before us. I tore into all of them, shocking man and beast. They had believed me a cool, methodical fellow, chary of speech. But I was in a fury that day.

With sufficient activity underway beneath our tentage, I decided to lead the ambulance train forward myself. The truth is that I wanted to see the battle (Will men never learn?), although I sincerely believed I might be of best initial service at the medical posts closer to the lines. Nor did I trust our teamsters to make their way with much speed unless attended, for we are sent the dregs of the service and the worst of the civilians hired on. Few teamsters wish to serve the medical arm, for there is less profitability than lies in ferrying general supplies.

Our first battle was with the roads. The ice cost us more mules than did hostile fire that day, and I took my poor horse along through the woods beside the track, since he found the going easier there, despite the snow's depth. We had to change teams and leave a pair of ambulances behind. I did have the presence of mind to order the derelict vehicles pushed off the road so they would not impede military movements.

My impression of battle is that it is, above all, confusing. We passed between regiments at rest, dawdling as if nothing unusual was afoot. Meanwhile, the blasts and crackle of battle had spread until the sound encompassed the entire world before us, although now and again we heard an individual shout distinct against the din. The first stragglers appeared, and the ambulatory wounded. No matter how light their injuries, each of the latter had one or two unscathed companions anxious to help them rearward. A number of them expected me to put them aboard a hospital wagon and turn the vehicle immediately. But I feared we would need those vehicles for men of lesser fortune and I scorched the selfish with language of which you would not have approved. Words were all I had, I fear, for in my anxiety to see that other men did their work properly, I had forgotten myself and rode off without buckling on sword or pistol.

I feared defeat. Healthy men came toward us at a run, their weapons cast away. The eyes of terrified boys swelled horse-like, while grown men wailed that all was lost and that the Rebels were on their heels. We worked our way through a good mile of deserters and debris, and gave way twice to line ambulances heading rearward packed with men who would never again be whole. Closer to the front, mounted troopers chased cowards with the flat of their swords and, sometimes, with the edge. We seemed in the midst of disaster.

Yet, the gunfire did not slacken or rush toward us. Some in Union blue were standing to put up a fight.

I hurried the ambulances along. Thinking on a thousand things, I looked casually to the side and saw blue ranks on a slope below me, visible only from the waists down, upper bodies blurred with smoke. One after another of them splayed backward. But the line held. I still saw no Confederates.

We had to pause while a regiment came on at the double, tripping in the slush the road had become. Then a battery nearly ran us into a ravine, racing forward like madmen. An officer screamed at me:

"Get those goddamned meat wagons off the goddamned road."

I pressed forward. In the background, I heard a wild keening, a high banshee scream, that chilled me. It was odd, you see. I do not recall a fear of the bullets spitting past—but that queer shouting made me want to flee.

Men surged back and forth across the road, sometimes moving by company but often in smaller groups. Lost officers shouted regimental numbers, while sergeants cursed their charges into line. I noticed how many soldiers lacked gloves, and remember thinking that their hands must be awfully cold on the steel and wood of their muskets.

A quartet of our soldiers came marching along, escorting three forlorn prisoners. You will not credit this, but only one of the captured fellows had proper shoes, while the worst off had only rags upon his feet. They looked crushed. And, yet, there was a residue of anger in them, but whether at themselves, their own superiors or at us I cannot say. They looked like they had been ill fed all their lives. I could not imagine that such ravaged creatures might make worthy soldiers.

The guns boomed all around us. Black smoke floated over white snow. We had taken on enough badly wounded men to turn three of my ambulances around, while another had lost a wheel to a ditch. Two went astray, and I had only a pair of vehicles left with me.

Down in the trees, men shouted for ammunition. I saw the orange belch of cannon, but could not see the guns themselves. It was midday, but the sky had burned twilight pink above the smoke.

A boy clawed at my bridle, asking me if he would be all right. I nearly slapped him off before I saw that his skull had been sliced away.

I would not have thought such a one could live. But he was standing upright, tugging at my horse and speaking clearly, if hastily. "Will I be all right, sir? Am I gonna be all right?" With half his brain exposed to the air and blood down the side of his head. He should have been dead, or at least unconscious.

I called for an orderly to help him into an ambulance.

The boy's face calmed and he smiled. He let go of my bridle. "Thank you, sir," he said. "Thank you a hundred times." With that, he pitched backward into the muck, eyes wide, brains squeezing out of him. He was dead, as he should have been well before. I was glad I offered him that last, false comfort.

I still could not find a proper line of battle. The fighting seemed all a-tilt. I thought I saw General McClernand in the distance, but may have been mistaken. We passed one of our batteries, where man and horse lay dead, the guns silenced. I wondered if the battle had somehow passed us by, if I had led us astray.

I had a sketch of the roads—no proper map—and I pulled off my gauntlets to draw it from my pocket. Then it happened. A gray-brown line swept over us, shrieking. That banshee howl came from the Rebels, you see. It is some sort of battle cry. You might have thought a tribe of primitives was attacking.

How do men manage battle? Everything happens so fast. One instant, I was unfolding my sketch of the tracks and lanes, the next the enemy flowed around us. Most of them rushed by, driven on by officers in proper uniforms. But a pack of ragged men surrounded me.

"Git off thet harse," a fellow in a farmer's hat called through broken teeth. Their speech is so curious I had difficulty understanding the man. Another of them, a boy in scavenged breeches, grasped my reins. I recall the redness—the awful redness—of his ankles in that cold, and the unmatched brogans on his feet. His rifle was as tall as he was.

"Git down, you sumbitch," the farmer fellow said.

I felt I needed my horse. To attend to my duties.

"Look here," I said. "I'm a doctor. I'm here to care for the wounded."

Farmer rammed his muzzle into my ribs. It hurt not a little.

"Git down, or yer gonna be a daid doctor. Git off thet harse."

It was no good arguing with them. I dismounted. I have no idea what they thought they had accomplished, for none of them climbed up in the saddle. They simply trailed after their comrades, leading their booty behind them.

I clambered up beside the teamster on the lead ambulance. His face was white. I had to manage the horses until he came around again.

"Damnation," the driver said, over and over.

In a swale of scrub timber, we found a devil's harvest. They must have stumbled upon one another. For every man shot, another lay in the snow with his head smashed or his face crushed inward. Now you have spoken to me of the bayonet, but few men use them here. They employ their discharged muskets as clubs, or use their fists, or rocks, or even their teeth. I did not see a bayonet unsheathed all day.

It is as well, for such wounds do not heal.

We loaded the ambulances without preference to the allegiance of the wounded. Some of my men complained, but I cut them short. A wounded man is a soldier no more. We left those whom I judged as doomed behind, for two ambulances were nothing to the numbers of the fallen. I will never forget that: Men with their guts strewn around them, pleading for succor, or lying broken-backed, or hemorrhaging beyond my capacity to aid them. A man may be fully sentient on his way to death, and damning eyes followed my progress. Those men will carry their hatred of me with them to whatever lies beyond the grave. For I was the one who walked among them, saying, "Take him, but not that one."

They cried for mothers and sweethearts, or wished me to Hell, as our wagons creaked away.

And then I found the horse. Not my own, but another. He was standing by the side of the lane, with his head down, as if sniffing for grass under the snow. I do not believe I have ever seen a more beautiful stallion outside of a racing paddock. That horse was bred for running, not for battle. What sort of man had brought him to the field? The saddle was no military issue, but sleek and oiled soft, and the thick cloth beneath it was gray with a yellow border. One of those high Southern gentlemen must have ridden him into battle. I knew not the rider's fate, but from that moment the horse belonged to me. I called him "Reb," which the fellows thought a great joke.

Mounted again, I guided the ambulances back along our route—or believed I did. I could not always recall which fork to take, and clouds of smoke had settled in the hollows, thick as a London fog. The battle continued at a furious heat, but we seemed well away from it again. I shall never understand war's turnings.

I led the wagons across a frozen stream bed, careful of the wheels and wounded—for the latter's cries and pleas wrenched the heart. At once, my spirits soared! I saw a ridge ahead of us and our flag waving handsomely between the bare trees. My horse, too, longed to run toward those dark blue ranks, as if he had changed allegiance with his change of rider. But I dared not hurry the second ambulance, which was having difficulty with the streambed.

A horseman broke from the ridge and rode for us at a gallop, slashing his horse with a crop. He applied great energy to his task and reached me just as the second ambulance pulled free.

"Sir," he cried, pulling up breathless, "General Grant sends his compliments and asks"—here a brief pause and pant—"if you could hurry these ambulances along"—pant—"so our guns may fire upon the enemy." He gestured to whence we had come.

A gray line of a thousand men stretched across the fields.

I moved the ambulances as briskly as I could, keeping the suffering of the wounded in mind. The moment we reached the shadow of the slope, our cannon opened fire over our heads.

Grant waited atop the ridge. His staff officers, most of whom I knew, wore pale and serious faces, but the general smiled and motioned me over.

"My apologies, sir," I said, saluting. "I did not comprehend the situation." I think he heard me, despite the discharge of a nearby battery.

His smile broadened.

He reined his horse closer to mine. Grant is, by the way, a superb horseman. He leaves his staff behind on their jaunts.

"Doctor," he said, "you are one brave fool."

Another section of guns released its salvo. My horse, to its credit, did not shy, and I leaned toward the general. I felt I must say something in response, for though clearly a fool, I had not the least bravery to my credit.

Grant spoke again before I could find appropriate words.

"Looks like you've picked up quite a mount there," he said. "But I can't have my officers making off with contraband. It's illegal, Doctor."

"Sir . . ." I stammered, ". . . General . . . the Confederates seized my own horse . . . they . . . I . . ."

He winked at me and called out above the shouts and volleys, "Well, I'm going to look the other way, Doctor Tyrone. This once. But the next time you come upon a horse of that quality, I want him turned in to my headquarters so I can induct him into Union service myself."

Just then, General Wallace trotted up, with a worried look. I believe I have mentioned him in a previous missive. He has a special fondness for the classics.

"General," I heard him say to Grant, "my apologies for the violation of your orders . . ."

Grant shook his head. "No apologies, Lew. You did just right. My thanks."

The battery fired canister down the road. The louder report made every horse prance or rear—except my mount and Grant's. General Wallace's bay took an effort to control.

Grant . . . seemed unshakable.

"What do you think, Lew?" he asked.

Wallace's horse had a last dance, then submitted. The general stared off toward the enemy, although there was little to see for all the smoke. "I believe we will hold, sir."

Grant nodded. "That we will. Got 'em now. Damned fool Pillow. Had his chance and lost it. Now he'll take his whipping." Then he remembered me. Looking up from a dispatch he had begun to scribble in the saddle, Grant told me, "You are dismissed, Doctor. With my compliments for your valor."

Now any man likes such words applied to him. But what shall we do, my friend, when we know our actions did not merit such a response? I rode off feeling a fraud.

You may hear complaints that Grant was not at his post when the attack began that day, for he was in conference with our Naval arm upon the Cumberland, some miles below the fort. But he "rode to the sound of the guns," as you old soldiers say. Lew Wallace was the hero of the hour, for he moved his regiments where they were needed without awaiting permission. He shored up McClernand's broken line. To those upon the field, it seemed a desperate day. But Grant was unperturbed from start to finish. A man of astonishing calm, he appears to see through the mystifications and confusions of battle with uncanny clarity. Medical Science would, I think, find him an interesting subject.

I rode back to my butcher shop. For such it was. The contest went on without me, but I saw its hideous residue. I like to think the note Grant was writing as he sent me off was the order to General Smith to counterattack the Confederate works. For hollow though we know such matters to be, we all would feel ourselves a part of history. And I had little else of glory.

With the Rebels contained and their defenses compromised by their own inadequacies, their surrender was only a matter of time. The night before they struck their colors, a cavalryman named Forrest slipped his command through our lines to escape, refusing ever to surrender to Yankees. But the remainder of them surrendered well enough. Their officers were full of bluster and nonsense, but the men wept in their shame. We captured nearly as many of them as we had soldiers of our own.

The following days were a blood-soaked blur to me. With human wreckage enough of our own, we had to take responsibility for the captured Confederate wounded, as well. The houses of the little town of Dover were full of bleeding men. We did our best for them, but there were not enough skilled hands or supplies. Despite Dr. Brinton's remarkable efforts, we are not yet a service fit for war. In the end, we will lose as many to gangrene and neglect as fell upon the field.

I cannot write of all the horrors that lay on my surgeon's table, for no language in my command contains words of sufficient description. I would need to make the noises of a brute. I began by trying to save limbs and ended by sawing away lives. I know, I know. You will insist that I must have done some good. But not enough, my friend. The carnage was too vast. For every two I cut, one died. And for every one I cut, another perished waiting for my knife. We buried the bodies or torsos in temporary graves, but the ground was frozen hard and willing hands were few, so we burned the mounds of limbs that fell from our surgery tables. That will always be my image of our great victory at Fort Donelson: a heap of limbs soaked down with kerosene and set ablaze, blackened fingers curling against the sky.

Grant wants to move south, but there are reports of jealousy over his victories. We are stopped, and know not when we will proceed. Perhaps it is as well. The next slaughter can wait.

Before I close, I must tell you of an incident that occurred this afternoon. The affair began a week ago, shortly after the surrender, when I rode into Dover to ascertain the needs of the Confederate wounded. I made my rounds, spending hours in makeshift hospitals that were little more than charnel houses. Not all of the attending physicians appeared to be men of advanced skill. Twice, I took over at tables where a country doctor was destroying the remnants of a life. I fear I was sometimes rude.

As I prepared to leave the village, a delegation of Confederate officers on local parole approached me, asking if I were not a surgeon. I told them that I was, indeed, although not as much of one as I had long imagined myself to be.

"Doctor," the ranking man began afresh, with the deceptive softness of the Southron gentleman, "I must swallow my pride and ask a service of you. As a gentleman and man of medicine, I hope you will not refuse me, sir." He was a small, upright fellow, bald-headed, with his hat held at his waist in supplication. His uniform, once fine, was tattered.

"What's the trouble?" I asked. Or snapped, perhaps. For I was weary. And his sort were the ones who made this war.

"Doctor, there is a young man who I fear will die if not attended. A young gentleman, sir. He requires a surgeon."

"Can't your surgeons do it, man?"

He lowered his eyes. In shame at the need to beg me. "Doctor—Major, sir—this here young man is the son of a senator from Miss'sippi. His father is a powerful man. Our doctors . . . are afraid to operate on Captain Barclay. They insist he cannot be saved, sir, and will not touch him. I fear they do not want the blame for his death under their knives, sir." He brushed a finger across his eyes, then cocked his head back proudly. "It is a disgrace, sir, and I am mortified to discover such cowardice among my own people."

I went to look at the officer. Now I always insist that patients be treated equally, whether rich or poor, as beautiful as Helen or ugly as mud. But our hearts are moved against our will. The young man, a captain while yet a boy, was blond and handsome to break the heart of every girl in his state. But his days of romance were over. He stank of urine, as he will for the rest of his life. Both his legs were shattered at the hip, and he had suffered dreadful local mutilations. His legs were rotting on him, and I have never seen a surer candidate for gas gangrene. He should have undergone amputation days before.

I made no secret of his advanced condition, yet I gave him a choice. I had no chloroform with me, and the Confederate supplies were long since depleted. I could either operate immediately with nothing to allay the pain, or return in the morning with an adequate supply.

The young man looked up at me with steady eyes of blue. "Doctor Tyrone"—he had instantly digested my name, as these "gentlemen" will—"I would not be so discourteous as to expect such a journey of you." He gathered himself for a moment. "But I would be grateful for your present services in relieving me of these legs. I have grown tired of them, sir."

We lugged him to a knacking yard. I made the bastards

wash their knives and saws, which had not seen water in days. Then I set to work. His friends held him down, although one of them soon found he was unequal to the task and left the table weeping. The young captain suffered dreadfully, I assure you, although I am a quick saw. He did not so much as groan. Nor would he even bite down on a rag. He closed his eyes and fought himself, ashamed at his body's quivering rebellion as I took his legs off. I have never seen his like.

Well, this afternoon, with time to spare at last, I looked the fellow up. I found him alive, bedded in a chapel that had been turned into a hospital. The other Confederate patients ignored me, turning their backs on my blue coat. Not one asked me to so much as examine a wound (their bandages, I must tell you, were filthy, and I will see to the matter). But the young captain recognized me at once, greeting me with a display of gentility. I fear I was a bit gruff, for I am no friend to aristocratic airs, but he pretended not to notice. He might have been holding court on a grand estate.

In fact, he lay on the floor, on rancid bedding stuffed with hay. But he smiled so easily you would have thought him on holiday. He barely winced when I examined my gory work. I think, by the way, that he will heal.

Suddenly, I sensed a change in the air. A cold curtain of hostility descended. I heard whispers, and noted that the men's eyes were fixed upon me.

An armless man with a massive beard knelt by the captain's head, bending—no, tottering—down to whisper in his ear. With sidelong glances at me.

The captain looked at me harshly, almost hatefully, for a moment. Then his face smoothed over again.

"Doctor Tyrone? The men say you are riding my Buster."

I failed to understand him. Theirs is a very foreign form of English.

"Buster," he whispered. "My horse. The boys say you are riding my horse."

I understood it then. I hastened to form excuses and explanations, but the captain reached out and closed a hand over my wrist before I could speak. He had lost his legs and more, but still had the grip of a man happiest out of doors.

I began to blather about finding the animal, but the young man did not let me finish a sentence.

"Buster loves his carrots, Doctor Tyrone." Tears glazed his blue eyes and he let his head sink back on the ticking. He released my arm. "You feed that horse plenty of carrots, hear?"

The captain called out then, not loudly, but in a voice accustomed to command since childhood:

"Boys, I have asked the doctor to look after Buster. He has kindly obliged me." But he sensed the men were still unhappy with the situation, so he continued, "We must be generous with our enemies. Doctor Tyrone here is going to need him a real, fine horse when we send him and all the rest of the Yankees skedaddlin' back where they came from."

The room was fiercely silent for a moment, then another voice said, "Damn right. Damn sure, you're right, Cap'n."

They all began to hoot, to shout and yelp. Next came that wild banshee call of theirs.

As I left that room of limbless men, they were singing a buoyant song about their flag. I fear this war will not end as soon as we might wish it done.

I am enclosing a list of books and a few banknotes. My dear friend, when next you pass through New York or Philadelphia, please inquire as to the availability of the titles. That is, of course, if you should find the time. Give preference to the medical works, especially those on vascular matters. Although I yearn to read of higher things, I am determined to make the most of my grisly profession. I will not accept that all this butchery should pass without an advance in knowledge.

Please think fondly of

> Yr. Obt. Servt.
> M. Tyrone
> Surg. U.S.V.

 IT WAS A LOVELY COW.

That is what my host said. I am sure of it. Standing there, brushing the animal's brown back, he looked my way and said, *"So 'ne schöne Kuh, nit?"*

I do not speak the German's weighty tongue, but my acquaintance with Mrs. Schutzengel, followed by my convalescence in this country household, had quickened my ears sufficiently to follow a bit of talk here and a scrap of chatter there. Ah, the mysteries of language! How little truth there is in any tongue, despite our ceaseless appetite for speech! All words are shadows. Only faith brings light. The Welsh know words are weak, and thus we sing.

Anyway, twas clear the fellow was fond of his animals. His kind would rather talk of cows than kings. And bless such men, says Abel Jones, if the wish be not presumption.

I was walking again. If slowly. Head a bit dazed and unwilling. But we cannot give in to our weaknesses, and I was supported in the flesh as well as in the spirit. *Herr* Kempf, my host, had whittled a cane to help me on my way.

If only the snow would have left us! We were prisoners. Deep into March, the south wind held its breath. You know how April's scouts ride out ahead, sneaking past the winter's sentinels to wake the earth into bright rebellion. The first scents rise, of earth and wet and life. All is reborn beneath a strengthening sun, and hearts swell in a hymn of wordless praise. This year, the earth slept on and whiteness reigned. March would not move, as if the very calendar had frozen. The snow still blocked the course to the main road. I ached to leave, to go back to my duty and stop Kildare before the deed was done. But the drifts had set in hard and kept us pinned.

Work done, *Herr* Kempf turned from the cow and sighed. His smile faded and earnestness overtook him. He gestured that I should follow him. Toward the gloom at the back of the barn.

Now, that was a well-kept barn, I will tell you. Neat as the family household. The animals were groomed, their stalls showed cleaner than the inns the county round, and the harness racked on the walls gleamed with oiling. The plow sat polished and ready, and fresh grease squeezed from the hub of the wagon wheels. Your German will not starve from neglect of his business.

Twas cold in the barn, yet I was delighted to be up and about. The smell of hay and even of horse sweat reeked life, and the wind crying through the boards sang of my good fortune. I was alive, though other men had not intended that I remain so. It was lovely just to be.

Still, my joy was tempered by dread. The world beyond spared no time for idylls. I feared what might have happened in my absence. I thought of Nellie, too. And between, behind and above all other thoughts, reveries of my Mary Myfanwy and young John haunted me as no ghost ever could. If ghosts there be, which I will not believe.

What if my sweet beloved thought me dead? What had my wife been told? How had she felt on the day no letter from me arrived, with none to come thereafter? I wished I had bought her that damnable—pardon me—sewing machine.

Herr Kempf beckoned me along, for I was not yet quick. I scuttled down between the hay bales, learning the length of my new cane. Though it was morning, musty twilight reigned. Fairy dust drifted between the eaves.

"Ist 'ne gute Scheune, nit?" he asked.

I understood only that something or other was good.

A stack of crates and chests rose against the back wall of the barn. He began lifting them down. I moved to help him—for I felt my strength returning—but *Herr* Kempf waved me off.

"Sollst ruhen," he said. *"War fast 'nen Totschlag, dass Du bekommen hast."*

He seemed almost bad-tempered now, which was not the fellow's nature. Twas as if he had been set to a task he longed to avoid.

I sat me down on a bench of hay, with the dust sweet in my nose.

At last, he reached the chest at the bottom of the stack. Before he opened it, the good man straightened himself and took a deep breath. Then he bent to lift the lid.

The container might have been full of serpents, the way he reached inside.

He lifted out my pistol, the Colt the boys from my old company had given me, with its fine engraving and embarrassing inscription. Now I do not love firearms, and might wish them gone from the world, but my heart swelled at the sight of that particular instrument. For we may think high thoughts all we want, but our sentiments will have their say.

He held the pistol out by the barrel. But he was not offering it to me. Only displaying it.

"Kommt nit ins Haus, die Waffe," he said. *"Verstehst?"* He tried, for the first time, to speak in English to me: "No in *unser* house." Shaking his head to make certain I understood.

I nodded. For I understood him better than he knew.

He stuffed the pistol back in its hiding place. If I had nursed any doubts, which I had not, they would have been vanquished by the sight of the weapon. The men who had attacked me had not bothered to search under my greatcoat, or even to pat along my sides. Thieves would have taken the pistol sure. My assailants had wanted to kill me only, and believed they had. But for the storm, they might have strung me up and given me the pitch cap.

Herr Kempf gestured toward the barn door. *"Gehen wir, ja?"*

I followed him back out. Into the sunshine. Twas bright enough to blind, and I stepped carefully. For even the best-tended barnyard remains a barnyard.

I was a steadier man than I had been the day before. And better I would be the next day, too. When a Welshman sets his mind on his improvement, stay out of his way.

That morning seemed to grace the world with confidence. The sky was a handsome blue. For the first time since my beating, the sun fell warm upon my shoulders. I stopped and raised my face in exultation.

An icy drop from the barn roof struck my cheek.

The snow was melting.

Herr Kempf looked at me.

"Morgen gehen wir zur Hauptstrasse. Ich helfe dir."

I did not understand a word he said. But his good wife come out just then, to take up the fresh-laid eggs.

She went by us at a perk, explaining:

"Tomorrow he helps you to the road."

• • •

The lady of the house made a chicken dinner that last night. This was on a weeknight, mind, when so rare a bird was forbidden the family pot. The hen died in my honor. The Kempfs were good souls, teachers of kindness.

What was I to them? Despite my uniform, I might have been a criminal, or otherwise deserving of my fate. Yet, I woke up in their own bed. The money had not been taken from my pocket by my attackers, so I offered to pay for my board. Neither man nor wife would hear of it, for they lived in mercy's dominion.

There is true religion, see. I speak not of Christian, Jew or Musselman, of Hindoo or the countless kinds of heathen. For

did not Jesus look beyond the name? Tis kindness, not sever-
ity, that lets us gain a little peek at Heaven. Now you will say,
"This Jones speaks like an infidel. Saved is saved, and damned
is damned, and done." But I will tell you: Those who would
put harshness in religion are no Christians worthy of the
name. Look at that young family, with poverty their neighbor
and lifelong work their fate. Were they not better Christians
than a prince? I say we must keep true religion from the grip
of the old and bitter, and place it in the hands of those who
love.

Father McCorkle did not err in all his judgments, I will give
him that. He understood why Jesus loved the poor. Had he
understood this world half so well as he understood our Lord,
we would have all been spared a share of misery. But let that
bide.

We sat and ate by the firelight, and snow broke from the roof.
Thump after whumping thump of it come down, with drips and
drops and drips between the avalanches. The night felt even
warmer than the day. I imagined the ice breaking on the canal,
and windblown waves on the lake, and boats and armed men
sailing to do wrong.

We ate the bird stewed up with homemade noodles, graced
with carrots and onions from the cellar. A bit of salt, and the
Hausfrau had a dish that would have tempted Adam out of the
Garden. Lovely puffs of biscuit sopped the leavings.

"There is good," I told them between bites.

Afterward, we prayed on our knees by the fire. The little one
lay solemn in the cradle and there was a heaviness upon my
hosts. You might have thought they saw what lay before me.
Yet, all I had told them was that I must reach the town as soon
as possible.

We sat by the hearth thereafter, drinking hot water and honey
pricked up with nutmeg and clove. The Germans have a way
with winter things.

"I must thank you again," I said, to liven the drowse into which we had sunk.

"*Nein!*" the woman said quickly. "The *Herrgott* you must thank. And the girl. Who is so strange. Without her, there is no finding of you."

Of a sudden, I remembered that earlier conversation, that other mention of a girl. My head had been spinning and my thoughts disordered with the seriousness of the injury upon me. But now the words rushed back. I recalled assuming a daughter was involved. Yet, daughter there was none grown in the house.

I felt uneasy.

"What girl?" I asked. "How was she strange?"

The woman glanced at her husband, but did not ask him again. She had heard the story often enough.

She shrugged. "The girl . . . maybe she is a woman. *Doch jung.* Young. By the road, she is standing. *Sehr komisch, hat sie ausgesehen.* She is looking not all right. Not with the right clothings for the coldness."

"Did he see her hair? Did the girl have red hair? Was she slender? A slender girl with red hair, was it?"

The woman asked her husband. He shook his head no.

That baffled me.

Herr Kempf read the befuddlement on my face and spoke to his wife. She weighed his comments for a moment, then said, "My husband does not understand these things still. He is only coming home. *Im tiefen Schnee.* All is snow. Then the woman is calling to him. With the hand only, not the talking. She is in the trouble, maybe, because so little clothings she has. He stops the wagon *und* is following after her. Then you are there. In the snow. With so much blood. *Mein Mann* looks up to ask the questions and—" the woman popped out a breath—"like this she is gone. In the snow *und die Nacht.* She must freeze, I am thinking. With her little clothings."

A chill gripped my heart.

"But what did she look like?" I demanded. "How did she *look?*"

The woman asked her husband another question. As he replied, he bobbed his hands, palms up, in a gesture of incomprehension.

"He says," *Frau* Kempf told me, "that he is not believing if he is not seeing. The girl has clothings like the *Prinzessin* of the Sultan, in the stories for the childrens. She is very beautiful, with the brown skin and her not many clothings." The good wife looked at me. "Is this not strange?"

• • •

We left in the morning, with my pistol returned to me. You guess my thoughts, so I will not report them. I was a man with one eye on the future, the other focused on a quitless past.

The going was hard. Later, they told me I had brought the winter of the decade with me to Yates County. Brown with mud, the high fields wanted plows, but the swales hid deep in snow. Now, humility is a virtue ever in short supply, so I will tell you frankly of my shame. I am not tall—though height is not everything in a man—and still lacked something of my normal strength. I could not have made my way without my guide. He helped me through the drifts where I stuck fast.

Once, he carried me like a child.

I wonder sometimes what it must be like to be tall and comely. I would not be envious, but look you. It must be an easier thing to be born long of leg and conquering handsome—though life is hard enough for all, I know. But think how it must be to go through life admired at first glance, body formed to overcome all challenges.

Well, we must be content with what we are given. We know what we are made of, you and I. Isn't it a miracle when someone loves us?

The day was not all trials. Birds sang. The melting went the faster for their songs.

The farm lay at the edge of the world, and it took us half the day to reach the main road. *Herr* Kempf stayed by me until a wagon come along headed south toward Penn Yan. A farmer fellow let me share his seat behind the horses. After helping me up and deflecting a last barrage of my thanks, my host strode off across the sodden fields.

The driver did not say much for a mile. Dour, he chewed tobacco, spitting off the side into the slush. When he did speak, it was to the horses, not to me:

"Damned foreigners are ruining this country."

• • •

The day was dying when we reached Penn Yan—a town I was not meant to see alive. The sky had clouded over and the farmer grumbled. He said a storm was coming, but I did not mind at all. I welcomed the prospect of more snow now. For snow would block Kildare. Until I could determine where we stood, and send my telegrams, and arrange for the militia.

My hopes were dashed. The storm arrived, but snow did not come with it. Just as I climbed down by the parsonage, I felt a drop of rain. I did not reach the porch before the Lord's artillery began to sound and bayonets of lightning cut the sky. The rain attacked as I slipped through the door.

It might have been the summer rains of India, the way the pellets come punching at the earth.

I heard sounds from the kitchen and rushed toward them. All were surprised. Myself at finding Mr. Douglass visiting, and the Noble Moor by my appearance alive. But Morris was the one who took the cake. The old expression never was more apt—the preacher looked as if he had seen a ghost. I fair thought he would take off at a run.

He began to stammer. "You . . . but . . . dead, you're dead . . .

we thought . . . my horse . . . no body . . . my horse, Priscilla came back and—"

I had a hundred questions I longed to ask. But one question had place before all others.

"Have there been any messages for me?" I fear I was shouting. For the slowness of the journey had set me to brooding. "Any messages, man?"

"Messages? Messages?" The poor fellow acted as if I had spoken in an exotic tongue.

"Yes. Messages. For me. It may be urgent."

He rose from his meager plate. "Yesterday . . . just yesterday . . . yes, yes . . . a message, a message!"

I nearly leapt upon him. "Where is it, man?"

"Where? Where?"

"Where's the message?"

He shook his head. Leaden raindrops struck the roof and walls. "Don't know . . . must think . . . you were dead . . . dead, you see . . . gone over Jordan . . . never thought . . ."

"On your desk, perhaps?" Mr. Douglass interposed. A boom of thunder followed on his words.

Mr. Morris looked as if he had been assaulted with yet another foreign term. "My desk? Desk? No, no. In the dustbin. Thrown away." His alarm grew even more intense. "I do hope Mrs. James hasn't emptied—"

"Where?" I shouted. "Which dustbin?"

Morris launched himself toward the next room. I followed, with Mr. Douglass trailing, caught up in the excitement.

". . . Dead . . ." Morris mumbled, ". . . gone over Jordan . . . everybody thought . . . over Jordan, passed over Jordan . . ."

He reached for a paper-stuffed cylinder beside his desk.

I took it away from him, dumping its contents on the old Turkey carpet. As I rummaged through the scraps, I had to slap poor Morris's fingers away. He only sought to help, but was a trouble.

The rain pounded at the windows. It come colder now. Sticking to the glass then sliding downward. Its sound was that of shots heard on a flank.

There it was! A sheet of schoolboy's paper, folded up and sealed. Inscribed, "to majur jones."

I tore it open.

> *if not ded hury Kildare leevs*
> *on canal barj tomorow after dark*
> *guns and men and gold he wil*
> *atak canady I am with him hury*

Chapter 18

"YOU WILL DO IT, SIR, IF YOU WISH TO SAVE OUR UNION!"

Mr. Douglass did not move. Behind his mighty shoulder, Mr. Morris leapt about in a dance of enthusiasm for the task I had assigned him, but the great Douglass only stared down at me. His hands tested the air at his sides, clenching and falling slack again, and his face had taken on the maroon hue of fine leather.

I know fear. I am not the blustering sort who will pretend he has never been afraid. Oft was the time when only the dread of failing in my duty saved me from abasement. I have seen fear gnaw at men, on the eve of battle or faced with disease. Some are afraid of serpents. Worst are those who see into themselves.

"I . . . my weapon is the pen . . . not the sword . . ."

I was abrupt with the poor fellow. For time was our enemy.

"Well, throw your inkpots at them, man. We need you with us."

"Need, need! We need you, Fred," Mr. Morris sang. "Union, save the Union . . ."

Now I do not suggest that Frederick Douglass was a coward, for he was not. Fear shadows us all like a padded-foot assassin and leaps out when our guard is down. For all his daring speech, Douglass long had led an ordered life, with the turmoil of bondage decades behind him. Twas the unexpectedness, see, of being asked to take a gun in hand that threw him. His was a world of boundaries, and well he knew the fate of the black man who lifts his hand against his white brother, no matter how just the cause. And I had made it clear we would be outnumbered.

Outside, the Lord's cannon boomed and lightning smote the earth. Sleet slapped the windows, clinging to the glass, and the wind wailed. When the world goes thus awry, old voices bid us keep to our firesides.

"I . . ." Douglass, never at a loss for words, could hardly begin. "I . . . dare not . . ."

I turned away. Brusquely, I'm afraid, for I have a heathen temper when there is a fight before me. It comes from my sergeanting days in India, when the lads needed to fear me more than the enemy. I waved to Morris to start him along on his errand. For the good preacher was to find John Underwood and bring him to meet me, along with any arms and men the sheriff had at hand. Just at the door, I turned again to Douglass.

"You will go," I told him, "to the livery stables. Tell John Brent to bring his horses, properly saddled and without delay, to the door of St. Michael's. Do that much at least, Mr. Douglass."

I did not know if we would be out-rifled ten to one or worse. I wanted every hand, and had drawn Morris and the Moor a sketch of the conspiracy in order to enlist their help. Morris had risen to the call with such alacrity that I feared for his welfare, should he be entrusted with a gun, but Douglass withered. When I needed him to swell.

Looking into the eyes of the bold orator one last time, I understood why slaves do not rise up. We men burn such deep fears into our fellows that they cannot overcome them in a lifetime. I have seen it in myself, when thrust among the rich. The onetime servant fears the master always.

If he would not raise his hand, I hoped Douglass would at least raise our horses. For we would have to ride hard to overtake the barge before it issued from the outlet canal. I dreaded that prospect more than I did the looming confrontation, for I am not happy on a horse in sunlight, let alone upon a night like this.

I pulled on my India-rubber cape, set my hat upon my head, and followed Mr. Morris out the door.

Heaven blasted us. Just as it did the old king on the heath. Colt hard against my hip, I told the preacher:

"Pray as you go, Mr. Morris. And have the sheriff show you how to load."

• • •

I had my own task before me, though twas one of little hope. I bent into the sleet, holding my hat to my head with a naked hand. My gauntlets had long been missing and my fingers stiffened as I marched through the town.

I was off to see the priest, you will have guessed. For only he could halt this wickedness now, by calling on his Irish to desist. I did not think he would help me, for he was in it deep. But we must do all we can to hinder bloodshed. And I will tell you: I felt my share of fear, just like Fred Douglass. I wanted to see my wife and child again, and to live long. I would have liked to call up the militia and let a thousand others share the burden. But look you: There was no time for dallying. A man must stand to his allotted duty, just as our gentle Savior stood to His.

McCorkle was the key.

I found him by his fire reading Scripture. I rushed inside without the slightest knock and stood there sodden, dripping like a fish.

Had the Angel of the Apocalypse come in with fiery sword, I do not think the priest would have been amazed one bit the more. He sat up as if pricked immodestly and his eyes went huge in the firelight.

"But . . . you're . . ."

I shook my head and spoke though numbed lips. "*Alive*, Father McCorkle. For the O'Hara boys are faulty executioners.

And now you are wanted, see. To put an end to this wickedness. For you have had the measure of these matters from the beginning, but do not know what lies behind the doings."

"Sure, and I haven't the one notion o' what you're raving about. Have ye been conked on the pate, then, and all disordered?"

"You do not know who stands behind Kildare. But I will tell you. For the sake of your Irish and the Union both. Kildare is paid with English gold. Your parish folk will cross the river, and the Royal Artillery will be waiting on the shore. To welcome them with canister. Those who do not fall under the volleys will throw down the rifles they know not how to use." Oh, how clearly I could see it! "And they will be Her Majesty's prisoners. But they will have done what is wanted of them by Kildare and those behind him. They will have served their purpose. The moneybags of Manchester and Birmingham will have their war and their cotton. And the Irish will be their fools again."

The priest's expression did not change. But his eyes narrowed. I would tell you they clenched, as if eyes were fists, to give you the sense of them.

"I don't know what all your blathering's about, Jones. But I'm beginning to think there's a touch o' the Irish in the vexed blood o' the Welsh, for it's a terrible gift for imagining ye have. And a great love o' the talk. Will it be banshees next? Or the Devil's Coach Devour at the door?"

Outside, the wind wailed. The little house fair shook under the storm's assault. Drops of wet fell down the chimney, hissing into the fire.

The priest glared into the burning. "You're a fool, Jones. A daft man. And no good to anyone."

But his voice was different. He spoke like a poor actor, mouthing lines in which he has no confidence.

"I am a fool," I said. "I give you that. But fools may be forgiven." I took a step toward the crumpled blackness of him. "And you, Father McCorkle? Will you be forgiven? For sending your boys to death or captivity? On a hopeless mission? Arranged by English gold?"

"Ye Welsh," he said. "Forever calculating, ye are. With your little paymaster souls. Our Lord's mission was hopeless, too."

"I will stop Kildare. With you or without you." Certainly, my voice sounded more confident than I felt. "I'm telling you it's all an English plot, man. To use the Irish to provoke a war. For the love of—do you really think they have a chance to conquer Canada? There'll be no rising of the Frenchies. Naught but a slaughter there'll be. And widows and orphans for nothing."

He turned on me. Face scorched by the fire. "Damn ye, Jones. *Damn* ye for a lackey and a dupe. It's nothing but their dancing dog, ye are. And not even fit for a jig, with the crook o' the leg on ye. They've crippled ye, and still ye beg their bones." His fist pounded the table and it shivered like an invalid. "The Irish will be free."

"Not in Canada, they won't."

"We'll rise. We'll rise and show the world."

"You'll rise to nothing. You've been betrayed."

"*Liar!* Tis nothing but a damnable liar I see before me. A Judas. Coming to bait me with your nonsense about English gold. A lying little Welshman, and a Judas."

I smiled a little, as we do when we are struck hard, and clutched the grip of the cane *Herr* Kempf had whittled. "Haven't you wondered where Kildare—Kilraine, I should say—where he gets his money? Do you think his bit of magic with the girl brings so much in, then? Do you know the price of an Enfield rifle in the middle of a war, man? Or of uniforms, or boats, or provisions? Do you know where the money comes from? From an English lord, I tell you. From a wicked dozen of them, most like. But twas only the one I saw in the streets of Rochester, giving Kildare his instructions. There is your Judas. Your informer. It's Kildare."

"You're a filthy Protestant liar."

I closed toward him. But not in anger. For my desperation was beyond the reach of insult. The commotion of horses out in the street told me it was time to go.

McCorkle began to rise. I think he would have liked to strike me a blow.

I slapped my hand down upon his Bible. Flat upon the Scriptures, may the Lord forgive me. Our faces come spitting close.

"Damn me for eternity, if I have spoken one false word, Father McCorkle. We *need* you to come along with us. To stop this. Before it ends in blood." I was pleading with every mote of my being. "I cannot say who will live and die. Only that your people will lose, one way or the other. And the price they pay will be a high one. There will be no freedom or glory in it, only shame and betrayal." How can you reach such a fellow? "I *beg* you, man. Come with me and talk to them. Tell them what I've told you. Stop this . . . this madness . . ."

He was a statue, not a man. A statue of a hard and vengeful prophet.

"I will not go with ye," he said. "And damn ye."

Twas time to do my duty, so I told him, "Damn me, you may. But stop me, you won't. And the blood will be on your hands."

The fiercest smile I ever saw deformed his lips.

"May it be your blood then," he said.

• • •

Hunched against the storm, four horsemen waited in the street. Their flesh and weapons shone beneath the lightning. I wished they were more, for there would be a plentitude of Irish.

Two empty mounts waited, heads lowered, on the flank of the little party. One was for me, the other for McCorkle. I cannot tell you in Christian words how I felt toward the priest at that moment.

John Underwood was there, massive, with a carbine slung barrel-down. Douglass had come, after all. A hunting piece lay across his saddle and, despite the weather, he looked like a prince at his sport. Morris carried a shotgun nearly the size of himself. I have never seen a man so ill matched to arms. A good gust might have blown him away. Last of the four was John Brent, whom I had not expected.

"The priest will not go with us," I told them all, casting my voice above the slap and spatter of the sleet.

"Oh, for crying in a bucket," the sheriff said. "I could've told you that."

"Well, we will leave the horse," I called. "The Lord may move him still."

Underwood shook his massive head in doubt. Water flew from the brim of his hat.

"And which shall be mine?" I asked John Brent, steeling myself to mount. I wondered at Brent's presence. I had not told Morris to ask for his participation, only for his horses. I worried for John Brent, see. For he must live on in the town as a black-skinned man, while Douglass could leave with the morning train. Even if we won the day, the Irish would never forgive him.

Brent tugged a canvas from the saddle of the horse that was to bear me. "Quickly," he told me. "Get up before it gets wet."

I rose at his command, with only a bit of trouble from my bad leg. I tucked my cane beneath my cape then spread the sour rubber around me. My stick would fair impale me, if I fell. But I had ridden off without my cane once and would not do so again.

The saddle was dry and snug. Brent was ever a thoughtful man. I wanted to say something to my benefactor, to give him a last chance to change his mind about coming along. Yet . . . was he not a subject of our Union? And was this not an hour of need?

Twas as if he read my mind. Leaning over, he spoke into my ear.

"I've driven for you all winter, Major Jones. You get to know a fellow along the road. If I didn't stand by you now, I'd never call myself a man again." Then he laughed. "Besides, ole Reg'lar John has to keep an eye on his horses."

I held onto the reins a bit too tightly and the horse shied.

"Her name's Betty," Brent told me. "Give her a little slack now."

I was about to call out to John Underwood, to ask him to lead our pursuit, when another horseman come slopping fast up the street. We sensed him, then heard him, but hardly saw him until he pulled up and the sky bleached white again.

Meeks, it was. The deputy. Spattered in mud, with melt soaking him and his horse.

So we were six in all.

"Eli Denton," Meeks shouted, breathless, "says they passed his way . . . maybe two hours ago."

Underwood straightened. Putting me in mind of a dog that has caught a scent.

"Two hours! Only two hours!" Morris crowed. For he knew more of canals and the speed of their traverse than did I.

"Who is Eli Denton, then?" I asked, with the icy rain striking my face. I had taken off my hat so I would not lose it at a gallop. For a proper hat costs money, and the braid and brass cost more, besides. The hat was stuffed beneath my rubber cape. For a head can dry more cheaply than a new hat can be purchased.

"Denton's got the keeping of the first lock," Underwood answered me. Then he turned his horse into the street and let a whoop. "Come on, boys. We've got 'em now."

I was glad that one of us was confident.

• • •

The sheriff was a lion. How sadly we misjudge our fellow men. I well recalled my alarm during our first interview, when he sat across the table from me, with his bulk and those ears and his doubts. I suspected then that he was composed of appetites only, a creature without a core, and not worthy of his occupation. He had proved me wrong that very day, and now, in the face of greater odds, he charged forward like a young hussar— though I had learned that he was over fifty, and not the man of forty that he seemed.

He had to wait for stragglers several times, for we were horsemen of different pedigree, and only John Brent rode with a skill equal to the sheriff's. Once, I will admit, Underwood had to come back after me, for my horse had strayed in the darkness and the storm. I was embarrassed to be the cause of the least delay. I bounced along behind him, with ice crusting my eyebrows and shame in my heart.

We rode across the heights, lashed by the heavens. Twas hard to see, and cold, and as desolate within a man as without. But I am an old bayonet and know that the weather is as hard on the enemy as it is on ourselves, and he who takes a grip has the advantage. They would not see or hear us, or expect us, and we might gain surprise to raise our chances.

The going was hard, for the roads were muddy ice and the fields icy mud. I mustered the courage to kick my mount in the flanks to spur her on, for riding behind the others left me a target for the clots their mounts kicked up. I must have looked a sad, ramshackle thing.

Sheriff Underwood stopped us in the center of a field. A wild place, it was. Lightning stabbed the earth and lit our faces. Horse eyes bulged.

"Stay here," Underwood told us. "Abel, you tell 'em about handling their guns, in case they don't know. Give 'em a dose of your soldiering business. I'm going to have a look along the gorge."

He would have done well on the Northwest Frontier, that John Underwood. He knew the scout goes best who goes alone.

"Look you," I said, as my horse strayed sideward, "the first thing is to clear the mud from the barrels."

Obediently, they swung their weapons into their arms.

"Don't point them at each other," I said quickly. "They are wet now, and likely will not fire. But one will take a friend's life out of spite. Point the barrels downward, gentlemen."

"Won't fire? Won't fire?" Morris exclaimed. He cradled the shotgun in his arms, as if it were a slighted child.

"Yours may do a damage, Mr. Morris. For it is a fine piece and has a hooded mechanism. But I cannot speak for those with caps exposed." I looked around me. The storm seemed to have weakened just a little. Or perhaps I was becoming conditioned to it, for a man can become accustomed to anything. "Remember, gentlemen: if your guns do not fire, theirs will not, either. And they do not know that yours are wet for certain. They will have their doubts, and doubts are fatal. Which of you have pistols in your belts?"

Meeks murmured, and John Brent raised his hand. No doubt Brent kept one loaded in his barn for the day the hateful came hunting. Underwood would have a revolver, as well. With my Colt, that made four.

"Do not take them out, but keep them dry. I will tell you when to draw them. For they will be our weapons in the fight, if fight we must."

"I have no pistol, sir," Douglass said, with just the least crack in his voice. "I would fulfill my role, Major Jones, and not stand idly by."

"Pick up the first that falls," I told him.

• • •

Underwood returned in a coat of mud. He must have gone crawling. When he spoke, he aimed his words at me.

"They're down there, all right. Don't I know it? Lanterns front and back of the barge, lit up like a society ball. Good thing, too. Still have to get snot-close to see anything. There's two mules drawing along the towpath on the near bank, with Napper O'Hara—the young one—on 'em with a switch. Mules are strung one behind the other, so they'll block a shot from up near the front. Half a dozen Irish out on the deck with staves, breaking up the last of the ice as they go."

"Armed?" I asked.

The sheriff shook his head. "Couldn't tell for certain. I'd bet that Napper's got a pistol tucked away. He's the wilder of the two, though Bull's the meaner. If the boys on deck have rifles, I didn't see 'em. But seeing's the problem down there."

"And Kildare?" I asked.

"Lamp's lit in the cabin, so I figure he's in there keeping dry. Probably with Bull O'Hara. Bull's the one I'd watch. He'll shoot straight."

"You know the ground, John," I said. "Where's the place to take them?"

"Next lock down," he said without hesitating. For he knew his business. "Deep one, sharp fall. Steepest part of the gorge, just about. Let 'em get into the lock, but we won't let 'em get out. Hard for 'em to get away on foot, with the banks so sheer."

If it would be hard for them to escape, that meant it would be equally difficult for us, should things go poorly. But I said nothing. For his spirit was up. And spirit has carried many a battle that should have been lost.

The sheriff was a sort I knew quite well, the man who moves briskly to keep a step ahead of his concerns. Such a man will carry the breastworks. Or fall before them.

"That's good, John," I said. "You have done us a fine reconaissance." But I was thinking: one O'Hara by the mules with a pistol. And Kildare was no trained fighter, so he would be over-armed. With two pistols, at least. And a gambler's gun concealed. If he was in the barge's cabin, his powder and caps would be dry. The same went for the other O'Hara brother, the one who worried the sheriff. And if the half-dozen Irishmen with the staves were armed, as well? What about those shut below the deck? Were the Enfields still in their packing cases? Or was each man primed to kill his way to Canada?

And where in God's name was Molloy? He had the sense to place himself discreetly, yet worried I was. For danger might come at him from either side if a battle erupted. Now a trouble he was, that one, with a past stained black as the devil's behind, begging your pardon. But he had done me fair and done me proud. I did not want to see a brave man fall.

And . . . and he was my *friend,* see. For friendship is a strange thing on this earth.

My companions sat on their horses, with the sleet down their necks and up their cuffs. Of a sudden, I realized they were waiting for me. Even Underwood looked for orders now. They saw me as the man who knew his killing.

It is a shameful distinction.

"Let's go, then," I said. "You will lead us to the spot, John. And I will set each soldier, begging your pardon, gentlemen, each *man*—"

"Can't hear ya," Deputy Meeks shouted.

I nodded. Twas just as well. "Let's go," I repeated with greater vigor. "We need time to put each man in his place."

The fields were muck and mire. Approaching the lip of the canal gorge, we dismounted. And I was glad of it, though walking had a queer feel after the ride. The mud wanted our boots. John Brent tied our horses. I asked him what might be done to keep them quiet, but he had thought that far without my bothering him. He paired each with a favored stablemate.

"I can't do anything about the thunder and lightning," he said. "But horses feel best in their preferred society. Just like people."

A single whinny might collapse our hopes. For a moment, I considered leaving Brent up with the horses, to soothe them. But we needed every man. Twas not so much a matter of *being* strong as of convincing Kildare and his boys that we were a mighty band.

"Careful now," Underwood said. He sent Meeks down the slope first, to test the way. Then Morris disappeared after the deputy. "Get your hand away from that trigger, Reverend," the sheriff called. "It's slippery going down."

He stepped up to John Brent, Douglass and me. "Be a miracle if Morris doesn't blow a hole in the boat then kill half a dozen of us for good measure."

"John?" I said to the sheriff. "It's a bit hard to tell, see. But I have a sense that I know this place."

"You go on down now, Brent," Underwood said. "You next, Mr. Douglass." He wiped a big hand across his face and a flash outlined those massive ears. "You know it, all right. Remember that poor little mick who drowned herself back in January? Down there in that lock, that's just where it happened." He sputtered a laugh and shook his head, as a man will when the world is unbearably hard. "Wasn't McCorkle a coot that day?"

I recalled the girl. The dark roses of blood where the grapples stabbed her. And the sheath of gold that wrapped her as a shroud. She had been thin, with the hair of a mermaid.

The thunder rolled down from the hills and across the heath. It seemed so odd to me, that winter thunder. For thunder is ever a summer affair in my memory, whether storms over the Black Mountains or the monsoon trumpets of India.

A horse moaned and shuffled.

I followed John Underwood down, and slid, and lost my cane in the brambles.

Well, I could stand without it. And shoot straight, if need be.

• • •

We were naught but pigs in a wallow after tumbling down the slope.

"His name is Jimmy Molloy," I told them, "and he must not come to harm. For he is a brave one, and has done good work."

"But how will we know him?" Morris asked. "How will we—"

"There is trouble," I said. "For he is a great one for disguises. Got up fancy, he is a fine-looking man, in a low and devious way. The last time I saw him he wore a Derby hat, but likely he'll be wrapped up for the storm. His hair is red, but you will not see that for the weather."

The sheriff grumbled. "Now I've got secret fellows running over my county. Oh, for—"

"He is a good man, John. And clever. He will find a way to let us know him."

I hoped that I was right.

I reconnoitered the site, while Underwood and Meeks checked the lockkeeper's shanty. Twas empty, but the upper gates of the lock were open wide. Ready to receive the barge. Perhaps Kildare had sent men ahead to open the locks. We never saw them, if he did. They may have taken shelter with a bottle, with the hard weather upon them. And good riddance. As for our position, it was poor. In the narrow defile, our ambush could easily be turned upon us, with a treacherous climb at our backs. We would take our stand at the foot of the embankment, in the underbrush, on ground slightly lower than the towpath. With naught but a ditch and the path between us and the conspirators.

Had they been soldiers and experienced, I would have spaced my comrades well apart, to make it seem the barge was all but surrounded. But these were simple men caught up in trouble.

I put each man in place, none more than a half-dozen paces from his neighbor, so each would have the comfort of sensing his fellow by him. I lined them up in a rank, to lessen the chance of them shooting each other. Although we did not separate, I divided us into wings of three men each, one centered on me and the other on the sheriff. I told them it was tactics. The truth is that I wanted those of less experience on either side of Underwood or me. The sheriff had Meeks to his left and Morris to his right, while I stood between Brent and Douglass. It would be our duty to bolster them.

We were crouched in the thicket, centered on the lock. The heavy gates made a fine prison for a boat. They would be trapped until the lower sluice was opened, and for a time thereafter.

Underwood called to me, in a reduced voice. "That light up there. That's them."

Twas no distance at all.

Hurriedly, I gave out final instructions. "Those of you with pistols, draw and prime. But keep them under your capes until they're needed. Do not touch the triggers until I challenge the barge. And do not point the barrels along your legs or at your feet in the meantime."

I scurried along our thin little line, twisting on my bad leg.

"Mr. Morris," I continued. "You will point your shotgun at any armed men who bunch together. Aim it at their bellies, and shoot if you feel menaced. But none of you must draw until I call the challenge, understand?" I lowered my voice. "Keep to your places. And keep you still. Do not stand to reveal yourselves. Let them wonder how many we are, and where."

I watched the lantern sway along the gorge, then made out its twin a bit behind. The lights seemed to grow in size with every second.

"No one is to fire unless Kildare's lot begins shooting," I said in a hushed voice. Only the slap of the sleet let me risk continued speech. Foul weather is the hard friend of the infantry. "Or if you hear my command, or that of the sheriff. Understand?"

The men made little noises of agreement, and I could sense their fear. Twas no longer a lark, or a fine gesture, or even a duty. Now it was living and dying. Twas easier for me, of course, as it always is for those in charge. We hear of the weight upon the colonel's shoulders, but the weak link in the battle is the private alone with his fears.

"Stay down now," I whispered, taking up my own position. "And be quiet. And don't forget Jimmy Molloy." Then I prayed.

A plan is nothing against fate. Our lives might end in a single volley.

A new sound come toward us. Almost a crying it was. Between the claps of thunder, we heard groans. As of a giant undergoing torment.

I wanted to ask what it was, but could not break our discipline. Later, I learned it was the noise of the barge grinding the last of the ice against the sides of the canal.

The lantern at the front of the barge disappeared, although its aura remained in the air. The lead mule had come between us.

They were that close. The first lantern reappeared, then faded behind the trailing mule, only to shine out again. Despite the blow and sleet, I could see figures straining on the deck, working with long poles. I saw no rifles. But all was still obscure.

I felt the wet come up through my boots. Cold as a widower's handshake. The wind screamed down the gorge.

Their voices come over, all Irish. *Would ye put yer back into it, ye wort'less bugger? It's frayzin' I am, Napper. Tell Boylan he's wanted. I'm frayzin', I'm frayzin' up dead. Swate Jaysus, would ye stop yer flailin'? Swate Jaysus . . .*

What were they but fools? McCorkle had been wrong. I was not the dupe, though fool enough. These were the dupes of empire and of wealth, of all the great lords and the cruel Kildares. Twas hatred blinded the priest, as hatred blinds all those who embrace it.

Damn it, me fingers! Push, would ye push? I'm frayzin' . . .

I did not want to fire on such fellows. But I would do what needed to be done.

And then a wicked voice broke out in song:

> *The swate-heart o' Dublin,*
> *'Er name was Light Sally,*
> *She'd do it for sixpence,*
> *Just back o' the alley . . .*

That Molloy. His lascivious tenor invited his fellow countrymen to join him. And the poor, benighted Irish did.

Singing, they come toward us.

I had a fix on Molloy now. But my companions would have no sense of him.

Napper O'Hara trailed the second mule. Just as the sheriff had said. I saw the lamplit cabin on the deck, imagining silhouettes on the oiled cloth behind its windows.

O'Hara stopped the mules, letting the boat drift into the lock.

A little time now, I thought. Easy, fellows, easy. I sensed the breathing of my comrades, for I could not hear it in the squall or over the wawling of the Irish. The sleet stiffened. It struck the wood of the boat and the trees like arrows, and left a cutting feel upon the face.

Twas shivering cold. My fingers would need prying from my pistol.

The lead mule started forward on its own, drawing the second animal behind it. The younger O'Hara, Napper, ran up and gave the first one the switch across its eyes. Angry, no doubt, that his brother was warm in the cabin and him king of the mules. Lucky I was that those boys had not killed me, for they were the sort that have joy of their meanness.

The boat moaned, timber against ice, against stone. The Irish with the staves were not in uniforms, but in rags, shabby even in the faint light of the lanterns. The uniforms were for Canada and death, not for the likes of us.

Twas miserable work they were doing, but that is the lot of the Irish in the best of times. They had to hook one great chunk of ice of the water, with six of them pulling, to let the boat snug to the lock. Their song broke down under the effort.

The barge was level with us now.

The poor navvies looked as if they were dancing as they worked. Though their feet were planted firmly on the deck of the barge. Twas the swaying of the boat that gave them their rhythm.

The wet upon me now was not the sleet, but sweat.

Jaysus, Mary and Joseph, would ye heave?

Perhaps Kildare had powers beyond the trick of Mesmerism. Perhaps a bit of the girl's gift had rubbed off. He stepped out of the cabin, pulling on his slouch hat. As if he sensed us. Or perhaps it was only to oversee the business with the lock.

Bull O'Hara followed him. Elder and thicker than his brother, with a beard to rival his master's.

Kildare peered into the darkness. Twas uncanny. He was looking almost exactly at the spot where I had crouched down.

Well, let him see. If the light was enough.

I rose and summoned up my old sergeant's voice.

"In the name of the United States Government, you are all under arrest. Surrender your weapons."

My boys ignored my earlier instructions and leapt to their feet beside me. Twas not proper doings.

Kildare and the Irish did not obey me, either.

Bull went for a pistol, and Kildare drew out two of his own.

"Drop 'em, Kildare," John Underwood shouted. "Or you're first."

Napper slipped behind the trail mule's haunches, fingering the trigger of his revolver.

I feared a slaughter.

"Don't shoot," I commanded. Or begged. "Hold your fire. Everyone."

Guns were up all round.

"Kildare, you'll not go farther. The militia are closing on the outlet," I told him, though it was a lie. "Surrender, and save yourself. Save the men who trusted you."

Twas as if two firing squads opposed each other. Kildare and the O'Haras against the rest of us. With the Irish dumb in wonder.

We faced off almost close enough for fists, weapons extended and gathering sleet.

Out of the corner of my eye, I saw Molloy ease toward the rear of the pack on the deck.

Thank the Lord, I thought, the rest of the Irish were not armed. They just stood gripping their staves. Waiting for a sign or an order.

The boat's rocking settled a little, though the storm churned on.

"You lied to them, Kildare," I tried. "Tell them how you lied."

I was just about to tell them myself, when the rest of the Irish emerged. Climbing up from the bowels of the barge. First two, and then a dozen. Then more.

They were armed with the Enfields.

Gunmen lined the barge, from the cabin back to the stern. I could no longer see Molloy.

"It would appear," Kildare said, "that my militia has arrived a bit earlier than yours, Jones. Now shut your mouth. And all of you put down your weapons, or we'll fire. Take aim, lads. Napper, collect their guns."

A line of rifle bores steadied their aim on us. Still dry enough to fire, most likely. The Irish did not look properly trained. Still, a volley from so many barrels would be deadly.

Napper eased out from behind the mule, pistol up and ready.

"Stay right there, O'Hara," the sheriff said. His voice was unshaken. And angry. "Or I'll shoot you dead as a lamb chop."

"Men," I tried again, "this is treason. You could be hanged. You've no hope at all . . ."

Just as Kildare mouthed the word to fire, I felt a new presence beside me. Now I am a veteran soldier, and should have heard him coming. I can only plead the darkness and the weather. And my fear.

"No hope at all!" McCorkle bellowed, shoving past me. He stretched out his arms, as if to gather in his flock. "Ye've been betrayed, me darlings, and by that one." He pointed to Kildare. "For he's in the pay of Englishmen and it's not but a trap ye will—"

Kildare shot him.

The priest fell. Beside a mule.

The animal kicked and brayed, driving Napper into the ditch.

"*Lies,*" Kildare screamed. "*He lied.*"

The world exploded.

I do not know who fired when, only that guns went barking. I shot Kildare, God help me. And put a bullet in his breast.

The mules were mad. High above the gorge, our horses shrieked.

Both O'Haras were blazing, and I heard the wrong voice cry. Then the O'Haras fell. One just after the other. Napper in the ditch and Bull on the deck.

And what of the Irish with their Enfields?

No rifle fired a shot. For none was loaded. Molloy had seen to that. Most of the Irish dropped their guns and jumped for the far bank. But half a dozen stayed to go after Kildare. Weapons raised as clubs.

His people knew McCorkle's worth.

The Great Kildare had climbed back to his feet. Pulsing blood in the lantern's light. Warning off the Irish with his remaining pistol. His eyes shone huge, despite the whip of the sleet.

"Don't kill him!" I shouted. "I need him alive!"

But the Irish have their own rules among themselves, and they were deaf to me. They closed toward their countryman.

"I'm shot," a voice cried. "Lord, I'm shot."

The rear mule slumped, belatedly feeling a wound and braying piteously. The harness dragged the lead mule down.

Kildare staggered backward to the bow of the barge. Lashed by the wind. Swaying. Struggling to keep his feet on the uncertain deck. He held his pistol out at arm's length. Pointing it first at one of the Irish, then another. Still, they edged closer.

Instead of firing at them, he turned to face the darkness.

"I'll kill you, Jones," he called, with the sleet punishing his eyes. His voice had weakened, but I heard him clear. ". . . kill you . . ."

He fired his pistol toward the bank, seeking me with bullets.

Mr. Morris stepped onto the towpath and triggered his shotgun.

Kildare flew backward over the lip of the boat. Plunging into the icy water, between the prow of the barge and the wall of the lock. Likely to be crushed, if not yet dead.

Swift as a cat, a figure shot across the foredeck, leaping into the water after Kildare.

Twas Jimmy Molloy.

The last of the Irish gave us a look-over, dropped their rifles, and fled after their fellows.

"I know you!" Sheriff Underwood cried. "I know every damned one of you."

"John," I shouted. "That's Molly in the water. My man. Help him. *Please.*"

For Underwood was stronger, and strength was needed now. Along with a good reach.

"Meeks is shot," the sheriff called to me as he dashed for the edge of the canal. "But he'll keep."

Douglass ran to aid the sheriff, peeling off his cloak. Poor Morris stood stiff in amazement, shotgun still in his hands, while John Brent calmed the mules.

I limped over to the priest.

He lay behind the crumpled mule, as still as the beast was a-quiver. I bent to move him to a more fitting spot. Thinking he was dead.

But he was not.

He opened up his eyes—just long enough to read my face—then they fell shut again.

"I damn you still," he said, and died.

The devil's own streak of lightning found the lock's machinery. Twas a great bolt and blast, blinding and deafening. I knew not what it was at first, for it turned me around and sat me on my hindquarters in the mud.

By the light of it, I glimpsed a figure up on the rim of the gorge. Standing where our horses had been tethered.

I did not imagine her, I tell you. I saw her plain, even to the red hair darkened by the wet of the storm. She had gathered her shawl about her, drenched skirt pressed by the wind. I saw her white face and white hands.

I *saw* her.

And then twas dark again.

I scrambled up the bank. Clumsy without my cane. Grasping limbs, brush, the mud itself.

"Nellie," I cried.

She had been right. I had killed Kildare. One way or the other.

"Nellie!"

When I reached the high fields, they were empty. And Nellie Kildare had vanished from the world.

• • •

Meeks was shot in the leg. I could not tell the quality of the wound for the filth of us, but the bone seemed unbroken. The deputy would likely live and prosper. One of the O'Haras would live, as well. Napper, the young one. But prosper he would not. His brother lay among discarded rifles, mouth open to the sleet as if it were whisky.

We did not find Kildare that night, but Molly bobbed up spitting and the sheriff fished him out.

We crowded around my old acquaintance, who was wet through to freezing. His brogans had come off in his struggle with the waters of the lock, and his rag of a coat was gone with his Derby hat. Douglass offered his cloak, which Molloy, shamelessly, accepted.

"Begging your pardons, gents," he said, "I'll just be going into the fine, warm cabin o' the barge for to be rid o' me rags. Oh, I'm cold as a beggar and worse."

I followed him. Queer, the things that strike you after a fight. The cabin smelled of kidneys fried in butter, Kildare's last meal. Perhaps it was the Lord's way of reminding me that, justice done or no, I had shot a man. It made me treasure Molloy's gesture all the more.

I diverted my eyes from his increasing nakedness and spoke my piece:

"Molloy . . . I must say . . . I . . . Jimmy, that was one of the bravest things I've ever seen. When you are properly dressed again, I would like to shake your hand."

Something made me look up. Perhaps I was too weary for propriety. And I saw the look of wonder on Molloy's face.

"Sergeant Jones—I mean, *May*-jor Jones, begging your pardon—what the devil are ye on about now? And what brave deed are ye praising me for? For I'm mystified by yer ramblings and fabulations."

"Why, your selflessness, Molloy. The raw courage of it. The Christian way you threw yourself into the water, risking certain death to save Kildare."

He shook his head slowly. In astonishment.

"Are ye mad, then, Major Jones?" he asked me. "I wouldn't have risked a splinter for Kildare. But didn't the man have his pockets loaded down with gold, and lovely English gold at that, and don't I hate the wasting o' good money?" Bare as the first of our kind, he slumped down in a chair cut from a barrel. "Oh, it broke me heart to see the man go over."

• • •

Nellie disappeared into a continent at war. I hope she found a little peace before the end, and that she was not harmed further by the hand of man. I never will forget her.

Nor did others discard her memory. There is strange, the way we are remembered. Twas long years later, in a time of peace, when I come up to visit the Falls of the Niagara with my Mary Myfanwy. We detoured to Penn Yan to visit my old friend John Underwood. He always kept a good table, and his wife was jolly. But that is not the matter of it.

Summer it was, and we had taken the buggy down to the lakeside to promenade with our ladies. Oh, slower we were, but fine men still, and of good heart. Well, there we were, strolling and watching the boats out on the water, when a grand fellow sauntered up, tipping his hat to the ladies. Underwood introduced him as the new sheriff. I looked hard at the fellow, for he seemed familiar to me, as if I might have known him as a boy. The face was Irish as cabbage at the end of the month, with a turned-up nose, but his speech was plain American.

Anyway, he invited us into a big, striped tent where a celebration was in progress. Underwood seemed to think the young sheriff a fine fellow, so we accepted. It was an Irish revel, got up by some charitable association. Times had changed, you understand, and the Irish were not entirely disreputable. Why, they even had tablecloths down. Nor was there the least scent of alcohol.

I remember that it was lovely and cool there in the shade, with the sides of the tent rolled up, and we indulged in a round of root beer, though it sometimes gives me wind. A handsome young fellow sang to a piano brought down from the town, fair weeping through their ballads full of loneliness, then turning the mood gay, but never saucy.

He closed with a mournful tune of local provenance—for the Irish make a song of all they touch—and the lyrics made me sit up proper. I still recall the refrain:

> *Soft as the lilacs,*
> *With long, fiery hair,*
> *Sweet, magical beauty,*
> *Sad Nellie Kildare . . .*

My Mary Myfanwy, who looked so lovely in her white summer dress, asked me why I was crying. I took her hand and told her I was a silly old man.

But I must tell you of my departure from Penn Yan. Not in those later years when life was golden, but in the midst of war.

Twas the lambkin end of March, when the brown earth ripens and a sniff of the air lifts your heart. The sun was out and shining. John Underwood come down to the station to see me off. Mr. Douglass had already departed, gone to New York City to pay a call upon Mrs. Stanton and to visit a German acquaintance. I had said my farewells to Mr. Morris, as well, who was off to the war. The regiment he had signed on to chaplain was leaving Elmira that very day. The good shepherd was proud as a field marshal in his regimentals, and I feared for the Rebels if they ever got within range of his sermonizing.

The sheriff stood there, grand and hale. We had worked well together, John and I, and we had saved most of the Irish from the gallows, though Napper O'Hara would hang and three more would see a prison. The traitors' ring was broken, for the present, and the English would not have their excuse for a war on our account. Much haunted me—not least Nellie and the priest—but still I felt a sense of satisfaction. Perhaps I had not done badly by our fine country. For if I could not lead again in battle, I wished to do my little bit behind.

All with the Lord's help, see.

I grazed my hand over the lovely walking stick John Underwood had given me as a parting gift. It was too fine to use, but his sort cannot be told such things. So I made a show of wielding it, although the rude cane carved by good *Herr* Kempf was more fitting to the likes of me.

"There is lovely," I said to him, admiring the stick in the sunlight. "I would call you 'friend,' John, if I may?"

"Oh, for crying in a bucket. If we're not friends after all we've been through, I—"

We heard the whistle of the train approaching.

I thrust out my hand. "You are a good man, John Underwood. May God bless you."

We shook, and if the big fellow did not go soft around the eyes! He dropped my hand and gave his ear a tug. "John Brent would've come down to see you off. But folks have their ways about them around here . . ."

"He is a good man, too."

Underwood nodded. "Don't I know it?"

The train chugged down upon us.

"And Meeks is convalescing properly?" I asked.

With a squeal of wheels on rails, the locomotive slid past us. Halting on cushions of steam. The coal smoke made me think again of home.

"His Sarah's driving him crazy. And then some. He'll get up as soon as he can, trust me. Here, let me give you a hand with that crate."

I let him help me, for the sewing machine was heavy. I had managed to persuade the shopkeeper to sell it even below the price he had posted as the "lowest ever," and the "bargain of the century." Leaving just enough of my husbanded pay for modest sustenance on the journey to my beloved—although she would need to spare me a dollar from the cup in the kitchen to get me back to Washington from Pottsville.

I had put on my good uniform for the occasion, and the conductor was respectful and did not hurry me. Still, I did not wish to keep others waiting, for that is inconsiderate. Underwood helped me up with my baggage.

We shook hands a last time, and he jumped—heavily—from the train step. Down on the platform, the conductor raised his wand to unleash the power of the locomotive. And then I heard a shout.

"Major Jones! Major Abel Jones! For the love of Pete, somebody find Major Abel Jones! Don't let that there train go!"

"A moment, please, and my apologies, sir," I said to the conductor as I stepped past him again. Underwood gave me a curious look. For a sheriff wants to know all that goes on.

It was a telegram from the President's office. I gave the breathless messenger a nickel, though it spoiled my economic calculations. What was to be done? Virtue is temperate, not miserly.

I opened the message and read:

AJ. Report immediately to Major General Grant, Army of the Tennessee. Present location southwest of Nashville. Authority to commandeer railroad stock, vessels, or other transport. Waste not a moment. Great danger. Trust no one. Go armed. JN.

THE ADVENTURES OF ABEL JONES WILL CONTINUE IN
CALL EACH RIVER JORDAN

History and Thanks

 THIS BOOK OWES MUCH TO THE GEN-
EROSITY OF OTHERS. Don and Donna
McIntire of Hammondsport, New York,
were my guides and flawless hosts as I
learned to love the land surrounding Keuka Lake. No country
could ask for better citizens, and no guest for greater hospitality.
Frances Dumas, the Yates County historian, gave time and
expertise, answering questions I did not yet know I had. She is a
credit to her office, deeply knowledgeable, ever helpful, and
determined that the past shall not wither. At the Yates County
Genealogical and Historical Society, Kevin Bates kindly made
period newspapers and other references available to me, offering
more than was asked. Matt Syrett, of the Hammondsport Public
Library, surfaced volumes I would not have had the wit to seek.
Marion Springer, assistant historian at the Steuben County Historical Society, responded generously when a blustering November wind carried me into her office. Each of these citizens clearly
love their land, its people and their past. Where I have erred or
"amended" history, the fault is mine, not theirs.

This novel is as accurate as I could make it, from patent medicines to battlefield details, but I have taken some liberties with
history and believe the reader has a right to know. While figures
such as Sheriff Underwood and Stafford Cleveland are loosely
drawn from historical persons, the Reverend Mr. Morris and
Father McCorkle are fictitious. I do not mind hanging great ears

upon a sheriff, but will not hang imaginary sins upon men of the cloth. While the schism in the local Methodist Church indeed took place, and Penn Yan hosted two Spiritualist conventions in the late 1850s, Mr. Morris's peculiarities are devised, not documented. As for the Catholic congregation of St. Michael's, they enjoyed the services of an Italian priest through much of the period. Civil War–era Fenian invasions of Canada are the stuff of historical fact and tragic failure, but Kildare's effort is early and invented.

Elsewhere, fact trumps fiction. The taverns of Bull Run and Manassas *did* stand at a crossroads on those high moors, and Yates County was divided into its own North and South, with violent confrontations. The Irish were troubled and troubling, for prejudices unthinkable to us were universal then. In the middle of the nineteenth century, Spiritualist beliefs and seances penetrated sober religious households by the tens of thousands, attracting many clerics with their promises. Those admirable souls struggling for women's rights often found inspiration in the spirit world, as well. And there *is* something inexplicable in those hills above that crooked lake. Yates and Steuben Counties even today attract religious dissenters, with an Amish migration from Pennsylvania to the less spoiled glens of western New York. Stafford Cleveland, a splendid newspaperman, wrongly predicted war with England, but rightly foresaw the rise of the United States as a world power . . . there is much more, and I encourage the reader to discover it for herself or himself on a visit to the Finger Lakes, with their evocative beauty, history, hospitality and ever-better wines (Abel Jones was wrong about the victory of Temperance, although the movement left us more temperate as a nation, and should be thanked, not mocked).

A last debt that must be acknowledged is to Rudyard Kipling. Those who have read that decent man's works will recognize the "quotations" from his masterful short story, "Without Benefit of Clergy," in the past of Abel Jones. I cherish Kipling. Attacked as a creature of imperialism by those who know him only through a hand-me-down reputation, he wants a fair reconsideration. Kipling transcended the petty hatreds of his times, and loved the world through which he passed with a naivety and joy worthy of Abel Jones. In his stories, novels and poems, love and friendship broke forbidden barriers—his best work was defiant of the givens of the Victorian and Edwardian ages in which he wrote. Even today, not one of the remarkable writers produced by India or Pakistan since independence has matched Kipling's portraits of old India, whether of the Grand Trunk Road in *Kim,* the commonplace dangers of a Northwest Frontier still wild today, or the unexpected love that crosses lines of color, religion and position. Nor has anyone written better of the common soldier. He was humane, true of heart, and less fallible than most. I wish only that those who dismiss him would read him first.

I hope this book will please the citizens of Yates and Steuben Counties. It is honorably meant. If I did not describe an Eden, I came as close as I could. For the highlands by their lake move me as they moved Abel Jones, and I found the people as worthy as he found them. God bless.

The **BLOCK SCHEDULING**
HANDBOOK

I dedicate this book to my high school senior English teacher,
Mary Shelton Drum of West Lincoln High School. Mrs. Drum was
a different teacher from many of my other teachers. She demanded respect,
but gave it. She expected excellence, but demonstrated it. She searched for
inspiration in her teaching, but inspired. Twenty-two years later, I had the
opportunity of working with her as a colleague sharing knowledge and
belief in a new way of teaching. This new way was block scheduling.
Thanks, Mrs. Drum.

The BLOCK SCHEDULING
HANDBOOK

J. Allen Queen

CORWIN PRESS, INC.
A Sage Publications Company
Thousand Oaks, California

For information:

Corwin Press, Inc.
A Sage Publications Company
2455 Teller Road
Thousand Oaks, California 91320
www.corwinpress.com

Sage Publications Ltd.
6 Bonhill Street
London EC2A 4PU
United Kingdom

Sage Publications India Pvt. Ltd.
M-32 Market
Greater Kailash I
New Delhi 110 048 India

Printed in the United States of America

Library of Congress Cataloging-in-Publication Data

Queen, J. Allen.
The block scheduling handbook / J. Allen Queen.
p. cm.
Includes bibliographical references and index.
ISBN 0-7619-4525-3 (c) — ISBN 0-7619-4526-1 (p)
1. Block scheduling (Education) 2. Curriculum planning. I. Title.
LB3032.2 .Q85 2002
371.2'42—dc21   2002005184

This book is printed on acid-free paper.

04 05 06 10 9 8 7 6 5 4 3 2

Acquisitions Editor:	Faye Zucker
Editorial Assistant:	Julia Parnell
Copy Editor:	Linda Gray
Production Editor:	Diane S. Foster
Typesetter/Designer:	Larry Bramble
Proofreader:	Eileen Peronneau
Indexer:	Teri Greenberg
Cover Designer:	Michael Dubowe
Production Designer:	Michelle Lee

Contents

Companion Website

Educators who have purchased this book will be able to visit Dr. Queen's website, www.blockscheduling.com, to download related materials for staff development with teachers and instructional ideas for students. One section will include detailed, colorful Powerpoint projections for instructional use. Teachers have a forum to share ideas and chat. Related links are also available. The website is updated on a monthly basis and a link allows you to contact Dr. Queen directly. He promises to return your email within 48 hours.

Acknowledgments

I would like to thank the many graduate students, principals, and classroom teachers who assisted directly and indirectly with the development of this book. Literally hundreds of individuals have used my designs and materials, testing these with thousands of students throughout the country. Thanks for sharing materials, ideas, research notes, and creative activities go to all those above and especially to those mentioned here.

Special thanks go to some special current and former graduate students who provided much direct input into the book. These include Wendy Tomberlin, Kimberely Isenhour, Kim Mattox, Elaine Jenkins, Walter Hart, Rick Hinson, and Ashlee Luff. All these individuals are educators who see the block schedule not only as a tool but also as a way of reforming education.

My most sincere appreciation goes to my colleague and editor, Jenny Burrell, for the many hours of reading, proofing and making constructive suggestions and changes to make the book more useful to you, the practicing educator.

Space does not permit the listing of all the educators nationally and internationally who have used many of these materials for teaching on the block, but I must list a few of the excellent teachers, principals, superintendents, and professors who have endorsed my work and encouraged the production of this book: These special individuals include Dr. Robert Algozzine, professor, UNC Charlotte; Dr. James Kracht, professor, Texas A&M; Bruce Smith, managing editor for *Phi Delta Kappan*; Dr. Martin Eaddy, North Carolina Director of Standards of Quality; Dr. Karen Gerringer, director of the North Carolina Principal Fellow Program; North Carolina superintendents—Dr. Jim Watson, Dr. Randall Henion, Dr. George Truman; principals—Michael Turner and Lloyd Wimberely, Charlotte-Mecklenburg Schools; Bret Robertson, Okaw High School, Bethany, Illinois; Don Kuntz, Stebbins High School, Riverside, Ohio; Pat Corbin, Nashua High School, Nashua, New Hampshire; Chris Settle, Reitz High School, Evansville, Indiana; and master teachers—Trish Scardina, Tom Watkins, Joyce Rex, Margaret Reynolds, Elaine Boysworth, Randi

Imbriano, Kristie Bullock, Bill Gustafson, Bonnie Obenchan, and Diana Brock. And the list continues. Thank you.

I would also like to thank all the professionals at Corwin Press. It has been an inspiration working with these folks, especially the editors. Thanks must go to Faye Zucker for her inspiration in making this book a reality. To Linda Gray, a special "thank you" for all the many, many hours you gave to making the book come alive; will you work on my next book? And final thanks to Diane Foster for your guidance in the production process.

About the Author

J. Allen Queen serves as a major consultant in block scheduling to school boards and school systems throughout the United States, working with them to train teachers, collect data, and evaluate the effectiveness of block scheduling. He is coauthor of *The 4×4 Block Schedule* (1998), many journal articles, and hundreds of presentations to educational groups interested in block scheduling, school discipline, and effective time management for instruction.

He has been a classroom teacher, principal, curriculum specialist, and college administrator. Currently he is Professor and Chair of the Department of Educational Leadership at the University of North Carolina at Charlotte. His Web site can be accessed at www.blockscheduling.com.

ONE

High Schools on the Block

T hose of us who have taught for years know that the traditional high school structure has remained fundamentally unchanged for most of the 20th century. Naturally, in our never-ending quest to improve education, some experimentation has taken place. In 1959, Trump proposed eliminating the rigid traditional high school schedule and instituting classes of varying lengths based on the instructional needs of students. The Trump Plan allowed for a science class to meet for a 40-minute lecture, a 100-minute lab, and a 20-minute help session per week, whereas other classes could be short periods of 20 or 30 minutes. With limited success, Trump encouraged teachers to experiment with a variety of instructional strategies in an attempt to provide flexibility in the educational process.

Tradition rather than proven educational success has guided administrators in scheduling classes for students. Even today, in spite of the awareness of problems with the traditional schedule, some of us continue to resist a change in the schedule, choosing a return to the traditional format—claiming failure due to limited training, preparation, time, and resources. In addition, generations of Americans have graduated from high schools requiring the successful completion of a prescribed number of Carnegie units, which are based on accumulated seat time (Canady & Rettig, 1995a). This high school tradition appeared trite when, in 1983, *A Nation at Risk* reported that our students were academically behind their

counterparts from a number of other industrialized nations. In response to the 1983 report, we began to examine alternatives that would result in higher student achievement and started a reform movement to restructure our schools. Block scheduling served as one avenue in this restructuring process.

While the various national education reports of the 1980s addressed the general condition of American education, including secondary schools, a few reports addressed high school exclusively. Ernest Boyer and Theodore Sizer wrote two of the most highly publicized proposals for high school reform.

High School: A Report on Secondary Education in America, written by Ernest Boyer (1983), was prepared for the Carnegie Foundation for the Advancement of Teaching. It was "based on a three-year study in which twenty-five educators collected data at fifteen diverse senior high schools" (Ornstein & Levine, 1989, p. 595). Boyer's proposals for improvement and reform included several themes. One of his main findings was "that high schools, lacking a 'clear and vital' vision of their mission, were unable to formulate 'widely shared common purposes' or 'educational priorities'" (Gutek, 1986, p. 347). Among Boyer's most important recommendations were those dealing with teacher's working conditions. "These recommendations included proposals that high-school teachers should have a daily load of only four regular classes and one small seminar, should have an hour a day for class preparation, and should be exempt from monitoring halls, lunchrooms, and recreation areas" (Ornstein & Levine, 1989, p. 595).

Theodore Sizer's (1984) major work, *Horace's Compromise: The Dilemma of the American High School*, was based partly on school visits he made to 80 high schools. "Sizer, former headmaster of Phillips Academy and former dean of Harvard's Graduate School of Education, created a synthesis that encompassed the liberating tendencies of the 1960s with the emphasis on academic competency of the early 1980s" (Gutek, 1986, p. 348). In his book, a teacher named Horace must choose between "covering" a multitude of low-level skills in the prescribed curriculum and in-depth teaching of important concepts and understandings. To develop in-depth learning, Sizer recommended that the curriculum be divided into four major areas: inquiry and expression, mathematics and science, literature and the arts, and philosophy and history. He also emphasized more active learning and reduced emphasis on what he considered mindless approaches to minimal competency testing. Sizer's particular concern was to eliminate the tacit understanding between students who say, "I will be orderly . . . if you don't push me very hard" and teachers who respond "You play along with my minimal requirements and I will keep them minimal" (Ornstein & Levine, 1989, p. 595). In addition, it is important to note that Sizer acknowledged the complexity of teaching high school. He pointed out that teachers could not effectively teach 150 to 180 students a day and recommended that a team of seven or eight teachers work with groups of about 100 students when teaching the four major curriculum areas he had prescribed (p. 595).

"Of all the reports of the 1980s, *Horace's Compromise* marked the greatest departure from the tendency to mandate more prescribed subjects in the curriculum. Sizer's recommendations were directed at raising expectations and achievement outcomes, but in a more flexible atmosphere" (Gutek, 1986, p. 349). As we move into the 21st century, Sizer's ideas for integrated learning are likely to remain significant since many schools in the United States are successfully teaming teachers to offer students a more interrelated curriculum.

In the 1980s, Mortimer J. Adler published his *Paideia Proposal* (Adler, 1982), which asserted that all students should have access to an intellectually-based curriculum. Adler argued that there exists a general learning that all human beings should possess. "Since American society is a democracy based on political and ethical equality, the same quality of schooling should be provided for all students" (Ornstein & Levine, 1989, p. 211). Adler and his Paideia associates considered the following subject matter as essential: language, literature, fine arts, mathematics, natural sciences, history, geography, and social studies. The subjects were viewed as a framework for developing a collection of intellectual skills necessary for all students. Some of the intellectual skills they wanted to focus on were reading, writing, speaking, listening, and problem solving. When the fundamental skills were coupled with the intellectual skills, a higher level of learning was reached. The *Paideia Proposal* allowed all students the opportunity to study the basics while achieving greater understanding of other ideas through Socratic teaching. In the late 1990s, the proposal reemerged in some schools as a means of teaching higher-order thinking skills and respect for others' opinions and views.

Perhaps the birth of the modern day block schedule began in 1984 when Goodlad argued in *A Place Called School* that the traditional high school did not allow enough time to individualize instruction, extend laboratory work, or provide much-needed remediation and enrichment to our students. He recognized then, as we do now, that an enormous amount of time and energy is wasted by changing classes from six to seven times a day. To be more effective, Goodlad encouraged schools to redesign their schedules into larger blocks of time. Six years later, Carroll (1994) suggested that we change to a format in which students concentrate on one or two subjects and encourage teachers to focus more on individual students. Block scheduling was beginning to take shape.

In 1994, Cawelti argued that by restructuring high schools, we as teachers could bring about fundamental changes in the expectations, content, and learning experiences provided to students. During the same year, we learned that 40% of schools in the United States were using some form of block scheduling. The number continues to grow nationally today with most states having more blocked schools than traditional schools.

In general, block scheduling is based on the idea of organizing a course around one semester in an extended class time of 90 minutes rather than the more typical 50 minutes. Following are the three major formats of block scheduling in use today:

1. *4x4*, four-block, compacted or accelerated model; the daily, four 90-minute periods per semester

2. *A/B*, eight-block, expanded model; the rotating daily, eight 90-minute periods per year

3. *Modified periods* with an array of block-scheduled and traditional classes taught over varying periods of three months, semesters, or the school year

The modified block classes can be scheduled in a variety of ways based on subject content or desired flexibility (Canady & Rettig, 1995a; DiBiase & Queen, 1999). Known as the modified block or the split block, this model is gaining popularity today in both middle and high school settings. While the modified model provides the most flexibility, it is the most difficult to schedule, and many teachers believe that many of the benefits provided by the 4x4 and A/B models are lost.

Teachers who instruct in block-scheduled schools have improved the academic environment for students by increasing the number of courses that can be completed in a four-year period. In the process, graduation rates have increased and discipline problems have declined. Since most students have been limited to four classes each day, lighter student loads can allow for greater immersion in the subject with less time spent changing from one class to another. An improved school climate can result in a more relaxed atmosphere with greater student-teacher rapport. In many cases, the schedule change has become a tool for curriculum improvement (Gerking, 1995). Teachers have learned quickly that both positive and negative results come with any change, and moving to a block schedule is a big adjustment. However, when weighing the advantages and disadvantages to the students, many schools have found that the change is worth the effort.

Educators who have purchased this book can go to my website www.blockscheduling.com (or directly to the site by typing block scheduling on Yahoo) to the section, "Block Scheduling Handbook Materials" and download the PowerPoint, "Introduction to Block Scheduling."

TWO

Benefits and Cautions

Block scheduling has advantages and disadvantages that must be considered from the perspectives of teachers, administrators, and most important, students—perspectives that, admittedly, overlap. The benefits to all those involved in the educational system are many; however, the disadvantages must be studied closely before implementation.

BENEFITS OF BLOCK SCHEDULING ■

One benefit to block scheduling is that students are usually able to take more classes, thereby broadening the scope of their course selection. Under the block schedule, students who may not have been able to take electives in a traditional schedule will be able to take them. Students' attendance in class improves, and they are less likely to show disruptive behavior because of reduced time spent in changing classes. In addition, more students complete advanced-placement courses, and on average, their course grades improve. The design of the block schedule allows students to receive more individual attention.

Teachers have more time to plan and prepare for classes under the block schedule. They become more effective by varying instructional strategies, thereby engaging students to a greater degree. Also, due to the increased length of the classes, more in-depth study of subjects is possible. Experience shows us that more than 70% of teachers go beyond the lecture approach and use interactive instruction (Queen, Algozzine, & Eaddy,

1997). With effective planning, teachers will have to spend less time organizing attendance sheets, receipts, report cards, and other business forms, thereby giving them further opportunities for planning instruction. In fact, some teachers, depending on the subjects, block design, and school size, may have only two course preparations daily. For example, she may teach two sections each of two different courses—say, two sections of advanced placement English and two sections of general English.

Administrators and teachers will be happy to know that block scheduling has a positive effect on school climate and requires less time spent on procedures, routines, and management. Teachers have more instructional time for extended laboratory investigation or classroom experiments. More guided practice and extra time are available for skill enhancement in music, art, and vocational classes. Field trips to locations close to the school may be taken during one period. Of the greatest importance, we know that the longer class period allows more time for interactive instruction using varied instructional strategies, such as cooperative learning, inquiry method, group discussion, concept development, simulations, and seminars, all of which can increase student interest and performance. In numerous studies and classroom observations, 70% to 80% of teachers, students, and parents believe that block scheduling is effective. As fears of school violence continue to grow, most of us believe that block scheduling also has increased school safety.

Students on the block are absent from class fewer times, but they have fewer classes to complete missed assignments. As a result, schools need to establish homework policies and guidelines for missed instruction. Students find they have another chance to remain with their peers if they fail a class, especially on the 4x4 block. If a student fails a class during the fall semester, the class may be repeated during the next semester. This second chance for some students may limit the need for summer school. Principals may find a higher probability for students to remain in school if they can keep pace with their peers to graduate on time.

Discipline is an important consideration in schools and can often be improved under the block schedule. When necessary, administrators can suspend a student for a semester instead of a year (in the 4x4 block) without putting the student behind for a full year. For example, depending on the infraction, a student could be suspended for an entire semester and still earn four credits for the year (Canady & Rettig, 1995a; Gunter, Estes, & Schwab, 1990; Hottenstein, 1998; Siefert & Beck, 1994). Historically, teachers throughout the United States have stated overwhelmingly the positive discipline results of being on the block (Canady & Rettig, 1995a; Queen, 2000).

■ RESEARCH BASE

Several researchers cite the advantages of the block scheduling in their studies. Day, Ivanov, and Binkley (1996) outline the benefits of a block schedule for science instruction. Day bases these benefits on her experi-

ence as the only science teacher at Center High School in Tennessee. The high school has an enrollment of 200 students and has used block scheduling for five years. The benefits she has found include increased student-teacher interaction, smaller classes, long blocks of instructional time with fewer interruptions per class, time for more in-depth study, and uninterrupted experiments. Also, block scheduling allows students and teachers opportunities to get to know each other better, which helps to keep a positive classroom climate, leading to fewer discipline problems. In addition, the teacher has time to introduce a concept, do an activity to reinforce the concept, and have follow-up activities for closure all in the same period.

Edwards (1995) cites the advantages based on his research at Orange County High School in Virginia where they have been using the 4x4 plan since 1993. Advantages for the teachers include a more manageable schedule by having fewer students at a time, fewer classes for which to prepare, and increased planning time. Advantages for students include fewer classes a day, which gives them fewer subjects to focus on at one time; the opportunity to earn up to eight credits per year; and the chance to repeat any failed courses without falling behind. He also found that grades went up, students completed more courses, and more students enrolled in and passed advanced placement exams.

Huff (1995) reports the advantages of block scheduling as evidenced at Scotland County R-1 High School in Memphis, Missouri. These include the following: (a) teachers have enough time to develop key concepts, (b) there is a greater range of classes for students to select from, (c) students have two evenings to complete assignments, (d) there is an increase in teaching and learning creativity, (e) a variety of teaching techniques can be used in each class meeting, (f) activities are diverse, (g) study halls can be eliminated, (h) new concepts can be applied immediately, and (i) both teachers and students have only four classes to prepare for each day. Huff found that both students and teachers agreed that block scheduling should continue. Seventy-nine percent of the students believed instruction under this schedule was superior to instruction under the traditional schedule.

Shore (1995), the ex-vice principal at Huntington Beach High School in California, cites some of the benefits of block scheduling at her school. These include students receiving personal attention because teachers see fewer students, an allowance for the implementation of a tutorial period before school, smaller classes, and happier students and teachers.

In late August of 2000, I was fortunate to conduct an interview with Dr. Dennis Williams, the former principal of West Mecklenburg High School, and we discussed his experiences with the first 4x4 school in the system when he began the program in 1994. He sited the benefits of implementing the 4x4 block plan. The school has experienced an increase in the number of students on the A and B honor roll and a decrease in the number of failing grades. There was also a decrease in the number of suspensions, both in school and out of school. At the end of the first year, over 90% of the teachers and almost 90% of the students did not want to return to the traditional schedule.

Gerking (1995), a science teacher at Laramie High School in Wyoming, states that on a block schedule, there are not as many contact minutes with the students over the entire semester but that the learning is far more intense and there is time available for group work and cooperative learning. Although not as much material is covered, what is covered is in depth and the important concepts are emphasized with less wasted time. The teachers, students, and parents have indicated that they would not want to return to the traditional schedule.

Picciotto (1996), the revolutionary guru of the San Francisco Urban Plan, compares the traditional schedule and the new block schedule at the Urban School of San Francisco, an independent progressive high school, where he works. The advantages he found include the following: (a) Teachers usually teach three periods and have two different preparation times, (b) teachers see fewer students so they get to know them better, (c) students juggle fewer subjects and can concentrate better on the ones they are taking, (d) the half-day period makes it possible to take field trips and pursue major projects, and (e) the three 70-minute periods allow enough time to do something in depth or to do more than one activity. The disadvantages are fewer homework opportunities because the class meets for only one semester, students' taking four academic classes creates a great deal of intensity, and the longer planning periods can be challenging for novice teachers.

In a study of 4x4 block scheduling at Wasson High School in Colorado Springs, O'Neil (1995) identifies the following advantages: a lower student-to-teacher ratio, a decline in discipline problems, and the creation of a less stressful climate. He concludes that the weaknesses are the teachers' failing to use scheduling effectively, inappropriate instructional strategies for the longer period of time, and the possibility of not as much curriculum being covered.

Wilson (1995), a teacher at Hope High School in Arkansas, states the advantages and concerns experienced with the 4x4-block schedule since its implementation during the 1994-1995 school year. The advantages were that students could earn more credits, the schedule was more flexible, homework was limited to four classes, and more work occurred in the classroom, with the teacher having the time to completely cover a concept before class is over. The concerns included students who transfer in and out of schools.

■ CAUTIONS ABOUT BLOCK SCHEDULING

While the promises for success have been numerous, many pitfalls have been identified. Block scheduling has been criticized for the loss of content retention from one level of a subject to the next and the extensive time required for independent study outside of class. Transfer students from schools on a traditional schedule, the limited number of new electives offered, and the increased overuse of lecture in the classrooms can be problems as well.

The first year on block scheduling is the most challenging for teachers and principals. Many teachers are anxious about the uncertainties associated with teaching in longer blocks of time. Many veteran teachers complain that the first year of block scheduling is much like being a beginning teacher again. As a result, careful planning is required for teachers to successfully adapt to the block schedule. Block scheduling requires teachers to prepare lessons that engage students during longer periods of instructional time. Depending on the subject taught, teachers have varying views and suggestions related to the block schedule.

Foreign language teachers continue to stress the importance of providing course sequencing in the block. These teachers believe that a long period of time between the first and second courses of a sequenced subject can be problematic and could hinder retention and seriously affect achievement. Principals may need to schedule students to take two sequenced courses in one subject area during the year in the block schedule format. Careful planning during the scheduling process will limit the time gap between the first and second courses of specific subjects.

Teachers of performing arts, particularly band instructors, complain that limiting instruction to one semester could hurt the quality of performance. However, many band teachers note improved quality when students with serious musical interests sign up in the program for the entire year. These teachers find increased student participation in music as additional elective opportunities become available.

Advanced placement courses that allow students to earn college credit while in high school present challenges to blocked schools. Problems emerge in the 4x4 design when these courses are offered during the fall semester, but the examination for awarding college credit is not administered until the end of spring semester. Schools using block scheduling have developed unique approaches to assist students in their exam preparation. For example, many schools conduct after-school and Saturday review sessions prior to administering the test. In some schools, students are allowed to take a related elective course during the semester preceding or following the advanced placement course to enhance their knowledge in that area. Advanced placement testing should become available on a semester basis. There are enough schools across the nation using the 4x4 block to warrant these tests each semester.

Many scheduling concerns involve students who transfer schools during the school year. In the beginning of block scheduling when most schools were on the traditional model, transfers were a major concern for some teachers. This is now becoming less of a problem because so many schools are on the block.

Block scheduling has been attacked because of the reduction of total instructional time per class. However, since blocked classes meet a little more than one-half as many times as traditional classes, the total amount of time lost for routine administrative tasks such as taking class attendance can be reduced by as much as 50%. Teachers find that the total time lost is negligible and that coverage of course content is not greatly reduced.

Students in a traditional course meet in 50-minute classes for 180 days, which is a total of 9,000 minutes of instructional time. Students in a block schedule meet in 90-minute classes for 90 days for a total of 8,100 minutes of instructional time. If 10 minutes are lost for administrative functions at the beginning and end of classes, then 1,800 minutes are lost under the traditional schedule (180 days [10 minutes] and 900 minutes are lost under the block (90 days [10 minutes]). Using these numbers, a teacher has 7,200 minutes of instruction under either format: $9,000 - 1,800 = 7,200$ minutes under traditional scheduling, and $8,100 - 900 = 7,200$ under block scheduling (Hackmann, 1995; Rettig & Canady, 1996; Shortt & Thayer, 1998).

Wasted instructional time becomes a key concern for schools using block scheduling. Instructional time is wasted when teachers fail to use a variety of learning activities and teaching strategies. The lecture method is overused in 30% of blocked classes. This problem can lead to parent and student complaints about the longer class periods becoming boring. Many teachers consider the overuse of lecturing the single most damaging factor to success of the block schedule. This issue will be covered in greater detail later in this section.

It is important to restate that the mere changing of the amount of time students spend in class through block scheduling does not guarantee school success. Unfortunately, it is possible for a school to change scheduling patterns without making appropriate changes in instruction practices. In some cases, modifications in classroom practices appear not to parallel the restructuring initiatives. Appropriate changes in instructional practices and the effective use of class time are the essential keys to the success of block scheduling. One may conclude that the major problem in block scheduling remains either the teacher's use of excessive lecture or the inability to employ more effective, engaging instructional methods in the classroom (Hart, 2000; Queen, Burrell, & McManus, 2000; Queen & Isenhour, 1998b; Schroth & Dixon, 1996; Skrobarcek et al., 1997).

■ OVERUSING LECTURE CAN DESTROY THE BLOCK SCHEDULE

As previously stated, the major problem in block scheduling today is the overuse of lecture. The lecture has become an "institution" in the American public high school, perhaps even to a greater degree than is found at the university level. When lecture is the major instructional strategy for teaching students, the time for using more appropriate instructional strategies is severely limited. Much of the research on the block schedule shows that teachers are better able to employ a variety of instructional strategies that address the learning needs of students in extended class periods. Some of these instructional strategies are more difficult to complete in a traditional class of 50 to 60 minutes. Unfortunately, the lecture method remains the most used instructional strategy in high school today. With public pressure to increase test scores, it is hard to eliminate

the lecture method, because it is used to facilitate coverage of the curriculum. Educators complain that they have to lecture more because there is limited time to use interactive methods with students given the amount of content to cover in preparation for state-mandated tests. Unfortunately, these teachers have missed a wonderful opportunity not only to have students gain a better understanding of the course content through student-engaging activities but also to have them retain more subject content and consequently perform more effectively on these very same mandated tests. Simply zipping through course content using lecture with passive learners is easier for teachers and students. However, the low retention and application of what is learned is alarming. Again, the block can provide more time for a variety of learning activities. With more time in class and an emphasis on action-oriented strategies, teachers have an opportunity to engage students in activities that allow them to apply content knowledge to real problems, to work together in teams, and to employ modern technology.

A 1997 study by Corley found that veteran classroom teachers (those having 15-20 years of classroom experience) were complacent about their teaching strategies in schools that had positive reputations for preparing students for college. These teachers saw no need to change their instructional approach because they were effective. Conversely, in the same year Adams and Salvaterra (1997) found that some teachers in specific subjects discovered most instructional strategies were easier to implement in a block schedule. The teachers surveyed stated that they used a variety of instructional methods, changing strategies as often as four times per class. Of no surprise was the fact that teachers who had used a variety of instructional strategies during longer class periods also did so during shorter periods. In this study, the researchers found that teachers from some school districts used significantly more instructional strategies than teachers in others. This phenomenon was related directly to the amount and quality of staff development prior to the change to the block schedule and the continued training opportunities that were provided by the school districts.

In another 1997 study, Queen, Algozzine, and Eaddy (1997) found that when appropriate staff development was provided, there was an increase in the variety of teaching strategies used in block scheduling. More specifically, it was discovered that, once prepared, two-thirds of teachers consistently used a variety of interactive instructional strategies. Comparatively, Khazzaka (1997) found that 77% of high school teachers surveyed agreed that they had received adequate staff development and implemented a variety of teaching strategies in the block schedule.

Obviously, if one-third of teachers in block-scheduled schools rely heavily on lecture and do not experiment with different instructional strategies, blocked schools will have greater barriers to success. In addition, many of these same teachers not using interactive methods also waste instructional time in the classroom by not instructing during the last 30 minutes of class. The success of block scheduling will be determined by the

degree to which teachers adopt instructional techniques that take advantage of the extended time blocks to create improved learning opportunities for students (Queen, 2000).

■ SUMMARY

To be a successful teacher in a blocked class, Queen, Algozzine, and Eaddy (1997) concluded that the most important teaching skills for instruction are as follows:

1. The ability to develop a pacing guide for the course in nine-week periods. This includes weekly and daily planning.

2. The ability to use several instructional strategies effectively.

3. The skill to design and maintain an environment that allows for great flexibility and creativity.

4. The desire and skill to be an effective classroom manager.

5. The freedom to share the ownership of teaching and learning with the students.

While it was important that all teachers master these skills, we discovered that beginning teachers needed special attention from mentors and principals (Queen, Algozzine, & Isenhour, 1999).

In reviewing block scheduling, it is apparent that principals and staff development personnel must provide initial and continuous training for teachers to master instructional strategies. Cooperative learning, synectics, Socratic seminars, concept attainment, case methods, inquiry methods, simulations, games, and role-playing strategies are excellent methods for teachers to use in blocked classes. Queen, Burrell, and McManus (2000) identified and reviewed several strategies in *Planning for Instruction: A Year Long Guide*. However, just as a 90-minute lecture is inappropriate, a 90-minute discussion session may be too long. We found that teachers should change activities about every 10 or 15 minutes. This prevents student boredom, elicits class interaction, and encourages teachers to meet the needs of diverse learners. Instruction in these extended periods should begin with a review, include various activities, and conclude with an adequate summary. Suggested instructional approaches for teaching in the block are presented in detail in Part III of this book. But before we focus on the instructional strategies, it is important to review some basic information on growth and development. Visit my website and download the material, Proper Ways to Use the Lecture Method and Related Materials.

THREE

Developmental Aspects of Growth and Behavior

Regardless of scheduling, teachers should understand the fundamental principles of child growth and development so that they can effectively instruct students. We know that children move from an immature and less complex and skilled dependent state to a mature and more complex and skilled independent condition. This process involves a series of invariant stages of physical, intellectual, and personal development. By understanding the stages of development that children invariably move through, teachers know what to expect of children, what and how to instruct, and how to communicate with children based on their stage of development.

Although part of the education and training to become a teacher focuses on these stages of development, it is imperative to keep these stages in mind when designing instruction. Without this knowledge, effective instruction is difficult. The goal of this chapter is to refresh understanding and give an overview of the various developmental stages.

■ PHYSICAL DEVELOPMENT FROM EARLY CHILDHOOD THROUGH ADOLESCENCE

We only need to watch young children for a short time to see that they tend to be unsteady. This instability is caused by several factors in their physical development. Children in the early childhood stage have a high center of gravity because their heads are out of proportion to their bodies, and their abdomens protrude, which makes balancing difficult. Gaining control over their motor activities is their biggest achievement, during which they also begin to favor the right or left side of the body. As their dexterity improves, children learn to perform fine motor activities, such as tying shoelaces and printing letters of the alphabet. Their ability to jump, run, and walk also improves significantly by the end of the preschool period.

By the time most children reach school age, they have already learned many skills such as buttoning and zipping pants and jackets, buckling belts, cutting with scissors, and coloring within borders. In addition, children print letters and words with greater accuracy. After the seventh year, most children continuously improve the quality of their fine and gross motor skills, but learn few completely new basic capabilities.

Through the primary years children experience comparatively small alterations in their weight and height. Until children reach age nine, boys are generally only slightly heavier and taller than girls. During the early elementary years, children need frequent exercise to accommodate skeletal growth and muscular development and to improve their physical skills. By the age of nine, children begin to participate in complex activities, such as playing musical instruments or constructing models.

From their 8th through 10th years, both sexes are similar in size. Although boys and girls are similar in size at the beginning of fourth grade, by the end of the year, many girls have begun to gain height and weight over boys. The rapid growth of their arms and legs, combined with the slower development of their torsos, causes girls to temporarily appear ungainly and lose a degree of strength and coordination. Most early-maturing females rapidly regain lost ground. By the end of fifth grade or the beginning of sixth grade, they are generally taller and heavier than most boys of the same age. By this point, many girls have reached the size that they remain until puberty.

With the onset of female menstruation at approximately age 13 and male ejaculation between 13 and 16 years, girls and boys enter puberty, a time of particularly significant and substantial changes. The order in which these changes occur is basically the same for each person, but the rate at which females and males mature can vary widely. Some adolescents may fully mature in as little as 18 months from onset, while others may require five or six years. During this period, almost every organ and system in the body are subject to change and stress.

Puberty is a particularly difficult time for children for many reasons. Their bodies change drastically in relatively short periods of time, making

them quite self-conscious; size, muscular development, amount and location of hair, and body proportions are all changed during this period. Since they are experiencing this stage at different rates, additional stress is placed on these adolescents. For those who experience puberty early, the notoriety caused by their advanced development is confusing and generally unwelcome. But as they successfully work through these changes, awkward self-consciousness diminishes and confidence improves. Those who undergo puberty "late" may experience even greater stress. An apparent lack of physical maturity can cause self-doubt, loss of self-esteem, and withdrawal from involvement with others. These problems can carry over into adulthood.

Cognitive Growth

Arnold Gesell notably achieved insight into the progressive nature of child development. Gesell (1971) established a center for research into child development at Yale University, where he worked on the premise that children's growth and development occur in an unvarying sequence within strict boundaries of time. Although his ideas were later found to be inadequate in explaining the true nature of development, his fundamental principle that children move through several phases of reorganization during which they develop new ways of understanding the world has been generally accepted.

While Gesell worked at Yale, psychologist and epistemologist Jean Piaget (1954) quietly explored the intellectual development of his children in Switzerland. His discoveries and the work that followed have become the basis of cognitive science in the fields of psychology and education. Piaget concluded that cognitive growth occurs in specific developmental stages, during which significant differences in the nature and substance of intelligence are developed over time. Piaget saw these differences as real transformations of consciousness.

Based on extensive observations, Piaget (1954) defined several stages of cognitive development. He described from three to six stages of development with several substages (see Table 3.1).

Characteristics of Piaget's Stages of Cognitive Development

Piaget (1954) established a general time frame for the onset of the stages of cognitive development. From birth to two years of age, a child is in the sensori-motor stage of development. The period of preoperational thought is active from the second year until approximately the seventh year. This is followed by the stage of concrete operations, which generally appears by the age of seven and continues through the 11th year. The onset of formal operations, the fourth stage, occurs sometime between the 11th and 16th birthdays.

Piaget (1954) determined that the onset of each stage is signaled by a major shift in intellectual activity from the preceding stage of develop-

Table 3.1. Piaget's Cognitive Stages

Cognitive Stages	Ages	Characteristics
Formal Operations	11 to adult	• Cognitive structures mature to the adult level • Capacity to engage all categories and classes of problems: the verbal abstraction, the hypothetical, and consideration of past and future conditions • Ability to evaluate a logical argument separate from its content
Concrete Operations	7 to 11 years	• Logical examination of the observable relationships between events, objects, and people • Involves the development of the cognitive structures of seriation and classification • Expression of a strong tendency to organize and apply strict rules to activities undertaken.
Preoperational	2 to 7 years	• Not restricted to immediate environment Expansion of use of mental images Application and understanding of vocabulary expands • Intuitive thought defines preoperational thought
Sensori-motor	0 to 2 years	• Period of simple reflexes • Restricted to immediate experience • Events are uninhibited by sight and feeling • Children build first cognitive structures

ment. Although the beginning of each stage varies for each individual, the sequence of the stages does not change. A child must navigate through the succession of stages; he or she cannot intentionally avoid or miss a stage through superior cognitive attributes. Piaget noted that although definable intellectual activities describe each period, mixing of capabilities from other stages, especially those from stages just experienced, would occur. In addition, as children age, there is an increasing variation in the age at which children begin a stage, with the onset of formal operations in adolescents subject to the greatest age variation. But before examining the four stages of development further, let us look at the ideas that describe the cognitive processes responsible for the changes within those stages.

Schemata and the Process of Assimilation, Accommodation, and Equilibration

In Piaget's (1969b) scheme of cognitive development, assimilation and accommodation are the ways children integrate new experiences into cognitive structures called *schemata* or schemes. According to Piaget, "A scheme is the structure or organization of actions as they are transferred or

generalized by repetition in similar or analogous circumstances" (p. 4). These structures develop from birth, at which time they are simple and undifferentiating. As a child develops and is more able to differentiate among stimuli, the number of schemata grows by absorbing additional relevant material that resulted from encounters with the environment. At major periods of transformation, schemata undergo significant changes that allow a child to deal competently with more complex problems.

The process of assimilation and accommodation is unending, and it reflects people's continuous interaction with an infinite number of stimuli. The process is "a constant filtering of input and modification of internal schemes to fit reality" (Piaget, 1969b, p. 6). Schemata expand as they encounter stimuli that fit into recognizable patterns. A change in the schemata may occur, however, when a child cannot assimilate an experience into the established structure. If the experience cannot be assimilated, then two alternatives are available to the child: (a) The insufficient schemata can be adjusted to accommodate the new material, or (b) a completely new structure can be established to accommodate the material.

The process of assimilation and accommodation (Piaget, 1969b) is the basis for cognitive growth and development that occurs during the life of the individual. Yet the process would be unworkable if the comparative quantities of assimilation and accommodation were not balanced. A person who assimilates everything would have too few schemata and be unable to differentiate experiences. Conversely, a person who accommodates experiences excessively would have too many schemata and would find too few commonalties to generalize to the broader world of experience. This balancing process is called *equilibration*. It is a process to which the engaging intellect is constantly drawn. Equilibrium must be sustained if the intellect is to develop effectively.

The Sensori-Motor Period

From birth through two years of age, children move through what Piaget (1969b) has called the sensori-motor period, which consists of six substages. During this period, children move from a period of simple reflexes to a period in which representation of unseen objects readily occurs. Within these first two years, children are restricted to immediate experience. Without any previous experience, children of this age group have no basis on which to build categories for organizing reality; rather, they experience events uninhibited through sight and feeling.

One of the most important events that a Stage 1 child experiences during the early months of life is the constant appearance and disappearance of familiar objects. From this activity, the child builds cognitive structures, such as object permanence, which are essential to continued mental development. Piaget (1969b) says that during the sensori-motor period,

> The system of sensori-motor schemes of assimilation culminates in
> a kind of logic of action involving the establishment of relation-

ships and correspondences and classification of schemes; in short, structures of ordering and assembling that constitute a substructure for the future operations of thought. But sensori-motor intelligence has an equally important result as regards the structuring of the subject's universe, however limited it may be at this practical level. It organizes reality by constructing the broad categories of action that are the schemes of the permanent object, space, time, and causality, substructures of the notions that will later correspond to them. (p. 13)

Adults who restrict or deny a child strong visual experiences during this period can cause deficits in the development of important cognitive structures. An environment filled with a variety of visual and reacting stimuli provides the most supportive conditions for developing a child's intellectual capabilities. An environment without appropriate stimuli can result in serious delays in a child's cognitive development that may not be easily corrected.

The Period of Preoperational Thought

The second stage of a child's development is called the period of pre-operational thought (Piaget, 1969b). To enter this stage, a child undergoes a major intellectual transformation. No longer restricted to their immediate environment, children expand on the use of the mental images that they began to develop during the previous stage. They quickly expand their capacity to store information, such as words and the implicit rules of language. During this period, children's application and understanding of vocabulary increase substantially. At two years of age, the average child can use a few hundred words, but by the age of five, that same child may be using over 2,000 words. This major advance in language capability is a distinguishing characteristic of intellectual development. Piaget (1969b) says this about the acquisition of language:

This has three consequences essential to mental development: (1) the possibility of verbal exchange with other persons, which heralds the onset of the socialization of action; (2) the internalization of words, i.e., the appearance of thought itself, supported by internal language and a system of signs; last and most important, (3) the internalization of action of such, which from now on, rather than being purely perceptual and motor as it has been, heretofore, can represent itself intuitively by means of pictures and "mental experiments" (p. 17).

The underlying mode of thought during Stage 2 is intuitive. During this period, children are experimenters, explorers, and imitators. They are unconcerned about the exactness of their pronouncements. Their use of sounds and language is often inventive and unique. Another aspect of speech during this period is that it is self-centered; children seem to be

talking "at" rather than "with" others. To stimulate their language growth, children need a verbally rich environment. Denying children the use of their language faculty can result in developmental delays that may be very difficult to correct.

Piaget (1969b) has observed that preoperational children's use of intuitive thinking often causes them to misinterpret reality. A child at this stage is generally unable to determine which container holds more water—a tall, narrow beaker or a short, wide one. Often a child's response to this problem is that the taller container holds more water simply because it appears so. According to Piaget, it would do no good to explain to a child at this stage why each container holds the same amount since the child is intellectually unable to process this information. Piaget also indicates that Stage 2 children have difficulties with reversible relationships. For example, Jennifer may understand that Matt is her brother, but she may not understand that she is Matt's sister. Regardless of its apparent lack of logic, the intuitive approach is powerful because it provides a way to learn language quickly and solve problems in imaginative ways.

The Period of Concrete Operations

The third stage of Piaget's (1969b) theory of child development is the period of concrete operations. Once again, children experience an intellectual revolution; progressing from the free-form thinking of the preoperational stage, they now logically examine the operative relationships among events, objects and people. Of operations during this period, Piaget says,

> The operations, such as the union of two classes or the addition of two numbers, are actions characterized by their very great generality since the acts of uniting, arranging in order, etc., enter into all coordinations of particular actions. They are also reversible (the opposite of uniting is separating, the opposite of adding is subtracting, etc.). Furthermore, they are never isolated but always capable of being coordinated into overall systems (for instance, a classification, the sequence of numbers, etc.). Finally they are not peculiar to a given individual; they are common to all individuals on the same mental level (pp. 96-97).

Unlike children in the intuitive state, Stage 3 children are not limited to understanding through perception. Children in concrete operations are able to focus their perceptions and to understand concrete transformations that events or objects undergo. They can now reverse operations. Communications also become less egocentric; children begin to talk with rather than at others. Language becomes functional and purposeful and begins to reflect the child's basic social nature. Piaget (1969b) also found that children in the concrete operations stage develop the cognitive abilities of seriation and classification. With this improvement, children's concepts of space, time, speed, and causality improve dramatically.

The development of logical operations and the associated capabilities of reversibility and classification allow children to solve problems more effectively and with more confidence than during the previous period. But the logic requires real and observable objects. Children at this stage still have great difficulty with verbal or hypothetical objects. Therefore, Stage 3 children are very literal-minded; they interpret situations concretely, failing to understand abstractions. Children presented with an abstract idea will convert the abstraction into a concrete event relevant to their experiences. A child will have a difficult time solving a problem presented in abstract verbal terms but will be able to apply logic to the same problem if it is presented in the form of real, observable objects.

During this period, children express a strong tendency to organize and apply strict rules to activities they undertake. The concrete operational child is often more concerned with establishing rules for an activity than with the activity itself. Working out the functional relationship among various elements in an activity is a focal point during the third stage of development. Once children establish relationships and rules for action, they have a particularly difficult time modifying their ideas during this period. They see things distinctly—things are or they are not; subtleties or shades of gray are not acceptable. Altering the rules of a game is a difficult undertaking for children in this category of intellectual development.

Unless children who are operating concretely are offered direct experiences, preferably hands-on, their learning will be inefficient. To support cognitive growth during this time, practical skills such as such as organizing, constructing, classifying, sorting, counting, and arranging should be taught.

The Period of Formal Operations

According to Piaget (1969b) formal operations is the fourth and final stage of intellectual development. During this period, the adolescent's cognitive structures mature to the adult level. Piaget predicts that no additional structural improvements will occur beyond the period of formal operations, although the efficiency and reach of those structures can be expected to improve during the course of adulthood.

> The great novelty of this stage is that by means of a differentiation of form and content the subject becomes capable of reasoning correctly about propositions he does not believe, or at least not yet; that is propositions that he considers pure hypotheses. He becomes capable of drawing the necessary conclusions from truths that are merely possible, which constitutes the beginning of hypothetical-deductive or formal thought (p. 132).

Logical operations, the onset of which began during the concrete operational period, are brought to their full development during Stage 4. This final period of cognitive development allows a considerably broader range

of logical applications to problem solving than the previous period did. During the period of concrete operations, a child was limited to applying logic to the solution of tangible problems as they occurred; he or she did not permit projection into the future or consideration of hypothetical situations. The child who has achieved formal operations, however, has the capacity to engage all categories and classes of problems. The verbal abstraction, the hypothetical, and consideration of past and future conditions are all subject to the power of the logic of formal operations.

The adolescent operating in formal operations can employ several strategies simultaneously in solving problems. Understanding the concept of causation, using scientific reasoning to approach a problem, and building and testing hypotheses are all hallmarks of the fourth stage of Piaget's theory. In addition, adolescents are able to consider problems involving a combination of several variables rather than focusing on one aspect of a problem as they did during the concrete period. They are also able to undertake complex verbal problems. Problems involving proportion and conservation of movement can also be solved with their advanced logic.

For the first time, a child can separate personal perception from objective reality. The result is the ability to evaluate a logical argument separate from its content. The child in concrete operations was restricted to dealing with the world according to personal perception; thus, a child would be unable to consider a problem involving yellow snow, for example. The more advanced child, however, is able to deal with such a hypothetical condition and, in fact, derive a logical and valid argument not dependent on the observable reality of white snow. As in the previous stages of development, formal operations evolve as a direct result of those intellectual abilities developed in preceding stages. With the transformations that occur from one stage to another, cognitive structures are continuously subject to structural changes. The assimilation, accommodation, and equilibration processes are constantly at work from the sensori-motor period through the period of formal operations.

Cognitive Theory and Block Instruction

According to cognitive theory, children's development is marked by periods when they are particularly sensitive and responsive to outside influences. However, children are not blank slates on which teachers compose whatever they desire. Children, who have inherent dispositions and tendencies and are subject to their external environments, develop and grow intellectually in an invariable sequence form birth through adolescence and beyond. To teach effectively, teachers should be aware of the materials and approaches most appropriate for a child's readiness to learn. Cognitive theory provides insights and guidance into these issues.

Piaget (1969b) suggested that children's cognitive structures should be carefully considered when presenting instructional materials. According to Piaget, intellectual capabilities are not set at birth; they are ultimately dependent on the appropriateness of the activities and the environment in

which a child develops. In preparing their lessons, teachers should pay close attention to the children's intellectual stages so that they can develop activities that stimulate cognitive development. If teachers do not consider the children's cognitive structure, the classroom experience will be less effective than it could be. A carefully tailored classroom experience produces cognitive growth and a successful child.

We tend to think that accelerating intellectual growth is always a positive step and one that teachers should pursue. However, attempting to push children beyond the level they are currently experiencing may serve only to frustrate a child. Children's intellectual accomplishments can be strengthened within each period of development. This improves a child's intellectual capacity and broadens the foundation for future growth. Expanding on learning opportunities that are relevant to each child's cognitive level improves learning conditions in the classroom by minimizing frustrating conditions for children.

■ PERSONALITY DEVELOPMENT

The development of personality coincides with physical and intellectual developments. Discussing the personal-psychological character of development helps us achieve greater depth in our understanding of the total child. The development of personality follows a sequence of interdependent periods that generally correspond to the stages of cognitive development. Satisfaction of needs during one stage determines the child's ability to progress to the next stage. When needs are not met, children have difficulty making the transition to the following stage and may be delayed or even prevented from continuing their personal advance to more mature stages of development.

As Jean Piaget's theories describe the area of cognitive development, Erik Erikson's (1980) ideas have become the basis for much of our understanding of personality development in children and adolescents. (See Table 3.2 for a comparison of Piaget's cognitive stages and Erikson's personality stages.) Erikson's (1980) ideas about human development arose out of his work in Freudian psychology. Sigmund Freud, originator of the concepts of the id, the ego, and the superego, believed that to understand adult personality and behavior, the experiences and relationships the adult had as a child must be analyzed. Within these experiences and relationships, Freud saw the basis for later emotional development. As the psychologist investigated child and adult behavior, he recognized that children and adults move through a series of emotional stages from birth to adulthood. Freud described five such stages: (a) the oral stage, from birth to 18 months; (b) the anal stage, from 18 months to three years; (c) the phallic stage, from three to seven years; (d) the period of latency, from seven to 12 years; and (e) the genital period, from age 12 through adulthood.

Table 3.2. A Comparison of Piaget and Erikson

Piaget's Cognitive Stages	Age and Erikson's Personality Stages	
	Ages 13 – 18	Identity vs. Diffusion
	Age 12	Industry vs. Inferiority
Concrete Operations	Ages 8 – 11	Industry vs. Inferiority
Preoperational	Age 7	Industry vs. Inferiority
	Ages 4 – 6	Inferiority vs. Guilt
	Age 3	Autonomy vs. Shame
Sensori-Motor	Age 2	Autonomy vs. Shame
	Age 1.5	Formal Operations
	Birth – 18 months	Trust vs. Mistrust

Freud found that as children undergo this sequence of emotional transformation, their experiences have a profound effect on the formation of adult personality. Specific areas of personality that are particularly vulnerable to alteration define these transformative periods. Based on these periods of change, Erikson (1980) developed eight stages that further define the contents and mechanisms operating in the maturing human being. In this section, the first five stages, from birth through adolescence, will be examined (see Table 3.3). For a comparison with Piaget's stages of cognitive development and Freud's stages of emotional development see Table 3.4.

Erikson's Stages of Personality Development

The first of Erikson's (1980) stages is concerned with the development of trust and mistrust. Erikson has defined trust as "what is commonly implied in reasonable trustfulness as far as others are concerned." He defines mistrust as characterizing "individuals who withdraw into themselves in particular ways when they are at odds with themselves or with others" (pp. 57-58). The stage of *trust versus mistrust* occurs during the infant stage, from birth to 18 months. Erikson has determined that during this time children develop varying degrees of trust and mistrust. To successfully establish a solid foundation on which to build a balanced personality, he believes that parents must provide a highly supportive and nurturing environment. The quality of attention and degree to which a parent attends to a child during this period will have a profound effect on the degree to which the maturing child expresses trust and dependability. When parents provide consistent care and affection during interactive periods, a child will be prepared to begin the next level of personal development successfully.

During the second stage of Erikson's (1980) theory, which he called the period of *autonomy versus shame and doubt*, children continue their emotional development. Between the age of 18 months and three years, chil-

Table 3.3. Birth Through Adolescence According to Erikson

Stage of Development	Approximate Age	Characteristics
V. Identity vs. Identity Diffusion	12 to 18	• Uses logic to solve hypothetical problems • Undergoes significant body system alterations, resulting in reproductive capability • Decisions made on objective evidence • Ideas of others considered less egocentrically • Capable of empathy • Need to improve things • Requires responsibility for growth
IV. Industry vs. Inferiority	6 to 12	• Focus turns to friends and school • Form social alliances reflecting growing interest in other people and in things outside family • Important to encourage children to actively explore the world, to test themselves, and to work hard to achieve goals
III. Initiative vs. Guilt	3 to 6	• Begin to explore sexual identity and identify with appropriate male and female models • Important to reinforce identity at this point, to establish a sense of self
II. Autonomy vs. Shame	18 months to 3 years	• Conflicted by attempts to gain a degree of independence and competence • Begin to express a strong sense of self • Intensely investigates environment • Should be encouraged to express themselves verbally
I. Trust vs. Mistrust	Birth to 18 months	• Develop varying degrees of trust and mistrust • Parents must provide supportive and nurturing environment • Quality of care has profound effect on the degree to which the maturing child expresses trust and dependability

Table 3.4. A Comparison of Freud and Erikson

Ages	Freud	Erikson
12 to 18 years	Genital	Identity-Identity Diffusion
7 to 12 years	Latency	Industry-Inferiority
3 to 7 years	Phallic	Initiative-Guilt
18 months to 3 years	Anal	Autonomy-Shame
Birth to 18 months	Oral	Trust-Mistrust

dren experience the conflict created by their attempts to gain a degree of competence and independence from their parents. Erikson describes the significance of this period:

> The overall significance of this stage lies in the maturation of the muscle system, the consequent ability (and doubly felt inability) to coordinate a number of highly conflicting action patterns such as "holding on" and "letting go," and the enormous value with which the still highly dependent child begins to endow his autonomous will. (p. 68)

While seeking independence, children begin to express a strong sense of self and engage in a period of intense investigation of their environment. At this stage, adults who prevent a child from fully developing personal autonomy can easily frustrate him or her. Therefore, adults at this stage should support a child's attempts to explore the world. Also at this time, children will begin to express themselves verbally. As noted in the discussion on cognitive development, vocabulary increases dramatically during this period; much practice is required to accomplish this. To increase the probability of success during this stage of development, children should be encouraged to express themselves verbally. Constantly correcting word pronunciations and grammatical forms will often hinder a child's development. Rather than inhibiting a child at this time by overcorrection, Erikson (1980) suggests that adults model the speech desired. Accordingly, adults should avoid speaking in unnatural ways, such as baby talk, which will only confuse a child's efforts.

There is a clear relationship between the way parents behave during this period and a child's self-confidence and sense of autonomy. The most productive patterns are those in which parents provide an imaginative environment that stimulates speech and exploration. Supportive parents constantly involve their children in stimulating activities during which they question and elicit a child's ideas. This indirect form of teaching, in combination with the experience of self-initiative, establishes the basis for a child's feeling of competence. As children learn independence and begin to see themselves as active and effective participants in the management of

their environment, they establish a strong foundation on which to build a healthy and maturing personality.

Unfortunately, a child will not always successfully navigate through the demands of this period. Sometimes children develop a sense of shame because of their failure to develop independence effectively. When parents or other adults fail to provide stimulating experiences, restrict activity too narrowly, ignore the need for attention and love, and deny or harshly criticize expression, children will not advance and may be prevented from developing a productive and well-balanced personality. Their sense of shame will limit their ability to engage life directly and confidently.

The third stage of Erikson's (1980) theory is concerned with *initiative versus guilt*. Children develop these personal characteristics during the third through sixth years. This period especially affects a child's gender identity. While in the previous stage of development children generally began to explore sexual identity, they now begin to identify with appropriate male and female models and behave in accordance with what they see. It is especially important to reinforce their sexual identity at this point so that they will establish the sense of self needed to successfully advance to the next stage of development.

Children naturally possess feelings of inferiority at this time. To avoid establishing a sense of guilt about their desires and inabilities, they should be assured that they will eventually be able to do what they see adults doing. Taking personal initiative is inherently connected to children's personal identity and overcoming this sense of inferiority. According to Erikson (1980), a child possesses the capacity to overcome the difficulties of this stage as the child

> (1) learns to move around more freely and more violently and therefore establishes a wider and, so it seems to him, an unlimited radius of goal; [as] (2) his sense of language becomes perfected to the point where he understands and can ask about many things just enough to misunderstand them thoroughly; and (3)[as] both language and locomotion permit him to expand his imagination over so many things that he cannot avoid frightening himself with what he himself dreamed and thought up. (p. 78)

When children have been successfully weaned of their sole reliance on adults for meeting their needs, adults will have been successful in supporting them in the development of their personal identities. As children express independence by effectively meeting the demands of various situations, they develop greater confidence in their own competence and enhance their growing sense of self.

During Erikson's (1980) fourth stage, *industry versus inferiority* are the primary issues. From approximately six until 12 years of age, children turn away from their focus on parents to a more generalized focus on the world in which they find themselves, most notably with friends and at school. During this period, children learn to communicate with others in an

increasingly less ego-centered approach. By behaving in this manner, children free themselves from the isolation and control related to their total dependence on parents. They become more socially oriented, forming social alliances that reflect their growing interests in other people and in things outside their family and home. During this time, they exert enormous amounts of energy trying to perfect their skills in dealing with the demands of the world. Erikson describes the focus of this period:

> While all children need their hours and days of make-believe in games, they all, sooner or later, become dissatisfied and disgruntled without a sense of being useful, without a sense of being able to make things and make them well and even perfectly: this is what I call a sense of industry. Without this, the best-entertained child soon acts exploited. It is as if he knows and his society knows that now that he is psychologically a parent, he must begin to be somewhat of a worker and potential provider before becoming a biological parent. . . . As he once untiringly strove to walk well and to throw things away well, he now wants to make things well. He develops the pleasure of work completion by steady attention and preserving diligence. (p. 91)

During this period of developing greater self-sufficiency and independence, children are particularly stable emotionally. Also during this period, children experience the concrete operational period, when the world is seen as stable and predictable and shades of gray are unwelcome intrusions into their ideas about the world. As children learn new social, practical, and academic skills, they enhance their sense of industry. When they fail to do so, they develop a sense of inferiority that further limits their ability to develop personal competence. At this time, it is important to encourage children to actively engage the world, to explore and test themselves, and to work hard to achieve goals. With success comes the knowledge that their efforts have results. Children who fail to develop a sense of industry based on their skills in achieving goals will not achieve independence. Their sense of inferiority will diminish their capacity to meet the demands of the world.

Development of industry during this period occurs to a large extent where children spend most of their active time—in school and among friends. The experience in school is particularly important to children's development of self-confidence and skill mastery. Within the classroom, children can be given the opportunity to learn many new skills that will result in a growing ability to solve problems competently. With this accomplishment, the promise of adulthood made in an earlier age comes closer to reality.

The final period of personal development relevant to this topic occurs between the ages of 12 and 18 years. According to Erikson (1980), the formation of *identity*, or the failure of that formation, which he calls *identity diffusion*, is the main issue of the adolescent age. During this period, chil-

dren undergo their most tumultuous changes, often causing them to behave in aggressive, confused, and unpredictable ways. It is a time of significant body system alterations that result in physically mature individuals capable of reproduction. But it is also a time when they begin to see the contradictions of the world more clearly, further increasing their emotional instability.

> But in puberty and adolescence all sameness and continuities relied on earlier are questioned again because of a rapidity of body growth, which equals that of early childhood, and because of the entirely new addition of physical genital maturity. The growing and developing young people, faced with the psychological revolution within them, are now primarily concerned with attempts at consolidating their social roles. . . . In their search for a new sense of continuity and sameness, some adolescents have to re-fight many of the crises of earlier years, and they are never ready to install lasting idols and ideals as guardians of a final identity. (p. 94)

Cognitively, adolescents leave the world of predictability where right and wrong are certain and where their skills have an immediate and direct effect on the environment in which they operate. As adolescents they begin to evaluate conditions, comparing what they see with what might be. They begin to separate the world around them from their own desires and perceptions. Objective reality begins to assert itself in the adolescent mind. They begin to understand and use metaphorical descriptions. The advancing adolescent considers the ideas and positions of others less egocentrically. They sometimes are able to put themselves in another's position, developing empathy and a need to change things.

Alternatively, with greater uncertainty and a heightened sense of self, children become particularly self-conscious as they advance into adolescence. In this state, they try to fit in by conforming to peer groups. They can be excessively egotistic, demand attention, and look for as many ways to conform as is possible. Their world becomes relativistic, where behavior is tested against rationalizations of their own and of their peers. Where they previously conformed to authorities' wishes, they may now rebel.

The effect of this change and uncertainty leads to an adolescent identity crisis. The successful evolution of personality during this period depends on the adolescent's ability to meet the demands of this stage of personal development successfully. If an adolescent overcomes the difficulties associated with this period, it is likely that he or she will have established a strong foundation for advancement into adulthood. If, on the other hand, a person has succumbed to these conflicts, the personality will not solidify. Instead, it will remain uncertain, diffuse, and alienated with little sense of purpose or satisfaction. To avoid this failure, Erikson (1980) strongly suggests that adolescents be given every opportunity to develop a sense of responsibility for themselves and others. Real, self-directed

experience, working to meet the needs of others, and satisfying the demands of society will help an adolescent to develop purpose and a strong identity on which to build a mature adulthood.

Implications of Erikson's Theory for Block Instruction

It is important to stress that a knowledge of the theories presented in this chapter is necessary for all teachers, regardless of the schedule their school uses. However, we now focus on these theories as applied specifically to block instruction. The scope of Erikson's theory permits us to see the needs and potential problems experienced by all children in their development toward adulthood. Each stage of development requires that adults provide the necessary environment and tools for children to succeed in overcoming the obstacles of the period in which they are operating. Children's behaviors and abilities expressed at each stage of development depend on the degree to which they successfully managed the issues of the preceding stage. If children fail to overcome difficulties or to learn the skills necessary to fulfill their growing responsibilities at any stage, problems will be compounded in each successive stage. It is important to make certain our instructional effort is effective and our knowledge and sensitivity to the transformations of childhood are substantial.

When Erikson's ideas about personality development are considered in conjunction with Piaget's theories about intellectual transformation, teachers have at their disposal a powerful perspective from which to view the conditions of childhood and adolescence. Teachers should evaluate their students from this theoretical perspective to determine children's readiness to learn. Teachers will have success in the classroom when they apply these ideas effectively. Dealing with a child's intellectual capacity as if it exists in isolation, separate from a child's personality, will not lead to effective instruction. This means that block teachers must consider the entire child, the cognitive and affective domains, and how to best use time when delivering instruction. All this must be kept in consideration if the faculty is going to build an effective culture for block scheduling. While blocking can positively affect the teacher, and that is important, we must keep our focus on the student.

Please visit www.blockscheduling.com to review and download additional materials about developmentally-appropriate procedures to use with varied age groups in extended periods of time.

FOUR

Building the Block Culture in the School

Increasingly, as more schools have moved to the block, a distinct culture has developed. For schools to be successful on the block today, the faculty must accept a change in the culture of the school. This cultural transformation is more than a simple change in when the bells ring. The block culture allows for a school environment in which teachers and students have greater freedom in the instructional process. This means that in addition to faculty members, students and parents have to be willing to accept change. But although student and parent input and concerns should receive great attention, those of us involved with the block for 10 years or more know that the ultimate key to a successful conversion is the classroom teacher; teachers make or break this transformation.

For schools on a traditional schedule that are planning to look at block models, principals can start by conducting a survey during a faculty meeting. Along with the survey, a simple discussion of present school needs can elicit the level of interest needed to change perceptions about the block. Many teachers have misconceptions about the block, so it is imperative to begin research on scheduling methods and have solid answers for any inquiries. The top five perceptions that traditional teachers state as advantages and disadvantages about the block include are these:

Advantages

1. Time to complete activities in one period

2. Fewer subjects for students at any one time

3. Increased planning time for faculty on a daily basis

4. Greater opportunity to practice effective teaching strategies

5. Time for review, teaching, and practice

Disadvantages

1. Limited staff development during the initial stages of implementation

2. Motivating students and keeping their attention for an extended period of time

3. Teachers being unwilling or unable to change instructional strategies

4. Possible larger gaps of time between sequential courses

5. Fear of not enough time to cover the complete course content

Once the decision is made to move to the block, it is imperative that the block culture in the school maintain faculty confidence. School leaders must ensure faculty members that the change process will be deliberate and will progress cautiously. The school should not move hastily into a block schedule without proper training of faculty and staff. Collecting research, visiting schools, and completing appropriate training take one to two years. During these planning years, various opportunities for training should include mastering a minimum of six major instructional strategies. Some strategies include synectics, cooperative learning, case method, inquiry, and concept attainment. (See Part III of this text for more in-depth coverage of instructional strategies.) In addition, the planning years should be spent realigning curriculum for instructional pacing.

Communication is essential. Positive communication among teachers helps to build confidence in block scheduling. Experienced teachers can help newer teachers work in teams in harmony. In addition, committees can be a vital tool in maintaining effective communication and monitoring success. They can also serve to keep the administration aware of developing activities and concerns. Maintaining effective communication should include frequent classroom visits and encouragement by the principal. Each faculty meeting should include a period of time allocated for talk on block scheduling success stories and problem issues.

When monitoring the implemented block schedule, lead teachers and school administrators should search for improved instructional techniques and successful classroom experiences. They should also monitor the degree to which test scores are affected and the extent to which students are adjusting. It is important to keep students involved and to know

their feelings about the block and their classes. A survey of the students as well as the parents is a good way to learn about their feelings concerning the block schedule.

In the unfortunate event that the administration requires a unilateral move to the block or fails to seek faculty support, teachers may feel under-valued, angry, and adversarial. Resenting the change, teachers will not benefit from the philosophy of block scheduling as a reform tool. Reassuring teachers that the cultural change to the block will be completed in an appropriately paced and orderly fashion can help eliminate their insecurity. Many teachers retain a degree of wariness of the unknown. This is usually mild and will subside with periods of success. In more severe cases, teachers who have major reservations, but who have agreed to make the change, must be given special attention and greater reassurance.

Visit my website for interactive discussion on how to build or improve culture in your school. See how others have done it.

FIVE

Selecting
the Best Fit

Currently, there are several organizational methods of block scheduling. These methods are divided into three types: the 4x4 block schedule, the A/B block schedule, and modified block schedule.

THE 4 X 4 BLOCK SCHEDULE MODEL ■

Classes in the 4x4 model of block scheduling are taught in longer periods of approximately 90 minutes and meet for only a part of the school year, usually one semester (see Table 5.1). The 4x4 model is also known as the semester, or accelerated schedule, because only four courses are taught per semester. Students have the opportunity to take eight different classes in one academic year. Teachers teach three classes per semester and use the fourth period of their day for planning, which is an advantage for teachers. "Educators have always been concerned about having enough time to complete the course content. Because of that, they found themselves looking for ways to change the traditional six- or seven-period day" (Queen, Algozzine, & Eaddy, 1997, p. 251).

Unlike the A/B schedule, the 4x4 model further limits the focus of students to four classes per semester so that there are fewer homework assignments, quizzes, and tests. This allows for concentration on new topics and time for mastery. Students also have the opportunity to repeat

Table 5.1. The 4×4 Block Schedule

Class Period (90-minutes)	First Semester	Second Semester
1st period	Biology	Algebra 1
2nd period	Chorus	Health/Physical Education
LUNCH	LUNCH	LUNCH
3rd period	ELP	English 1
4th period	Freshman Seminar	French II

failed classes within the same year and still graduate on time, which is an incentive to remain in school. Where applicable, many students opt for advanced study on and off campus since greater freedom is possible within the 4x4 block. For teachers, the 4x4 block reduces the preparation to three classes having a total of between 50 to 90 students, depending on the size of the school. Planning must involve more than preparing the usual lecture. Various instructional strategies that meet individual learning styles, alternative assessments, and integration of content should be planned for students. Lunch periods in smaller schools have sometimes been reduced to a single 45-minute period that serves for club meetings, teachers' office hours, detention, transfer student remediation, and general remediation.

The 4x4-scheduling model does, however, raise questions about the ability of students to retain information over the long periods of time that may occur between courses. It is possible for a student to finish Algebra I in the fall of his or her 9th-grade year and then take the next math class in the spring of the 10th-grade year. Although it is advisable to take sequential building courses as closely together as possible, teachers on the 4x4 block have not noticed any great difference between students who had recently finished a prerequisite course and students who finished the same course some time earlier.

■ THE A/B BLOCK SCHEDULE MODEL

Alternative day schedules or A/B block schedules alternate periods within the day or week. The classes usually meet every other day for extended blocks of time or a combination of alternating blocks and shortened classes taught every day for the entire year. Other modifications may be made to the A/B model by doubling a blocked class so that "A" days are Monday and Tuesday, followed by "B" days on Wednesday and Thursday. Fridays are rotated each week between "A" and "B" courses (see Table 5.2). Problems may arise with the A/B schedule; because the course load for students is not focused on four courses at a time, the students are enrolled in eight courses for an entire year. Many students have also expressed confusion as to keeping up with whether a day is "A" or "B."

Table 5.2. The A/B Block Design

"A" Day MONDAY	*"B" Day* TUESDAY	*"A" Day* WEDNESDAY	*"B" Day* THURSDAY	*"A" Day* FRIDAY	*"B" Day* MONDAY
Course 1 Language Arts	Course 5 Spanish 1	Course 1 Language Arts	Course 5 Spanish 1	Course 1 Language Arts	Course 5 Spanish 1
Course 2 Introduction to Computers	Course 6 Math	Course 2 Introduction to Computers	Course 6 Math	Course 2 Introduction to Computers	Course 6 Math
Lunch	Lunch	Lunch	Lunch	Lunch	Lunch
Course 3 Science	Course 7 Social Studies	Course 3 Science	Course 7 Social Studies	Course 3 Science	Course 7 Social Studies
Course 4 Health/P.E.	Course 8 Band	Course 4 Health/P.E.	Course 8 Band	Course 4 Health/P.E.	Course 8 Band

THE MODIFIED BLOCK ◼

In the modified block, classes arranged in differing lengths of time during a quarter, semester, or year might be found in many schools throughout the country. The modified block offers students the opportunity of taking a variety of classes ranging in periods of 30 to 180 minutes in length. For example, if classes are typically 90 minutes in length on a particular block schedule, one period of the day may be modified by dividing it into two 45-minute sections, allowing students to take an additional course (see Table 5.3). Carroll (1990) asserted that every high school in the nation could increase course offerings and reduce the total number of students with whom a teacher works each day by more than half. Seminars dealing with complex issues can be offered with greater flexibility for a more productive instructional environment. This flexibility is the strength of the modified block schedule. From my experience of working with schools throughout the United States, I find that there really are few pure 4x4 or A/B models used. Most schools have modified a grade level, subject area, or both to accommodate their students and provide the best fit for their schools.

In 1994, Carroll reported his findings from a study of eight high schools that used a type of modern, block plan known as the Copernican Plan. His findings included improved student attendance, a decrease in suspensions, reductions in dropout rates, greater content mastery seen in higher grades and credits earned, and a favorable rating for the Copernican Plan compared with the traditional schedule. With these approaches becoming more widely used, educators began pushing for and rushing to the block. After high school teachers learned the value and benefits of the block, middle school educators raised the banner for block scheduling in their schools.

Register your opinions about the best type of block scheduling. Go to my website, under "Block Scheduling Handbook" and select the button for THE BEST FIT. Share stories about your successes with a particular model. Talk with other teachers around the United States and other countries about block scheduling models.

Table 5.3. The Modified Block Schedule

Class Period (90 minutes)	First Semester	Second Semester
1st period	Biology	Algebra 1
2nd period	Chorus	U. S. History
LUNCH	LUNCH	LUNCH
3rd period	English 1	English 2
4th period	Band (45 minutes)	Band (45 minutes)
	P.E. (45 minutes)	Art (45 minutes)

SIX

Block Scheduling in the Middle School

THE MIDDLE SCHOOL DEFINED ■

There is really no established or set definition for the middle school. Typically, school systems place Grades 6, 7, and 8 in the middle schools. Nevertheless, the main purpose behind the middle school movement is to recognize that early adolescence is a distinct stage in development. The task for middle schools is to protect, nurture, counsel, and teach the individuals at this unique stage of life (Farmer, Gould, Herring, Linn, & Theobold, 1995). Many educators believe there are five to seven program characteristics that make the middle school unique. The more characteristics or concepts that are present, the greater the chance that the purpose of the middle school can be achieved.

The characteristics of the middle school are usually described in programmatic terms such as:

Team teaching/interdisciplinary teaching

Block classes or periods

Advisor program/advisor/teacher or student mentor

Exploratory studies/ electives

Interactive instructional strategies

Basic subjects or core curriculum

Effective transitions

While all of these characteristics are important in their various forms, I am focusing on the first three in this chapter. Instructional strategies will be discussed in detail in later chapters. (Queen, 2002; Rettig & Canady, 2000; DiBiase & Queen, 1999; Russell, 1997; Farmer et al., 1995; George & Alexander, 1993).

■ CHARACTERISTICS OF THE MIDDLE SCHOOL

Team Teaching/Interdisciplinary Teaming

The grouping of students and teachers is an important characteristic of the middle school concept. One of the most important grouping concepts is interdisciplinary teaming. Students are organized into heterogeneous teams of 70 to 150 students (Farmer et al., 1995). It is important to note that they are not grouped by ability, race, sex, or any other specific characteristic. The teams can be established by grade level or they can be multiage. Multiage grouping allows students to stay on the same team with the same teachers throughout their middle school years (McClure, 1998). The teaming approach allows teachers to meet the individual student's needs by providing a variety of groupings within their teams.

Two to five teachers are usually organized in areas of math, science, social studies, and language arts. In this professional collaboration, teachers are involved in an interactive process that brings staff members together to make decisions (Gable & Manning, 1997). The teaming approach allows for better communication and understanding among the disciplines. There are also nonacademic benefits to interdisciplinary teaming. For example, teachers can better deal with discipline issues when they work together on a regular basis. Students tend to be more comfortable discussing problems or asking for advice because they interact with fewer teachers. Consequently, teachers are better able to serve the needs of those students.

Block Classes or Periods

One of the most important concepts in middle school is the schedule. The schedule serves many functions. According to Rettig and Canady (2000), the schedule

provides a more reasonable workload for teachers and students . . . determines the number of student/grades/records for which a teacher must be responsible. . . can reduce how frequently students and teacher teams change classes . . . determines how many teachers a student must interact with on any given day/term/year

. . .[and] can fundamentally affect the relationship among staff and between staff and students. (pp. 6-7)

Although the schedule is a critical component for middle school, it must not be allowed to dominate and must still be flexible enough to meet the students' needs.

Interdisciplinary teams cannot use the traditional schedule if they truly want to meet the needs of the adolescent student. With a block scheduling approach, the academic courses are scheduled within a large block of time, and other subjects, such as art, music, drama, physical education, and foreign language, are scheduled during shorter time periods. These other subjects are designed to be, and should remain, exploratory in nature. The focus of the schedule should be on the core academics.

Block scheduling in the middle school setting offers many advantages. For example, teachers have a common planning time for team collaboration and conferencing. The interdisciplinary teams have the flexibility to schedule classes to meet student needs. Other advantages to consider are that teachers can team teach in any given subject area, can more easily integrate the disciplines, and can more easily schedule field trips, speakers, and community projects (Farmer et al., 1995).

There are many block scheduling models for the middle school. Some use variations of the 4x4 or A/B designs used by the high schools. Rettig and Canady (2000) recommend a simple procedure that allows each interdisciplinary team to create its own schedule for the school year. First, the specific number of time modules needs to be determined. The schedule of events that occur outside "team time" must be plugged in. These events include lunch and exploratory time slots for specific teams (Rettig & Canady, 2000). It has also been recommended that once the core subjects are plugged in, the academic courses rotate. This prevents a course from meeting exclusively in the early morning or late afternoon (Rettig & Canady, 2000).

Advisory Programs

One of the most important characteristics of the middle school concept is the adviser/advisee program. The program developed from a commitment to meet the needs of the adolescent student. One teacher works with a small group of students—typically, between 20 and 30. All teachers, including art, physical education, and life skills teachers have a group of students as advisees. Every student needs to have a positive relationship with at least one adult in the school. This is such an important concept that time is provided for advisement daily. Students are provided with an "adult advocate" who knows each one personally and can help in making responsible choices.

Student academic progress is monitored on a regular basis, and parents are contacted to provide information about the student's progress. When teachers take this responsibility seriously, students have someone in the

school with whom they can talk and who can arrange help for them, both of which help to prevent student problems (Farmer et al., 1995).

Benefits of the Block Schedule in the Middle School

DiBiase and Queen (1999) believe that the middle school is prime for gaining the benefits of the block. In the middle school model, block-scheduled classes involve blocking math/science and language arts/social studies with the expectation that instructional time within the blocks be adjusted as needed. However, any additional time provided to one of the paired subjects is at the expense of the other.

Many reform documents recommend lengthening the amount of time that middle grades students spend in a learning environment. In its report *Turning Points: Preparing American Youth for the 21st Century*, the Carnegie Council on Adolescent Development (1989) cautioned against limiting classes to 40 or 50 minutes and emphasized the need for concentrated time blocks of learning: "Students need time to learn and teachers should be able to create blocks of time for instruction that best meets the needs of students, responds to curriculum priorities, and capitalizes on learning opportunities such as current events" (p. 52). Furthermore, the report asserts that for most adolescents, the shift from elementary to junior high or middle school means moving from a small neighborhood school and the stability of one primary classroom to a much larger, more impersonal institution. In this new setting, teachers and classmates will change as many as six or seven times a day. This constant shifting creates formidable barriers to the formation of stable peer groups and close, supporting relationships with caring adults. The chances that young people will feel lost are enormous (Hackmann, 1995).

Time management is usually perceived as the most important tool that administrators use in scheduling the school day. Time management, however, is not the only concern that educators have in developing a successful schedule. A continual search for the best way to meet the needs of all students remains a primary focus. Block scheduling makes time more than just a tool. As such, block scheduling provides choices and various alternative means to address key factors in middle schools today. In addition, block or flexible schedules can be configured to meet any middle school's physical plant, student management, accountability, assessment, instructional, and fiscal needs. As such, block scheduling plays an integral role in helping define the school's climate.

■ SHORTFALLS OF THE TRADITIONAL SCHEDULE

Traditionally-scheduled middle schools are generally organized around six to eight daily periods of instruction. The length of these periods ranges anywhere from 40 to 55 minutes, with three to five minutes for changing classes. In these short instructional periods, course content rather than the

students' learning needs becomes the teachers' focus. Middle grade students find themselves overwhelmed by six to eight different teachers, a disjointed curriculum, several sets of class rules, multiple homework assignments, and stacks of books. The typical day for a middle school student with this type of schedule consists of several different classes, an advisory period, and lunch—all in different locations—in a six-and-a-half-hour day. Students are expected to accumulate fragments of information and are tested on how well they can memorize details and facts. This is not a schedule that fosters reflection (Carroll, 1990).

Not only do the students languish in the 40- to 55-minute period, teachers are limited in the types of instructional strategies they are able to use. Just as in the high school, lecture is the most efficient way to expose students to a large amount of information in a short time frame. Highly effective teaching strategies such as cooperative learning, exploration, concept attainment, inquiry, role-playing, and simulations are difficult to implement in a span of 20 to 35 minutes (Canady & Rettig, 1995a). In addition, a six- to eight-period day promotes isolation of teachers and works against teaming, a practice that is integral for effective middle school instruction. Also, short periods favor the compartmentalization of knowledge rather than an integration of the curriculum. Teachers are unable to get to know their students as individuals because a great deal of their daily energy is spent monitoring student movement through the halls up to eight or nine times a day, recording attendance in as many as eight classes, and recording grades for as many as 150 or more students (Miller, 1997). As the student population increases in diversity, teachers must struggle to meet the emotional and academic needs of heterogeneous classes in which they may not have time for either effective instruction or authentic assessment.

THE FLEXIBLE/ALTERNATE/NAVIGATE (FAN) MODELS   ■

Queen's flexible/alernative/navigate (FAN) block models, particularly the 3x2 FAN, are the most effective block schedules to implement at the middle school level. The 4x4 and the A/B block are better suited to meet the teaching and learning needs at the high school level. The 3x2 and related modified models of block schedules meet the needs of middle grades learners. In the FAN models, classes meet either every day or every other day. The master schedule includes an advisory and a combination of core and elective classes. Classes meet for either extended or shortened blocks of time. Classes are taught on a yearly or semester basis. Teachers teach four or five periods per day and use the remaining period(s) for both individual and/or team planning. Students carry anywhere from five to six classes. Table 6.1 depicts the basic framework of the 3x2 model. By way of example, the scheduling of science and social studies is highlighted.

In the basic 3x2 schedule, three classes meet in 90-minute blocks (Blocks A, B, & C) and two classes meet for 45-minutes a day (Block D).

Table 6.1. The 3×2 Model

A. The Basic Schedule

	Monday	*Tuesday*	*Wednesday*	*Thursday*	*Friday*
90 min.	**Block A** Language Arts	**Block A**	**Block A**	**Block A**	**Block A**
90 min.	**Block B** Mathematics	**Block B**	**Block B**	**Block B**	**Block B**
90 min.	**Block C** Science/ Social Studies	**Block C**	**Block C**	**Block C**	**Block C**
(90 min.) 45 min. 45 min.	**Block D** Elective Elective	**Block D**	**Block D**	**Block D**	**Block D**
	Advisory	Advisory	Advisory	Advisory	Advisory

B. Science/Social Studies: Alternate Days

Block D Week 1	Social Studies	Science	Social Studies	Science	Social Studies
Block D Week 2	Social Studies	Science	Science	Social Studies	Social Studies

C. Science/Social Studies: Semester

Block D Semester 1	Social Studies	Social Studies	Social Studies	Social Studies	Social Studies
Block D Semester 2	Science	Science	Science	Science	Science

Classes can meet every day or alternate on an A/B schedule. In the A/B configuration, Monday and Wednesday are "A" days and Tuesday and Thursday are designated "B" days. Fridays can rotate each week between "A" and "B" courses or contain a shortened schedule during which all classes meet. Blocks A through C meet for the whole year, whereas the classes in Block D can meet on either a yearlong or semester basis. Science and social studies are offered during Block D. In addition, Fridays can be used to implement special exploratory and research courses, electives, seminars, clubs, or assemblies.

Queen (1999) has developed eight major FAN block scheduling models. Tables 6.2 and 6.3 demonstrate two such examples.

The FAN block model provides the middle school with an almost limitless number of scheduling options. Classes can be offered in combinations of 90-, 45-, and 30-minute blocks of time. This allows for core and elective classes to be configured in the format that best serves the needs of the students. Table 6.2 shows how the FAN model can be embedded into

Table 6.2. The Eight-Period Queen Model

A. The Basic Schedule

Period	Time Allotment	Description
1 & 2	90 minutes	Language Arts: Block A—This class meets daily or on alternating days for a 90-minute block of time.
3 & 4	90 minutes	Mathematics: Block B—This class meets daily or on alternating days for a 90-minute block of time.
5	45 minutes	Mini-Block C Science/Social Studies
6	45 minutes	Mini-Block D Science/Social Studies
7	45 minutes	Mini-Block E Elective
8	45 minutes	Mini-Block F Elective Advisory

B. Science/Social Studies: Alternate Days

Mini-Blocks C&D	Monday	Tuesday	Wednesday	Thursday	Friday
Per. 5 Week 1	Social Studies	Science	Social Studies	Science	Social Studies
Per. 6 Week 2	Science	Social Studies	Science	Social Studies	Science

C. Science/Social Studies: Semester

	Monday	Tuesday	Wednesday	Thursday	Friday
Per. 5 Semester 1	Social Studies	Social Studies	Social Studies	Social Studies	Social Studies
Per. 6 Semester 2	Science	Science	Science	Science	Science

an eight-period day. In this model, the school day is divided into two 90-minute and four 45-minutes blocks of time.

- Classes in Blocks A and B meet daily for 90 minutes.
- Classes in Mini-Blocks C through F meet either daily or on alternating days for combinations of 45- and/or 90-minute blocks of time.
- Mini-blocked classes are either yearlong or semester length in duration. In this model, science and social studies are scheduled during Periods 5 and 6.

Table 6.3 depicts a FAN block schedule configured around a seven-period day:

- The class in Block A meets daily or on alternating days for a 90-minute block of time.
- The classes in Mini-Blocks B through D meet daily and/or on alternating days for combinations of 30- and/or 60-minute blocks of time.
- The classes in Mini-Blocks E and F meet daily and/or on alternating days for either two 45-minute or one 90-minute block of time.

The model in Table 6.3 provides a great amount of flexibility when scheduling classes. This model allows for the scheduling of core and elective courses, an advisory, one or more exploratory classes, and club meetings, as well as seminar classes. In this model, science and social studies can be offered either during Periods 3 and 4 or during Period 6.

■ ADVANTAGES OF MODIFIED SCHEDULES IN THE MIDDLE SCHOOL

There are many advantages to moving to a modified block schedule, a number of which are presented below. The list was gleaned from comments made by middle school teachers who are teaching in schools that have adopted block scheduling (Queen, 1999). The 3x2 block schedule achieves the following:

- Relieves the fast-paced, pressurized atmosphere found in many middle schools
- Offers teachers and students innovative ways to interact with one another and accomplish their objectives
- Provides opportunities for creativity in classroom instruction designed to promote in-depth learning (inquiry, research, cooperative learning groups, thematic units, computers and other learning technologies, and hands-on learning experiences)
- Supports teaming by providing time for individual and/or team planning
- Facilitates integration of the curriculum
- Cuts the number of class changes and movements that large groups of students make in one day
- Reduces the number of administrative tasks performed in one day by teachers and students
- Improves the student-teacher ratio so that teachers can know more about each student's individual learning and social needs
- Helps teachers make effective use of planning time by reducing the number of courses taught in one day
- Matches learning time to the learner and to the course content
- Results in fewer discipline problems

- Provides time for one-to-one interaction between students and teacher
- Provides time for teachers to get to know their students and develop better rapport
- Establishes a classroom environment that is more amenable to students

Table 6.3. The Seven-Period Queen Modified Model

A. The Basic Schedule

Period	Time Allotment	Description
1	45 minutes	Block A—Language Arts
2	45 minutes	
3	30 minutes	Mini-Block B
4	30 minutes	Mini-Block C
5	30 minutes	Mini-Block D
6	45 minutes	Mini-Block E
7	45 minutes	Mini-Block F

Block A: Meets daily or alternating days for a 90-minute block of time (Language Arts)

Mini-Blocks B-D: Meet daily and/or on alternating days for combinations of 30- and/or 60-minute blocks of time (electives, math, science, social studies)

Mini-Blocks E &F: Meet daily and/or on alternating days for combinations of 45- and/or 90-minute blocks of time (electives, math, science, social studies)

B. Science/Social Studies: Alternate Days

	Monday	Tuesday	Wednesday	Thursday	Friday
Per. 3&4 or Per. 6 Week 1	Social Studies	Science	Social Studies	Science	Social Studies
Per. 3&4 or Per. 6 Week 2	Science	Social Studies	Science	Social Studies	Science

C. Science/Social Studies: Semester

	Monday	Tuesday	Wednesday	Thursday	Friday
Per. 3&4 or Per. 6 Semester 1	Social Studies	Social Studies	Social Studies	Social Studies	Social Studies
Per. 3&4 or Per. 6 Semester 2	Science	Science	Science	Science	Science

The major advantage of the FAN model is that it allows for the schedule to be configured so that it meets the individual and collective needs of middle grades learners. FAN block scheduling gives individual students the opportunity to experience a wide variety of innovations, and this can bring about a positive change in the school's climate.

The positive change in school climate is a result of the reduction in class size, the ability of students to engage in open-ended learning experiences, and the ability to flex schedules to meet the needs of an increasingly diverse middle grades student population. The change in the school and classroom is also positive when teachers move away from the "introduction-lecture-review" format and vary the presentation of content. If the class structure changes every 20 to 30 minutes, interest can be maintained. An experiential-based curriculum encompassing reflection, cooperative learning, critical thinking, process writing, and active learning experiences will keep the pace brisk and the students engaged. Teachers and students are often surprised by the positive change in the classroom climate; the atmosphere is charged with energy and bustling with activity.

Evidence of improved school climate can best be seen in the decrease of reported discipline problems and in the cleanliness reports of the custodial staff. Students move around the school fewer times throughout the day, and that produces a safe and less frenzied atmosphere, which can be significant for student motivation and management. The pace of the school day is slowed, while active learning and interaction among teachers and students is increased (Queen & Gaskey, 1997).

By varying instruction, teachers are able to reach students from diverse backgrounds and learning styles. Methods such as cooperative learning increase positive social attitudes, increase self-confidence and self-efficacy, and foster open-mindedness and appreciation of others. Class projects require interdependence, individual responsibilities, and specified goals. Along with varied teaching methodologies, block scheduling provides students with the time to demonstrate what they know.

■ TEACHING IN THE BLOCK IN THE MIDDLE SCHOOL

Planning in block scheduling involves more than preparing a traditional classroom lecture. Instead, teachers need creative ways to actively engage students in learning. Various strategies that meet individual learning styles, authentic assessments, and integration of content can now be planned and implemented. Lunch periods can be reduced to 45 or 30 minutes, with the remaining time used for advisory time, club meetings, detention, and remediation.

One of the biggest concerns among teachers of block-scheduled classes is effective organization of instructional time. It is almost impossible to keep students' attention for a full 90 minutes. Passive sitting is especially inappropriate for the physical needs of middle school students (Hackmann, 1995). As such, teaching strategies in blocked classes must

include more than the traditional chalk and talk. Cooperative learning, group problem solving, learning centers, and discovery learning are methods consistent with what is known about the social and emotional nature of middle grades learners. Following is a list of strategies designed to improve the quality of instruction in blocked classes:

- Make certain that all learning experiences are developmentally appropriate for middle grades students.
- Include topics of interest for the students. Make the content real and relevant.
- Have the students work alone and in collaborative groups.
- Incorporate the use of computers and other learning technologies.
- Use pacing guides for long-term planning.
- Structure learning experiences in a learning cycle format of pre-assessment, exploration, concept development, and concept application. This method of instruction incorporates the use of discovery and open-ended inquiry. This will allow the students to discover personal meanings and understandings and construct their own knowledge.
- Do not let the adopted text drive the curriculum.
- Use a variety of resource materials, including, but not limited to, texts, trade books, magazines (such as *Cable in the Classroom*), newspapers, and the Internet.
- Use assessment alternatives, including journals, portfolios, traditional pencil-and-paper tests, and performance-based tasks. This will provide students with more than one way to demonstrate what they know, what they can do, and what they have learned.
- Use higher-level questions.
- Engage the students in a variety of student-directed activities.
- Let students do the work. Teachers become assistants to the learning process. "Do not do anything that students can do!"(Bohince, 1996, p. 21).
- Make students take responsibility for a variety of tasks.

SUMMARY ■

With more schools adopting block scheduling to restructure the school day so that time is used more effectively, I proposed the following question for research: What is the effectiveness of block scheduling when compared with traditional scheduling? After reviewing the work of several researchers, I found the following advantages most often: increased instructional time, smaller classes, fewer classes to prepare for, more in-depth study of concepts, a decrease in the number of discipline problems, increased student-teacher interaction, students and teachers getting to

know each other better, students earning more credits per year, increased planning time for teachers, better grades earned by students, and an opportunity for students to take more electives. The disadvantages found most often included less curriculum being covered, a decrease in the number of contact minutes with students in each class, difficulty in placing transfer students, and problems with the succession of courses. When asked, most students and teachers believe the block schedule to be successful and would not want to return to the traditional schedule. With so many schools finding success with the block schedule, its adoption is becoming increasingly popular. It has proven to be an effective means of restructuring the school day to use time more effectively. With more changes being made every day to increase its effectiveness, more schools will adopt the schedule, possibly making the traditional schedule obsolete. But before all this can happen, there is a need for further research on the long-term effects of block scheduling.

Middle schools exist to meet the educational and social needs of young adolescents. As such, middle school programming concepts need to be aligned with the social, biological, and cognitive development and achievement needs of middle grades learners. The programming concepts that middle schools have adopted to meet these needs include interdisciplinary teaming/blocked classes, advisory, exploratory, developmentally appropriate teaching strategies, and a core curriculum. There is a growing ethnic, racial, linguistic, and socioeconomic diversity within the middle school population. As such, there is a growing consensus that collaboration, student grouping, and scheduling options are essential if the needs of all middle grades learners are to be met.

Before the implementation of blocked classes, middle school schedules were generally organized around six to eight daily periods. In these short instructional periods, the teacher's focus is on course content and not on the student's learning needs. In addition, teachers are limited to the types of instructional strategies they are able to use. Block scheduling provides choices and alternative means to address these issues as well as other key factors in middle schools today.

The modified models are the most effective block schedules to implement at the middle school level. These models meet the needs of all middle grades learners by supporting each of the five middle school programming concepts. In addition, FAN block models provide middle schools with an almost limitless number of scheduling options. This allows for core and elective classes to be configured so that the individual and collective needs of middle grades learners are met. Adoption of either a 3x2 or some variant model will bring about a positive change in a middle school's climate.

Visit the special middle school link on my website and check out additional suggestions and ideas for teaching block at the middle school level.

SEVEN

The Elementary School on the Block

The elementary school is an important breeding ground for the educational pursuits of children. It is the place where the schooling process begins, so the elementary school must be inviting and exciting to all students who attend. Its history dates back over two centuries in the United States and even further on the continent of Europe. The young child, between the entrance into kindergarten and the exit of fifth grade, experiences myriad developmental changes. The effective principal is aware of these changes in the student body as a whole and accounts for them in the vision and mission of the school. Also, the curriculum taught at this level is crucial because it is probably the initial student encounter with an organized body of study. An understanding of its distinct parts and programs is needed by the principals and teachers to implement the mandated curriculum effectively and efficiently. Various strategies exist to organize the elementary school, and each school, through its uniqueness, has that one best way to be arranged for instruction. The principal must identify this particular arrangement and implement it with all deliberate speed.

■ HISTORICAL EVENTS IMPACTING THE ELEMENTARY SCHOOL

Johann Heinrich Pestalozzi (1746-1827) was a working-class Swiss who believed that the best educational process was to move away from traditional methods. One of his central tenets was that children learned best through their senses and when they are motivated through their own interests. "His conviction that children's learning is essentially self-motivated gave rise to a teaching methodology that de-emphasized schoolbooks and most of the traditional school subjects, attempting to stimulate and reinforce the child's naturally inquisitive behavior" (Woods, 1998, p. 307). Pestalozzi contended that a child's education began at birth and contained graduated steps that built on prior knowledge (Green, 1969). His thoughts and ideas centered on the principle of *Anschauung*, which can be translated as observation, intuition, contemplation, sense experience, perception, and sense impression (Downs, 1975). Teaching needed to be inductive, which Pestalozzi believed was the introduction of unknown material to the students based on what they knew. Pestalozzi began a school at Stans in 1799 where there were no lesson plans and no books and he taught whatever he saw the moment dictate. A distinct portion of his instruction was called "object teaching," which basically consisted of nature walks during which the students could learn by exploration (Woods, 1998).

Pestalozzi's educational ideas first began to surface in the United States during the early part of the 19th century. William Maclure, a businessman from Philadelphia, traveled to Europe and observed the teaching style and strategies of Pestalozzi. Maclure tried to persuade Pestalozzi to immigrate to the United States and establish a school that he would fund. He could not convince Pestalozzi to come, but Joseph Neef, Pestalozzi's former assistant, did come and establish the first Pestalozzian School in the United States in 1806. Neef used no textbooks in his new school and provided only oral instruction from the blackboards (Downs, 1975). The school eventually failed, and evidence of Pestalozzi disappeared for the next half century.

Beginning in 1860, the educational ideas of Pestalozzi began to reappear in different parts of the country. Horace Mann, considered the leader of the common school movement, traveled to Europe to visit Pestalozzian schools and returned to America highly recommending these teaching methods. The first evidence of an entire school system adopting the Pestalozzian method was in Oswego, New York. In 1861, Superintendent Edward A. Sheldon implemented these instructional practices in his system and even had his teachers formally trained in the methods of Pestalozzi. Also, William T. Harris, Superintendent of the St. Louis Public Schools, used the ideas of Pestalozzi as the basis for the instructional practices in the elementary schools (Downs, 1975).

Friedrich Froebel (1782-1852) was a German educator credited with the first use of the kindergarten—a garden where children grow—for young

children (Zais, 1976). Froebel's approach to the education of young children was rooted deeply within his religious (Christian) beliefs. He contended that the education of the child should lead to a harmony with God and nature (Woodham-Smith, 1969). He believed that the child needed a special environment in which to grow and learn. "The educator needs to be highly conscious of his own intentions and actions and finely sensitive to the child's total needs" (Lilley, 1967, p. 23). Froebel stressed the importance of play in the overall development of the child and used it as the basis for his kindergarten curriculum. Along with the "play" aspect, Froebel contended that the children's schooling should be organized around individual and group interests and activities (Ornstein & Hunkins, 1998).

Froebel wrote extensively about his ideas concerning education, but he often considered that his greatest work was *The Education of Man*, published in 1826. In his writing, Froebel emphasized the importance of character development and the need for the child to prosper in accordance with nature. "He wanted the kindergarten to be centered around the whole child and contended that every human being, even as a child, must be recognized, acknowledged, and fostered as a necessary and essential member of humanity" (Woodham-Smith, 1969, p. 21).

NATIONAL INITIATIVES ■

The elementary curriculum has changed greatly over the years. Beginning as a basic study of how to read the Bible and civic documents, it has now evolved to such an extent that it contains many goals and objectives directly related to technology. Computer and information-processing skills are commonplace around the nation in various state curriculums. There have been pushes for national curricula where students in all states would study and learn identical material and information. America 2000 and Goals 2000 are examples of acts and legislation attempting to set high goals for the United States and, in doing so, would standardize the curricula of all states.

America 2000

President George H. W. Bush and the National Governors Association met in 1990 and established six national education goals for United States to accomplish by the year 2000. The President was calling on all Americans to be accountable for the youth of America. "The America 2000 strategy depends on the strong, long-term commitment of all Americans" (*America 2000*, 1991, p. 7). *America 2000: An Education Strategy* was the Bush Administration's four-part plan to meet those goals. A list of goals and a detailed account of the initiative follows:

1. Every child will start school ready to learn.

2. Raise the high school graduation rate to 90%.

3. Students will leave Grades 4, 8, and 12 showing competence in core subjects (English, math, science, geography).

4. Make our students first in the world in math and science.

5. Ensure that all citizens are literate and have the skills needed to compete in a global economy and exercise rights of citizenship.

6. Free schools of drugs and violence.

PART 1: FOR TODAY'S STUDENTS, BETTER, MORE ACCOUNTABLE SCHOOLS

There will be an emphasis on comparing the nation's schools to hold them more accountable to the stakeholders. The mission of the schools will be to prepare the students for college or the workforce. National and state report cards shall be issued to increase accountability to the public. Parents will have choices as to where to send their children to school; this competition will hopefully improve all schools. Local boards will be given more authority and responsibility to manage the schools thereby reducing the entanglement of the federal government and education. Also, there will be differential teacher pay based on his/her progress toward meeting the six outlined goals of America 2000.

PART 2: FOR TOMORROW'S STUDENTS, A NEW GENERATION OF AMERICAN SCHOOLS

Resources for extensive research and development will be employed in an effort to provide the best schools for future students. Business partnerships will provide much of the capital to develop these schools. In this new generation of schools, there will be a creative use of time, space, staff, and technology to maximize the educational opportunities available to the students. The governor of each state shall be responsible for the oversight of school development to ensure that they are constructed in the best way possible.

PART 3: FOR THE REST OF US (YESTERDAY'S STUDENTS AND TODAY'S WORKFORCE), A NATION OF STUDENTS

In the beginning of the 21st century, 84% of the workforce is empolyed. Although impacted to a degree by the depression influenced by the 9/11 terrorist attack, 78% of mothers with children over age six are in the workforce (Bryson, 2001). Workers need to adopt an attitude of lifelong learning and instill in their children a value for learning and education. Industries should establish skill standards for all employees to meet. There needs to be an overall skill upgrading of the workforce in order to keep pace with the competitive global marketplace. As a nation, we should strive for a substantial increase in adult literacy.

PART 4: COMMUNITIES WHERE LEARNING CAN HAPPEN.

America needs a "renaissance" of her values—strength of family, parental responsibility, neighborly commitment, and caring of churches, civic organizations, business, labor, and the media. Every level of government can facilitate these activities to solidify the fusion of strong communities. Developers can play a vital role in this revival by the implementation of effective community planning. Communities provide the breeding ground for learning and can benefit greatly from an educated populace.

Goals 2000: Educate America Act

The Goals 2000: Educate America Act was passed in 1994 under the Clinton administration. It basically reiterated the six goals of America 2000 issued three years earlier and added the goals of better teacher preparation programs and more parental involvement in education (Table 7.1). The act called for a change in the way children are educated. It started with the preschool child because Goal 1 stressed a belief in the importance of early childhood education (Lunenburg & Irby, 2000). Like America 2000, Goals 2000 stressed accountability, performance, and assessment. The United States had always considered itself the world's elite nation, and this legislation was an attempt to make our educational system world-class.

"The passage of Goals 2000 represents an important victory for the 'cosmopolitan centralists' of educational policy who advocate a stronger role for the federal government in improving schools" (Cookson, 1995, p. 405). Goals 2000 is a prime example of the federal government attempting to influence educational practices in the states. In prior decades, because the Constitution remained silent concerning the federal role in

Table 7.1. America 2000 and Goals 2000

America 2000	*Goals 2000*
1. Every child will start school ready to learn.	1. Every child will start school ready to learn.
2. Raise the high school graduation rate to 90%.	2. Raise the high school graduation rate to 90%.
3. Students will leave Grades 4, 8, and 12 showing competence in core subjects.	3. Students will leave Grades 4, 8, and 12 showing competence in core subjects.
4. Our students will be first in the world in math and science.	4. Our students will be first in the world in math and science.
5. All citizens will be literate and able to compete in a global economy.	5. All citizens will be literate and able to compete in a global economy.
6. Schools will be free of drugs and violence.	6. Schools will be free of drugs and violence.
	7. Teachers will have access to programs to enhance skills.
	8. Increase parental involvement.

education, states had held the responsibility and accountability for the educational decisions affecting their schools. In addition, the United States, unlike numerous other countries, does not maintain a federal agency with control over the national curriculum. However, with Goals 2000, the federal government with its vast financial resources has tried to influence the policymakers in the states. For school districts that showed significant progress toward the implementation of Goals 2000 on average $700 per child in federal funds were available in 1995. Cookson (1995) terms this practice the new "educational federalism" with federal politicians attempting to influence state-level decision makers in their legislative priorities. The pressure has come from the federal level to standardize the curriculum nationwide, but the results and success are yet to be determined and decided.

■ A STATE EXAMPLE: THE ELEMENTARY CURRICULUM IN NORTH CAROLINA

The North Carolina Standard Course of Study (2001) outlines the curriculum for all elementary students. The North Carolina Department of Public Instruction uses this document as a basis for all classroom instruction in the state.

Technology

North Carolina has three competency goals for technology in Grades K-5 (Table 7.2). They are as follows:

- Competency Goal 1: The learner will understand important issues of a technology-based society and will exhibit ethical behavior in the use of computer and other technologies.

- Competency Goal 2: The learner will demonstrate knowledge and skills in the use of computer and other technologies.

- Competency Goal 3: The learner will use a variety of technologies to access, analyze, interpret, synthesize, apply, and communicate information.

Table 7.2. Technology Objectives for North Carolina Elementary Students

1st Grade	Objective 2.4 • Indentify key words and/or sentences using word processing.
2nd Grade	Objective 3.1 • Collect, sort, and organize information to display as a graph or chart.
3rd Grade	Objective 2.6 • Identify the parts of a spreadsheet.
4th Grade	Objective 1.3 • Identify violations of the Copyright Law.
5th Grade	Objective 3.6 • Participate in curriculum-based telecommunications projects as a class activity.

Grades K-2. The objectives for grades K-2 mainly address basic computer skills and knowledge. The student will learn the physical parts of a computer, know correct care and use of the equipment, and become familiar with the keyboard. Some examples of basic skill objectives are being able to manipulate the cursor, arrange a picture, keying words and sentences, and using various drawing tools.

Grades 3-5. In the intermediate grades, the objectives become more complex and interrelated. Students will begin to learn copyright laws and how to telecommunicate. They will learn how to retrieve and edit a word processing document. The spreadsheet is introduced, and students study the parts of a spreadsheet and how to perform calculations. E-mail is used as a means of communication, and the learner becomes aware of the damage caused by computer viruses and vandalism.

English Language Arts

Grades K-2. A primary goal of the K-2 curriculum is the development of oral and written language abilities. A focus is placed on reading, and students are taught skills in decoding different texts. Also, the skill of reading comprehension is a focus for instruction. At this level, the students are inexperienced in the realm of structured learning, so they are exposed to strategies for learning how to learn. The main goal is for students, upon leaving second grade, to be able to independently read a text they have not seen before while using appropriate decoding skills.

Grades 3-5. The intermediate grades provide the opportunity for students to learn how to communicate critically, creatively, and effectively. The teacher attempts to make the crucial connection between school setting, personal experience, and real-world application. Students at this level are progressing toward automatic word recognition and strategic comprehension of read material—comprehending for a purpose. As the students' reading experiences increase, they become consumers of various types of literature, so they are taught how to make judgments on fiction and opinions. Metacognition is introduced as the students learn to think about their own thought processes.

Mathematics

Grades K-2. Initially, the student will learn how to read, write, and count using whole numbers. Next, the skill of comparing and ordering whole numbers is emphasized along with a basic understanding of place value. The learner will use tools to represent the mathematical operations with a concentration on addition and subtraction. These tools are important because many students at this early age are not able to write all of the mathematical operations. They learn simple shapes such as circle, square, rectangle, triangle, sphere, cylinder, and cube and practice drawing them. The concepts of length, width, and height are explored in addition to

money. The primary student will also perform simple probability experiments.

Grades 3-5. During the intermediate grades, students learn the meaning of equivalent fractions and decimals along with the properties of special numbers like 0 and 1. Problem-solving skills are furthered as students practice estimating answers to problems and practice basic multiplication and division. Children begin to tell time on both analog and digital clocks and understand the concept of elapsed time. Geometric terms such as *perimeter, parallel, perpendicular, congruent,* and *similar* are introduced. Students learn to use calculators and to construct tables and graphs—bar, circle, and pictograph.

Science

Grades K-5. Five unifying threads encompass all science instruction for Grades K-5:

1. Nature of science: Students will view science as a human endeavor.

2. Science as inquiry: Students will develop abilities to do and understand scientific inquiry.

3. Science as process: Students will learn and practice the science process skills—observe, classify, use numbers, communicate, measure, infer, predict, interpret, experiment, use space-time relations, control variables, formulate hypotheses, formulate models, define operationally.

4. Science and technology: Students will understand technology and design and be able to distinguish between natural and man-made objects.

5. Science in personal and societal perspectives: Issues such as personal health, changes in populations, and changes in the environment are developed and explored. Science and technology are discussed in regard to their local influence.

Social Studies

Grades K-3. The social studies curriculum begins with a study of what is most familiar to students. The students learn about the family and the home and then proceed to a survey of the characteristics of neighborhoods and communities. The student, by studying his or her immediate surroundings, can now make generalizations about other children in other parts of the world. History is introduced with the concept of "here and now." The primary curriculum is an interactive program consisting of relationship skills and the duties of citizenship and civic participation.

Grades 4-5. The intermediate level is when students begin their study of regions. The concentration of this regional study is North Carolina, the United States, Canada, and Latin America. In the Western Hemisphere,

half the instruction focuses on the United States and the other half on Canada and Latin America. The students learn how societies are organized along economic, social, and political lines. These studies are intended to equip the students to answer the following questions about their state, nation, and hemisphere:

1. Who are the people of this society, and what are their values and beliefs?

2. What is the environment in which the people live?

3. How is the society organized?

4. How do the people of this society make a living?

5. How has this society changed over time?

Fine Arts: Dance

Grades K-5. The elementary dance curriculum contains four strands that are relevant across all grade levels:

1. Creating: expressing ideas and feelings through dance

2. Performing: formal or informal—using technical, expressive, and interpretative skills

3. Responding: observing, describing, analyzing, critiquing, and evaluating dance

4. Understanding: relating dance knowledge to history, culture, and heritage

Fine Arts: Music

Grades K-5. The elementary music curriculum uses the four strands present in the dance curriculum:

1. Creating: expressing feelings through composing or arranging music

2. Performing: presenting an existing work, formally or informally; calls upon technical, expressive, and interpretative skills

3. Responding: listening, analyzing, critiquing, describing, evaluating, and moving to music

4. Understanding: application of knowledge of music to history, culture, and heritage

Fine Arts: Theater

Grades K-5. The theater arts program has skills that guide the instruction at each grade level. These skills are perceiving, thinking, comprehending, applying, integrating, communicating, creating, analyzing, and critiquing. There are two focus areas for theater instruction at the elementary level:

1. K-2. Imitating: to use or follow as a model the actions or mannerisms or speech of others

2. 3-5: Presenting: to offer or share, usually in a classroom or informal setting, a portrayal or other theater work for consideration or display

Fine Arts: Visual Arts

Grades K-5. The visual arts curriculum has skills and processes that guide the teaching and learning sequence for the elementary school. They are as follows:

1. Perceiving: to be aware of surroundings

2. Producing: to use art to communicate

3. Knowing: to understand historical perspective of art

4. Communicating: to use multiple intelligences to use artistic expression to interchange ideas

5. Evaluating: to produce critical responses to artistic expression

6. Connecting: to understand relationships between art and other aspects of life

■ ORGANIZATIONAL PATTERNS

The elementary school of today is arranged by grade, which is basically an age grouping. The students start kindergarten at age five and exit the elementary school around the age of 11. The movement from grade to grade is according to age, and this process is called the vertical organization plan (Reinhartz & Beach, 1997). The curriculum of each grade contains a specific set of skills and topics to be covered and mastered before promotion to the next grade.

There is a long history behind the graded system of organization. During the 1830s Samuel Burnside, Henry Barnard, and Horace Mann urged schools to adopt this type of organization to increase the efficiency of operation (Noble & Dawon, 1961). The initial example of this practice occurred in the New Quincy Grammar School of Boston in 1848. John Philbrick, school principal, had a new building erected with 12 classrooms. Therefore, the instruction was graded, and students were distributed equally based on achievement among the 12 assistant teachers. This practice was more common in urban areas around the country for decades; it was 1900 before it appeared in many of the rural schools.

Disadvantages of Graded Arrangement

Although the graded arrangement has been used for many years, its disadvantages bring its true effectiveness into question. One problem is

that students are placed into grade levels regardless of their development and ability. Many times, the students and grade levels simply do not match. The curriculum is lockstep and not paced accordingly for the students (Reinhartz & Beach, 1997). Too often, textbooks dominate the curriculum, and teachers are more concerned with covering the grade-level material instead of differentiating their instruction to meet individual student needs.

Alternative Possibilities for Scheduling

Looping

Looping is generally defined as a teacher remaining with a group of students for more than one year. This practice is quite common in the elementary schools of the United States, and it greatly benefits the students and teachers. Because the teacher-pupil relationship has time to develop over a two-year time period, academic achievement tends to be greater (Forsten, Grant, & Richardson, 2000). Also, the teacher has an extended time frame in which to learn the strengths and weaknesses of the students and can differentiate instruction to better suit a group of learners (Crosby, 1993). The curriculum now can be dominated less by the notion of covering everything during the year, and the teacher can focus more on cooperative learning strategies and group project assignments (Burke, 1997). These processes give the learners more authentic activities that will greatly increase their retention of knowledge and information.

Multiage Classrooms

Another alternative to the traditional graded program is the multiage classroom in which the teacher has students of different ages in the classroom working each at their own pace. A benefit from this arrangement is that students move from easy to more difficult material when they are ready, and peer tutoring is readily available because of the differing ages of fellow classmates (Leslie & Halpert, 1996). "Advancement to the next unit depends on the mastery of subject matter, regardless of age or attendance, and students who have mastered content can help those in need of additional assistance" (Kolstad & McFadden, 1998, p. 14). Students learn to take responsibility for their own learning because they work individually and in groups on a daily basis, this is necessary for classmates who work at different levels. The high rate of language skill development is evident because of the continuous interaction with older students who have mastered more complex skills (Kolstad & McFadden, 1998).

4-BLOCKS MODEL FOR ELEMENTARY EDUCATION ■

The 4-blocks model is an instructional model based on the premise that there are four fundamental ways that all children learn to read. The model

ensures that students are exposed to all four methods every day, thereby addressing the individual learning styles of children. The four blocks are (1) guided reading, (2) writing, (3) working with words, and (4) self-selected reading. Most elementary teachers would agree that it is important to construct a balanced approach to literacy instruction that could address the individual needs of children to create a community of learner in a heterogeneous classroom setting.

The 4-blocks model is a literacy framework that can be used in isolation by an individual teacher in a school, even without the support of his or her peers and administrators, although the most successful teachers are those with a strong network of support from the staff and other faculty members.

Although it's important to use this model in a supportive environment, the 4-blocks model probably best serves a self-contained classroom. Keeping the blocks under one teacher's guidance is the best plan. One disadvantage of the model is that, often, teachers and or administrators change the design for various reasons. Sometimes the changes are minor; however, if the intent of the blocks is altered, the expected results may change as well (Sigmon, 2001).

■ PARALLEL BLOCK SCHEDULING

The elementary curriculum continues to evolve with more content being added and little subtracted. Teachers are required to teach more content in the same amount of time while incorporating such strategies and interdisciplinary instruction. Parallel block scheduling is a way of structuring time within a school day to facilitate instructions and to reduce the student-teacher ratio during designated time periods. Large and small blocks of time can be distributed among several teachers in a grade level by giving each teacher more minutes each day (i.e., 90 minutes) for whole-group instruction in language arts and social studies, with less time (i.e., 50 minutes) each for reading and writing in smaller groups.

During whole-group instruction, the teacher may use social studies content to teach a language unit on research skills. The students may reinforce those skills in small groups during reading or writing time and also in extension center. Students may also be assigned to the library during extension center time where a media specialist will instruct them on effective use of the card catalog or an online computer search. There are many options for instruction in the parallel blocking model.

According to Canady and Hopkins (1997) parallel block scheduling produces the following instructional benefits: (1) smaller class size during critical instructional periods; (2) less reliance on strict ability grouping; (3) less fragmentation of the school day due to better integration of support programs such as special education, gifted education, and Title I; (4) more efficient and effective use of instructional staff; (5) significantly higher student engagement rates in learning activities; and (6) increased test scores.

With parallel block scheduling, the benefits of flexibility can be achieved with few additional expenditures. The schedule is built basically around half-class instruction groups in reading and mathematics. Homerooms are usually comprised of approximately 25 students, with reading and math taught in groups of fewer than 15, thereby magnifying instructional time and increasing student achievement (Canady & Rettig, 2001).

SUMMARY ■

Restructuring of time occurs as educators capitalize on the potential of innovative scheduling as a means to improve schools. "With open minds and equal doses of creativity and technical expertise, school administrators, teachers, parents, and students can harness this power" (Canady & Rettig, 1995b, p. 12). It is my estimate that every two of three schools, elementary through high school, are using some form of blocking or alternative scheduling practices. From the first one-room schools to the most modern, schools within schools, have blocked a particular period of extended time for a specific subject. It may not have been called block scheduling, but in essence, it was blocking. This has been especially true in elementary schools where large sections of time exceeding 60 minutes have been used to block language arts or mathematics.

Visit my website for using block scheduling in the upper elementary grades.

EIGHT

Aligning Standards and Course Content

Curriculum alignment is an essential element in the total success of implementing the block. The first elements in curriculum alignment include scoping out and sequencing the units or content to be taught.

In sequencing, educators examine the order of information or skills that must be taught to achieve the desired outcomes. For example, in the language arts program, teachers instruct readiness skills in reading at kindergarten to basic skills in elementary and middle schools to English in the high school. Teachers strive to put content in a meaningful order. Some courses such as mathematics and science are sequential and require a step-by-step approach. In processing skills such as observing, comparing, and inferring, there can be a definite order in which higher-order processing skills are developed. In the sequencing, evident patterns emerge at various levels in the high school. In high school courses, the sequencing becomes extremely important, to include all of the desired content. Most subject content has been prescribed by the various state departments and the local boards of education. In most states, teachers will find biology being taught in the 10th grade; however, in other places, it may be taught in 11th or 9th grade. However, the scope of the content is similar. To be educationally sound, the material is taught in a sequence; the basic biology class is taught before advanced biology and usually before chemistry and physics courses. Once courses have been developed for scope and sequence, scheduling is the next step.

Scheduling is where administrators and curriculum leaders become involved in the process. Their role is to make sure that course offerings are presented at a particular time and offered on a regular basis to ensure all students the opportunity to take the classes. Scheduling becomes more important as we move from curriculum alignment to instructional alignment in that if the courses are not aligned in the schedule in the right fashion, it will be difficult to implement the desired curriculum.

■ MODELS FOR USE OF INSTRUCTIONAL TIME

As stated in Chapter 2, moving to a block schedule causes teachers to lose some overall instructional time that needs to be examined in the process of curriculum alignment. When realigning their courses with the curriculum, teachers can examine three basic models that will prove to be time wise and will allow for the maximum use of desired content. These include limiting content, assigning outside content, and integrating content.

Limiting Content

In these three approaches for curriculum alignment, the one often used as default is limiting the content. A decision is made to limit what is to be taught and to focus on the priorities of the course. Teachers tend to spend more time on the content they like and less on content they either dislike or have limited instructional materials for teaching.

The concept is similar to the concept of abandonment found in the effective schools research of the 1980s. Researchers found that to succeed in designing an effective school, some part of the content had to be abandoned to allow time to implement the remaining content in an orderly and appropriate fashion. When examining the abandonment model, we refer to this as the prioritizing approach. When analyzing any curricular model, whether from the state department, the local board, or even the textbook alone, teachers begin to plan what to teach in a course. They begin by listing their intended topics, usually in the order they plan to teach. (These usually have a sequence and may be skill related.) Many topics are arranged by units.

What teachers should be striving to do is eliminate, move, or modify the competencies or guidelines in curriculum. The first step in prioritization is to list or group patterns of concepts, units, or mini-units. The teacher prioritizes these as shown in Table 8.1. In the table, 12 basic groupings of items are presented. (These numbers will be more or less in most cases.) Sometimes we can do a factor analysis on this and break down the content in particular areas. In most cases, these are listed in the local curriculum. A goal may be to abandon two or three in the list of 12. In the block schedule, 10% to 15% of class time will be lost in the course of a year. In comparison, we find from our research and observations that teachers using traditional models often fail to use their time effectively and are teaching beyond the prescribed curriculum. Therefore, although some

overall instructional time is lost in the block schedule, the abandonment model and the use of various instructional models will actually cause an increase in interactive learning time. For example, one can focus on a total of 12 concepts for the course and decide to abandon two components that could be eliminated from the course. Often, this is material that has been added by the teacher over the years. Teachers implement the curriculum but should not add to the curriculum. In a case where the curriculum is tightly outlined and the teacher strives to cover all material, he or she may choose one or two areas where similar competencies may be combined and taught simultaneously. For example, the Civil War and the Revolutionary War competencies may be taught together within the concepts of restoration. In the English classroom, epic poetry may be taught as a part of a general poetry unit. I recommend that teachers find two or more concepts to abandon or combine with similar items.

Notes to Remember

1. Teachers must not use the abandonment model to cut required content or competencies. The only content that should be abandoned may include superfluous examples, excess content, or information outside the content area that teachers may have added over the years.

2. Group competencies together that may be taught in one unit instead of separate lessons, such as process skills or English short stories. Two or three short stories will enable students to understand selected literary terms and the general concept of short stories. It is not necessary to inundate them with 10 or more short stories.

3. Isolate the strengths and weaknesses of teaching styles, content examples, and student ability. Create recommendations to deal with the weaknesses.

Assigning Outside Content

Assigning outside content is the second curriculum alignment model. With this approach, the teacher assigns content to students to investigate on their own or in pairs or groups outside class. Creative teachers use course contracts or instructional packages for students to complete this content by, for example, clarifying in their course syllabus specifically what

Table 8.1. Prioritization in Ninth-Grade English

9th-Grade English –Abandonment			
Speech	~~Epic Poems~~	Film	~~Advertising~~
Poetry	Technology	Drama	Short Story
Fiction	Nonfiction	Research	Novel

must be completed outside class. Students often keep portfolios and/or journals to respond to share the content with the teachers. An excellent example would be that a student reads a novel that cannot be covered in class, but the teacher wants to hold the student responsible for the content.

Pretend there are 12 blocks of similar items, such as units or skills, content, and various situations or classes. In this model, the content is blocked and placed in order. Teachers can mark their use as "T" for teacher directed, "T/S" for teacher and student directed, and "S" for student directed (Table 8.2). Most will be teacher directed, meaning that the teacher plans to include this content within the course. The teacher will be responsible for preparing all the material. There may be an area where teachers and students can share teaching. The teacher could start a basic content, such as pollution, and have students research thermal, water, and air pollution. Learning stations, product or instructional packages, use of contracts, use of library—all are helpful to responsible students and also serve as good tools. The teacher provides perimeters and materials. This works well when students work on this over a period of time, alone or with peers. The student is held accountable for the content, and the assignments can be completed as cooperative projects. In my opinion, only 10% of the content should ever be taught in a student-directed manner. Another alternative would be to use the T/S, giving teachers more variety and flexibility in selecting contents.

Integrating Content: C-Clustering

The integrating model, which groups, or clusters, subject content, is shown in Table 8.3. The same 12 items are used as in Table 8.2. This model is known as the thematic approach. The 12 items are clustered into three categories or themes patterns, three basic sections of the course. These three major units may be carried over a long period of time.

Content is merged into a more meaningful pattern. For example, in a U.S. history course, there could be a grouping of wars. All the content of war can be taught in one long cluster to look for patterns of prewar climate, the political manifestations, causes, restoration, and postwar reconstruction. In a master plan or unit on war, timelines should be drawn and posted for students to see the sequence of time. To compare the similarities

Table 8.2. Assigning Outside Content in Ninth-Grade English

9th-Grade English—Blocking			
Speech T/S	Epic poems T	Film S	Advertising S
Poetry T	Technology T	Drama S	Short Story T/S
Fiction T	Nonfiction T	Research S	Novel T/S

Table 8.3. Integrating Content in Ninth-Grade English

9th-Grade English–Clustering		
Unit 1: Literature	Unit 2: Communication Skills	Unit 3: Media & Technology
Fiction	Research Writing	Advertising
Novel	Speech	Technical Writing
Nonfiction	Creative Writing	Electronic Research Methods
Poetry	Formal Presentations	

of the various wars, highlight mini-themes or curricular threads, such as politicians, taxation, and so on. In an English classroom, a cluster of media and technology could group together computer technology, advertising, and film. The cross correlation among these topics can result in student investigations into advertising on the Internet, in films, and in print media. Selecting content is difficult in the beginning; however, this approach is compelling when students see the relevance of what they are learning and how information may be linked. This approach can be implemented to focus on higher-order thinking skills. Weaknesses may occur in not being able to see the chronological order of events.

As teachers begin to redesign their courses from a traditional schedule to the block model, the following steps and related forms can be used. Sample models are included in the figures in Chapter 9 in the two subject areas of geometry and French II.

CURRICULUM ALIGNMENT ■
AND INSTRUCTIONAL PACING

Curriculum Alignment Phase 1

Step 1: Scope out the course as it has been taught in the traditional schedule (see Figures 9.1–9.3).

Step 2: Place a minus sign over one or two areas or units on which you spent more time than you intended in the traditional model. Usually we do this when we have more materials or we like this part of the content more.

Step 3: Place a plus sign over one or two areas or units on which you spent less time than you intended or that you were unable to get to in the traditional model.

Step 4: Now mark the amount of time IN DAYS that you have used compared to time used for the traditional use for each unit. For example, 10 days on the introduction of the animal cell. Scope out each unit with respect to time needed for the traditional schedule.

Step 5: Now mark each unit using the following formula: For the areas in a unit not marked with a plus or minus sign, divide the number of days in a traditional schedule for the unit by half to determine how much time to spend in a blocked schedule on those areas; for the areas on which you spent more time (areas with a minus sign), divide by half and subtract one day to determine how much time to spend; and for the areas that you spent less time on (areas with a plus sign) divide by half and add one day to determine how much time to spend. This is one way to help teachers begin realigning their courses. This is refined in Phase 2.

Curriculum Alignment Phase 2

Step 1: Further develop each unit according to the content on the Phase 2 form (see Figures 9.4–9.6). List content, vocabulary, and other material to be covered in the unit. Mark items that may be learned outside class in an alternative assignment. Make any notes that will help you organize your instructional plan or pacing.

Step 2: From the above formulas, begin further prioritizing content to be taught.

Mark areas where some content must be limited, assigned outside class, or integrated with other content. At this stage, don't worry about the instructional processes or activities that will be used in or out of class. We will complete this element in the pacing process, which follows. NOTE: Use a pencil with all of this because you will be making changes as you develop the plan.

Instructional Pacing Phase 1

Step 1: Transfer the topics from Phase 2 of curriculum alignment to Phase 1 of instructional pacing. Use a day-by-day approach in the transfer (see Figures 9.7-9.9).

Step 2: Keep Days 3 and 8 as "safe days." These are days that no instruction is planned because over 90% of teachers are behind at these days, and this allows them to get caught up and feel less frustrated. I recommend that a half day for catching up be included every week thereafter. If you are one of the few who are not to behind, just go to the next day of the plan and you are ahead. Keep the last three or four days as safe days for reviewing, catching up, and exams. Most teachers actually teach about 86 to 87 days per 90-day semester.

Step 3: Now that you have safe days to include, be sure to revisit the actual days planned and make adjustments. This may change again as you select specific activities to use for teaching. That is why it is important to be very processed oriented with this approach. Move now to the last stage, which is Phase 2 of instructional pacing.

Instructional Pacing Phase 2

Step 1: Use this model as a weekly and daily lesson plan. Complete the content information as shown in the samples in Chapter 9 and then project activities that you will be using by minutes on a daily level (see Figures 9.10–9.12). It is important that you have the first three weeks of lessons completed before the students arrive and that you remain three weeks ahead throughout the semester or year. Most teachers use one day per lesson, but it is important to know that some lessons may exceed one day or that there may be two lessons in one day.

Step 2: As you learn more about interactive methods and assessment, you will have to make adjustments in your plan.

IMPORTANT NOTE: This is a well-tested procedure that has been used by thousands of teachers in the United States to develop appropriate pacing of instruction. Do not take any of the steps lightly, or you will have difficulty pacing and being successful. Of equal importance, it will make your planning and teaching less stressful, and by the second and third time you teach the course and make appropriate modifications, you will have a master plan.

NINE

Samples of Curriculum Alignment and Pacing

In this chapter, you will find blank forms and samples for curriculum alignment and pacing. The figures in this chapter are grouped according to phases. Each group of figures contains a blank form and two completed samples. Use them as shown or adapt them as necessary. It is my hope that these pages will enhance the information presented in Chapter 8 and ease your journey into block scheduling.

The first step in aligning curriculum for block scheduling involves modifying a unit of study from the traditional schedule so that it can be taught in the block schedule. Figures 9.1, 9.2, and 9.3 address courses as they have been taught in the traditional schedule. Figure 9.1 is a blank form for teacher use and Figures 9.2 and 9.3 are samples of completed forms. For more detailed instructions, refer to Chapter 8, pages 69-70, Curriculum Alignment Phase 1, Step 1-5.

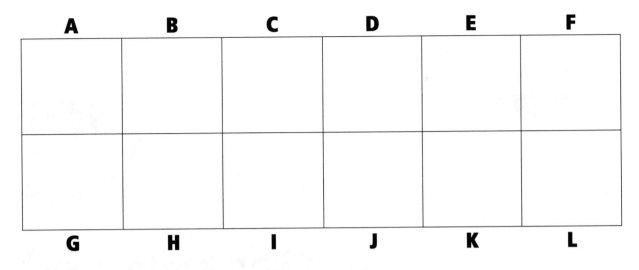

Figure 9.1. Curriculum Alignment: Phase 1 Form

A	B	C	D	E	F
Points, lines, planes, and angles	Deductive reasoning	Parallel lines and planes	Congruent triangles	Quadrilaterals	Similar polygons
Right triangles	Circles	Areas of plane figures	Surface area and volume	Coordinate geometry	Transformations
G	H	I	J	K	L

Figure 9.2. Curriculum Alignment: Phase 1—Geometry Sample

Subject: French II
Grade Level: 10-12
Teacher(s): _____

A	B	C	D	E	F	G	H	I	J	K	L
Describing your city	Finding your way around	Describing your home and family	Making plans to do things in town	Talking about clothes	Discussing shopping plans	Buying clothes	Discussing leisure activities	Describing vacation travel plans	Narrating what happened	Talking about your favorite foods	Shopping for food
Planning a meal	Eating out with friends										

M	N	O	P	Q	R	S	T	U	V	W	X

Figure 9.3. Curriculum Alignment: Phase 1—French II

Figures 9.4, 9.5, and 9.6 are for Phase 2 of curriculum alignment. They are used to further refine the content and materials of the unit of study. See page 70, Curriculum Alignment Phase 2, Steps 1 and 2, in Chapter 8 for detailed instructions.

Subject _____

Grade Level _____

Teacher(s) _____

Goal/Topic

1	2	3	4
Notes:	Notes:	Notes:	Notes:
(a)	(a)	(a)	(a)
(b)	(b)	(b)	(b)
(c)	(c)	(c)	(c)
(d)	(d)	(d)	(d)

Figure 9.4. Curriculum Alignment: Phase 2 Form

Subject: Geometry
Grade Level: 9-12

Goal/Topic

Points, Lines, Planes, and Angles

Points, Lines, and Planes	Segments, Rays, and Distance	The Coordinate Plane	Angles
1	**2**	**3**	**4**
(a)	(a)	(a)	(a)
(b)	(b)	(b)	(b)
(c)	(c)	(c)	(c)
(d)	(d)	(d)	(d)

Figure 9.5. Curriculum Alignment: Phase 2—Geometry Example

Subject: French II
Grade Level: 9-12

Goal/Topic

Describing Your City

1	2	3	4	5	6	7	8	9	10
Streets and public buildings	Places you often go to	How you get around							
28.B.2b	28.D.2a	28.B.3a							

Goal/Topic

Finding Your Way Around

1	2	3	4	5	6	7	8	9	10
Asking and giving directions	Indicating the floor								
28.B.3a	28.D.2a								

Goal/Topic

Describing Your Home and Family

1	2	3	4	5	6	7	8	9	10
Your address	The inside and outside of your home	Your family							
28.D.2a	28.D.2a	28.D.2b							

Figure 9.6. Curriculum Alignment: Phase 2—French Sample

Figures 9.7, 9.8, and 9.9 are used for Phase 1 of instructional pacing. The topics from curriculum alignment Phase 2 are transferred day-by-day to this form. See pages 70-71, Instructional Pacing Phase 1, Steps 1-3 in Chapter 8 for detailed instructions.

Subject _____   **Teacher** _____

Day	Topics/Goals/Objectives	Textbook/Materials/Resources
1.		
2.		
3.	Safe day	
4.		
5.		
6.		
7.		
8.	Safe day	
9.		
10.		
11.		
12.		
13.		
14.		
15.		
16.		
17.		
18.	½ Safe day	
19.		
20.		

Figure 9.7. Pacing: Phase 1 Form

Day	Topics/Goals/Objectives	Textbook/Materials/Resources
21.		
22.		
23.		
24.		
25.		
26.		
27.		
28.	Safe day	
29.		
30.		
31.		
32.		
33.		
34.		
35.		
36.		
37.		
38.		
39.		
40.		
41.		
42.		
43.	Safe day	
44.		
45.		

Figure 9.7. Continued

Day	Topics/Goals/Objectives	Textbook/Materials/Resources
46.		
47.		
48.		
49.		
50.		
51.		
52.		
53.		
54.		
55.		
56.		
57.		
58.		
59.		
60.		
61.		
62.		
63.		
64.		
65.		
66.		
67.		
68.		
69.		
70.		

Figure 9.7. Continued

Day	Topics/Goals/Objectives	Textbook/Materials/Resources
71.		
72.		
73.		
74.		
75.		
76.		
77.		
78.		
79.		
80.		
81.		
82.		
83.	Safe day	
84.	Safe day	
85.	Review	
86.	Review	
87.	Safe day	
88.	Unit 8 test	
89.	Safe day	
90.	Safe day	

Figure 9.7. Continued

Subject: Geometry   **Teacher** _____

Day	Topics/Goals/Objectives	Textbook/Materials/Resources
1.	Points, lines, and planes	Geometry figures poster
2.	Segments, rays, and distance	Geometry figures poster
3.	Safe day	
4.	The coordinate plane	
5.	Angles	Protractors
6.	Review	
7.	Unit 1 test If-then statements, converses	
8.	Safe day	
9.	If-then statements, inverses and contrapositives	
10.	Properties from algebra, Introduction to proof	
11.	Midpoint, angle bisector	
12.	Special pairs of angles	
13.	Perpendicular lines	
14.	Mixed practice	
15.	More on proofs	
16.	Review	
17.	Unit 2 test Terms in parallel lines and planes	
18.	½ safe day	
19.	Properties of parallel lines	
20.	Properties of parallel lines cont'd	

Figure 9.8. Pacing: Phase 1—Geometry Sample

Day	Topics/Goals/Objectives	Textbook/Materials/Resources
21.	Proving lines parallel	
22.	Angles of a triangle	
23.	Angles of a triangle cont'd	
24.	Angles of a polygon	
25.	Review	
26.	Unit 3 test Congruent figures	
27.	3 ways to prove triangles Congruent: SSS, SAS, ASA	
28.	Congruent triangles and proof	
29.	Congruent triangles and proof cont'd	
30.	Isosceles triangles	
31.	2 more ways to prove triangle congruent: AAS, HL	
32.	Proving triangles congruent practice	
33.	Medians, altitudes, and perpendicular bisectors	
34.	Review	
35.	Unit 4 test Algebra review: quadratics	
36.	Properties of parallelograms	
37.	Ways to prove quadrilaterals are parallelograms	
38.	Parallelogram practice	
39.	Theorems involving parallel lines	
40.	Special parallelograms	
41.	Special parallelograms cont'd	
42.	Trapezoids	

Figure 9.8. Continued

Day	Topics/Goals/Objectives	Textbook/Materials/Resources
43.	½ safe day	
44.	Review	
45.	Unit 5 test Algebra review: fractions	
46.	Ratio and proportion	
47.	Properties of proportion	
48.	Similar polygons	
49.	Similar polygons cont'd	
50.	A way to prove triangles similar: AA	
51.	2 more ways to prove triangles similar: SAS, SSS	
52.	Proving triangles similar practice	
53.	Proportional lengths	
54.	Proportional lengths cont'd	
55.	Review	
56.	Unit 6 test Algebra review: radicals	
57.	Simplifying radicals Similarity in right triangles	
58.	Similarity in right triangles cont'd Pythagorean theorem	
59.	The converse of the Pythagorean theorem	
60.	Special right triangles	

Figure 9.8. Continued

Subject: French II   **Teacher:**_____

Day	Topic/Goal	Textbook/Materials Resources	Strategies
1.	Describing your city, directions, address, and your house	Lesson 21, pp. 188-197	Diagram of house
2.			
3.	Safe day		
4.			
5.			
6.			
7.	Things to do Verb *aller*	Lesson 22, pp. 198-209	
8.	Safe Day		
9.	Places you go How you get around		
10.			
11.			
12.			
13.	Asking others to come along	Lesson 23, pp. 210-219	
14.	Saying where you have been		
15.	Contradicting someone Expressing surprise		
16.			
17.			
18.			

Figure 9.9. Pacing: Phase One

Day	Topic/Goal	Textbook/Materials Resources	Strategies
19.	Making plans to do things in town	Lesson 24, pp. 220-229	
20.	Expressing doubt Your family		
21.	Unit 6	Lesson 24 (Suite)	
22.			
23.			
24.			
25.	Review		
26.	Unit 6 Test		
27.	Padding		
28.	Padding		
29.	Talking about clothes	Lesson 25, pp. 246-255	
30.	What people are wearing		
31.			
32.	Whether their clothes fit		
33.	Where to go asking for help		
34.			

Figure 9.9. Continued

Day	Topic/Goal	Textbook/Materials Resources	Strategies
35.	Discussing shopping plans	Lesson 26, pp. 256-265	
36.	What to buy		
37.	Emphasizing a remark		
38.			
39.			
40.			
41.	Paying for clothes	Lesson 27, pp. 266-273	
42.	What clothes look like		
43.	Deciding what to choose		
44.	Comparing time		
45.	Introducing an opinion		
46.			
47.	Clothing	Lesson 28, pp.274-285	
48.	Where to go		
49.	Finding out price		
50.	Talking about what you would like		
51.			
52.			
53.			

Figure 9.9. Continued

Day	Topic/Goal	Textbook/Materials Resources	Strategies
54.	Review		
55.	Unit 7 Test		
56.	Padding		
57.	Discussing leisure activities	Lesson 29, pp. 296-305	
58.	Going out with friends		
59.	Sports		
60.	Helping around the house		
61.			
62.			
63.	Describing vacation plans	Lesson 30, pp.306-317	
64.	How you and others feel		
65.			
66.			
67.			
68.			
69.	Narrating what happened	Lesson 31, pp. 318-327	
70.			
71.	How long to stay		
72.			
73.	What to see		
74.			

Figure 9.9. Continued

Day	Topic/Goal	Textbook/Materials Resources	Strategies
75.	Narrating what happened	Lesson 32, pp.328-337	
76.	Things you never do		
77.	Travel dates		
78.	Where you went and when you returned		
79.			
80.			
81.			
82.			
83.	Safe day		
84.	Safe day		
85.	Review		
86.	Review		
87.	Safe day		
88.	Unit 8 test		
89.	Safe day		
90.	Safe day		

Notes_____

_____

_____

_____

_____

_____

_____

Figure 9.9. Continued

Use the samples and blank forms to complete Phase 2 of instructional pacing. Phase 2 is completion of daily and weekly lesson plans. See page 71, Instructional Pacing Phase 2, Steps 1 and 2 of Chapter 8 for detailed instructions on completing the forms.

Time Period _____
Day(s) _____

CONTENT FOCUS		REQUIRED RESOURCES
DESIRED OUTCOME(S)/OBJECTIVE(S)		**ASSESSMENT/EVALUATION**
DESCRIPTION OF ACTIVITIES/PROCEDURES		

Figure 9.10. Pacing: Phase 2 Form

TIME LINE (Minutes)

DAY	0	20	40	60	80
	5	25	45	65	85
	10	30	50	70	90
	15	35	55	75	

DAY	0	20	40	60	80
	5	25	45	65	85
	10	30	50	70	90
	15	35	55	75	

DAY	0	20	40	60	80
	5	25	45	65	85
	10	30	50	70	90
	15	35	55	75	

DAY	0	20	40	60	80
	5	25	45	65	85
	10	30	50	70	90
	15	35	55	75	

DAY	0	20	40	60	80
	5	25	45	65	85
	10	30	50	70	90
	15	35	55	75	

Figure 9.10. Continued

Time Period
Dates: _____

CONTENT FOCUS (1)		REQUIRED RESOURCES (4)
Segments, rays, and distance		Geometry figures poster

SPECIFIC OBJECTIVES (2)		STUDENT ASSESSMENT (5)
Identify, name, and draw		Transparency questions Decoding activity—distance on a number line

DESCRIPTION OF ACTIVITIES/PROCEDURES (3)

Review key points from previous lesson. Short lecture with transparency sample questions. Guided practice. Small assessment of transparency questions for groups of 3-4 students. Decoding activity dealing with calculating distance on a number line. Teacher points to a geometric figure on a large poster and asks students to name it without giving the students any information about the figures prior to discussion. Review of the day's lesson.

Figure 9.11. Pacing: Phase 2—Geometry Sample

DAY 1 IN MINUTE INTERVALS

0 Review 5 10 15 Definitions and examples of terms	20 25 30 35	40 Student practice (transparency ?s) 45 50 Decoding activity (distance on a # line) 55	60 Check student work 65 70 75 Poster	80 85 Summary 90
DAY 0 5 10 15	20 25 30 35	40 45 50 55	60 65 70 75	80 85 90
DAY 0 5 10 15	20 25 30 35	40 45 50 55	60 65 70 75	80 85 90
DAY 0 5 10 15	20 25 30 35	40 45 50 55	60 65 70 75	80 85 90
DAY 0 5 10 15	20 25 30 35	40 45 50 55	60 65 70 75	80 85 90

Figure 9.11. Continued

96

Time Period
Day(s): 1-5

CONTENT ANALYSIS AND FOCUS		REQUIRED RESOURCES
Describing your city Finding your way around Describing your home		Textbook Workbook

DESIRED OUTCOME(S)/OBJECTIVE(S)		ASSESSMENT/EVALUATION
Students will learn to describe building, asked to give directions, describe their house		Graded interviews Graded group exercises Drawing of house Composition—written description of house Map of city

DESCRIPTION OF ACTIVITIES/PROCEDURES	
Lecture discussion Paired exercises Composition Drawing	Generating conversations from drawings

Figure 9.12. Pacing: Phase 2—French II

DAY 01

Time	Activity	Time	Activity	Time	Activity	Time	Activity	Time	Activity
5	Rules & expectation	20	Students reintroduce themselves—name, where from, age, interesting facts	40	Read over p. 188 French cities	60		80	
10		25		45		65		85	
15		30		50		70		90	
		35		55		75			

DAY 02

Time	Activity	Time	Activity	Time	Activity	Time	Activity	Time	Activity
5	Students draw bldgs. in their cities	20	Identify the building in French	40	Vocab. p. 190	60	Work in pairs Interviews p. 190	80	Present interviews
10		25		45		65		85	
15		30		50	Ex. 1, p. 190	70		90	
		35		55		75			

DAY 03

Time	Activity	Time	Activity	Time	Activity	Time	Activity	Time	Activity
5	Do Ex. 1, p. 181 Wkbk. Cassette A-B	20	pp. 165-166	40	Ex. 3-4, p. 192	60	Pairs Ex. 5, p. 193	80	Present group exercise to class
10		25		45		65		85	
15		30	Divide class in half—one asks, the other answers	50	Asking directions	70		90	
		35		55		75			

Figure 9.12. Continued

97

TEN

Effective Instructional Strategies for Block Scheduling

To be a successful teacher in a blocked class, Robert Algozzine, Martin Eaddy, and I (Queen, Algozzine, & Eaddy, 1997) concluded that the most important teaching skills for instruction are as follows:

1. The ability to develop a pacing guide for the course in nine-week periods, including weekly and daily planning

2. The ability to use several instructional strategies effectively

3. The skill to design and maintain an environment that allows for great flexibility and creativity

4. The desire and skill to be an effective classroom manager

5. The freedom to share the ownership of teaching and learning with the students

In another study, while we (Queen, Algozzine, & Isenhour, 1999) found that it was important that all teachers master the preceding skills, we discovered that beginning teachers need special attention from mentors and principals. This was most evident in the area of effective classroom management.

Principals and staff development personnel must provide initial and continuous training for teachers to master instructional strategies. Cooperative learning, synectics, Paideia seminars, concept attainment, case method, inquiry methods, simulations, games and role-playing strategies are excellent methods for teachers to use in blocked classes. Jenny Burrell, Stephanie McManus, and I (Queen, Burrell, & McManus, 2000) identified and reviewed several strategies in *Planning for Instruction: A Year Long Guide*. However, just as a 90-minute lecture is inappropriate, a 90-minute discussion session may be too long. We found that teachers should change activities every 10 or 15 minutes. This will prevent student boredom, encourage class interaction, and promote teaching to the needs of diverse learners. Instruction in these extended periods should begin with a review, include various activities, and conclude with an adequate summary. Briefly described below are some instructional strategies that teachers should be aware of and trained to use for teaching in the block. These instructional approaches are presented in greater detail in *The 4x4 Block Schedule* (Queen & Isenhour, 1998b).

■ COOPERATIVE LEARNING

Cooperative learning, developed by Slavin in the early 1980s, is a very useful teaching method and classroom management tool (Slavin, 1987). A block schedule allows for group meetings, various grouping structures, and team presentations. Cooperative groups can include competitive subject reviews or timely coverage of material. Groups can be created by a random selection or a prescribed mix established by the teacher. For specialized activities, cooperative groups can be formed by the students. For optimal benefits, groups should stay together for at least four weeks. However, many class activities call for quick group formations. Limiting the time periods for groups can decrease problems resulting from personality conflicts within the groups.

For the most efficient use of time while grouping, teachers must inform students of the objective of their work together and explain the grading procedures that will be used for evaluating their performance. Group members should have an individual set of responsibilities and be held accountable for their actions in all activities. The teacher and students evaluate performance using self, peer, and teacher assessment in a cooperative evaluation model.

Cooperative learning can be structured in a variety of ways for a block schedule. However, inappropriate use of cooperative groups can lead to increased discipline problems and may result in excessive student competition. I believe the most effective grouping structure is the "jigsaw" method. In a jigsaw, each student prepares an assigned activity, then meets with the group to teach or inform other members. Each student has individual accountability and special responsibility to listen and learn the new material from the other group members. Another approach used is the

project groups. Groups are assigned a specified project to analyze completely or a specific problem to solve. Project groups conclude with a presentation to the class and, often, written documentation of the project. I find that this type of group construct works well with the case method.

THE CASE METHOD ■

The case method is used to stress introspection, higher-order thinking, and individual accountability. It also creates the type of layered class structure needed in a block schedule. Once the initial narrative or case is presented to the class, individual students sign contracts for their roles in the case study. Groups negotiate with the teacher for final presentations, meet for daily discussions, or seek guidance for research. Portfolio development is possible on an individual and group basis. Many different activities can be incorporated into the case, which achieves the variability aim of teachers in the block. For example, a case study on Thomas Jefferson in a history class can include individual research projects, a jigsaw share of expert knowledge, group presentations on contemporary leaders, and Socratic seminars on several of Jefferson's accomplishments (Queen & Isenhour, 1998b).

SOCRATIC SEMINAR ■

In 1982, Mortimer Adler introduced *The Paideia Proposal* by using a group discussion model that can be easily incorporated into a blocked class. Each member of the class reads a selection from the material provided by the teacher prior to the seminar. The teacher avoids directing the discussion of the seminar. The teacher's role is to record the participation and degree of preparedness of each participating student. Students are instructed to explore their ideas about a particular topic and question other members of the class in an open discussion. Students thrive in these seminars once they discover that their opinion is valued and that the teacher is not searching for a specific, "right answer." The teacher usually asks the first question, or it can be elicited from a student experienced with the seminar format. Teachers avoid evaluation, direct the discussion toward topic relevancy, and clarify arguments if there seems to be no solution. The Socratic seminar often leads to further issues, thus extending the learning opportunities beyond one classroom discussion.

SYNECTICS ■

Through the use of metaphor, Gordon in the early 1960s developed an approach by which students learn to associate a new topic with prior experience (Gordon, 1961). In analogy form, the teacher asks students to

describe the similarities between a given topic (the concept) and some unrelated item (the analogue). For example, a biology teacher may ask her students to describe the similarities between the parts of an animal cell and the parts of a city. After reviewing these similarities, students are asked to "become" the concepts and analogues by using first-person statements of feeling. The teacher may elicit statements such as "I feel strong when my cell membrane keeps out impurities," or "I am the nucleus and I feel very powerful." If obvious differences exist between the topic and the comparative element, the teacher may address these differences while being careful not to destroy the link previously made. Finally, students create their own new analogies to better retain the original concepts. This method serves well as a review activity and can be a valuable tool in assisting students to retain facts and concepts.

■ CONCEPT ATTAINMENT

In the concept attainment model, initially developed by Bruner in the early 1960s, teachers prepare and present a series of positive and negative examples in order to lead students to a definition of a concept and its essential attributes (Bruner, 1966). After the teacher presents the students with the first set of examples, students brainstorm a list of similarities between the positive examples and formulate a definition of the concept. The teacher then presents the students with a second set of examples for the students to test their predictions. The final concept is gradually attained by students who develop a greater understanding of the concept than if they were merely expected to memorize it from a lecture or book. Joyce, Weil, and Calhoun (2000) continue to advance different formats of the model.

■ INQUIRY METHOD

In using the inquiry method, the teacher presents students with a problem to solve using the scientific process. Students gather data by posing yes-no questions to the teacher and use their results to formulate a theory on relationships or the solution to the problem presented. Typically, as Eggen and Kauchak state in *Strategies for Teachers* (2001), inquiry is using facts and observations to solve problems. The teacher then directs the students to test their theories and discuss the steps used to solve the problem. Inquiry is an attention-getting approach useful as an anticipatory set and often works well at the beginning of an extended period. Teachers using inquiry can become masters at asking thought-provoking questions. Inquiry can lead to group or individual study and may serve as the motivational element for a case study.

SIMULATIONS ■

Simulations can be used in a blocked class to create the effect or reality of a real situation or experience. Students participate in simulations of the real world by solving problems, completing developed packages of materials, or taking part in organized role-playing. Because of the extended time in a blocked class, students use short field trips to related sites as a part of simulations without being absent from an entire school day. Games, while more competitive than simulations and role-playing, are often included in the simulation family. Although it takes more time to plan, design, and implement a simulation, the increased student motivation and involvement are well worth the investment for greater student learning.

RECOMMENDATIONS FOR IMPROVING BLOCK SCHEDULING FOR THE FUTURE ■

Listed below are important recommendations for maximizing the positive effects of block scheduling:

1. Teachers must develop and follow monthly, weekly, and daily pacing guides.

2. Teachers must master a minimum of five instructional strategies that engage students directly in the learning process and should aim to master seven or eight strategies.

3. Teachers should pace each lesson by changing grouping patterns, varying presentations, and using different instructional activities every 10 to 15 minutes. In most cases, a teacher should use a minimum of three instructional strategies during any period.

4. Teachers should incorporate alternative and authentic assessment practices when evaluating students.

5. Teachers must use the entire class period for instruction. Every day. Period!

6. Teachers should strive to be creative and flexible in assigning activities.

7. Teachers should coordinate and incorporate outside assignments into regular classroom activities.

8. Teachers should monitor individual students consistently to be sure of total student participation.

9. Teachers should mentor, formally or informally, beginning teachers and veteran teachers having difficulty with instruction in block scheduling.

10. Principals (and/or staff development personnel) must provide continuous staff development for all teachers throughout the year on the topics of curriculum/instructional alignment, instructional pacing and strategies, and time management.

11. Principals must develop a monitoring team to verify that all teachers are using pacing guides, instructional strategies, and class periods effectively.

12. Principals must take appropriate disciplinary action with teachers unwilling to follow the basic principles and procedures necessary in block scheduling.

13. Principals should work with less effective teachers in the development of an instructional improvement plan.

14. Superintendents should contact colleges of education in their regions and demand that block scheduling methods be included in teacher and principal training programs.

15. Superintendents should require that before schools move to a block scheduling format that principals and teachers spend from one to two years in effective staff development. (Queen, 2000)

In essence, the success of block scheduling depends greatly on the professionals who implement the model in their schools. It is imperative that the teachers, principals, students, and parents give the same attention and effort to block scheduling that they would to any other school schedule. Using instructional methods effectively will assist students to learn at an optimal level, as affirmed by Joyce et al. in the 2000 edition of their book *Models of Teaching*. Thoughtful planning, organization, implementation, and evaluation are imperative to maximize success in the block. All shareholders involved in education must provide the opportunity for the continued improvement of a scheduling format that has great potential for increased success in the future.

ELEVEN

Teacher-Directed Instruction

Direct instruction is a teaching method in which teachers direct the instruction from one lesson to the next within a fixed time period. It is sometimes referred to as a formal lesson. Direct instruction has come to have a number of different meanings, ranging from a type of classroom management system to any type of structured teaching to a set of specific steps to be followed in teaching a lesson. This instructional strategy is widely used and is a member of the behavioral systems family. In teaching models that have developed from the behavioral family, the focus is on the definition of the task and the analysis of the task. "Analysis of the task" refers, in this sense, to approaching the task from the perspective of the learner. The instructional design principles proposed in models such as direct instruction focus on (a) conceptualizing learner performance into goals and tasks, (b) breaking these tasks into smaller component tasks, (c) developing training activities that ensure mastery of each subcomponent, and (d) arranging the entire learning situation into sequences that ensure adequate transfer from one component to another and achievement of prerequisite learning before more advanced learning (Joyce, Weil, & Calhoun, 2000).

DIRECT INSTRUCTION AS A TEACHING MODEL ■

Direct instruction is a teaching model that places a great deal of emphasis on the completion of academic tasks. Its purpose is to maximize student

learning and to achieve a high rate of student success. Direct instruction involves a high degree of teacher control and high expectations for student progress. One of the major goals of direct instruction is to maximize learning time. When using direct instruction, the teacher arranges the learning environment so that there can be a predominant focus on learning.

As mentioned earlier, direct instruction is primarily teacher directed, and that is a factor in determining how it is used. The teacher is responsible for asking the questions in the lesson and leading the student to the desired answers. This is one reason it is recommended that direct instruction not be used as the only method of instructional delivery. It is most applicable to teaching a well-structured body of knowledge or the steps in a process or skill. It was once thought that direct instruction was beneficial only to young students, but recent studies have demonstrated that direct instruction may be successfully used for teaching skills such as comprehension in reading to both elementary and secondary students (Klesius & Searls, 1990).

The most common applications of direct instruction are in the study of basic information and skills in the core curriculum areas (Joyce et al., 2000). Recently, there has been a resurgence of interest in direct instruction. It has been touted as a successful way to teach ESL students—those for whom English is a second language. Direct instruction has been seen as extremely beneficial for those students identified as being from low socioeconomic status homes and therefore "at risk." Jere Brophy (1996) has suggested that direct instruction of social skills is an appropriate way to work with shy or withdrawn students.

The phrase "direct instruction" has been used by researchers to refer to a pattern of teaching that consists of the teacher's explaining a new concept or skill to a large group of students, having the students test their understanding by practicing the skill or concept under teacher direction, and encouraging them to practice under teacher guidance. In a direct instruction lesson, structuring comments are made at the beginning of the lesson. The comments may take the form of introductory activities that capture the students' attention immediately, or they may simply involve a discussion of the objective for the day's lesson. During the lesson introduction, the teacher provides explicit instructions for how the work is to be done. Then students are informed about the materials they will use and the activities they will work on. Finally, the teacher provides an overview of the lesson.

In direct instruction, the teacher often models a "finished product." The purpose of these introductory comments is to provide clarification for the student about what the procedures will be and the actual content of the lesson that is to follow. The next step is for the teacher to present the lesson. The teacher has decided in advance what information students are to learn. In the presentation portion of the lesson, the teacher explains the new concept, providing demonstrations and examples, along with the rules or definitions that help students to remember the concept. The teacher directs the questioning, always bringing the student to the correct answer. When

incorrect answers are given, there is immediate correction. After the presentation, the teacher demonstrates what he or she wants students to do in practicing what has just been taught. The teacher demonstrates each step in the correct order. When the teacher feels secure about the students' understanding, he or she assigns guided practice. This is an opportunity for students to practice the new learning under the teacher's guidance as the teacher circulates around the classroom, checking for student comprehension. The guided practice will be informally assessed so that the teacher is assured of student understanding. The aim is to master the skill. After this, independent practice is assigned. This is often done as homework. Whether the work is done as independent seatwork or at home, the objective is for the student to work independently. In a direct instruction lesson, the student works independently 50% to 75% of the time. The independent work is also assessed. The goal is 85% to 90% mastery.

The components of a direct instruction lesson design have appeared in other lesson designs as well. Dr. Madeline Hunter's (1982) research has shown that effective teachers have a methodology when planning and presenting a lesson. She has suggested various elements that might be considered in planning for effective instruction. In what has become known as the "Madeline Hunter model," we see the following elements:

- Anticipatory set
- Purpose
- Input
- Modeling
- Guided practice
- Checking for Understanding
- Independent practice
- Closure

It is not difficult to see the similarities in the design of a direct instruction lesson and the Madeline Hunter design. Others have also added to the basic lesson design of direct instruction, and direct instruction basics can be used in other teaching models. In fact, there are those who would argue that the components of direct instruction provide the background that is necessary before other models are used and that the lesson design can be used as a shell for any instructional lesson or unit.

The beginning of direct instruction is often credited to Siegfried "Ziggy" Englemann (Becker & Englemann, 1971). Englemann was a philosophy major who worked in the field of advertising. While exploring literature on the behalf of clients who marketed to children, he became interested in what type of input was required to induce retention of learning. Englemann began by working with small focus groups that included neighborhood children as well as his own sons. He outlined sequences of instruction that formed the nucleus for his later curricula. The early components of this sequence of instruction looked very much like the components of direct instruction today. Skills were precisely communicated in small bits, there was measurement to determine mastery, mistakes of

learners were quickly corrected, learners adhered to a strict schedule, and there was continual and repetitive review for the purpose of incorporating old material with new material. Englemann's early focus was on computational skills and phonetic skills. Eventually, Englemann's research was purchased by Scientific Research Associates (SRA), a division of McGraw-Hill, and was published in the form of kits that contained everything needed for presenting a lesson. The material was marketed under the trade name of DISTAR.[1]

In 1968, direct instruction enjoyed national attention for a brief time. Nixon's White House initiated a federal study called Project Follow Through. The Office of Economic Opportunity and the Office of Education joined forces to organize and fund this endeavor. The study was the largest controlled comparative study in pedagogical techniques in history, and its purpose was to work to isolate the "best practices" in education. The cost of the study was $1 billion.

At the same time that Englemann was publicizing information about direct instruction, Jean Piaget was expounding his theory of developmental learning. The two ideas were in direct opposition to each other. Becker and Englemann (1971) were positing that regardless of a student's age, if information was transferred in small enough bites and with enough repetition, learning could be accomplished. Piaget believed that even with the very best instruction, student learning would not occur until the student was developmentally ready.

■ DIRECT INSTRUCTION AS A CONTINUUM OF TEACHING BEHAVIORS

Several studies have shown that a strong academic focus produces greater student engagement and subsequent achievement (Joyce et al., 2000). Direct instruction plays a limited but important role in a comprehensive educational program. Some proponents of direct instruction say it is a way to target specifics of learning and to teach children what you want them to know. But opponents argue that direct instruction thwarts the development of higher-order thinking skills. One way for an educator to examine direct instruction is on a continuum. At one end of this continuum is the very directed and carefully sequenced lesson. This would be the type of lesson that one finds in materials such as Mastery Reading or other SRA publications. The lessons are scripted, and the teacher is taught how to signal for correct responses from the student. The questions asked are not open-ended, and there is one right answer that the teacher is seeking. The middle of this continuum is where one finds lessons such as the ones included in most textbooks. The lesson is partially scripted, and the students may be encouraged to think of different responses to questions, but the lesson is teacher directed, and the students are acquiring information in small bits. The learning theory is that the acquisition of small pieces of knowledge can eventually be constructed into the larger concept. At the

other end of the continuum is direct instruction used as an introductory mini-lesson in a writing workshop. The components of direct instruction are still there, but they are used as a part of the lesson, not as the whole lesson. The teacher directs the student to specific information that will assist in completing the rest of the lesson, which may actually use another instructional strategy.

Barak Rosenshine addressed the topic of direct instruction in 1978 at the annual meeting of the American Educational Research Association. He is credited with introducing the phrase "direct instruction" into the mainstream of educational research. When direct instruction was viewed at this time, Rosenshine had this to say:

> Direct [a concept] is related to the concept of academic engaged time. The term is relatively new, and apparently was developed independently by a number of researchers in the last three years. The meaning of the term is still being developed, and the definition is still loose. I use it to refer to those activities which are directly related to making progress in reading and mathematics and to those settings which promote those activities.
>
>   . . . Direct instruction refers to levels of student engagement within classrooms using sequenced structured materials. . . . [D]irect instruction refers to teaching activities focused on academic matters where goals are clear to students, time allocated for instruction is sufficient and continuous; content covered is extensive; student performance is monitored; questions are at a low cognitive level and produce many correct responses; and feedback to students is immediate and academically oriented. In direct instruction the teacher controls instructional goals, chooses material appropriate for the student's ability level, and paces the instructional episode. Interaction is characterized as structured, but not authoritarian; rather, learning takes place in a convivial academic atmosphere. (Rosenshine, 1985)

As Rosenshine continued to research student achievement, he and others found that students acquire structures for learning when the following take place:

- Information is presented in small steps so that the working memory does not become overloaded.
- Students are helped to develop an organization for the new material.
- Students are guided through practice and given opportunities for extensive processing.
- Students are provided with cognitive strategies as they approach higher-level tasks.
- Students are given opportunities for extensive practice.

Direct instruction is a highly structured approach to teaching content, whether for math, history, or biology, in a highly structured environment in which the information is given to the students and they learn by prac-

ticing their knowledge under the teacher's direction until the content and associated skills are mastered. For instance, a teacher provides the information on how to balance a mathematical equation, and the students learn by practicing their knowledge. Rosenshine (1985) describes the process in steps, such as reviewing, stating the objective, modeling, providing numerous examples and reteaching. He and others have attempted to identify those teaching behaviors related to student achievement for the purpose of improving the quality of learning that takes place in school.

There is often disagreement about what constitutes a pitfall or a promise with direct instruction, depending on whether or not one sees merit in direct instruction as a method. Some see scripted lessons as evils that destroy the creative nature of the classroom. Proponents of the scripted lesson argue that there is no doubt that what is important will be conveyed to the student. With lessons of this nature, lesson plans are also available. Again, for some, this is a disadvantage, while others see a constructed lesson plan as a great time-saver and advantage. Direct instruction is by definition teacher-directed. Many educators feel that children learn best when the teacher tells them what they need to know. This kind of instruction has had a revival of popularity with the advent of high-stakes testing. As one would expect, opponents of direct instruction include those who regularly employ instructional strategies such as cooperative learning, discovery learning, and group investigation. However, direct instruction, as stated earlier, can be viewed on a continuum that allows movement away from the "all or none idea" to understanding the ways that direct instruction can become a part of any lesson. Student mistakes are corrected quickly in a direct instruction lesson, but some educators would argue that this is a negative. Direct instruction is easily evaluated, which is usually seen as an advantage for two reasons. First, most people have been taught by this traditional method, so it is familiar. Second, most evaluation instruments "fit" with this model. The components of a direct instruction lesson are not hidden; they are very obvious. Parent involvement is not emphasized in direct instruction. Many see this as negative, but it is one reason that direct instruction is seen as a strategy to be used in low socioeconomic populations and in ESL settings. In both situations, parents are often not capable of helping their child. No technology is necessary to teach a lesson using direct instruction.

■ SUMMARY

Direct instruction is a teaching model that is beneficial to students and that certainly has validity. It is important to remember that it is not a model to be used for all instructional delivery. Students will benefit from direct instruction but only up to a certain point. It is beneficial to student learning to balance direct instruction with models that encourage discovery of concepts and ideas. Models that engage students in more sophisticated cognition should be used as well.

The chapter ends with a sample lesson related to direct instruction titled, "Our Mr. Jefferson."

NOTE

1. Direct Instruction, a packaged learning program published by SRA but that was developed by Ziggy Englemann and supported by other researchers like Wes Becker (Becker & Englemann, 1971) should not be confused with direct instruction, a teaching strategy that has broad implications.

OUR MR. JEFFERSON: A SAMPLE TEACHER-DIRECTED LESSON

Following is a sample teacher-directed lesson. When delivering a directed lesson, it is important to have visuals to maintain the students' attention as well as to accommodate the visual learners in your classroom. For this lesson, one could use slides or pictures of Thomas Jefferson, the Jefferson Memorial, the Declaration of Independence, Monticello, and so on as part of the presentation of the material, which is broken into short sections of boxed text. Remember that, to be effective, the lesson must be well planned and focused, should not be more than 30 to 45 minutes in length, and should maintain students' motivation. In addition, check frequently for understanding and modify the pace accordingly.

LESSON TITLE:
AN AMERICAN ENIGMA: THOMAS JEFFERSON

Sources: *Thomas Jefferson: An Intimate History,* by Fawn M. Brodie (1915–1981) and *American Sphinx: The Character of Thomas Jefferson,* by Joseph J. Ellis (1943–)

Who was the *real* Thomas Jefferson?

- If Thomas Jefferson were a monument, he would be the Sphinx
- If he were a painting, he would be the Mona Lisa
- If he were a character in a play, he would be Hamlet

Thomas Jefferson was . . .

- A violinist, farmer, scientist, lover of fine wines
- A restless architect who couldn't bring himself to ever finish building his home
- A politician with a voice so soft that he could barely make himself heard from the podium but who founded the first political party
- A man who denounced the moral bankruptcy he saw in Europe, but delighted in the gilded salons of Paris
- A statesman who was twice elected president of the United States but didn't think it worthy for the listing on his gravestone

Thomas Jefferson . . .

- Brought about fiscal stability to the country but died facing personal bankruptcy
- Was a lifelong champion of small government who took it upon himself to more than double the size of his country
- Endured the loss of nearly everything he held dear but somehow never lost his faith for the future
- Distilled a century of Enlightenment thinking into one remarkable sentence that began, "We hold these truths to be self-evident that all men are created equal" yet owned more than 200 human beings and never saw fit to free them

Early life

- Born in Albemarle County, Virginia on April 13, 1743
- Mother—Jane Randolph Jefferson
- Father—Peter Jefferson

Schooling

- Received a classical education with the Rev. Maury
- Attended William & Mary in Williamsburg and was influenced by William Small (mathematics, science, and philosophy)
  George Wythe (law)
  Governor Francis Fauquier (friend)

The beginnings of a patriot

- Colonists thought of themselves as British citizens with the privilege of British liberty
- Stamp Act of 1765—a dictate of a far-off parliament that had no colonial representatives
- Jefferson in the Virginia House of Burgesses—signed a boycott of British goods to end the "enslavement" of the colonists

As a young adult

- Practiced law for 7 years
- Married Martha Wayles Skelton on New Year's Day 1772
- Received land, slaves, and debt from his father-in-law

THE AMERICAN REVOLUTION

Before the Revolution

- 1774—Summary of the Rights of British America
- June 1775—Left for Philadelphia
- The Continental Congress and committee work
- Declaration of Independence
  "We hold these truths to be self-evident that all men are created equal, that they are endowed by their creator with certain inalienable rights, that among these are life, liberty and the pursuit of happiness."

During the Revolution

- House of Delegates in Virginia: Sponsored the law to overturn primogeniture and wrote the Establishment of Religious Freedom in Virginia
- Governor of Virginia
- Mentor of the next generation of statesmen: James Madison, James Monroe, William Short

After the Revolution

- Martha Jefferson died in September 1782
- 1784: Wrote *Notes on the State of Virginia*

Jefferson in Paris

- Went to Paris in 1784—took daughter Patsy and slave James Hemings
- Friendship with John & Abigail Adams
- Paris: A close view of monarchy and the salon society
- Daughter Polly comes to Paris, accompanied by slave Sally Hemings
- Maria Cosway: "My Head and My Heart" (letter to Maria on a dialogue between his head and his heart)

Secretary of State

- 1789: Secretary of State for Washington's administration
- Conflict: Alexander Hamilton
- Political parties: The Federalists vs. the Democratic-Republicans

Home to Monticello: Before returning to politics

- Monticello his home and safe haven
- Focused on his farm, his home, and his inventions
- 1786: Ran for president—became John Adams's vice president
- Opposed the Alien & Sedition Acts of 1796

Revolution of 1800

- 1800: Candidates for president: Adams, Pinkney, Jefferson, and Burr
- Election thrown into the House of Representatives
- A legacy of Federalists judges for the Jefferson administration

Jefferson as president . . .

- Worked to decrease federal spending
- Negotiated the Louisiana Purchase
- Sent Lewis & Clark and the Corps of Discovery to explore the West
- James Callender publishes rumors about Jefferson and Sally Hemings
- Daughter Polly dies—1804
- Imposed an embargo on exporting American goods and the economy suffers
- Endured a tormented second term
- Left Washington in 1809 for Monticello, never to return

Did He or Didn't He?

- Sally Hemings had five children: Tom, Beverly, Harriet, Madison, and Eston; all were reported to be mulattos
- Jefferson was present at Monticello nine months prior to the births of Sally's last four children; Sally was said to be in Paris when she became pregnant with her first child
- Jefferson's descendents claim that the father was one of the Carr brothers

Genetic evidence

- A man receives a "Y" chromosome from his father and an "X" chromosome from his mother.
- The Y chromosome has polymorphisms—the "glue" holding the actual genes together.
- Fathers pass on polymorphisms (the "glue"), which have specific characteristics, to their sons.
- If two men have identical polymorphisms, the chances are great that they have a common ancestor.
- Field Jefferson and Eston Hemmings had identical polymorphisms.

Retirement at Monticello

- His plants and garden
- Constant visitors
- A household with grandchildren

The North and South Poles of the Revolution

- 1812: James Madison negotiated a "truce" between John Adams and Jefferson
- 1812–1826: The most important correspondence between public figures in United States history

University of Virginia

- Founded the University of Virginia—an "academic village" in Charlottesville
- First university in the world that did not begin as a religious or theology school

Mounting debt

- 1815: Forced to sell his library—became the nucleus of the Library of Congress
- At the end of his life, owed over $100,000 and knew that Monticello would be lost to his descendents

"Is it the 4th?"

- July 4, 1826, was the 50th anniversary of the Declaration of Independence.
- Thomas Jefferson died on July 4th around 1:00 p.m. at Monticello.
- John Adams died in Massachusetts the same day around 5:00 p.m.—his last words were, "Jefferson still survives."

Indeed he does.

TWELVE

Discovery
and Inquiry

DISCOVERY LEARNING ■

Although the phrase "discovery method" has been used to describe a variety of instructional techniques, most definitions include the learner's discovering what is to be learned without much assistance from the teacher. After discovering the rule that underlies the example, the student must apply that rule to a new example or concept. Because of its many uses, discovery learning is sometimes called the inductive method, guided discovery, problem solving, activity learning, or learner-centered instruction (Blake, 1984). Although these are used as synonyms for discovery learning, there does exist a difference between it and the inductive, guided-discovery, and problem-solving methods. The inductive method is a mental process, whereas discovery learning is an instructional strategy. In guided discovery, the teacher guides students by using hints, questions, and other devices. This differs from pure discovery in that students receive no help. Finally, problem solving requires students to discover or find many different rules they may have already known in isolation and craft them into a solution (Blake, 1984).

Discovery learning can be broken into the following two parts: (a) the amount of guidance and (b) the sequence of rules and examples. The variable regarding guidance is straightforward and deals with how much

assistance a teacher gives a student in the learning process. This can range from providing no help to providing many clues and hints. To understand the second variable in sequence, it is important to understand what a rule is and where it came from. In Bloom's domains and categories of learning behaviors, the three domains are psychomotor, affective, and cognitive. Discovery learning is located within the cognitive domain and primarily deals with the last three categories of learning behaviors—concept, rule, and problem solving. A concept is a class of objects, things, or events. A rule is the interaction of two or more concepts. Problem solving involves selecting, combining, and/or generating rules to solve a problem (Blake, 1984). Therefore, in discovery learning, the student is trying to discern the rule having to do with the interaction of the concepts in the example. The sequence of rules and examples in discovery learning is always example, then rule—referred to as "egrule." This contrasts with the sequence in the expository method. Here, the teacher supplies the student with all of the content to be learned, and the student applies that knowledge to an example. Expository learning results in a rule-to-example sequence—"ruleg" (Blake, 1984).

David Ausubel stated that the rationale for discovery learning was that all true knowledge is self-discovered (Blake, 1984). This echoes an earlier belief of John Dewey, whose rationale for discovery learning lay in the distinction between knowledge and the record of knowledge. To Dewey, knowledge was gained when students created or discovered that knowledge for themselves while being actively engaged (Davidson, 1971). Proponents claim that by experiencing the example first, abstract ideas become more concrete and easier to understand (Blake, 1984).

The lesson design for discovery learning is simple. First, students are presented with an example. This can be an interaction between any two or more concepts. The students study the example and attempt to discern a rule. During this process, the teacher plays a very limited role and does not provide content. Once the rule has been established, students are then asked to apply this rule to a new example or concept.

History and Research

The discovery method has been around for many centuries. Socrates engaged in a dialog of questions to the slave boy in an effort to help him discover the principle of geometry. In more modern times, discovery learning grew out of the progressive education movement. The method saw a large growth in interest during the post-Sputnik era when schools were encouraged to use discovery methods so students could become more "scientific" (Blake, 1984).

Although other proponents for discovery learning included Rousseau and Montessori, the two major designers of the method were John Dewey and Jerome Bruner (Blake, 1984). Dewey believed that education should be based on personal experience and that knowledge should be discovered. His book *Experience and Education* (1938) proved a major force in discovery

learning (Blake, 1984). Bruner's works in the 1960s helped to give discovery learning a boost in popularity (e.g., see Bruner, 1966). He has been credited with starting the experimentation necessary to establish discovery learning as a valid instructional method (Blake, 1984).

One of the loudest critics against discovery learning was Ausubel. His main contention had to do with whether discovery learning was more efficient in helping students learn given the large amount of time necessary for the method. He argued that if students could learn the material without discovery learning in less time, then discovery learning was inefficient (Hermann, 1969).

Research findings in discovery learning have often been contradictory. The primary reason is that researchers have been unable to agree on a single definition for discovery learning. Taking this into consideration, Hermann (1969) and Blake (1984) conducted two extensive meta-analyses of discovery learning research. Most of the research compared discovery learning with expository learning. Both researchers found that discovery learning assisted students in transferring the knowledge to a new problem. It was also more effective when the transfer task was more complex or when background knowledge was limited. They also found that discovery learning resulted in better long-term retention. In addition, research showed that discovery learning was appropriate for all subjects. It was more effective with low-ability groups than with high-ability groups. Finally, guided discovery was more effective than pure discovery.

Promises and Pitfalls

Discovery learning has several advantages. It is appropriate for all subjects and ages and uses students' own personal associations as a basis for understanding. It also allows students the opportunity to reconcile any misconceptions about a topic. Discovery learning has also proven easier for beginners in a field since understanding is constructed and not received. This learning method places the responsibility of learning on the learner (Svinicki, 1998).

A disadvantage of discovery learning is that it is time-consuming and does not lead to immediate retention. In addition, it is difficult for administrators to observe, and it demands teacher creativity.

Summary

The discovery learning model is designed to let the learners realize knowledge for themselves. Although there has been conflicting research, this method has been shown to be effective when the background knowledge is limited and the transfer task is difficult. It is more efficient than expository learning for overall task transfer. This method is a good way to begin a lesson and can serve as an advanced organizer.

NOTE: See the end of this chapter for a sample discovery learning lesson titled "How Do We Build the Tower?"

■ THE INQUIRY TRAINING MODEL

The inquiry training model (inquiry) is designed to teach students how to learn an inquiry process by asking questions and developing hypotheses concerning a puzzling problem, called a "discrepant event." Inquiry is a model of teaching in the information processing family. This model specializes in causal reasoning that helps students sharpen their scientific inquiry skills. Information processing models assist students to make sense of their world by acquiring and organizing data, identifying problems, and generating solutions. These models are designed to help students develop a conscious awareness of strategies for learning that will help them reflect on the world in which they live.

Inquiry builds on a child's natural curiosity. Students develop skills that are relevant and useful in helping them become autonomous learners. Using this method, students solve problems by asking a series of questions, collecting and verifying data, developing concepts, and building and testing hypotheses. With practice, students develop into independent, autonomous learners who become increasingly conscious of their process of inquiry. Students participate in the process of scientific inquiry, questioning why events happen, logically processing and analyzing new data, and in the process, developing intellectual strategies to use in the acquisition of knowledge. Although inquiry training is not in the social family of teaching models, students do collaborate with others to solve problems, and this collaboration helps them enrich their thinking and tolerate views other than their own.

There are five stages in the lesson design structure of inquiry training. In Phase 1, confrontation of the problem, the teacher explains the inquiry procedures and then presents a discrepant event. Teachers and students must use the language of the inquiry process. Students are told that they will be able to ask the teacher questions with a "yes" or "no" answer. If the questions require more than "yes" or "no," students will be asked to rephrase them. Because students may feel uncomfortable asking questions and developing theories on their own, the teacher will not evaluate student theories; teachers will encourage students to make precise statements and will ask students to support their theories with facts. Interaction among students will be allowed during the inquiry process. Once the inquiry procedures are explained, the teacher presents the discrepant event. A discrepant event is anything that is puzzling or unusual. Joyce, Weil, and Calhoun (2000) state that "the ultimate goal is to have the students experience the creation of new knowledge, the confrontation should be on discoverable ideas. . . . bending a metallic strip held over a flame begins the inquiry process" (p. 177). An example of a discrepant event is the following scenario: You are traveling across the Golden Gate Bridge in San Francisco, and you realize that there is nothing under the bridge. What is holding it up?

In Phase 2, data collection, verification takes place. This is the stage in which students begin asking questions such as "What holds the bridge

up?" The teacher answers the students' questions to verify the nature of the objects and conditions and to verify the occurrence of the problem situation. Phase 3, data gathering and experimentation, requires students to isolate relevant variables and begin to restate their questions in the form of a hypothesis that could explain the discrepant event. To continue the example, an explanation may be, "Is the bridge held by the steel cables that are anchored at both ends?" A fact sheet, used in Phase 4, organizing, formulation, and explaining, is useful in helping the students understand the explanation for the discrepant event.

Phase 5, analysis of the inquiry process, has the teacher questioning the students regarding the process of inquiry. The main purpose of inquiry training is not to help students acquire knowledge; instead, the purpose is to teach the process of inquiry. In this final stage, the teacher might ask these questions: What questions were most effective in leading you to a hypothesis? What questions were not effective? What have you learned about this process? What suggestions do you have that would make this inquiry more effective? Students continue to use inquiry methods to learn more about their world because new knowledge is continuously available. Both teachers and students are engaged in a never-ending quest for new information. The inquiry training model is one tool teachers and students need in their acquisition of knowledge.

History and Research

In 1962, Richard Suchman developed the method of teaching called inquiry training. Suchman defined inquiry as "learning that is directed and controlled by the learner." All students should be responsible for their own learning. Since he believed that "all knowledge is tentative," students need well-developed inquiry skills so they can become life-long learners. Students begin to understand that there is not always only one right answer. When questions are asked using new tools and technology, knowledge once considered a "truth" might turn out to be false or inaccurate. In the inquiry technique, students learn the art of asking questions and the science of searching for answers. The tools of inquiry include an inquiring mind, the ability to ask questions to collect more data, and the ability to analyze findings to determine possible reasons or discover solutions to a problem. Since students are naturally inquisitive, teachers should present information in such a way as to help students increase their power of inquiry. Most of Suchman's work dealt with children of high intelligence. Using inquiry training, highly verbal students more than doubled their ability to inquire effectively to solve problems, and they increased their use of analytical procedures when learning new information (Suchman, 1962). Suchman's research showed that inquiry training was very beneficial to gifted students, but other research studies showed that all students could benefit from inquiry training.

Another researcher, Howard Jones (1966), studied the effects of planned guidance on the problem-solving abilities of elementary-age stu-

dents. The results showed a significant relationship between inquiry training and changes in the problem-solving behaviors of elementary students, but there was no significant relationship between inquiry training and concept transfer or changes in recall of factual knowledge.

Ivany (1969) and Collins (1969) studied two modes of teaching science —the expositional and the hypothetical. The Illinois Inquiry Training Program developed by Dr. Suchman was implemented with their experimental treatment groups. Their study showed that inquiry training worked best when the discrepant event was strong and the topics under consideration were especially instructional. For example, in determining how a suspension bridge works, students' knowledge deepens if they can build a model of a suspension bridge. One of the instructor's responsibilities prior to the lesson is to select appropriate puzzling events for inquiry—discrepant events suitable for capturing the students' interests. The selection of the discrepant event is crucial for the success of the lesson.

Emily Elefant, a science teacher at a school for the deaf, conducted a study to determine the strategies that would be acquired by deaf students involved in an inquiry training program modeled on Suchman's design (Elefant, 1980). As in Suchman's study involving gifted students, behaviors exhibited by the deaf students were no different from those of the hearing students. The actual number of inquiry behaviors and experimenting behaviors increased over an eight-week period.

Studies by Schlenker (1986) showed that inquiry training increased the understanding of science, creative thinking, and skills for obtaining and analyzing information. Inquiry training proved as effective as recitation or lectures accompanied by laboratory experiences, but not more effective than any other information processing method.

Donald Hansler (1985) conducted a series of studies over a three-year period to determine whether inquiry was effective for teaching problem solving, thinking, and decision making. He concluded that inquiry training was a potentially highly effective method of teaching cognitive skills and was appropriate for use with elementary-level to college-level students. Although many educators feel inquiry methods of teaching are best in science courses, Hansler's studies showed that inquiry could be used with almost any subject. With some modifications and teacher training, inquiry can be one of several strategies in a teacher's repertoire.

Promises and Pitfalls

Implementing inquiry training as a teaching strategy has numerous advantages. Inquiry can be used successfully with elementary, secondary, and college-age students. It is adaptable to all elementary and secondary curriculum areas, although inquiry training seems most suitable for science curricula. Like the social family models of teaching, inquiry encourages cooperation, although it provides students with more intellectual freedom. Because the teacher does not evaluate students' questions and theories, students feel a greater sense of equality in the learning process.

Where inquiry training is a prevalent method of teaching, schools report an increased use of their school libraries.

Disadvantages of implementing inquiry training are important considerations. First, the method takes time—time to train students in the process and time to train teachers in the method. Inquiry is not one of the most familiar of the teaching methods, especially among teachers of nonscience curricula. Second, inquiry training involves risk taking on the part of students, who must develop the skills and courage to question and verbalize possible theories. It also involves risk taking on the part of the teacher, who must be willing and able to turn over the direction of the learning process to the students. Third, lower-level students may have difficulty generating questions. In addition, some students in all ability levels have difficulty working with and expressing theories. Since the major focus of inquiry is on students' developing inquiry skills, some teachers and administrators may have difficulty using a model that emphasizes the process over the acquisition of specific facts or concepts. However, if implemented correctly, inquiry training could do both—teach the inquiry process as well as the content.

Summary

All teachers need a selection of teaching tools from which to choose to meet the various needs of their students. Inquiry training is not a model of teaching with which many teachers feel comfortable, but that should not be a reason for not using it. Administrators should create a school environment in which teachers are willing to take risks and try new methods of teaching. Some teachers teach only the way they were taught or teach only the way they learn best, but not all their students learn best using these methods. Traditionally, teachers have felt responsible for directing instruction and learning, but current thought is that students should be accountable for their own learning, although this paradigm shift may be difficult for some educators and students to accept. All students in all curriculum areas need to possess inquiry skills. Since research shows that students of all abilities and ages can benefit from inquiry training, this method should be used in all classrooms. As our society enters the 21st century, more and more jobs require employees to be problem solvers and analytical thinkers. Schools have the responsibility to equip students with the skills they will need to be productive citizens. If all knowledge is tentative, as Suchman believed, citizens will have to be lifelong learners whether they want to be or not.

BUILDING THE TOWER:
A SAMPLE DISCOVERY METHOD ACTIVITY

This activity is one that covers all the components inherent in the discovery method. It is learner centered and requires brainstorming and the formation and testing of hypotheses. The conclusion of the activity is a debriefing process that requires learners to evaluate their performance.

The materials needed for this activity are several packs of 100 4×6 index cards and a yardstick. The learners are grouped into teams and given an unopened pack of cards. They are told that they will have five minutes to build the highest-standing structure using only the index cards that they have been given. No "tools" of any sort are allowed; they can fold the cards, but that is all.

The first round of "play" is a five-minute planning stage. The learners cannot yet open the package of cards, but they can strategize and determine how best to build their structure. After the five-minute planning stage, the instructor gives the students a 10-minute experimental phase. The participants are able to open their cards and test the strategies they devised in the planning session. After 10 minutes of experimentation, the instructor takes up the used index cards and provides each team with a new unopened package. The students are then given five minutes to build the tallest structure they can. At the end of the building stage, the structures are measured and the winners are announced. Then the participants are given a 15-minute debriefing stage in which they determine what they could have done differently, what went well, and so forth. Finally, a reporter from each team takes a turn discussing the knowledge gained in the debriefing session.

THIRTEEN

Simulations and Role Play

SIMULATIONS ■

Simulations belong to the behavioral family of instructional strategies. They are constructed using real-life situations in a simulated environment. Simulations can be used to learn how to fly a plane, develop international negotiations skills, or resist peer pressures. Their applications for classroom use are numerous and are designed to enhance the cognitive and affective domains of learning.

Simulations are considered a form of experiential learning. Although they are sometimes called games or role play, a distinction needs to be made between role playing, games, and the simulations model. Games and role play are forms of simulations. Simulations can involve games, using rules and competition, but they do not use drama as is the case in role play. The learner is himself or herself, perhaps serving in another role, in a simulated environment but is still himself or herself. Any reaction from the simulated environment should be the learner's own natural behavior so that the consequences of actions can be learned while experiencing the simulation. Simulations are experiential learning, not direct instruction or rehearsed events. In simulations, mistakes are inevitable and desirable because the participants learn through these mistakes. In fact, sometimes the greater the disaster, the greater the learning (Jones, 1987).

Forms for the Simulation Model

There are several forms of the simulation instructional model. Simulations can use machines or people. For example, there are machine simulations for flight instruction, driver education, military combat, or simply trekking through the Oregon Trail. Most simulations are used to teach technical skills for learning to drive a car or to use machinery that can be both expensive and dangerous. Simulations teach technical skills in a safe, inexpensive way. Some simulations teach personal skills. Examples might be having students keep an imaginary bank account or play the stock market with fake money. Furthermore, some simulations have more of a gaming flavor, such as Monopoly or Trivial Pursuit. Today, several simulations can be used on the computer. Educators are split on the definitions and consider simulations, games, and role playing all to be the same or to have similar characteristics. Call them what you like, but use them. Students love them and they learn a great deal from them.

Machine simulations involve simulators or readily available software. The simulator is a type of training device that represents reality but that has controlled events. An example of this would be a driving simulator with which students learn to drive in a simulated automobile. The automobile simulator has the same mechanisms as an automobile—namely, a steering wheel, brakes, a clutch, and a gearshift. A moving picture represents the road, and realistic noises accompany the driving. This type of driving simulator mimics actual events that could occur while driving without the consequences in real life, thus enabling the student to acquire the skills needed later for actual driving. A flight simulator is another example; students can learn how to fly and master certain aspects before actually piloting a plane (Joyce, Weil, & Calhoun, 2000). Less complex machine simulations include computer games, such as the popular Where in the World or USA Is Carmen Sandiego, Oregon Trail, or SimCity software programs.

There are simulations involving both aspects of a game (roles and competition) with the components of a simulation. In gaming simulations, roles are defined for the players, a scenario is used to describe the situation, and a type of accounting system is used. The accounting system monitors and records the status of the players and provides appropriate feedback. In simulation games, success is defined in terms of player's goals with a prescribed criterion for winning (Dukes, 1978). These gaming simulations are usually competitive in nature, involving both the accumulation of points and clear winners and losers.

All-people simulations are another type of simulation. These simulations extract certain elements of a social or physical reality in such a way that students can interact with and become a part of a simulated reality (Dukes, 1978). True simulations represent a real-life situation, which duplicates selected parts of an environment along with its interrelationships. A common mistake is to believe simulations involve role playing. In simulations, students are not performing in a dramatic role. It is the environment

that is simulated. The students participate as themselves in a role and are given the key facts, not asked to invent them (Jones, 1980, 1987).

Reality can be manipulated in numerous ways. Simulations can be used to demonstrate how governments work, teach economic concepts, or gain career knowledge. Simulations can be structured to demonstrate the adverse effects of prejudices, socioeconomic power, or unethical decisions. Simulations can help students learn about competition or cooperation and empathy or apathy (Joyce et al., 2000).

Joyce et al. (2000) describes the following four components of the simulation instructional model: orientation, participant training, simulation operation, and debriefing. In the orientation phase, the teacher presents the topic and concepts to be explored and explains the type of simulation in which the students will participate. In the second phase, the rules and procedures are established. The third phase involves the actual simulation activity. The students participate, and the teacher serves as a referee or coach. The final stage is the participant debriefing, in which the events are summarized and analyzed by the teacher and students.

Simulations are based on social situations so that cooperative interaction can flourish. The overall success of the simulation depends on the cooperation and participation of members. While some simulations can be disconcerting to individuals because they have the potential to reveal negative characteristics, the overall social system should be nonthreatening and one of mutual cooperation.

Rationale for Appropriate Use

Simulations can be used in numerous contexts and to teach numerous process skills, especially in the affective domain. Simulations have the unique ability to help students achieve attitudinal objectives more effectively than any other instructional model. It is possible for students to observe emotions through the use of texts or other media; however, no other instructional design format is capable of permitting participants to actually experience them (Thiagarajan & Stolovitch, 1978).

Thiagarajan and Stolovitch (1978) recommend the use of simulation games as a way of introducing instructional content; they consider it especially applicable for the social studies curriculum. Students become interested in the variables influencing an individual's behavior, making them eager to learn the background or content of the simulation's real-life counterpart. A simulation may also be used as the cumulative activity to provide students an opportunity to try out the skills and knowledge they have acquired during the unit of study. Maximum effectiveness can be achieved through the participation in the same simulation prior to and preceding the unit of study.

Simulation games are effective ways to assess the student's ability to transfer content skills and knowledge in a realistic context. The teacher will need to observe students and use an evaluative rubric, which can be somewhat complex; however, simulations are valid and authentic assessments.

Thiagarajan and Stolovitch (1978) found that they can also be used for instructional improvement. Used as a preassessment tool, educators can determine which skills need to be emphasized or de-emphasized depending on the observation and analysis of the performance of students during the simulation. By identifying student's strengths and weakness, the instructional delivery can be tailored to meet individual needs.

Simulations have a practical value for the classroom and, used correctly, can help students achieve affective objectives as well as introduce and integrate authentic learning and assessments for meaningful long-term learning.

Lesson Design

Simulations can be structured into three basic areas for the lesson design: the *briefing*, the *action*, and the *debriefing*. These are the terms commonly used in all simulation models. The teacher can serve as the controller-facilitator or referee-coach and is responsible for moving the students through the three stages of the lesson.

The briefing should be used to provide an overview of the simulation. The rules, roles, procedures, scoring, goals, and levels of decisions should be discussed. Roles should be assigned, followed by a short practice session to check understanding. During the briefing stage, the teacher should be cautious about disclosing too much information. If answers are available in reading materials or documents for the students, more learning will occur if they are encouraged to investigate on their own. One of the functions of simulations is to provide students with the opportunity to find out the facts. The teacher-facilitator will also need to explain the rules sufficiently for the students to carry out the simulation, but it is not essential for students to have a total understanding of the simulation at the start. Rules can be revealed as needed, imitative of real life (Joyce et al., 2000). Should the simulation involve various stages, a briefing should be included with each consecutive stage.

The action stage involves the actual simulation. Students participate in the simulation, and the teacher functions as a coach. Occasionally, the simulation may need to be stopped to provide feedback or evaluate performances and clarify tasks. If a new stage or round is required, the teacher briefs the class prior to starting it.

One possible danger involves inappropriate behavior by the students. This may happen if the facilitator fails to clearly explain the rules of the simulation. In ordinary teaching, the instructor will step in and correct the behavior or mistakes. There are arguments suggesting that this makes the activity ineffective and an instructor-controlled exercise (Jones, 1980). Additional arguments state that students should have the opportunity to make mistakes, take the consequences, and learn (Joyce et al. 2000).

After the action, the debriefing stage occurs, during which the events are summarized and analyzed. During the debriefing, students explain their parts, their perceptions of the problem, and how they dealt with it.

Each participant contributes without any comments from the others. The teacher then leads an open discussion. The teacher should structure questions in advance to guide students to the expected outcomes. The simulation is compared with the real world and related to the curriculum content.

The debriefing is a crucial stage and one that should not be rushed through, especially if the simulation had a hidden agenda. Simulations dealing with prejudices, ethics, or power plays can sometimes stir up emotions, with the participants feeling exposed or humiliated. These individual insights may not be pleasant, requiring a supportive teacher to guide students through the process.

History and Research

Simulations can be traced back to ancient war times. Ancient China had a war game called Wei-Hai, and Chaturanga was a war game first played about 1,500 years ago in India. Chess, developed during the Middle Ages, simulates battles between nations with the game pieces representing competing forces with various degrees of strength and flexibility. In these games, which were played primarily for enjoyment until the 18th century, the game pieces were useful in the planning and predicting war outcomes. Following its defeat by Napoleon, Prussia pioneered the development and refinement of war gaming. Chess pieces were replaced by pieces representing actual infantry, artillery, and cavalry units. Teams of players replaced two single opposing players, and judges monitored the game activity (Heitzman, 1983; Maidment, 1973).

During the 20th century, the U.S. military refined the Prussian model, and the development of the computer led to technical improvements in national security efforts. During the 1950s, experimentation began with other social simulations. Economists and business theorists used quantitative models of simulations. Soon, political scientists, sociologists, and psychologists discovered the practical value of simulations. Crisis games were developed and created possible future international disasters in various parts of the world. This simulation provided foreign policymakers with a set of alternatives in the event of an actual crisis (Maidment, 1973).

Harold Guetzkow and his colleagues at Northwestern University created an international relations simulation during the late 1950s and the early 1960s. Guetzkow introduced simulations into the educational arena. This simulation was known as the 'Inter-Nation Simulation.' It re-created the main structural and dynamic features of an international system. His model was used to explain the operation of a system, and it advanced the theory of international relations. Student teams represent countries and act as decision makers. Information is provided to the teams about the nation's economic, consumer, and military bases. Then trading and the development of various agreements begin. Organizations can be established or trade agreements made. Nations can make war, with the outcome being determined by the military force of the group. The negotiation stage helps

students develop an understanding of the principles in international relations (Joyce et al. 2000; Maidment, 1973).

Simulations are designed using cybernetics, a branch of psychology. Cybernetic psychologists compare humans to machines and conceptualize the learner as a self-regulated feedback system. Cybernetic psychology operates on the principle of sense-oriented feedback that is intrinsic to the individual, in which the ability to feel the effect of one's decisions is the basis for self-corrective choices. According to this theory, human behavior has covert behaviors, such as thinking and feeling, and overt behaviors, or actions. Actions are created by the received feedback. When the choices are played back, the consequences can be felt. Simply put, simulations in cybernetic terms are designed to create an environment in which feedback is given that results in self-corrective behavior.

Numerous books and research articles recommend the use of simulations; however, there is no recent empirical research to substantiate the claims of the effectiveness of the simulation model for instruction. Several documents state that more research was needed; however, none is forthcoming. Jones (1988) offered this reasoning for the shortage of empirical data, claiming that the studies are confined to one simulation only, making it difficult to measure results. Furthermore, Jones contends that the articles are full of hypotheses and statistics from the tests but usually say little about what actually happened.

Boocock and Schild (1968) also identify several research issues that confound studies. A simulation evaluation requires the use of experimental and control groups, which Boocock and Schild find difficult to implement in school settings. Likewise, they cite a variance in the degree of teacher capability, claiming that researchers cannot be sure that sample teachers are using the same techniques or are presenting the materials in the same way. Boocock and Schild hypothesized that teacher bias or preference for one teaching method would also confound the results.

Boocock and Schild conducted a study on the use of simulation techniques in the fall of 1964, as simulations were being introduced in the schools. The purpose of the study was to test students' role empathy and feelings of efficacy after participation in the simulation. Pre- and posttests were used to compare responses and measure the effectiveness of simulation activities. The study involved the use of two games. *Life Career* introduced students to labor, school, and marriage decisions and the consequences of those decisions, and the *Legislative Game* allowed collective decisions to be reached on issues with which members of society have differing interests.

Boocock and Schild concluded that the career game provided role empathy, especially with the boys who took the feminine role or role of the high school dropout. The male students developed a sympathetic attitude toward those roles after their experiences. The image of political roles was not changed by the legislative game, although feelings of political efficacy were greater. The most convincing evidence supporting the use of simulations was produced by the career game, for which actual cognitive learn-

ing gains were measured. Boocock and Schild stated that although their study was far from conclusive, they believed the results showed promising effects for positive results of the simulation, based on the stated objectives for the learner.

Promises and Pitfalls

Simulations hold much promise as an instructional method because they incorporate both the cognitive and affective domains of learning. Simulations help students develop process-thinking skills. Simulations can enhance decision-making abilities, communication skills, the use of persuasion, or to influence resisting. Simulations can be used for learning in general or be designed to integrate ideas and information students already have. A simulation experience leads students to see the interconnectedness of political, social, interpersonal, cultural, economic, and historical factors. Simulations are especially useful to help students understand the idea of social systems.

Simulations can be designed to affect attitudes. Participants can gain empathy for real-life decision makers, learn that life is more complicated than ever imagined, or decide that they can do something important about affecting their own personal lives or the lives of others. Simulations provide participants with explicit and experiential ideas and with concepts and words to describe human behavior. They act as an information retrieval device to help bring dormant knowledge to consciousness.

Simulations affect the social setting in which learning takes place. The physical format alone produces a more relaxed natural exchange between teacher and students. During simulations, the control of the classroom goes from the teacher to the structure of the simulation, allowing for better student-teacher relations. Simulations are engaging, helping students to drop their usual interpersonal facades, which leads to a more open classroom atmosphere.

The use of simulations leads to personal growth (a) through the discovery of personal skills, abilities, fears, and weakness that weren't apparent before and (b) by providing opportunities to express affection, anger, and indifference without suffering permanent consequences.

Joyce et al. (2000) claim that simulations have several advantages. One is the practice of complex activities prior to the application in real life. Simulations have the ability to help students learn from self-generated feedback and, consequently, learn necessary corrective behaviors, another distinctive feature of this instructional strategy.

Dukes and Seidner (1978) describe how simulation activities reach cognitive and affective educational objectives. They contend that simulations can incorporate a body of factual knowledge in the structure and functioning of the game so that the knowledge can be transmitted to the student through participation in the simulation. Simulations can be designed for students to use higher-order thinking concepts, principles, and processes. According to Dukes and Seidner, many objectives in the affective

domain may be attained only through the use of simulations, causing changes in attitudes or empathy and efficacy.

Maidment and Bronstein (1973) state that simulations have three advantages over other teaching methodologies: (a) an increase in student motivation and interest brought about by (b) the creation a favorable learning environment by having the teacher behave in a nonauthoritative role and (c) the presentation of realistic and relevant learning experiences.

Although simulations are a promising instructional strategy, possible drawbacks should be considered. First, there is a lack of evidence to support the effectiveness of simulation activities in the classroom, especially for cognitive skill attainment. A careful study of the practicalities of this model may suggest that in this day of high-stakes testing and accountability, there is no time to use models that do not guarantee success. For this argument, an assertion can be made that numerous instructional standards require the use of process skills, which can be obtained through simulation activities. In addition there is a strong need for our schools to have a positive influence on students' character building and value systems—something that may be achieved only through participation in simulation activities.

Experts note other potential problems with this instructional strategy. First, simulations can be defective, producing a lack of validity or playability. According to Maidment and Bronstein (1973), there is little educational value in a simulation game that does not in some way accurately reflect events in the real world or that creates a false sense of reality. The lack of playability refers to the lack of clear directions or rules that are too complex or confusing, requiring the teacher to continuously interrupt the flow of the simulation.

Jones (1987; see also 1980) also cautions educators on the use of correct terminology for simulation activities, stating that the wrong wording can lead to wrong expectations, which in turn can lead to wrong student behavior. Words can often be interpreted in numerous ways based on prior knowledge. For example, telling students they are going to play a game and having the students expect fun and games may create disappointment because it wasn't their expectation, or students may decide to interject a little fun through inappropriate behavior. Jones also warns that saying the simulation is a role play can be interpreted as a need for students to play a role and so not behave as they naturally would. Simulations are simulated environments, not behaviors. To avoid confusion, it is helpful for educators or the simulator presenters to use appropriate terminology. Jones recommends the words *simulation, event, participant, behavior, action, issues,* and *ethics* and not the use of the words *game, drama, play, player, act, winning,* or *losing* to describe simulations.

No matter which terms are used, simulations provide active and engaged learning for students. The lesson at the end of this chapter should

validate this model as an effective instructional strategy for helping students attain learning objectives.

Summary

Simulations provide relevant learning opportunities for real-life situations. They have numerous applications for classroom use—all designed to enhance the cognitive and affective domains of learning—and should be a regular part of a master teacher's instructional strategies.

NOTE: See the end of this chapter for a sample lesson titled "The Gifted and Talented Simulation."

ROLE PLAY ■

Role play is a method of learning based on role theory. In this instructional method, students adopt assumed positions and interact in a simulated life situation. Role play takes on different meanings for different people. These range from highly controlled, guided conversations to improvised drama activities to highly complex simulated scenarios (Ladousse, 1987).

Role play has roots in both the personal and social dimensions of education. On a personal level, it helps students find personal meaning within their social worlds and resolve personal dilemmas. Socially, it allows students to work together to analyze social issues and develops democratic ways of coping with these situations (Joyce et al., 2000).

To really understand the instructional model of role play, one must understand the concept of *role*, one of the central theoretical underpinnings of the role-playing model. Students must understand roles and how they are played to truly understand themselves and others. It is the teachers' responsibility to teach students to recognize different roles and to think of their own and others' behaviors using the concept of roles.

The role of the teacher is critical to the success of the instructional model of role play. It is not the time for teachers to check papers or do remediation with students while students participate in role playing. First, teachers may need to provide initial props to support the role play. These props make the role play more realistic and will engage the students in the instructional model. Teachers should also challenge the children to use the skills they are learning in other curriculum areas to apply them during the role play to assist in the problem-solving process. Sometimes, it may be necessary for teachers to enter into the role play to encourage the students to think more deeply and play their roles more realistically. By intermittently assuming roles in the children's play, a teacher can assess the students' understanding of their roles and their ability to solve problems.

Finally, it is important for teachers to provide enough time for the children to interact with the materials and with one another. Teachers should not rush the children; they need time to build understanding (Jarrett, 1997).

The instructional value of role playing is that students learn to analyze their personal values and behaviors. They learn empathy and respect from participating in the nine steps involved in the Shaftels' (Shaftel & Shaftel, 1967) model of role-play (see Table 13.1 later in this chapter). In addition, students learn strategies for solving interpersonal and personal dilemmas they encounter. Role playing also has nuturant effects as students learn skills in negotiating and comfort in expressing their own opinions (p. 73).

A teacher may use role play for two basic reasons. First, it can be used to develop a social program that teaches children to problem-solve as they work through social issues students will experience as they develop into adults. Teachers may also use role play to counsel a group of students who are experiencing a human relations problem (Shaftel & Shaftel, 1967, p. 70). This instructional method can also be used to increase the efficiency of academic learning through the portrayal of current events or historical circumstances or through the use of the dramatization of plays or novels (Chesler & Fox, 1966).

History and Research

Many people have designed models for role play. Each model has its own series of steps for conducting a role play. Fannie and George Shaftel, Mark Chesler and Robert Fox, and Gillian Ladousse are just a few names associated with the instructional model of role-play.

Mark Chesler and Robert Fox (1966) argue that role playing in the classroom works best when there is an attempt to follow a definite sequence of steps. The steps allow for a logical ordering and development of the role-playing session. The first step is preparation and instruction. During this step, the problem is selected, a warm-up is conducted, and instructions and roles are given to the students. The second major step involves dramatic action and discussion. The actual role playing itself and the subsequent discussion and interpretation of the action are conducted during this step. Evaluation is the final step in Chesler and Fox's model. This is the time for the students and the teacher to review the successes and failures of the role-playing experience.

Fannie and George Shaftel's (1967) model of role play has nine steps that involve assigning students to be either role players or observers during the enactment. Each of the steps has a clear purpose that contributes to the richness and focus of the learning activity. The collection of steps ensures that a line of thinking is maintained throughout the role play, that roles are assigned and understood, and that the discussion is rich.

Gillian Ladousse's (1987) model of role play is structured around a lesson design for teachers to follow while using the instructional model. First, teachers decide the aim of their role play, which focuses the children's attention. An example may be to encourage students to interpret a scene in

different ways through the use of photographs. Once the teacher explains the aim to the students, he or she warms up the group with an activity that introduces the students to the aim for the day. For example, in a lesson on the three branches of the government, the teacher may do an activity about how we would make a new rule for the class. Following the warm-up, the teacher moves onto the procedure part of the lesson. At this point, the teacher explains the problem and passes out role cards that describe the roles students are to take during the role play. The students then participate in the role play using their role play cards to support them. The lesson ends with the teacher conducting a follow-up discussion to allow the students to debrief the role play.

In their book *Models of Teaching*, Bruce Joyce, Marsha Weil, and Emily Calhoun (2000) describe the role play model created by Fannie and George Shaftel. The Shaftels' model of role play includes nine steps (Table 13.1). To begin the role play, the teacher should warm up the students. To support the children in their understanding of the problem, the teacher should assist the children in expressing the problem vividly through the use of examples that the students generate based on reality, imagination, or literature. The Shaftels (1967) wrote *Role-Playing of Social Values: Decision Making in the Social Studies*, which presents problem stories that can be used by teachers to support Step 1 of the model. The problems the Shaftels present in their book are open-ended problems without solutions. It is the job of the students to use role play to generate solutions to the problem presented. Step 1 concludes with the teacher asking probing questions that will require the students to make predictions concerning the outcomes of the problem story.

Following the presentation of the problem, a brief discussion of examples that relate to the problem, and predictions about the outcome of the problem, the teacher moves on to Step 2. In this step, characters involved in the role play are clarified and students are assigned roles. The teacher can assign roles or students can volunteer for them. Once the roles are assigned, the next step involves the students and the teacher creating the setting to support the problem that has been presented. Next, in Step 4, the students who are not assigned roles in the role play are assigned as observers who are responsible for examining how students are playing their roles, the solutions that the role play demonstrates, and the feelings and emotions shown by the role players.

In Step 5, the role players conduct the role play in front of the observers. The role play should be short and allow for the role players to respond to each other. The purpose of this step is to ensure that the role players and observers really understand the problem they are dealing with. A discussion and evaluation of the role play that was just conducted make up Step 6. The observers discuss what they observed, how the role players solved the problem, and the consequences of the way the problem was solved during Step 5.

Following the discussion and evaluation of the first enactment of the role play, the students reenact it, which is Step 7. This time, the information

Table 13.1. Components of Role Play

Step 1	Warm up the group
Step 2	Select participants
Step 3	Set the stage
Step 4	Prepare the observers
Step 5	Enact
Step 6	Discuss and evaluate
Step 7	Reenact
Step 8	Discuss and evaluate
Step 9	Share experiences and generalize

that was discussed and evaluated in Step 6 is incorporated into this reenactment. Once again, a discussion and evaluation is conducted on the reenactment that just took place (Step 8). The role play ends with Step 9 as the teacher helps the students produce generalizations that can be made about the problem and the appropriate solutions to the problem presented by the teacher. The teacher may have to guide the students to the generalizations and how they can apply to their personal lives.

Promises and Pitfalls

Role play has many advantages over traditional ways of problem solving. First, the traditional approach to problem solving involves only having the children think about the possible solutions. Role playing requires the students to use cognitive and affective skills to generate solutions to problems. For children who are bored and find school a waste of time, role playing simulates the real conflicts of the child's world, which makes school more meaningful and relevant for them. Children who are engaged in role play are not involved in competition activities, so children feel more relaxed and friendly while they are learning. In traditional instruction, students learn concepts from listening to their teacher lecture

to them. In role play, students learn by doing. It converts ideas into direct experiences. One of the most important advantages of role play is that it makes students aware of the possibilities of alternative choices as they observe and participate in ways other than their own of resolving problems. Finally, role play allows students to examine their own values, defend them, and possibly make changes to their values as a result of looking at a problem from a variety of perspectives (Furness, 1976).

Role play does have disadvantages that administrators and teachers need to be aware of when using this instructional model. First, compared with traditional instructional models, the teacher turns over a lot of the responsibility of learning to the class and individual students. The teacher presents a problem, but the students generate solutions to the problems through the role play. The teacher can indirectly influence the solutions through the discussions that follow the first and second enactment, but he or she turns over most of the control of learning to the students. Role playing does take a lot of time. Students need time to fully explore the problems, problem-solve solutions, and enact their role play. If a teacher rushes this process, the purpose of the role play can be lost because insufficient time was provided. Many times, role play may be seen as too entertaining or frivolous. It looks different from the traditional classrooms where students sit in their seats and do their work without any noise. Finally, if the students have not had many experiences with problem solving, the solutions generated during the enactments may not be what the teacher wants the students to learn. Problem solving is a skill that needs to be worked on prior to engaging in role play so that students have prior knowledge of generating and supporting solutions to problems presented to them (Van Ments, 1999).

Summary

Role play leads students to understand social behavior, their role in social interactions, and ways of solving problems effectively. The model involves students acting out conflicts, learning to take the roles of others, and observing social behavior (Joyce et al., 2000).

Role play is best used when the teacher wants students to experience and become involved in the situation they are studying and to formulate their attitudes toward it. It is an excellent way for students to develop interpersonal and communication skills, and it provides highly motivating and memorable lessons.

In the following staff development activity for teachers, there are 10 applicants who have applied for the National Gifted Program in Washington, D.C. This is a free school that selects only three or four new students per year. The school is nongraded and defines *gifted* and *talented* loosely. Tell the teachers that the objective of the simulation is to devise their own selection criteria and procedure and then select the top three applicants. They must be able to defend their choices. Next, the teachers should rank order the applicants from 1 to 10, with 1 being the top selec-

tion and 10 being the last. They should then defend their positions for this ordering. Finally, share with the group what these selectees grew up to become (1. university professor in physics; 2. brilliant scientist; 3. famous wife of a president; 4. congressman; 5. satirist; 6. most famous president; 7. famous inventor; 8. famous dancer; 9. inventor; 10. famous congresswoman).

The following abbreviations are used in the exercise:

AQ = achievement quotient

IQ = intelligence quotient

SQ = social quotient

CQ = creative quotient

For the sake of the simulation, 100 is average for all four quotients. As a follow-up activity, have the teachers try to figure out who the individuals really were. Variations can be done with students on who would be the best scientist, the best artist, best farmer, and so on.

Gifted and Talented Simulation:
A Sample Lesson Using Simulation

Applicant #1

FATHER

MOTHER

Name: Bill Grost
Address: Lansing, Michigan
Age: 30 **Race:** Caucasian
Place of birth: East Lansing
Nationality: American
Occupation: Accountant
Religious preference: Catholic
Educational level: M.S.
Interests: Sports, reading

Name: Audrey Grost
Address: Lansing, Michigan
Age: 28 **Race:** Caucasian
Place of birth: East Lansing
Nationality: American
Occupation: Housewife
Religious preference: Catholic
Educational level: B.A.
Interests: Sports, music

Applicant #1
Child applying for N.G.P

Name: Mike Grost **Age:** 10 **Educational level:** Grade 6
Height: 4'11" **Weight:** 75 lbs. **Appearance:** Average
IQ: 180 **SQ:** 140 **AQ:** 170 **CQ:** 165

School adjustment: Aloof from age peers, organizer
General physical health: Excellent
General emotional health: Excellent
Congenital abnormalities: Requires glasses
Evaluation of family stock: Above average
General political beliefs: Conservative but futuristic
Special interests: Chess, math
Special skills: Eidetic memory
Vocational goals: Make a commitment to education
Personal goals: Personal fulfillment and make significant contribution to society
Vocational contributions: Published an original mathematics theorem (Accepted by the American Association of Mathematics)

Applicant #2

FATHER

Name: Herman Edder
Address: Gary, Indiana
Age: 31   **Race:** Caucasian
Place of birth: Germany
Nationality: American
Occupation: Self-employed
Religious preference: Agnostic
Educational level: High school
Interests: Reading

MOTHER

Name: Anna Edder
Address: Lansing, Michigan
Age: 30   **Race:** Caucasian
Place of birth: Germany
Nationality: American
Occupation: Housewife
Religious preference: None
Educational level: High school
Interests: Music

Applicant #2
Child applying for N.G.P

Name: Sam Edder   **Age:** 9   **Educational level:** Grade 4
Height: 5'1"   **Weight:** 74 lbs.   **Appearance:** Homely
IQ: 82   **SQ:** 74   **AQ:** 82   **CQ:** 110

School adjustment: Very poor, considered unsociable, disturbed
General physical health: Often sickly
General emotional health: Certified emotional breakdown, removed from
     school temporarily
Congenital abnormalities: None
Evaluation of family stock: Average
General political beliefs: Quiet child, beliefs not known
Special interests: Frequently withdraws into fantasy world
Special skills: Plays violin, likes to be alone to read
Vocational goals: No evidence
Personal goals: Independence from family
Vocational contributions: None

Applicant #3

FATHER

Name: William Hall (deceased)
Address: Lives with grandmother
Age: —   **Race:** Caucasian
Place of birth: New York
Nationality: American
Occupation: Itinerant
Religious preference: Presbyterian
Educational level: B.A.
Interests: —

MOTHER

Name: Rosemarie Hall (deceased)
Address: Lives with grandmother
Age: —   **Race:** Caucasian
Place of birth: New York
Nationality: American
Occupation: Chores
Religious preference: Catholic
Educational level: High school
Interests: —

Applicant #3
Child applying for N.G.P

Name: Mary Hall   **Age:** 10   **Educational level:** Grade 5
Height: 5'8"   **Weight:** 76 lbs.   **Appearance:** Unattractive
IQ: 110   **SQ:** 76   **AQ:** 83   **CQ:** 95

School adjustment: Erratic, withdrawn, seeks attention, fails often
General physical health: Sickly, bedridden, hospitalized often
General emotional health: Bites nails, phobias, attention-seeking behavior, dominates
Congenital abnormalities: Wears back brace from spinal defect
Evaluation of family stock: Average or better, father alcoholic
General political beliefs: Conservative
Special interests: Daydreams, prefers to be alone, wants to be center of attention
Special skills: Patience with children, elderly or infirm
Vocational goals: None
Personal goals: Altruistic, prefers to help elderly or poor
Vocational contributions: None

Applicant #4

FATHER	MOTHER
Name: James Horn	**Name:** Jane Horn
Address: Indianapolis	**Address:** Indianapolis
Age: 29 **Race:** Caucasian	**Age:** 29 **Race:** Caucasian
Place of birth: Philadelphia	**Place of birth:** Philadelphia
Nationality: American	**Nationality:** American
Occupation: Banker	**Occupation:** Housewife
Religious preference: Protestant	**Religious preference:** Protestant
Educational level: B.A.	**Educational level:** B. A.
Interests: Sports, chess	**Interests:** Swimming, reading

Applicant #4
Child applying for N.G.P

Name: William Horn   **Age:** 10   **Educational level:** Grade 5
Height: 5'4"   **Weight:** 125 lbs.   **Appearance:** Attractive
IQ: 169   **SQ:** 155   **AQ:** 166   **CQ:** 128

School adjustment: Good, organizer, and leader
General physical health: Excellent
General emotional health: Excellent
Congenital abnormalities: None
Evaluation of family stock: Above average
General political beliefs: Conservative
Special interests: Basketball, math
Special skills: Leader, self-motivated
Vocational goals: To teach math
Personal goals: Wants to make a personal contribution to society
Vocational contributions: None

Applicant #5

FATHER

Name: Van Gunther
Address: Oklahoma
Age: 51   **Race:** Am. Indian
Place of birth: Oklahoma
Nationality: American
Occupation: Rancher
Religious preference: None
Educational level: High school
Interests: Ambitious

MOTHER

Name: Mary Gunther
Address: Oklahoma
Age: Deceased **Race:** Am. Indian
Place of birth: Oklahoma
Nationality: American
Occupation: Housewife
Religious preference: —
Educational level: High school
Interests: Religion/philosophy

Applicant #5
Child applying for N.G.P

Name: William Gunther   **Age:** 11   **Educational level:** Grade 4 (3 times)
Height: 4'11"   **Weight:** 135 lbs.   **Appearance:** Unkempt
IQ: 110   **SQ:** 85   **AQ:** 82   **CQ:** 115

School adjustment: Dislikes school, does not mind, has caused extensive damage to school yard and building through carelessness
General physical health: Good
General emotional health: Shy and bashful, prankster
Congenital abnormalities: None
Evaluation of family stock: Healthy, low-middle class
General political beliefs: Inconsistent and critical
Special interests: Horse riding, roping
Special skills: Good sense of humor
Vocational goals: Perform in wild west show (parents want him to be a minister)
Personal goals: Wants to see world, perform for people
Vocational contributions: Participates in local rodeos

Applicant #6

FATHER

MOTHER

Name: Joseph Wright
Address: Indiana
Age: 45   **Race:** Caucasian
Place of birth: Virginia
Nationality: American
Occupation: Rancher
Religious preference: Baptist
Educational level: Uneducated
Interests: Horses

Name: Mary Wright (deceased)
Address: Indiana
Age: Deceased **Race:** Caucasian
Place of birth: Virginia
Nationality: American
Occupation: Housewife
Religious preference: Baptist
Educational level: Uneducated
Interests: Cooking, state fairs

Applicant #6
Child applying for N.G.P

Name: Albert Wright   **Age**: 17   **Educational level**: High school dropout

Height: 6′4″   **Weight**: 170 lbs.   **Appearance**: Plain
IQ: Unavailable   **SQ**: Unavailable   **AQ**: Unavailable   **CQ**: Unavailable

School adjustment: Good, well-liked, respected, attendance irregular
General physical health: Good, large for his age
General emotional health: Pleasant, easygoing, poor self-concept
Congenital abnormalities: Opthamuscular weakness (eye wanders)
Evaluation of family stock: Mother illegitimate, father involved in several lawsuits
General political beliefs: Very conservative
Special interests: Physical sports, wrestling, practical jokes
Special skills: Likes to argue, fairly well-read, good debater
Vocational goals: Interested in retailing
Personal goals: Wants to own his own business and have a good family
Vocational contributions: Manual labor, clerked in store, longshoreman, considered lazy by employers

Applicant #7

FATHER

Name: Sam Ridell
Address: Michigan
Age: 54   Race: Caucasian
Place of birth: Nova Scotia
Nationality: Canadian
Occupation: Unemployed
Religious preference: Baptist
Educational level: None
Interests: None

MOTHER

Name: Nancy Ridell
Address: Michigan
Age: 49   Race: Caucasian
Place of birth: Ontario
Nationality: Canadian
Occupation: Teacher
Religious preference: Baptist
Educational level: B.A.
Interests: Literature, crafts

Applicant #7
Child applying for N.G.P

Name: Bill Ridell   Age: 11   Educational level: Withdrawn
Height: 4'5''   Weight: 75 lbs.   Appearance: Pleasant
IQ: 81   SQ: 79   AQ: 87   CQ: 110

School adjustment: Withdrawn from school after three months,
                considered backward by school officials
General physical health: Enrolled in school two years late due to scarlet
                fever, respiratory infections, going deaf
General emotional health: Stubborn, aloof, shows little emotion
Congenital abnormalities: Enlarged head at birth
Evaluation of family stock: Father lower class, mother intelligent
General political beliefs: Unconcerned
Special interests: Mechanics, likes to build things, flying, likes to play with
                fire (burned down father's barn)
Special skills: Manual dexterity, reads well, poor grammar
Vocational goals: Scientist or railroad mechanic
Personal goals: Works hard, wants to earn money
Vocational contributions: Sold magazines

Applicant #8

FATHER

Name: Bill Hawkins
Address: Los Angeles
Age: 55   **Race:** Caucasian
Place of birth: California
Nationality: American
Occupation: Entrepreneur
Religious preference: Catholic
Educational level: Not known
Interests: Writing

MOTHER

Name: Valerie Hawkins
Address: Los Angeles
Age: 51   **Race:** Caucasian
Place of birth: California
Nationality: American
Occupation: Teacher
Religious preference: Catholic
Educational level: B.A., music
Interests: Traveling, sewing

Applicant #8
Child applying for N.G.P

Name: Elaine Hawkins   **Age:** 12   **Educational level:** Elementary
Height: 5'2"   **Weight:** 99 lbs.   **Appearance:** Attractive, mature
IQ: 108   **SQ:** 84   **AQ:** 94   **CQ:** 115

School adjustment: Dropped out at age 10, claimed to be 16 years old
General physical health: Very good
General emotional health: Talked back, stubborn, rebellious, behavior problem
Congenital abnormalities: None
Evaluation of family stock: Broken home, mother works, rarely home, migrants
General political beliefs: Radical, outspoken
Special interests: Reading, art
Special skills: Dancing
Vocational goals: To teach dance
Personal goals: Wants a career in dance
Vocational contributions: Likes to play at being a dance teacher with neighborhood children

Applicant #9

FATHER

Name: Samuel Krebbs
Address: Indiana
Age: 34   **Race:** Caucasian
Place of birth: Indiana
Nationality: American
Occupation: Farmer
Religious preference: Methodist
Educational level: High school
Interests: Playing the fiddle

MOTHER

Name: Sally Ann Krebbs
Address: Indiana
Age: 32   **Race:** Caucasian
Place of birth: Indiana
Nationality: American
Occupation: Housewife
Religious preference: Methodist
Educational level: Jr. high
Interests: Sewing, canning

Applicant #9
Child applying for N.G.P

Name: Lloyd Krebbs   **Age:** 11   **Educational level:** Grade 5
Height: 4'11''   **Weight:** 142 lbs.   **Appearance:** Average
IQ: 108   **SQ:** 98   **AQ:** 112   **CQ:** 105

School adjustment: Good average performer
General physical health: Very good
General emotional health: Good
Congenital abnormalities: None
Evaluation of family stock: Conservative, rural family, active in church
General political beliefs: Mostly conservative
Special interests: Sports, fiddle
Special skills: Active in 4-H
Vocational goals: Farming
Personal goals: Get married and own good farmland
Vocational contributions: None

Applicant #10

FATHER

Name: Ben Jackson
Address: Texas
Age: 47   **Race:** Black
Place of birth: Texas
Nationality: American
Occupation: Minister
Religious preference: Baptist
Educational level: High school
Interests: Music

MOTHER

Name: Arlyne Jackson
Address: Texas
Age: 46   **Race:** Black
Place of birth: Texas
Nationality: American
Occupation: Housewife
Religious preference: Baptist
Educational level: High school
Interests: Wants daughter to be a
music teacher

Applicant #10
Child applying for N.G.P

Name: Pearl Ruth Jackson   **Age:** 16   **Educational level:** Grade 10
Height: 5'11"   **Weight:** 195 lbs.   **Appearance:** Heavy, unattractive
IQ: 138   **SQ:** 126   **AQ:** 149   **CQ:** 108

School adjustment: Top 5% of class, ghetto school
General physical health: Good, obese
General emotional health: Good, confident
Congenital abnormalities: None
Evaluation of family stock: Conservative parents, opposed to program
General political beliefs: Politically active in school
Special interests: Rock music, student government
Special skills: Debate team
Vocational goals: Wants to be a lawyer
Personal goals: Ambitious, hardworking, wants to participate in National
Gifted and Talented Program
Vocational contributions: Has participated in local "get out and vote"
efforts

FOURTEEN

Cooperative Learning

Cooperative learning has been attributed to gains in three major areas—academic achievement, intergroup relations, and social and affective development (Gillies & Ashman, 2000; Slavin, 1996). Academic achievement has been expressed in terms of higher grades, better retention of information, and more long-term learning; it benefits both high and low achievers, and it benefits all races and genders. The success of cooperative learning strategies is evident; moreover, it has been shown to cross all barriers of race, gender, and ability. It aids in the cognitive growth of all children at all levels.

The intergroup aspect of success is exhibited by better race relations in desegregated settings, more tolerance of different cultures, and an appreciation of diversity. Cultural diversity is an issue confronting all of society, and cooperative learning can assist in more positive interactions between the races in the future.

Students also display substantial affective development by showing higher self-esteem, an increased "liking" of school, better attendance, increased socialization skills, increased ability to work effectively with others, and a better understanding of people as individuals. It is important for schools to impart cognitive knowledge and skills to students, but it is also crucial for students to become contributing members of society. Cooperative learning can make these social processes second nature to

children, and they, in turn, can become better citizens making positive impacts on society.

The literature identifies essential components necessary for successful implementation of the cooperative learning model. Lyman and Foyle (1998) and Ngeow (1998) contend that seven elements contribute to the whole of cooperative learning:

1. Designed learning tasks based on shared learning goals

2. Groups consisting of two to six members

3. Prior teaching of effective group processes

4. Teacher initiation of concept

5. Cooperative learning behavior within the groups

6. Positive interdependence within groups

7. Individual accountability of all group members for the final outcomes

The teacher and student develop the intended learning task based on the shared goals of the school and the classroom. This allows students to take ownership in their learning through the establishment of the task. An essential aspect of cooperative learning is the structure of the group itself. A teacher must be aware of the situational aspect of group assignment and place students accordingly. The situational aspect refers to the role that each student has within a group. For example, different students within a group have different areas of academic strength. In most group situations, the teacher needs either to assign or approve individual, specific roles in cooperative learning settings for the purpose of balancing the group dynamic. The group task also contributes significantly to the composition of the group, and the potential group structures are innumerable—homogeneous, heterogeneous, mixed ability, equal ability, culturally diverse, and ranging in size from two to six members.

The teacher is responsible for the next two processes in the continuum of cooperative learning. Before group learning is to happen, the teacher must model and discuss certain group processes for students to be successful in the assignment. Communicating with others and being able to work well in groups are topics that must be explored and explained. The initiation of the cooperative learning task will occur when the teacher introduces the concept. This process provides students with some amount of prior knowledge or cognitive structure on which to base their group learning. Although the teacher is not directly involved in the cooperative learning, he or she initiates the concept discussion and establishes the framework on which the learning is built.

True cooperative learning can happen only when collaboration among all members of the group is required to accomplish a given task. This cooperative behavior and positive interdependence among the group members are crucial for successful learning. The promises of this method

are rooted in these two factors. Students are "forced" to cooperate and establish positive relationships as a means of reaching that predetermined end. Finally, individual accountability must be used to ensure that all students are learning and contributing. Within this strategy, it is too easy for a student to become passive and allow the other members to provide the learning, but teachers who encourage and mandate accountability for every student will find the most success with cooperative learning.

Cooperative learning has established its effectiveness across grade levels and curricular areas. Gillies and Ashman (2000) contend that "it has been used successfully to promote learning achievement in collaborative writing, problem solving in mathematics, comprehension in reading, and conceptual understanding in science" (p. 19). The affective domain has also shown positive growth, and Gillies and Ashman point out that "it promotes socialization and positive student interactions, improved attitudes to learning, and improved acceptance of children with disabilities by their nondisabled peers" (p. 20). These findings signify gains and growth in multiple cognitive and social domains.

Often, cooperative learning is viewed as solely an elementary strategy that works only with younger students. But this teaching model can promote growth in middle and high school students, who many times are attempting to establish independence from adult authority figures. Cooperative learning gives adolescents some degree of independence within their groups and creates a situation in which the progress of each member contributes to the group's success (Slavin, 1996). The adolescent is searching for an identity that conforms to the peer group, and cooperative learning can help the student with this quest.

Similar to other teaching models, cooperative learning has a "best" structure by which to organize the lesson. Stahl (1994) outlines five basic parts for a well-developed cooperative learning lesson:

1. A clear set of outcome objectives

2. A complete set of task completion instructions

3. Heterogeneous grouping

4. Individual accountability

5. Time for reflection and debriefing of the learning

Students must know beforehand exactly what they are expected to learn from the activity. This may be basic knowledge, social skills, or cognitive processes, but the teacher should dictate this information to students prior to initiation of the lesson. How are students supposed to accomplish the learning objectives? The teacher must provide concise and clear instructions for the activity so that students will be cognizant of the means with which to meet the end. This also has to be done before any group activity is started to avoid infinite questions after the activity begins.

The groups should be as heterogeneously mixed as possible. Academic ability, race, gender, ethnic backgrounds, and socioeconomic status are

characteristics to consider when grouping. Students will learn how to work effectively with different students and with classmates who probably are not "regular" friends. The diversity of the group exposes all students to viewpoints different from their own and provides the opportunity to appreciate the differences present in the human race.

The rationale for cooperative groups is to have the whole be greater than the sum of its parts. However, each member must be held personally accountable for the work completed and for internalization of the content. The teacher should develop appropriate devices to assess the learning and long-term retention of each student.

The last step is to allow time for reflection on the group process as a whole. This forces students to analyze not only the group dynamics used to achieve a goal but also how they individually contributed to the group's success. The stage is now set for improved cooperative learning in the future because students have reflected on the past "mistakes" and can use them as a springboard for continuous improvement.

■ HISTORY AND RESEARCH

John Dewey (1910) was the first to advocate the teaching methods combining academic inquiry and democratic learning. "Dewey viewed the school as a miniature democratic society in which students could learn and practice the skills and tools necessary for democratic living" (Ornstein & Hunkins, 1998, p. 46). Dewey also contended that one of the philosophies of education is not only to learn to acquire information but to bring that learning to bear on our everyday actions and behaviors (Ngeow, 1998).

More recently, renewed research efforts have been made to further develop cooperative learning models. Researchers and theorists who currently study the effects of cooperative learning are David and Roger Johnson, Robert Slavin, and Shlomo and Yael Sharan.

David and Roger Johnson, based at the University of Minnesota, have published numerous articles and books on the effectiveness of cooperative learning models. They contend that the education of cooperation is an important aspect of the entire schooling process. Their "learning together" (Johnson & Johnson, 1994) model, where groups hand in a single assignment and receive a group grade based on this product, has proven beneficial to student learning (Slavin, 1996). They have also searched for the effects of cooperative tasks and reward systems, the effect of peer teaching, and the improvement of intergroup relations and behavior (Johnson & Johnson, 1994).

Robert Slavin, codirector of the Center for Research on the Education of Students Placed At-Risk at Johns Hopkins University, has studied how cooperative learning can benefit children for which traditional teaching methods have been unsuccessful. The focus of his research is to find "best practices" for teachers to use to enhance student learning. Slavin has experimented with various types of grouping and differing group tasks.

His efforts have also focused on the implementation of heterogeneous groups and the importance of both intrinsic and extrinsic rewards for students.

At the University of Tel Aviv, Shlomo Sharan studies the impact of cooperative learning with regard to student achievement. His "group investigation" model (Sharan & Sharan, 1992) involves students in the planning, researching, and presentation of information to the class on a topic chosen by the group (Slavin, 1996). Students take ownership of the learning process because they are given the opportunity to chose interesting topics to study. Shlomo and Yael Sharan, along with Rachel Hertz-Lazarowitz, have intensely studied the outcomes derived from the group investigation model (Hertz-Lazarowitz, 1990; Sharan & Sharan, 1992).

PROMISES AND PITFALLS ■

Although the strengths or promises of cooperative learning are evident, educators are also identifying the negative consequences of using this method. Randall (1999) has contended that this model contains the following three challenges to learning:

1. The responsibility of members for each other's learning

2. The design of the cooperative learning group

3. A tendency toward lower-level fact-based activities

That students have responsibility for other members' learning may be too much for younger children who struggle themselves to learn. Also, if this arrangement is in place, students may work equally, or they may rely too much on their peers to provide conceptual understanding.

Frequently, the membership of the cooperative learning group includes one high achiever, one low achiever, and two average achievers. The result is that the high achiever becomes bored because he or she has to explain the information many times for the entire group to understand. Consequently, the lowest achiever can become a passive learner simply waiting for the other members to provide the needed information and learning.

In addition, the general nature of the cooperative learning activity is basic lower-level knowledge acquisition. Students need to develop and train their minds to be critical thinkers and problem solvers, and group work traditionally neglects this need. Simply stated, cooperative learning does not address the higher-level cognitive structures that students need to be a successful, contributing citizenry in the future.

The Case Method

It is important to note in this chapter on cooperative learning an offshoot of this instructional strategy—the case method. Case studies are a special form of the cooperative learning technique. In this instructional

method, students study individual cases representative of a type of institution, issue, problem situation, or the like in order to draw conclusions about the type as a whole (McBurney, 1995, p. 36). Examples of topics suitable for case studies include the following: the similarities of the causes of wars; the formation of clouds; the structure and function of the Krebs Cycle; the measurement of angles in a circle; effects of a recession on the economy; investigating the concept of the corruption of power; comparing Julius Caesar with Alexander the Great, Napoleon Bonaparte, George Patton, and Dwight Eisenhower; the mechanics of writing; the elements of literature; comparing synonyms with metaphors. Case studies allow students to focus on a situation or topic that is a prime example of its type. In this way, they learn specifics about individual cases and learn about the overall type as well. In addition, case studies offer opportunities to deal with specific diversity issues in the classroom such as prejudice, gender bias, poverty, and cultural misunderstandings. By acknowledging students' previous experiences and attitudes in response to multicultural and diversity issues, the teacher gains a clearer picture of strategies to use to introduce and integrate additional information and heighten cultural awareness. The case method also promotes and advances students' ethical and moral reasoning (Sudzina, 1993, p. 5). Meaningful learning occurs when a learner has a knowledge base that can be used with fluency to make sense of the world, solve problems, and make decisions. Higher-order thinking skills are important for all students; teaching them is not a frill, nor is it a skill that only *gifted children* can or need to develop (Lewis & Smith, 1993, p. 42). An important benefit of the case study method is its responsiveness to the varying developmental differences of students (Sudzina, 1993, p. 4). There are a variety of differences in today's classrooms. The case study method is responsive to all student reflections and opinions.

It is important for teachers, prior to assigning case studies, to discuss evaluation procedures with their students. Teachers should prepare students before lessons so that they will have a clear understanding of the teacher's expectations. If students are going to be tested on their grasp of the concepts discussed in a case study, they need to know. Ground rules are a necessity. Teachers may choose to let students set their own goals and work to meet them. Goal setting requires both creative and critical thought, as well as a sense of evaluation of what is important and what is not. Goal setting also requires time management and an organization of ways to assess whether the goals have been met at the end of the assignment (Parsons & Smith, 1993, p. 21).

After selecting a topic for study and materials, students can be divided into groups or pairs. Ground rules must be established. The teacher must clearly state the case, so students will not be confused during the lesson. If cases have been previously assigned, it is a good idea to briefly summarize the facts of the case for the benefit of those who may not have prepared. Teachers should emphasize the importance of reasoning during the assignment, rather than emphasizing the solution of the case study (McBurney,

1995, p. 37). Once students begin discussing the case, teachers should remain silent so that they don't give their conclusions or opinions. The teacher's role is to pose questions, draw out incomplete answers, and probe inconsistencies (McBurney, 1995, p. 37). So often, students will become anxious and sometimes dispirited when a teacher refuses to tell them the right answer. The case study method is designed to teach students that there is no one right answer, an important lesson unto itself.

SUMMARY ■

Cooperative learning is an instructional model adaptable to all grade and cognitive-ability levels. The effective teacher can propose the specific modifications needed in a particular classroom setting, and if this is duly accomplished, the lesson will extend knowledge and learning to students. An understanding of group processes is desperately needed for one to function effectively in society, and the more opportunities that students have to practice these processes, the more success they will experience in school and in life.

Cooperative learning has been proven to foster academic achievement, better intergroup relations, and social and affective development. These three areas give students an excellent knowledge and skills base that will help them develop into productive, contributing citizens ready to meet the future.

BUILDING THE PERFECT SCHOOL: A COOPERATIVE STAFF DEVELOPMENT ACTIVITY

Every educator at some point in his or her career has said or thought, "I could do things better. If only I ran this place, things would be done differently." This staff development idea allows teachers that opportunity, if only for a short while.

Divide teachers and staff members into groups and tell them that they are in a committee for the purpose of designing the perfect school. They need to determine roles and make sure that each committee member has an equal part. At the end of a set amount of time, they are to come to a mutual decision as to the perfect school. The key word is, of course, *mutual*. This activity allows teachers to see the cooperative method in action while they are actually involved in it. The relevancy of the activity to their real-life experience is obvious. It also puts them in their students' shoes for a change. Teachers can present their "perfect schools" upon completion, making sure to rationalize to the audience the choices they made during synthesis. This activity also gives teachers a chance to focus on and refine their educational philosophies. See Table 14.1 for a sample handout for participant consideration during this activity.

Table 14.1. Educational Philosophies

Educational Philosophy	Method of Teaching	Exam	Preferred Architecture	Seating	Educational Outcome
Perennialism	Lecture Discussions Seminars	Essay	Classical	Students grouped around teacher (philosopher)	Philosopher
Essentialism	Lecture Teaching Machines	Objective	Efficient Functional	Students grouped around teacher (scientist)	Technician Scientist
Progressivism	Discussion Projects	Gauge how well people can solve problem	Flexible Natural	Group	Good problem solver
Reconstructionism	Real-life projects Action projects	Gauge ability as activist	Nonschool setting "Schools without walls"	Outside involvement	Social activist
Existentialism	Learner is encouraged to discover the best method for himself or herself	Student should learn to examine himself or herself	Individual preference	Individual preference	Inner-directed person "Authentic individual" Committed, involved person

TABLE 14.1 Continued

Educational Philosophy	Root Philosophy	Rationale	Curriculum	Teacher
Perennialism	Idealism	Deals with that which is lasting—stresses intellectual attainment	Great books liberal arts	Philosophically oriented—knowledges about great ideas
Essentialism	Realism	Deals with basic knowledge—facts	3 R s, history, science, foreign language, English	Fact oriented Knowledgeable about scientific and technical data
Progressivism	Pragmatism	Search for things that work—experimental—democratic	Core, flexible Revolves around interests and needs, student-centered	Guide one who can present meaningful problems with skill
Reconstructionism	Pragmatism	Seeks to reconstruct society through education	Current events Social problems	Social activist Utopian oriented
Existentialism	Existentialism	Importance of the individual—"existence precedes essence"—paradox, subjectivity, anxiety	Individual preference	Committed individual I Thou—person who is both teacher and learner—one who provides a free environment

FIFTEEN

Synectics

Synectics is a teaching model for information processing that stimulates creative thought and problem solving through the use of metaphoric activity, attempting to break set ways of thinking to address familiar material in new ways or to introduce new material through previously learned concepts (Rettig & Canady, 2000). The word *synectics* is derived from the Greek *son*, meaning "to bring together," and *ectos* or *ectics*, meaning "diverse elements" (Weil, Joyce, & Kluwin, 1978). There are two main strategies or approaches in the synectics model. The first, making the familiar strange, seeks to assist students in looking at tasks or ideas in new ways. The second, making the strange familiar, is used to connect prior learning with new concepts. Synectics is rooted in metaphoric activity and seeks to increase students' capacity for creative thought.

Each strategy—making the familiar strange and making the strange familiar—attempts to help students connect prior knowledge with new concepts. Both strategies involve numerous steps that must be followed to elicit the desired metaphoric activity and conceptual distance needed to be creative. Both involve the three analogy types—direct analogy, personal analogy, and compressed conflict—although variations of each do exist.

Also called "creating something new," the first method, making the familiar strange helps students see familiar things in new ways, to view old problems or ideas in a more creative light. Possible objectives include

developing new understanding, empathizing, designing a new product, addressing social or interpersonal problems, and prewriting. Analogies are used to create conceptual distance, and steps are followed to ensure that students cycle through Gordon's stages of creativity, discussed later in this chapter.

■ HISTORY AND RESEARCH

William J. Gordon, known for his work in creativity, developed the synectics model, publishing *Synectics* in 1961 (Joyce, Weil, & Calhoun, 2000). The method was originally used for business and industry in "creativity groups." It was believed that by participating in creative exploration, new ideas could be formed and creative solutions for problems could be found. The model was later modified for the classroom. Synectics has deep roots in creativity, metaphoric activity, and Gordon's assumptions about the creative process.

Citing that creativity is important in everyday activities, Gordon proposes three assumptions about the creative process (Weil et al., 1978). First, the creative process is not mysterious; it can be described, and it is possible to train persons to increase their creativity. Gordon believes that teachers can directly train students to be aware of their own creative processes and that students can be taught to engage in metaphoric and creative activity on their own to assist in understanding topics and ideas. Next, creative invention is similar in all fields. Although most people associate creativity with artists, writers, and musicians, Gordon argues that we all possess the ability to be creative. Scientists call it invention; writers, inspiration; others, creativity. Finally, individual and group invention (creative thinking) are similar. The same processes that individuals go through to tap their creative potential are mimicked in creative group interaction.

A scholar in the psychology of creativity, Gordon adds additional holdings to his assumptions to further describe the creative process. He states that by bringing the creative process to consciousness and by developing explicit aids to creativity, we can directly increase the creative capacity of both individuals and groups. Gordon contends that in creative thought, the emotional component is more important than the intellectual, the irrational more important than the rational. He does explain that the rational mind should be used to evaluate alternatives and make decisions but that the creative process affords the individual or group a wider range of solutions. Gordon also argues that emotional and irrational elements must be understood in order to increase the probability of success in a problem-solving situation. From these holdings and assumptions, Gordon introduced metaphoric activity as paramount in the synectics model.

Metaphors establish a relationship of likeness, the comparison of one object or idea with another object or idea by using one in place of the other. By engaging in such activity, participants are able to make connections between prior knowledge and new concepts. Metaphor introduces "con-

ceptual distance" between the student and the object or concept and prompts original thought. This distance is presumed to increase the mental flexibility of participants. Just as the two strategies in synectics imply, metaphoric activity can make the familiar strange and make the strange familiar, offering participants a new view of an old topic or a way of relating new information to prior learning.

There are three basic types of metaphoric activity: direct analogy, personal analogy, and compressed conflict. A direct analogy is a single comparison of two objects or concepts (Joyce et al., 2000). The comparison need not be identical in all respects, and students would be expected to identify similarities and differences between concepts to strengthen the analogy. Direct analogies function to transpose the conditions of the real topic or situation to another topic or situation to afford new perspectives. Differing levels of strain are involved in analogical activity. Comparing oneself to a dog is a lesser degree of strain than comparing oneself to a car engine or other inanimate object. Participants involved in direct analogy are said to progress through stages of creative activity. Detachment from the situation, deferment of easy or obvious holdings, speculation about different approaches and framing, and finally, a return to the original situation make up these stages.

Personal analogy requires students to become involved empathetically with the ideas or objects compared (Weil et al., 1978). There are four levels of empathetic involvement: (a) first-person description of facts, (b) first-person identification with emotion, (c) empathetic identification with a living thing, and (d) empathetic identification with a nonliving object. The greater the conceptual distance attained through each type of analogy, the more likely that students have been creative or innovative in their thinking and in their work. Synectic success depends on the quality of analogies developed and mental stretching that students achieve.

"Compressed conflict" is generally a two-word description of an object in which the words seem to be opposites or contradict each other, sometimes called an *oxymoron* (e.g., "jumbo shrimp"). Gordon maintains that these contradictory terms provide the broadest insight into a new subject (Weil et al., 1978). Compressed conflict incorporates two frames of reference in viewing a single object and encourages the distance desired in the detachment and speculative stages. The greater the conceptual distance achieved, the greater the mental flexibility.

There is a paucity of research on synectics, aside from the studies commonly mentioned by instructional methods texts. In one study of college students, synectics was found to enhance both immediate and long-term learning (Joyce et al., 2000). Another study makes similar findings about learning and adds that although synectics is effective across domain boundaries, specific training in some domains increases the likelihood that students will master concepts. A study done in science revealed that the use of synectics with text materials bolsters short- and long-term learning (Glynn, 1994).

Gordon's Stages of Creativity

In Gordon's model, creativity includes seven stages, or phases. Phase 1 is the description of a present condition. The teacher has students describe a situation as they see it now. Students should be encouraged to flesh out the concept or topic and note specifics that can be used for comparison later in the lesson. Phase 2 is direct analogy, and the teacher prompts students to suggest direct analogies, select one, and explore and describe it further. Phase 3 involves personal analogy during which students are to "become" the analogy they selected in Phase 2. Empathetic involvement and a focus on the other three types of personal analogy is important because students must move through more pronounced levels of strain to flex their creative muscles. Phase 4 is compressed conflict. Students take their descriptions from Phases 2 and 3, suggest several compressed conflicts, and choose one on which to focus, preferably a grouping that reflects the truest ring of conflict. Phase 5 is direct analogy; in this phase, students generate and select another direct analogy, based on the compressed conflict and explore it in detail. The students then come to Phase 6, which is the reexamination of the original task. Finally, students move back to original task or problem and use the last analogy or the entire synectics experience to create new products or solutions. Students should exhibit more creative artifacts or solutions as a result of the model. Differences in perceptions, writings, and thinking should be noticeably different than at the beginning of the lesson.

Alternatively, aimed at increasing understanding and internalization of new or difficult material, the strange-to-familiar strategy makes use of similar phases but involves a different end. Metaphoric activity is used for analyzing, not for creating "conceptual distance," and while the first method involves a great deal of divergent thinking, this second method encourages students to converge thinking in creative ways (Lasley & Matczynski, 1997). Making the strange familiar involves defining or citing both the characteristics that are present and those that are lacking in analogies and comparisons. Through these comparisons, students gain a better understanding of new concepts because they have prior knowledge to build on, even though it may be seemingly unrelated in the beginning.

Phase 1 of making the strange familiar involves the provision of substantive input about the new topic by the teacher. Phase 2 is the direct analogy step; the teacher suggests a direct analogy and asks students to describe the analogy in as much detail as possible, in hopes of achieving some conceptual distance in the process. Phase 3 moves the students into a personal analogy, one in which the teacher has students "become" the direct analogy in the previous step. Phase 4 involves a comparison of analogies. Students identify and explain the points of similarity between the new material and the direct analogy. Phase 5 is concerned with explaining differences. To contrast the two frames of reference, students explain where the analogy does not fit. In Phase 6, exploration, students reexplore the original topic on its own terms, applying what they have

learned from the experience. Finally, Phase 7, generating an analogy, requires students to provide their own analogy and explore the similarities and differences found in the new pairing. Students should exhibit the ability to make connections and point out discrepancies in creative ways. The goal of this strategy is to make the strange familiar, and students should be able to evidence a more comprehensive understanding of the new material or concept.

Teachers have much to consider when tackling a synectics lesson. First they must master the process and operational procedures of each method. They must also take care to avoid premature analyses and limited mental stretching (Queen & Isenhour, 1998b). Teachers should explain the vocabulary to students and give them an idea of the purpose of each phase, as well as taking students through the process numerous times to build familiarity with the model. Teachers employing this method should strive to be well versed in evocative questioning and ready in advance to facilitate lesson flow and encourage spontaneity. Because of the "playful" nature of the activities, teachers must be proficient in time and behavior management. They must be sure to involve all students and accept all responses, and they should be prepared for nontraditional student and teacher interaction and dialogue. Done correctly, this model is fun and immediately productive. Results are obvious, and teachers can begin to ascertain the increase in student creativity fairly quickly. Done poorly, the model is a nightmare and will likely prove counterproductive.

In evaluating a synectics lesson, administrators or evaluators must understand the difficulty inherent in mastering all the steps and in stretching students to think divergently. The evaluator should be aware of what to look for in lesson presentations. Administrators should provide ongoing staff development in synectics and should be aware that the methods take time to master. Synectics is not direct instruction and may appear to be fluff during valuable instructional time. Evaluators not privy to the model and its form are likely to dismiss creative learning as "silly banter." This method requires strong classroom management skills. Evaluators observing teachers consistently using this model should develop an approach to instructional evaluation for this method and perhaps obtain forms or guide sheets to assist them.

Synectics does not require that a canned curriculum be purchased or that teachers bring in tons of equipment and materials. The two main resources necessary for success in the model are time and operational skill, both of which are necessary to realize all the benefits of the model. This method also requires an open and inviting classroom climate in which all students feel comfortable in contributing. Most of the time, needed materials will already be present. Although synectics is possible with large groups, smaller groups are recommended, and the classroom and teacher must support this type of grouping.

Peer teaching and observation is widely recommended in synectics literature as a way to train staff and help teachers master the method. The model is difficult, and care must be taken to offer thorough and continuing

staff development. Synectics materials and training groups are available as resources for schools or groups interested in learning the model. Training for synectics should include focus on the questioning and classroom management skills necessary for successful implementation, as well as training in the theory and processes undergirding the model. Short, brief introductions to this model may cause frustration and attrition.

■ PROMISES AND PITFALLS

There are many purported promises in the synectics method. Proponents argue that synectics stimulates and promotes creativity, encourages divergent thinking, addresses higher-order thinking skills, and bolsters students' ability to problem solve (Dallman-Jones, 1994). Synectics can be used in any subject or content area or for any activity, and the strategies work with all student types—high or low achievers, withdrawn or outgoing personalities, and students with varied learning styles. Synectics combines easily with other models and affords both instructional and nurturant effects. Users of the model claim that it promotes empathy and interpersonal closeness because all students are allowed to participate without fear of delivering an "absurd answer" and students gain deeper understanding of classmates and their views. Synectics requires students to synthesize and analyze, and the strategies can be used to introduce new concepts or to expand or review previously learned material. Synectics is alleged to bolster self-esteem because there is no "right" answer, and the model can be used individually or in groups. Finally, synectics improves self-expression—in oration, writing, and other areas.

Synectics has its drawbacks as well, and many teachers find themselves unhappy with the number of steps and the "weird" nature of the students and their interactions with metaphor and analogy. The methods, with their phases and steps, take some time to master and much preparation to implement. Younger children may have trouble with emotional expression or understanding the process and will probably have difficulty understanding the terms and activities involved. All levels of students may find the steps cumbersome and the operational vocabulary intimidating (Dallman-Jones, 1994). Students partial to left-brain, concrete, sequential thinking may be stretched out of their comfort zone in synectics, and teachers may be uncomfortable with letting student thinking "run free" or the fact that there is no "right answer."

■ SUMMARY

Synectics is not for the faint of heart. It involves a great deal of time and energy both in mastering the method and in instruction. Synectics is effective if it is implemented correctly and is useful in almost any setting, for any content, and at any point in the teaching of a unit. Synectics activities

often transfer to students who pick up the processes and begin to use them on their own, ultimately producing students who can use the approach as a system to create or remember any time they want. At the very least, synectics offers a viable alternative for instruction and addresses many of the skills and processes that educators want to deliver to students. Whether making the familiar strange or making the strange familiar, synectics stimulates creative thought and helps students make connections that may not normally go together well. Synectics, although involved and difficult to master, promises to continue to be an effective instructional method and alternative.

Following is a sample synectics lesson. Remember that the foundation of the synectics method includes developing various types of analogies—direct, personal, and new. This metaphoric activity is the central concept of this instructional method. *To Kill a Mockingbird* is especially appropriate because even its title is metaphoric.

After reading the book, students view the movie starring Gregory Peck. The presentation is used to help the students determine the direct analogy in a general way. First, students should consider the following question, "Who would be like the mockingbird?" Then the lesson moves to the second, personal, phase in which students empathize with the character by "becoming" him or her. Finally, the students can compress their own feelings into a new analogy in order to better understand the concept.

To Kill A Mockingbird
By Harper Lee

Harper Lee

- Born in 1926 in Monroeville, Alabama
- *To Kill a Mockingbird* was her first and only novel
- Was awarded the Pulitzer Prize in 1961
- Now lives a very private life in Alabama and avoids press interviews

Characters

Atticus Finch

- Lawyer in Maycomb, Alabama, in the 1930s
- Widower and father of two children, Scout and Jem
- Defends Tom Robinson, a black man who is accused of raping a poor white woman

Jean Louise "Scout" Finch

- Narrator of the novel
- An intelligent six-year-old tomboy
- Younger sister of Jem and daughter of Atticus

Jem Finch and Dill Harris

- Jem is Scout's ten-year-old brother who is fascinated with "Boo" Radley, their neighbor
- Dill is a "goin' on seven" friend of Jem and Scout who visits during the summer

Characters

Arthur "Boo" Radley

- A mysterious and reclusive neighbor of the Finches
- The children are terrified of him because of untrue rumors, but they try to get him to come out of his house

Tom Robinson

- A black farmhand who is wrongly accused of raping a poor white woman
- Defended in court by Atticus Finch
- His only "crime" was saying that he felt sorry for a white woman

Bob Ewell

- The main "villain" in the novel and known as the "trash" of Maycomb
- Charges Tom Robinson with raping his daughter, Mayella
- Threatened to get even with Atticus after the trial

Major Themes in
To Kill a Mockingbird

Racial Injustice
- A man's guilt or innocence was determined by his skin color
- Atticus demonstrates moral courage by defending Tom Robinson

To Kill a Mockingbird
- "Mockingbirds don't do one thing but make music for us to enjoy. They don't eat up people's gardens, don't nest in corncribs, they don't do one thing but sing their hearts out for us. That's why it's a sin to kill a mockingbird."
- Tom Robinson and "Boo" Radley were "mockingbirds"—they didn't harm anyone but were victims of injustice and cruelty.

To Kill a Mockingbird:
The Movie

- The movie was filmed in 1962 in black and white.
- Gregory Peck won an Oscar for Best Actor for his portrayal of Atticus Finch.
- Robert Duvall, who played "Boo" Radley, made his film debut in this movie.
- Harper Lee was pleased with the movie and the portrayal of its characters.

SIXTEEN

Socratic Seminar

In 1982, Mortimer Adler introduced *The Paideia Proposal,* using a group discussion model that can be easily incorporated into a blocked class. Each member of the class reads a selection from the material provided by the teacher prior to the seminar. The teacher avoids directing the discussion of the seminar. The teacher's role is to record the participation and degree of preparedness of each participating student. Students are instructed to explore their ideas about a particular topic and question other members of the class in an open discussion. Students thrive in these seminars once they discover that their opinion is valued and that the teacher is not searching for a specific, "right answer." The teacher usually asks the first question, or it can be elicited from a student experienced with the seminar format. Teachers avoid evaluation, direct the discussion toward topic relevancy, and clarify arguments if there seems to be no solution. The Socratic seminars often lead to further issues, thus extending the learning opportunities beyond one classroom discussion.

GROUP DISCUSSION AND STUDENT PARTICIPATION ■

The success of the Socratic seminar can be attributed to the stark contrast it provides to the normal classroom setting. Students are used to teachers being in front of them, perhaps at a podium, whereas the teacher is literally on the same level as the students in the Socratic method. Students are also typically seated in rows but are placed in a circle during a Socratic

seminar. Rather than teachers talking for the majority of the class time, students talk approximately 95% of the time during this instructional method.

In a comparison of a typical class discussion and the Socratic seminar method, student responses increase from 2 to 3 seconds in a typical discussion to 8 to 12 seconds in a Socratic seminar. Teachers are not to provide feedback during the seminar to ensure maximum student discussion time. This "silence" tactic works well in getting even those students who do not typically speak up to contribute. It also encourages students to think their way through their own ideas and speak up without concern about being incorrect; open exploration of thoughts is paramount.

Following is a list of the nine steps involved in the Socratic seminar.

- *Step 1:* Students arrive and form a circle prepared for the assignment
- *Step 2* The teacher presents opening question
- *Step 3:* Students respond to each other (Phase 1, about 15 minutes)
- *Step 4:* The teacher probes or clarifies *only*
- *Step 5:* The teacher asks core questions
- *Step 6:* Students respond to each other (Phase 2, about 30 minutes)
- *Step 7:* The teacher presents closing question
- *Step 8:* Students personalize discussion (Phase 3, about 30 minutes)
- *Step 9:* Seminar evaluation (Phase 4, usually 15 minutes)

■ WHAT HAPPENED? A SOCRATIC SEMINAR

This activity is one that may begin simply and in an unassuming way, but as so often happens in the Socratic seminar method, the relevance becomes serious and encourages deep introspection.

In preparation for this activity, the book *The True Story of the 3 Little Pigs* by A. Wolfe (Scieszka, 1999) should be read aloud. This book, available in any library or bookstore, is a twist on the traditional fairy tale in that it is told from the point of view of the wolf, who believes himself to be innocent of the crimes of which he has been accused.

To begin the seminar, the opening question is presented: Should the wolf be charged for the crimes? After approximately 15 minutes, in which the students have control and the instructor merely clarifies or probes only when absolutely necessary, a core question is asked, such as, "What should the punishment be?" or "Do you believe in capital punishment?" In the next phase, the teacher asks a closing question, such as, "Should Osama bin Laden be executed?" It is important to personalize the closing question in some way, such as having the students pretend, if necessary, that they lost a loved one in the terrorist attacks on the World Trade Center and the Pentagon on September 11, 2001 (using the bin Laden example from before).

Most teachers have thought that the Socratic seminar could be used for limited areas in English and perhaps the arts. As a teacher, I have found that the Socratic seminar can be used in any subject. It is great for

the social sciences and even the sciences. I know of teachers who even do specific problems in advanced mathematics. Feel free to modify the time periods, and in some cases, math for example, only the first and third questions can be used, omitting the second question. One thing is important: Experiment—and then experiment some more. What works for one teacher will not always work for another.

SEVENTEEN

Instructional Assessment

Instructional evaluation, or assessment, was once exclusively the teacher's domain. It consisted mainly of predetermined paper-and-pencil testing. Periodically, the students read a book, wrote a report, or gave an oral presentation, activities that all had to live up to the expectations of the individual teacher. Now assessment is not necessarily based on the sole, personal judgment of the teacher. Students are included. As the community demands more student accountability, students are becoming more involved in their own learning process, including evaluation and assessment.

Instructional evaluation occurs through the assessment of student achievement, which often depends on the effectiveness of the instructor. For example, does the teacher choose the right delivery system? Are the teacher's objectives clear? Do test items relate to objectives? Evaluation of instruction is also evaluation of the curriculum. It reveals the success of one dimension—how much the student achieves in areas that are assessed. It may also indicate whether the content has been adequately covered. Evaluation of instruction does not answer curricular concerns as to whether the subject matter was the right choice, whether its content is relevant, whether it meets student or societal needs, and whether it has been selected wisely.

■ METHODS OF INSTRUCTIONAL EVALUATION

Measurement is the means of determining the degrees of achievement of a particular competency. Testing is the use of instruments for measuring achievement. The three phases of instructional evaluation are (a) preassessment, evaluation that takes place before instruction; (b) formative evaluation, evaluation that takes place during the instruction process; and (c) summative evaluation, assessment that takes place at the end of instruction.

Preassessment

The tool used in preassessment is the criterion-referenced test or pretest. The criterion-referenced test measures the entry skills that have been identified as critical to beginning instruction. This is also known as a pretest. The pretest is criterion-referenced to the objectives the designer intends to teach. A pretest by itself is not sufficient to address all needs at the beginning of instruction. If students perform poorly on a pretest, the instructor may not be able to gauge whether they did poorly for lack of general knowledge or for lack of the knowledge required for entry-level instruction.

A second type of test is designed to help students measure their skills against the skills of others. These types of tests are called norm-referenced tests. Norm-referenced measurement compares a student's performance on a test with the performance of other students who took the test. Norm-referenced testing is necessary when a limited number of spaces are to be filled from a pool of applicants. Norm-referenced measurement permits comparisons between people, with the primary purpose of making decisions about the qualifications of individuals.

Formative Evaluation

Formative evaluation consists of formal and informal techniques of assessing the learning of students. Formative evaluation occurs during the process of instruction. It may include questions at different points during the instruction or checking students' responses to parts of the instruction. Instructors use formative evaluation to determine if the skills to be learned are being addressed. It allows instructors to determine whether they need to provide remedial instruction to overcome difficulties.

Summative Evaluation

Summative evaluation is the assessment that occurs at the end of a course or unit. The tools used are final exams, a posttest, or an actual demonstration of a skill or operation. It is used to determine whether students have mastered the instruction.

ASSESSMENT OF STUDENT ACHIEVEMENT ■

Several new ways are available to evaluate student achievement. The new tools are called performance-based or authentic assessment. *Authentic* means "worthy of acceptance or belief, trustworthy" (Engel, 1994, p. 24). Assessments are authentic because they are valuable activities within themselves and involve the performance of tasks directly related to real-world problems.

Portfolios, authentic assessment measures, and *alternative assessment activities* are the latest buzzwords used to describe activities other than standardized tools for determining a student's achievement. Educators, parents, and students have come to realize that standardized tests do not truly represent a student's academic growth in the content knowledge, skills, and instructional activities in the classroom. Following is a more detailed explanation of these methods of assessment, beginning with a definition of *assessment*.

- An *assessment* is an exercise such as a written test, portfolio, or experiment that seeks to measure a student's knowledge in a subject area.
- A *portfolio* is a systematic and organized collection of a student's work throughout a course or school year that measures the student's knowledge and skills and often includes some form of self-reflection by the student.
- *Alternative assessment* is any form of measuring what a student knows and is able to do other than traditional standardized tests, including portfolios, performance-based assessments, and other means of testing students. These alternative assessments show actual growth over a period of time that the students, parents, and teachers can physically see. Tests do not show this growth as it occurs.
- *Authentic assessment* allows the student to "become progressively self-disciplined as a thinker . . . (and) to acquire the habit of inquiring and engaging in discourse with care and thoroughness" (Wiggins, 1993, p. 211). Its purpose is to get students to take control of their own learning while maintaining relevance and a meaningful connection to what they are learning. Student contracts, for example, enable students to take responsibility for their own learning while giving them freedom to explore; these contracts also teach organizational control of the lesson content.

Portfolio

The portfolio, a collection of student writing samples assembled over a period of a course or longer, is the most popular form of alternative assessment and is authentic assessment when done correctly. It is like a collection of photographs of a student's writing. Analyzing each writing sample singularly does not give one a complete picture. The portfolio allows for a

comprehensive evaluation of a student's growth and the creation of individual goals for future work.

A portfolio is called a performance-based assessment because the intent of the portfolio is for students to assemble a collection of samples of their work, which in essence shows evidence of their accomplishments. Portfolios may contain creative writing, tests, artwork, exercises, reflective essays, notes on topics, and whatever other materials portray achievement. Standards and criteria for achievement in portfolios should be set. Some of the criteria may include completeness, effort, neatness, and creativity. Portfolios reveal students' patterns of learning and thinking as the year progresses; they also allow both teachers and students to work in the most productive ways possible. There are almost as many approaches to compiling and evaluating portfolios as there are proponents of this form of assessment. Portfolios can be used both formally and informally. Ideally, the portfolio captures the evolution of the student's ideas and can be used instructionally and as progress markers for the student, teacher, and program evaluator.

Portfolios are adaptable to a variety of educational settings. In Fort Worth, Texas, a fifth-grade teacher used them in his math class. Kentucky and Vermont educators have made portfolios a part of their statewide assessment of students. Pittsburgh educators have used portfolios to assess learning in imaginative writing, music, and visual arts.

A portfolio has three major parts: biography, range of works, and reflections. The biography shows the developmental history of the child's progress and gives the reader an impression of how the student has progressed from the beginning to that point. The portfolio contains a range of assignments. These could be the student's "best," "most important," "satisfactory," and "unsatisfactory" pieces of work, as well as revisions. The student critiques his or her work by reflecting on how his or her performance has changed, what he or she has learned, and what he or she needs to do to improve. See Box 17.1 for three portfolio models.

Educators who use portfolios in the 4×4 block believe that these are practical and effective assessment tools for several reasons. Portfolios are easy to design, durable, and reusable. This form of assessment influences the teacher's way of teaching and testing by problem solving, communication, application, and so on and promotes worthwhile learning while expanding the dimensions of education. It provides a developmental perspective that is easily observed by students, parents, and teachers. Finally, it documents a student's progress through school until graduation. Members of the NEA (National Education Association) support the portfolio's use because it accurately reflects what the student has learned.

Not all educators support the portfolio. Some teachers use it to display the best of a student's work. Used this way, it will not accurately reflect performance and rate of progress and cannot be called an assessment measure because, rather than including a representative sampling of a student's work, teachers may guide students about what to write and include. Storage is difficult because a portfolio, if used appropriately, can be big

Box 17.1

Three Portfolio Models

Model 1

I. Introduction—title page
II. Student Portrait—photo or video montage of student
    A. Attendance record
    B. Discipline record
    C. Self-esteem rating
    D. Test scores
III. Educational Goals
    A. Student goals for the year
    B. Career goals
    C. Copies of exceptional work—all discipline areas
IV. Conclusion—reflection
    A. Evaluation of portfolio
    B. Summary paper at end of year—student self-evaluation

Model 2

I. Writing
    A. Submissions from English: literature response, personal essay, research paper
    B. Submissions from history: cause-and-effect paper, defense paper
    C. Submissions from science: classification paper, lab report
    D. Submission of student choice
II. Reading List
III. Conclusion
    A. Self-evaluation of writing and reading goals
    B. Teacher analysis of writing ability—establish goals for next school year

Model 3

I. Student Goals for the School Year
    A. Writing goals
    B. Reading goals
    C. Communication goals
II. Writing Samples
    A. Literature response
    B. Comparative analysis
    C. Journal entry
    D. Research paper
    E. Essay test
    F. Creative writing—poem, short story, etc.
    G. Student choice
III. Editing
    A. Peer evaluation
    B. Self-evaluation
IV. Future Goals for Writing and Reading
    A. List of future goals
    B. Summary of career goals

and bulky. Scoring is time-consuming as well as inconsistent, and even if the scorers do agree, that does not guarantee that the portfolio measures what it was supposed to measure (Viadero, 1995). In Vermont, for example, it took more than 160 scorers five days to assess 7,000 portfolios. In addi-

tion, these scorers were, understandably, influenced by their personal beliefs.

Teachers participating in 4×4 seminars expressed the following suggestions for evaluation success:

Assessment and Evaluation
- Reports
- Team competitions, research projects
- Skills
- Role playing
- Portfolios
- More oral response time, debates
- Team projects
- Self-assessment
- Individual
- Pre- and posttests
- Teacher-student evaluation, one-on-one
- Practical hands-on skill evaluation, theory into practice
- Peer evaluations
- Standardized testing
- Parent conferences
- Ongoing evaluation of program, formative evaluation
- More home involvement
- Nonthreatening evaluations for teachers, opportunities to try things without fear of failure or accountability

Unit Evaluation

Unit evaluation includes two major types of evaluation: diagnostic and summative. Diagnostic evaluation allows the teacher to learn what the students' learning potential is prior to the start of the instruction. Summative evaluation measures what the students have learned through implementation of the unit. The usual form of evaluation is a written test. The unit test can contain a mix of objective (answer with the facts) and subjective (essay) questions. These two types of evaluation assist with the planning of future methods of teaching a unit by providing, through student response to test items, information about how the instruction can be organized to become more effective.

Lesson Evaluation

Lesson evaluation occurs daily. Informal and formal evaluation occurs while the lesson is going on as well as at its completion. Some informal ways of evaluation are observations of the students both individually and as a group, assessment of students' contributions, review of homework, and overall impressions of the level of student understanding and success. Some formal methods of evaluation are quizzes, debates, and rating scales. These evaluations are done constantly throughout the lesson to verify that

the lesson is being comprehended by the students. They allow for modifications to be made at any point in the lesson.

A POSITIVE CLASSROOM CLIMATE ■
THROUGH INSTRUCTION

Students and teachers learning in a 4×4 model of block scheduling become more active and engage in hands-on activities. The classroom climate is positively affected by this active learning. During the lengthened class period, students and teachers have the opportunity to get to know one another better. Teachers have fewer students in one day and spend longer periods of time with individual students. This one-on-one time helps to build strong relationships between students and teachers.

To improve the classroom climate, a strong management program is important. The classroom management program puts boundaries and limits on student behavior and gives opportunities for the students to learn in a safe environment. Along with more engaging and hands-on learning, students benefit from a warm and inviting environment. The classroom climate will improve if teachers have a positive attitude, are approachable, can create learning activities that are student-friendly, and decorate the classroom in a pleasing and educational manner. The school building itself can also be a warm and nurturing place. Bulletin boards that clearly display upcoming events, lists of students with perfect attendance, lists of awards and honors, honor roll lists and athletic achievements are both visually interesting and communicative. Giant calendars, club-sponsored bulletin boards, and festive holiday decorations make the school more personal and aid in creating a positive learning environment.

EIGHTEEN

Program Evaluation and Student Assessment

Evaluation is the process of determining the worth of any given thing. Evaluation of school programs and of the curriculum is done in order to establish their value. Throughout the history of education, evaluation in these areas has been assessed either formally or informally. Many trends and issues affect evaluation. Evaluation must be carefully considered before, during, and after implementation of a block schedule. In this chapter, I address the "how" and "why" of evaluation in general since the methods and reasons can be applied to any type of program.

Evaluation has many definitions. It can be seen as a product of the work of evaluators, but it is more commonly viewed as a process. The process of evaluation primarily involves two basic acts. It is first the process by which data are gathered so that decisions will be informed. Second, evaluation is the process of applying criteria to the available information in order to arrive at justifiable decisions. In *Perspectives of Curriculum Evaluation*, Michael Scriven (Tyler, Gagné, & Scriven, 1967) explains that evaluation itself is an activity that is essentially similar whether we are trying to evaluate coffee machines or teaching machines, plans for a house, or plans for a curriculum. The method for the activity consists simply in the gathering and combining of performance data with a weighted set of goal scales to obtain either comparative or numerical rat-

ings and in the justification of (a) the data-gathering instruments, (b) the weightings, and (c) the selection of goals.

When evaluating a curriculum or a program, it is necessary to distinguish between the roles associated with evaluation and the goals associated with evaluation. When discussing roles, distinctions must be made as to the role of the principal, the role of the teacher, and the role of the evaluation itself. What will the evaluation be used for? What evaluative instrument will be used? When the question is asked, "What is the goal of evaluation?" the question "Whose goal?" must be answered. The point is that when discussing evaluation, it must be acknowledged that this is a complicated, multifaceted subject, and the terms and their particular usage must be clearly defined every step of the way. The reality is that evaluation should be a continuous process that is part of every stage of curriculum development, program development, and implementation of the two.

■ REASONS FOR EVALUATION

Evaluation provides the information needed to make changes. Evaluation gives (or should give) direction to everything that is done in school. Evaluation should guide decisions about staffing, materials and equipment, facilities, and scheduling. Evaluation of curriculum and of programs must be done systematically in a way that can be easily explained and replicated. Only then can all involved stakeholders learn from the process. Too often, only those conducting the evaluation have knowledge of the instrument and, later, of the findings. If the information is not shared and understood, there was little reason for conducting or imposing an evaluative process in the first place. In the book *Supervision and Instructional Leadership*, Glickman, Gordon, and Ross-Gordon (2001) discuss the importance of evaluation in education and the way it has recently changed. The public demand for accountability and the advent of high-stakes testing has added new interest to the subject of evaluation. National reform efforts such as Goals 2000 have drawn attention to education. There is great concern over what the children of the nation are learning. Right now, the focus with regard to student learning is performance on standardized tests. Administrators, teachers, and parents want to know how to enable their students to achieve higher test scores. Evaluation is a large part of this. An example shared by the authors of *Supervision and Instructional Leadership* (Glickman et al., 2001) is a look at 15 exemplary elementary and middle schools in three districts that all made significant improvements in mathematics and reading over a three-year period. The common characteristic of these schools was found to be that information about student progress was regularly gathered, and the information was used schoolwide to make decisions about changing curriculum. Every school did not change curriculum in the same way but changed based on the determined needs of the students. The information obtained was also used to guide professional staff development.

DEFINING PROGRAM EVALUATION ■

The terms *curriculum* and *program* are sometimes used interchangeably but are usually not considered the same thing. A program is often viewed as a specific component of a curriculum. A program can mean an organized set of ideas and plans within a certain discipline that may be used to provide information for students. For example, the term may be used to detail what will be done with a particular group of students in reading. The reading program is only a component of the total curriculum. The word *program* may also be used to mean the overall instructional program. It is acceptable to use the terms in either way as long as the definition used in a particular instance is made clear and the definition is used consistently.

Evaluation must be applied to the programs used within a curriculum. As evaluation is used to determine the worth of anything, evaluation of a program is used to see if the programs have merit, if the programs are working for the students for whom they are used, and if changes need to be made. Glickman et al. (2001) discuss six components that may be considered as one conducts a comprehensive program evaluation. The components are as follows:

Evaluation of Needs Assessment. It is important to determine whether or not there is a need for a program. While this may seem obvious, there is evidence that schools often succumb to good salesmanship and "bandwagon" popularity rather than responding to actual need when choosing programs. Teachers report the frustration that occurs when asked to implement new programs without old programs first being phased out. Layering program on program is confusing. The needs assessment will assist in determining what should continue to have a valid place in the curriculum and what has outlived its usefulness.

Evaluation of Program Design. An essential part of program evaluation is to look at the written plan of a program. It is important to ask if the goals and objectives are consistent with the needs the program is to meet. And it is critical to determine *before* implementation of the program what human and material resources have been committed to the program.

Evaluation of Readiness. When a program fails, it is usually because one or more of the stakeholders (principals, teachers, students, parents, and/or other community members) were not prepared to support implementation of the program. This lack of support may stem from disagreement with the program, lack of understanding about how to implement the program, or a lack of communication about the program. Many times, a good program has had no success because a stakeholder did not understand, like, or feel competent to implement the program as designed.

Implementation Evaluation. The key question to be asked here is, "Was the program implemented as planned?" If the answer to this question is no,

then what was responsible for the error? When a program is implemented, three phases should be considered: (1) the initiation of the program, (2) the continuation of the program, and (3) integration of the program with the school culture. Implementation according to the directives of the program is key. Many programs fail to produce desired results because they are not executed as intended. Principals must fully understand the programs that are to be put into operation in their buildings. Regular monitoring of instruction and program implementation can control what evaluators refer to as "loss of program fidelity."

Evaluation of Outcomes. Two types of outcomes can be measured with program evaluation. *Intended outcomes* are the goals and objectives of the program. *Unintended outcomes* are results that came about but that were not planned for. Unintended outcomes can be positive or negative. Unintended outcomes should be carefully studied, for they provide valuable insight as the "next step" is contemplated.

Cost-Benefit Analysis. When an analysis is applied, evaluators are comparing the benefits of the programs to the cost in terms of the use of human resources, material resources, and dollars spent. Most schools operate with limited resources in all areas, so this is very important.

Program evaluation may be used effectively to make the changes that benefit students whether the changes are for a short time or are more permanent. A principal in North Carolina whose elementary school had adopted a popular mathematics program tells a story about the importance of program evaluation. A prepackaged mathematics program was chosen for use because (a) most of the elementary school leaders in his particular district felt that the program would raise end-of-the-year test scores and (b) the program, since it incorporates the use of many manipulatives and "real-life" situations, would improve math instruction in the school. Teachers follow a script to deliver instruction with this particular package. The program was implemented at the beginning of the school year. The training for how to use the program was very brief because all the material did not arrive until a few days after school had started. Teachers were told to "read the script" and to "stay a couple of days ahead of the kids." After a few weeks of using the program, the fourth-grade teachers approached the principal with the disturbing news that 12 children in the grade level could not keep up with the program. Parents had been contacted about the problem, and the students had been supported in a variety of ways, but the difficulty remained. These particular students had learning difficulties in mathematics, but the discrepancy between ability and performance was not substantial enough to allow them to qualify for diagnosis of a specific learning disability. Therefore, the students could not be placed in a separate learning environment, which would have helped to address their needs. A few of the students struggled because of very low IQs, but again, that alone did not allow them to receive services outside the

regular education classroom. These boys and girls were the students with whom educators constantly struggle. They were the children who fail to meet any criteria for additional services. These were the children who are often referred to as "at-risk" or "falling through the cracks." Their math skills were significantly below grade level, and after two of the program assessments, it was apparent that a change must be made for the struggling students. The principal supported the teachers in their request, trusting in their collective professional abilities to recognize that a change needed to be made. A great deal of time was spent as the principal and the teachers, along with the special education teacher, discussed solutions to the problem. At the heart of each discussion was the desire to create a situation that would provide for the needs of the students who were experiencing such difficulty. The principal provided support as classes were reorganized. He also provided an extra teacher to work in the classroom with the 12 students. The important lesson to be gleaned from this case study is that (a) teacher input was valued, (b) the children for whom the program *was* working were not affected, (c) teaching support was provided so that the group of students working below grade level could make progress faster, and (d) the integrity of the mathematics program was not compromised. The outcome of this program evaluation was that the school gained valuable knowledge about the ability level of these at-risk students. The decisions to act and to support student learning were made, and as a result, there were increased skills for those students as well as significant gains on the end-of-year standardized tests.

When evaluating the overall instructional program, many areas within the school must be looked at because the areas are appreciably related to the success of the program. Glickman et al. (2001) address this issue in *Supervision and Instructional Leadership*. Box 18.1 illustrates the areas they recommend be considered.

INSTRUCTIONAL EVALUATION ■

A program has been defined as a component of the curriculum. A program may be further broken down into a unit of study. Classroom teachers implement and present information to students in units of study. This presentation is commonly referred to as instruction. Instruction of a unit must also be evaluated. In *Curriculum Practice in the Elementary and Middle School* (Queen, 1999), reference is made to the two major types of evaluation— diagnostic and summative. Through diagnostic evaluation, the teacher identifies what the learning potential of a student is prior to the start of an instructional unit. A summative evaluation is a way of measuring what a student has learned from the presentation of an instructional unit. These methods of evaluation are valuable to the classroom teacher and should not be overlooked by the instructional leader of the school. Regular instructional evaluation is the piece of the evaluation process that should

---

Box 18.1 Areas to Consider When Evaluating an Overall Instructional Program

Educators must ask themselves . . .

1. What are the characteristics of the community, parents, teachers, and students?

2. What programs are in place that involve parents, the community, and professional development?

3. What are the standards for student achievement, and are students meeting those standards?

4. What is the climate and culture of the school?

5. How is the school governed?

6. What kind of relationships exist between other schools, the central office, and external organizations?

SOURCE: Glickman, Gordon, and Ross-Gordon (2001).

---

regularly inform the classroom teacher about how to proceed so that the needs of students are met.

The focus today for most school principals is "alignment." This refers to the prescribed objectives of the curriculum "matching up" with instruction delivery, textbooks, and scheduling. There may be the perception that in a state where there is a standard course of study, very specific curriculum and program objectives, and an evaluation that measures these objectives, there is very little that the principal has any control over, at least in the area of curriculum and instruction. This is certainly not the case. An instructional leader in this instance is responsible for knowing the course of study. While it would be ridiculous to imagine a building administrator who has detailed knowledge of the content objectives for every grade level, the principal must have an overall knowledge of what is to be taught at his or her building. Certainly this requires time and effort, but a lack of this knowledge translates to teachers in a very negative way. A principal who is incapable of demonstrating knowledge of what teachers should be teaching cannot be viewed or respected as an instructional leader. It is imperative that principals have knowledge of effective teaching strategies and that they are comfortable sharing those strategies. Principals must recognize the needs that teachers today have and work to create the best possible instructional environment for them.

Important in this era of accountability and reform is the need for the principal who can lead a school community as all involved work to

achieve their greatest potential. More important is the principal who has the ability to communicate a vision to all members of the school community so that boys and girls get the best that entire educational community has to offer. This is sometimes referred to as the ability to transform.

Principals interested in taking their place as the instructional leaders of their schools must consider three key features, according to Henderson and Hawthorne (2000) in *Transformative Curriculum Leadership*. The first item to consider is action research. When principals examine their own practices and encourage teachers to do the same, there is a greater understanding within the entire community about what is happening and why. The second item to consider is dialogue. Good dialogue can help educators avoid the type of curriculum activity that serves no purpose. When dialogue is focused around the needs of the students and teachers of the school, then everyone is supported in doing the best possible work. Dialogue that is helpful acknowledges the contributions of all involved, recognizes the merit of alternative viewpoints, and subscribes to a theory that different is just different—not good or bad. Finally, principals and other members of the educational community recognize the ongoing nature of evaluation. The gathering of information is ongoing, the interpretation of the information is ongoing, and the practical application of the gathered information is ongoing.

The reality for today's school principal is that there is little hope for the school without an instructional leader. And the losers, when there is no instructional leader, are the children within that school. Administrators who understand the value of evaluation can begin the transformation within the school.

SUMMARY ■

Evaluation is an important part of the issue of school reform and school transformation. The entire educational community must be a part of any change that is to take place, but change cannot be made simply for the sake of change. Instructional leaders of the schools must know what needs to be changed and must be able to guide the school community through change. Decisions must be based on careful and intentional evaluation. The instructional leader must also understand the dynamics that occur when change is introduced into an organization. Evaluation means assessing the value of something. Regularly determining the value and the effectiveness of the curriculum, the programs, and the instruction in a school is the way to ultimately offer the best to the students in the school.

The chapter ends with two tools for evaluation before and after a school implements block scheduling. Evaluation Resource 1 is a preassessment survey that can be used to determine a school's interest in and attitudes toward block scheduling. Evaluation Resource 2 can be used to assess the use of, preference for, and training in classroom instructional practices for teachers from schools that use block scheduling.

EVALUATION RESOURCE 1
Block Schedule Teacher Survey

Please take a few minutes to complete the items on both sides of this sheet. Thank you.
Use the following scale to answer each question:
1 = Very High (VH), 2 = High, 3 = Average, 4 = Below Average, 5 = Low, 6 = Very Low (VL).

	VH				VL	
1. Effectiveness of block scheduling relative to student achievement?	1	2	3	4	5	6
2. Effectiveness of block scheduling relative to use of instructional time?	1	2	3	4	5	6
3. Effectiveness of block scheduling relative to instructional pacing?	1	2	3	4	5	6
4. Effectiveness of block scheduling relative to "completeness" of course?	1	2	3	4	5	6
5. Overall rating of the effectiveness of block scheduling?	1	2	3	4	5	6

Use the following scale to respond to these items:
1 = Very Strongly Agree (VSA), 2 = Strongly Agree, 3 = Agree,
4 = Disagree, 5 = Strongly Disagree, 6 = Very Strongly Disagree (VSD)

As a result of block scheduling,

	VSA				VSD	
6. Fewer class changes result in safer and more secure school grounds.	1	2	3	4	5	6
7. I am able to vary the instructional methods I use to keep students actively engaged.	1	2	3	4	5	6
8. I am more involved in my school's curriculum and decision making.	1	2	3	4	5	6
9. I am better able to meet the needs of students at differing levels of ability.	1	2	3	4	5	6

Tell us about yourself and how you teach:

10. Total years of teaching experience?
     a. first-year teacher   b. 2–5 years   c. 6–10 years   d. 11–20 years   e. more than 20 years

11. Typical percentage of time spent in interactive instruction with students?
     a. less than 20%   b. 21–40%   c. 41–60%   d. 61–80%   e. more than 80%

12. Typical percentage of time spent monitoring independent work of students?
     a. less than 20%   b. 21–40%   c. 41–60%   d. 61–80%   e. more than 80%

13. Typical percentage of time spent handling classroom management problems?
     a. less than 20%   b. 21–40%   c. 41–60%   d. 61–80%   e. more than 80%

Tell us what you think of block scheduling.

14. List in priority order characteristics or teaching skills of a master teacher in block scheduling.

a. _____   b. _____

c. _____   d. _____

e. _____   f. _____

15. List some benefits of block scheduling.

a. _____   b. _____

c. _____   d. _____

e. _____   f. _____

16. List some problems with block scheduling.

a. _____   b. _____

c. _____   d. _____

e. _____   f. _____

17. What kind of assistance do teachers need to better deliver instruction when using a block scheduling model?

_____

_____

EVALUATION RESOURCE 2

TEACHER SURVEY: HIGH SCHOOL INSTRUCTION

The following sections request information about your classroom instructional practices, your recent staff development experiences, and your teaching experience/workload. Please provide answers directly on the survey.

I.   Classroom Instructional Practices

Please select the statement that *best describes* your level of use, preference, and training for each of the following instructional practices.

Cooperative Learning *(Cooperative learning is the practice of grouping students in small, mixed-ability learning teams. The teacher presents the group with a problem to solve or task to perform. Students then work together to achieve a group performance score by helping one another and praising and criticizing one another's contributions.)*

Level of Use

A.   I *do not use/do not have time to use* cooperative learning in my classroom.
B.   I use cooperative learning activities *very seldom* (e.g., once or twice during the course I teach).
C.   I use cooperative learning activities *seldom* (e.g., once or twice during each grading period).
D.   I use cooperative learning activities *often* (e.g., once a week).
E.   I use cooperative learning activities *very often* (e.g., every day).

Level of Preference

A.   I do not prefer cooperative learning as a teaching practice for my subject.
B.   Cooperative learning is an appropriate practice that can be used occasionally in my subject area.
C.   Cooperative learning is a practice that is well suited to my course content.

Level of Training

A.   I have had *no training* in cooperative learning.
B.   I have had *some training* but not enough to implement.
C.   I have had *extensive training* in cooperative learning and understand it well.

Discovery Learning *(Discovery learning involves hands-on, experiential, intentional learning through teacher-directed problem solving activities.)*

Level of Use

A.   I *do not use/do not have time to use* the discovery learning in my classroom.
B.   I use discovery learning *very seldom* (e.g., once or twice during the course I teach).
C.   I use discovery learning *seldom* (e.g., once or twice during each grading period).
D.   I use discovery learning *often* (e.g., once a week).
E.   I use discovery learning *very often* (e.g., every day).

Level of Preference

A.   I do not prefer discovery learning as a teaching practice for my subject.
B.   Discovery learning is an appropriate practice that can be used occasionally in my subject area.
C.   Discovery learning is a practice that is well suited to my course content.

Level of Training

A.   I have had *no training* in the discovery learning.
B.   I have had *some training* but not enough to implement.
C.   I have had *extensive training* in discovery learning and understand it well.

Lecture *(A lecture is an instructional practice in which the teacher gives an oral presentation of facts and principles, with the students frequently being responsible for note taking.)*

Level of Use

A.   I *do not use/do not have time to use* lecture in my classroom.
B.   I use lecture *very seldom* (e.g., once or twice during the course I teach).
C.   I use lecture *seldom* (e.g., once or twice during each grading period).
D.   I use lecture *often* (e.g., once a week).
E.   I use lecture *very often* (e.g., every day).

Level of Preference

A.   I do not prefer lecture as a teaching practice for my subject.
B.   Lecture is an appropriate practice that can be used occasionally in my subject area.
C.   Lecture is a practice that is well suited to my course content.

Level of Training

A. I have had *no training* in lecture.
B. I have had *some training* but not enough to implement.
C. I have had *extensive training* in lecture and understand the concept well.

Direct Instruction (*When using direct instruction approaches, the teacher structures lessons in a straightforward sequential manner, discussion, worksheets, and drill.*)

Level of Use

A. I *do not use/do not have time to use* direct instruction in my classroom.
B. I use direct instruction *very seldom* (e.g., once or twice during the course I teach).
C. I use direct instruction *seldom* (e.g., once or twice during each grading period).
D. I use direct instruction *often* (e.g., once a week).
E. I use direct instruction *very often* (e.g., every day).

Level of Preference

A. I do not prefer direct instruction as a teaching practice for my subject.
B. Direct instruction is an appropriate practice that can be used occasionally in my subject area.
C. Direct instruction is a practice that is well suited to my course content.

Level of Training

A. I have had *no training* in direct instruction.
B. I have had *some training* but not enough to implement.
C. I have had *extensive training* in direct instruction and understand the concept well.

Simulation (*A simulation is a representation of a manageable real event in which the learner is an active participant engaged in acquiring a new behavior or in applying previously acquired skills or knowledge.*)

Level of Use

A. I *do not use/do not have time to use* simulation in my classroom.
B. I use simulation *very seldom* (e.g., once or twice during the course I teach).
C. I use simulation *seldom* (e.g., once or twice during each grading period).
D. I use simulation *often* (e.g., once a week).
E. I use simulation *very often* (e.g., every day).

Level of Preference

A.   I do not prefer simulation as a teaching practice for my subject.
B.   Simulation is an appropriate practice that can be used occasionally in my subject area.
C.   Simulation is a practice that is well suited to my course content.

Level of Training

A.   I have had *no training* in simulation.
B.   I have had *some training* but not enough to implement.
C.   I have had *extensive training* in simulation and understand the concept well.

Field Trips *(When using field trips, teachers take students to a specific location where they may study or observe real things in direct interaction with specified concepts and/or skills to be learned.)*

Level of Use

A.   I *do not use/do not have time to use* field trips in my classroom.
B.   I use field trips *very seldom* (e.g., once or twice during the course I teach).
C.   I use field trips *seldom* (e.g., once or twice during each grading period).
D.   I use field trips *often* (e.g., once a week).
E.   I use field trips *very often* (e.g., every day).

Level of Preference

A.   I do not prefer field trips as a teaching practice for my subject.
B.   Field trips are an appropriate practice that can be used occasionally in my subject area.
C.   Field trips are a practice that are well suited to my course content.

Level of Training
A.   I have had *no training* in integrating field trips into instruction.
B.   I have had *some training* but not enough to implement.
C.   I have had *extensive training* in field trips and understand the practice well.

Student peer coaching/peer tutoring *(Peer coaching/peer tutoring involves students teaching other students either in cross age grouping or within their own class.)*

Level of Use

A. I *do not use/do not have time to use* peer coaching/peer tutoring in my classroom.
B. I use peer coaching/peer tutoring *very seldom* (e.g., once or twice during the course I teach).
C. I use peer coaching/peer tutoring *seldom* (e.g., once or twice during each grading period).
D. I use peer coaching/peer tutoring *often* (e.g., once a week).
E. I use peer coaching/peer tutoring *very often* (e.g., every day).

Level of Preference

A. I do not prefer peer coaching/peer tutoring as a teaching practice for my subject.
B. Peer coaching/peer tutoring is an appropriate practice that can be used occasionally in my subject area.
C. Peer coaching/peer tutoring is a practice that is well suited to my course content.

Level of Training

A. I have had *no training* in peer coaching/peer tutoring.
B. I have had *some training* but not enough to implement.
C. I have had *extensive training* in peer coaching/peer tutoring and understand the practice well.

Audiovisual Experiences *(When providing audiovisual experiences, teachers use films, videos, tape recordings, and other media presentations to deliver the content of their instruction.)*

Level of Use

A. I *do not use/do not have time to use* audiovisual resources in my classroom.
B. I use audiovisual resources *very seldom* (e.g., once or twice during the course I teach).
C. I use audiovisual resources *seldom* (e.g., once or twice during each grading period).
D. I use audiovisual resources *often* (e.g., once a week).
E. I use audiovisual resources *very often* (e.g., every day).

Level of Preference

A. I do not prefer audiovisual resources as a teaching practice for my subject.
B. Audiovisual experiences are an appropriate practice that can be used occasionally in my subject area.
C. Audiovisual resources are a practice that is well suited to my course content.

Level of Training

A. I have had *no training* in integrating audiovisual resources in instruction.
B. I have had *some training* but not enough to implement.
C. I have had *extensive training* in audiovisual resources and understand the practice well.

Technology Assistance (*Technology-assisted instruction involves the use of computers to assist in instruction of basic facts, skills, and concepts related to the subject as well as drill and practice, tutorial, gaming, simulation, discovery, problem solving, and other activities.*)

Level of Use

A. I *do not use/do not have time to use* technology assistance in my classroom.
B. I use technology assistance *very seldom* (e.g., once or twice during the course I teach).
C. I use technology assistance *seldom* (e.g., once or twice during each grading period).
D. I use technology assistance *often* (e.g., once a week).
E. I use technology assistance *very often* (e.g., every day).

Level of Preference

A. I do not prefer technology assistance as a teaching practice for my subject.
B. Technology assistance is an appropriate practice that can be used occasionally in my subject area.
C. Technology assistance is a practice that is well suited to my course content.

Level of Training

A. I have had *no training* in computer/telecommunications.
B. I have had *some training* but not enough to implement.
C. I have had *extensive training* in technology assistance and understand the use of computers well.

Small Groups/Structured Pairs (*Students are organized into small groups to discuss/review a concept/learning objective or to complete a teacher-directed assignment.*)

Level of Use

A. I *do not use/do not have time to use* small groups/structured pairs in my classroom.
B. I use small groups/structured pairs *very seldom* (e.g., once or twice during the course I teach).
C. I use small groups/structured pairs *seldom* (e.g., once or twice during each grading period).
D. I use small groups/structured pairs *often* (e.g., once a week).
E. I use small groups/structured pairs *very often* (e.g., every day).

Level of Preference

A.   I do not prefer small groups/structured pairs as a teaching practice for my subject.
B.   Small groups/structured pairs is an appropriate practice that can be used occasionally in my subject area.
C.   Small groups/structured pairs is a practice that is well suited to my course content.

Level of Training

A.   I have had *no training* in small groups/structured pairs.
B.   I have had *some training* but not enough to implement.
C.   I have had *extensive training* in small groups/structured pairs and understand the practice well.

Projects *(When using projects, teachers have students work on a task for an extended time period, alone or in small groups, usually to produce a tangible product.)*

Level of Use

A.   I *do not use/do not have time to use* student projects in my classroom.
B.   I use student projects *very seldom* (e.g., once or twice during the course I teach).
C.   I use student projects *seldom* (e.g., once or twice during each grading period).
D.   I use student projects *often* (e.g., once a week).
E.   I use student projects *very often* (e.g., every day).

Level of Preference

A.   I do not prefer student projects as a teaching practice for my subject.
B.   Using projects is an appropriate practice that can be used occasionally in my subject area.
C.   Using projects is a practice that is well suited to my course content.

Level of Training

A.   I have had *no training* in student projects.
B.   I have had *some training* but not enough to implement.
C.   I have had *extensive training* in student projects and understand the use of projects well.

II.   Staff Development Experiences

Please indicate whether you have participated in staff development (at least 4 hours) within the last five years on the following topics and the extent to which the staff development was helpful to you in your classroom.

Helpfulness Scale

	Did Not Participate	Not Helpful	Helpful	Very Helpful
Pacing guides	NO	A	B	C
Curriculum alignment/audit	NO	A	B	C
Discipline-specific planning within departments	NO	A	B	C
Alternative assessments/evaluation methods	NO	A	B	C
How to make effective use of class time	NO	A	B	C
Dimensions of learning	NO	A	B	C
Models of teaching	NO	A	B	C
Student learning styles	NO	A	B	C

Do you have adequate access to technology (e.g., computers, CD ROMs, etc., to use in support of instruction?

_____ Yes   _____ No

III.   Teaching Experience/Workload

How many years have you been teaching?   _____

How many classes do you currently teach this semester?   _____

How many course preparations do you have this year?   _____

How are you involved in instructional decision making in your school?

Serve on school improvement team	YES	NO
Serve as a department chair	YES	NO
Serve on an instructional planning committee	YES	NO
Serve on an instructional technology committee	YES	NO
Serve on a SACs Committee	YES	NO

NINETEEN

A Guide to Traditional and Authentic Assessment

I t is clear that measuring student achievement constitutes a substantial portion of the practitioner's charge. I believe that block scheduling contributes substantially to student achievement, but measuring students' progress is necessary no matter what type of schedule a school has. How else will the institution determine if its curricular presentation and instructional practices are producing results? Although one may choose from many forms of assessment, all have the common end of evaluating programs and instruction. Politicians, parents, practitioners, and students have a considerable interest in measuring student performance. Basic knowledge of the various phases and types of assessment present in today's educational world is essential in understanding the assessment process and the need for multiple approaches. Following is a guide to both traditional and authentic assessment. It may be used to create checklists, slides, or other useful tools for student assessment.

When it comes to student assessment there tends to be an overuse of one or two procedures. It is important for teachers to realize that regardless of the scheduling format, the major purpose of assessment is to check to see how the student is mastering the content. Block scheduling allows the teacher more time to do more hands-on assessment such as presentations, projects that can be done in class—not just pencil-and-paper tests.

STUDENT ASSESSMENT

PART ONE

Writing and Evaluating Test Items

OVERVIEW

- Parts of a Test Item
- Categorizing Items
- Evaluating Test Items

Parts of a Test Item—Stems

The Stem

- The part of the question that gives the situation and delineates the task to be addressed.

Two Types of Stems

- Open stem
  An incomplete sentence is provided and the answer choices must finish the sentence.
- Closed stem
  A complete question is provided.

Parts of a Test Item—Stems

General Rules for Stems

- Keep the stem concise to minimize reading time
- Include only relevant information
- The stem should be as complete as possible
- Use present tense whenever possible
- Students should know exactly what the question is asking of them

AVOID

- Stereotyping any age or gender group
- Using "politically incorrect" terms
- Using negative stems such as except, not, least, etc.

DO

- Use a nonsexist writing style; if it is impossible, write the stem clearly and concisely without using the pronouns "his," "her," etc.
- Have an equal number of males and females in the stems
- Resist the use of clever names that may distract students
- If names are used, restrict them to first names or surnames

Parts of a Test Item—Options

Options

- All of the answer choices for a question.

Two types of options

- Key
  The correct option.
- Distracters
  The incorrect options.

Parts of a Test Item—Options

General Rules for Options

- There should be one single best option that students *with the appropriate knowledge* will recognize
- Distracters should not be easily recognizable as choices
- Distracters should be plausible to students *without the necessary knowledge* required to answer the question correctly
- Options should be about the same length, level of complexity, and detail
- If all options can't be the same length, make two long options and two short options
- Word the distracters clearly and concisely
- Distribute the position of the key randomly
- If applicable, use a logical basis for ordering options

AVOID

- Using disparaging remarks in options so that the options are obviously wrong.
- Making the key part of a pair of similar or contrasting options
- Using the words "never" "ever" and "always" as an option
- Using the terms "all of the above" or "none of the above"
- Using "multiple multiples" as options
  Example: A & B, C & B
- Making a distracter wrong for a minor reason causing an answer error under the stress of testing

DO

- Make sure the key does not include one of the distracters
  Example: the distracter is "mix the chemicals" & the key is "mix the chemicals and turn on the Bunsen burner"
- Make sure the distracters do not include the key within their range
  Example: the distracter is "more than 5" and the key is "more than 10"
- If you find that the options begin with the same words or phrases, put this in the stem
  Example: Every option begins with the words "add the . . ."
- If any words from the stem appear in the key, make sure they appear in the distracters as well

Categorizing Items on Cognitive Levels

Knowledge

- Remembering or recognizing appropriate terminology, facts, ideas, materials, trends, sequences, methodology, principles, and generalizations

  The capital of Turkmenistan is:
  - A.) Ulaanbaatar
  - B.) Bishkek
  - C.) Astana
  - D.) Ashbagat *

Categorizing Items on Cognitive Levels

Comprehension

- Understanding written communication, reports, tables, diagrams, directions, regulations, maps, etc.

  The exploration to Lake Tanganyika began at
  - A.) Dodoma
  - B.) Arusha *
  - C.) Ujiji
  - D.) Tabora

Categorizing Items on Cognitive Levels

Application

- Applying ideas, rules of procedure, methods, formulas, principals, and theories in situations

  In a walkathon to raise money for charity, Laura walked a certain distance at 5 mph, then jogged twice that distance at 8 mph. Her total time walking and jogging was 2 hours and 15 minutes. How many miles long was the walkathon?
  A.) 10 miles
  B.) 12 miles
  C.) 15 miles *
  D.) 17 miles   <u>Formula</u>: rate x time= distance

Categorizing Items on Cognitive Levels

Analysis/Synthesis

- Breaking down or putting together material or information in relation to its constituent parts and detecting the relationship of the parts and the way they are organized

  What was a major reason many former colonies in Africa experienced internal strife after achieving independence?
  A.) Colonial borders had separated culturally similar people and enclosed traditional enemies.*
  B.) The new nations wanted to form governments which were radically different.
  C.) The new governments wanted to nationalize the many industrial complexes.
  D.) There were too many diverse languages in the former colonies for effective communication.

Evaluating Test Items

Reliability

- The consistency of test scores
  Would a student score about the same on the test if he/she were to take it today and again next month?

- Improve the individual items through the process of item analysis
  Item analysis includes the following:
  - A review of the item's difficulty level
  - Discrimination data
  - The effectiveness of the distracters

Evaluating Test Items

Difficulty Level

- The *p*-value (or difficulty level) refers to the percentage of students who answered the question *correctly.*
  Therefore, a *p*-value of 0.95 means that 95% of the students answered it correctly

- Items that are too easy or too difficult take away from the test's reliability—they *don't discriminate* between those who know the material from those who do not

Evaluating Test Items

Determining Difficulty Level

- To determine the difficulty level, use the following formula:
  <u># of students answering correctly</u>
  total # of students

- Look at any questions that have
  <u>*p*-value of 0.30 or less</u>
  *Check to make sure the key is correct first!
  <u>*p*-value of 0.90 or more</u>
  *Criterion-referenced questions should be above 0.90.

Evaluating Test Items

Discrimination Index

Item discrimination indicates how well the item discriminates between the high-scoring and low-scoring students.

- Index of 0.00 means the item didn't discriminate at all between groups.
- Index of 0.20 to 0.29 indicates a reasonably good item.
- Index of 0.30 or higher is great!
- Negative discrimination occurs when the low group scores better on the item than the high group.

Evaluating Test Items

Determining Discrimination Index

To determine the discrimination index, use the following formula:

% students high group* − % students low group* = discrimination
    answering correctly   answering correctly   index

*Use the top 27% and bottom 27% of the scores on the test

Example:
10 of 14 high students got the item correct = 0.71
7 of 14 students got the item correct = 0.50
0.71 − 0.50 = a discrimination index of 0.21

Evaluating Test Items

Effectiveness of Distracters

- Look at the distribution of answers among the distracters given in the item
- If a distracter has not been chosen, it may not be effective and needs to be changed to something more plausible
- If student numbers taking the test are low, you may want to wait for another testing with the item to see if the distracter is chosen with the second group
    Remember to keep the first data!

Evaluating Test Items

Analyzing Item Data

- Review the Difficulty Index
    Look at the items that have either very low or very high *p*-values
- Review the Discrimination Index
    Look at items that have low or negative values of discrimination
- Review the Effectiveness of Distracters
    Look at distracters that were not chosen by students
- Review the "history" of the item's data
    Data may change with teaching techniques, the "student grapevine," etc.

Example:

For a community project, an advanced biology student chose to teach groups about the prevention of various urinary and kidney diseases. When preparing material about the prevention of acute glomerulonephritis, the student will stress prevention through the proper treatment of

A) Influenza   B) High cholesterol
C) Strep throat*   D) Gonorrhea

Item Data

Data came from 2 testing times that were 1 year apart
    Total # of students: 135
    Difficulty index: 0.77 and 0.68
    Discrimination index: 0.33 and 0.36
    Effectiveness of distracters: All distracters chosen

STUDENT ASSESSMENT
PART TWO

Using Authentic Assessment for Student Evaluation

The trouble with tests is . . .

- "I'm just not good at taking tests."
- "You asked all the wrong questions."
- "I know a lot more than the test tells you."
- "Let me prove to you that I have learned."
- "Tests are dumb."

What is authentic assessment?

- Movement from paper and pencils tests
- Includes genuine, useful, applicable, practice-based, transferable, and demonstrable items
- Includes skills, knowledge, and attitudes that can be carried beyond the classroom
- Goes beyond true/false examination

(For more information see Merrell, 1998)

Why do students need authentic assessment?

- It helps to develop better brains!
  1967—Brain pioneer Marian Diamond of UCLA discovered that the brain can literally grow new connections with environmental stimulation:

  "When we enriched the environment, we got brains with a thicker cortex, more dendritic branching, more growth spines, and larger cell bodies."

  This indicates the brain cells communicate better with each other and have more support cells.

- This research suggests that the environment impacts the wiring of the brain as much as the person's actual experiences.

(For more information see Jensen, 1998)

How to Maximize Brain Growth

William Greenough, an expert on brain enrichment, emphasizes that two things are vital components of growing a better brain:

Challenge

- Learning should include opportunities for problem solving and critical thinking.
- Provide new information and/or experiences in projects that are relevant to the students.
- If there is too much or too little information or experience, students will get bored or give up.
- Vary time, materials, lessons, pedagogy.

Feedback

- Feedback reduces uncertainty and increases coping abilities.
- Brain self-references: It decides what to do based on what has just been done.
- Feedback is most useful when it is immediate and specific, when it is learner controlled, and when it is presented in several ways.

(For more information see Jensen, 1998)

Brain Enrichment

- Challenging problem solving: Problem solving not limited to one part of the brain

  Can solve a problem on paper, with an analogy or metaphor, with a model, by discussion, with statistics, through artwork, or during a demonstration

- Critical to expose students to a variety of approaches to solving a problem

Enrichment & Attention

- Students must be primed: They will learn better if they are told to look for new information or prompted to its location
- Learning must be relevant, engaging, and chosen by the learner

Direct Instruction Learning Times

- Grades K-2: 5-7 minutes
- Grades 3-7: 8-12 minutes
- Grades 8-12: 12-15 minutes

After learning, the brain needs time for processing and rest; teachers must rotate activities.

(For more information see Gardner, 1993; Jensen, 1998)

How Do We Enrich Student Learning?

Authentic Assessment

**Effective Implementation of Authentic Assessment
(Rural School and Community Trust, 2001)**

- Articulate the goals of instruction clearly.
  1. What should students know, understand, and be able to do? What important cognitive skills do you want students to develop?
     - Communicate effectively orally and in writing
     - Analyze issues using primary source and reference materials
     - Use the scientific method
  2. What social and affective skills do you want students to develop?
     - Work independently and also cooperatively with others
     - Be persistent in the face of challenges
     - Have confidence in their abilities
  3. What metacognitive skills do I want my students to develop?
     - Discuss and evaluate their problem-solving strategies
     - Formulate efficient plans for completing independent projects
     - Reflect on the writing process they use, evaluate its effectiveness, and derive their own plans for how it can be improved
  4. What types of problems do you want them to solve?
     - Know how to do research
     - Predict consequences
     - Make healthy choices
  5. What concepts and principles do I want them to be able to apply?
     - Understand cause-and-effect relationships in history and everyday life
     - Criticize literary works based on plot, setting, motive, etc.
     - Understand and recognize the consequences of substance abuse

Effective Implementation of Authentic Assessment

- Determine valid and appropriate evidence for meeting instructional goals.
    1. How will we know when students understand what we most want them to understand?
    Standards for Student Work in Mathematics (Newmann, Lopez, & Bryk, 1998)
        - Mathematical analysis: Students demonstrate thinking by going beyond simple recording and reproducing of algorithms.
        - Mathematical concepts: Students demonstrate understanding by representing concepts in different contexts or real-world application.
        - Written mathematical communication: Students demonstrate elaboration of their understanding in the form of diagrams or symbolic representations.
        - Habits of study and work: Students demonstrate skills by using time wisely, completing work on time, and showing initiative.

- Ensure that assessment tasks are complex, realistic, and generate multiple sources of data.
    1. Does the task require students to display their knowledge on multiple dimensions?
    2. Are the genres, contexts, and content typical of real-world work in this area?
    3. Does the task produce evidence that can be evaluated upon completion?

Effective Implementation of Authentic Assessment

- Construct clear, well-understood rubrics for assessing student products.

  What differentiates levels of student performance—from excellent to insufficient—on the various components required by the task?

Three types of rubrics

Particular Trait Rubrics	Analytic Rubrics	Holistic Rubrics
Single out one or two criteria to evaluate in a complex performance and ignore other elements for purposes of assessment.	Track all the criteria or standards demonstrated by students in a performance and allow for individual ratings of each one.	Merge all the criteria into a comprehensive description of the performance.
They provide especially targeted information.	They require more than one score for each piece of student work, providing more detailed information about a student's performance.	The benefit is to assess the student's overall performance on a particular task; they also allow for comparing work over time.

Effective Implementation of Authentic Assessment

- Involve students in developing rubrics and evaluating their own work.

Self-Evaluation Check List for Expository Essay

Initial each statement that you feel describes your work. Explain any things you cannot initial, giving reasons. Attach this to your paper.

_____ My paper has a definite purpose: it works.

_____ My title indicates my point or slant.

_____ I had a specific audience in mind as I wrote and revised.

_____ The details and word choices paint the right picture and give the right feel.

_____ I can explain why I placed every punctuation mark as I did.

_____ Each paragraph contains a clear idea and topic sentence.

_____ I checked each sentence to make sure it was complete.

_____ The transitions are smooth.

_____ The ending is effective in wrapping things up.

(For more information see Perrone, 1992)

Multiple Intelligence and Authentic Assessment

- Multiple intelligences and authentic assessment are natural partners.
- Several optional assessment formats may be implemented based on a student's dominant intelligence.
- Optional assessments blend cohesively with the many types of authentic assessment.

Multiple Intelligences

Verbal/Linguistic

- Debates
- Portfolios
- Quotation reactions
- Rough drafts/final drafts
- Vocabulary
- Word associations

Logical/Mathematical

- Experiment logs
- Logic exercises
- Pattern games
- Rubrics
- "What if" exercises

Visual/Spatial

- Flow charts/graphs
- Hands-on demonstration
- Photo albums
- Scrapbooks
- Murals/montages

Body/Kinesthetic

- Case studies
- Charades/mimes
- Dramatizations
- Skill demonstration
- Physical exercise routines

Musical/Rhythmic

- Checklists
- Creating raps/songs
- Musical performances
- Orchestrating music
- Dances

Multiple Intelligences and Authentic Assessment

Interpersonal

- Buzz sessions
- Group jigsaw puzzles
- Project rosters
- Scavenger hunts
- Think/pair/share

Intrapersonal

- Autobiographical stories
- Feelings diaries/logs
- Individual conferences
- Reflections
- Self-study reports

Naturalist

- Recognizes flora and fauna
- Makes consequential distinctions in the natural world
- Includes farmers, botanists, conservationists, biologists, environmentalists

Types of Authentic Assessment

Graphic Organizers

- The mind spontaneously organizes information as it is learned
- Graphic organizers help to visually organize new information.
- Represent similarities and differences
- Detect patterns and relationships
- Relate new information to previous learning
- Link interdisciplinary topics
- Display information, ideas, and concepts
- Types of Graphic Organizers
  Webbing
  Cause/Effect
  Story Map
  Venn Diagram
  Double Bubble

(For more information see Tombari & Borich, 1999)

Types of Authentic Assessment

Self-Assessment

- Self-assessment allows students the opportunity to evaluate their performance or product.
- Evaluation leads to self-correction and improvement.
- Self-assessment provides student ownership and analysis of products.

Methods

- Video Reflection
- Student-Led Conferences
- Journals

Types of Authentic Assessment— Self-Assessment

Video Reflection

- Use of videotape to assess and improve performance in areas of chorus, band, physical education, or the arts
- Teacher or proficient student models the desired production
- Use rubric for presentation

Implementation of Video Reflection

Application: High school chorus
Objective: Students will sing a ballad in stratified vocal sections. Teacher will model a ballad demonstrating the criteria needed for the production

- Video is made of students singing in groups of mixed vocal sections
- Students use teacher-generated rubric to assess strengths and weaknesses upon review of the video

Types of Authentic Assessment— Self-Assessment

Student-Led Conferences

- Conference with parents led by students
- Teacher = Facilitator
- Several conferences conducted at once in classroom (teacher circulating in room)
- Discussion centered around student portfolio of work
- Collection of student work
- Shows academic progress over time

(Bailey & Guskey, 2001)

Types of Authentic Assessment— Self-Assessment

Implementation of Conferences

BEFORE	DURING	AFTER
Set learning objectives and work with students to create portfolio of work.	Circulate around to each family group and make individual student comments.	Schedule extra time with parents if follow-up needed.
Build in reflection/edit time and role-play conferences with students.	Facilitate when needed.	Read and process evaluations from parents and students.
Prepare a family-friendly environment.	Express gratitude for parental involvement.	Debrief process with students.

Types of Authentic Assessment— Self-Assessment

Journals

- Use of non-structured writing to evaluate short stories and novels
- Permits personal reflection/writing
- Allows for synthesis of ideas and evaluations rather than rigid mechanical corrections
- Can be used as a dialogue between student and teacher

Implementation of Journals

Application: Middle school Language Arts
Objective: Students will reflect in their journals using the following questions from Chapter 14 and 15 of *A Day No Pigs Would Die:*

1. If faced with the same dilemma as Rob, would you have had the courage to act as he did?
2. Do you think the ordeal with Pinky made Rob a stronger young man? How?
3. What do you perceive as Rob's new challenges as man of the house at 15?

Types of Self-Assessment

Rubrics

- A guide for evaluating student work
- Use specific criteria to assess project mastery
- Allow for a variety of student skills to be assessed
- Hold learners to high levels of achievement
- Minimize scoring subjectivity and bias
- Can be generated by both teacher and student

Types of Rubrics

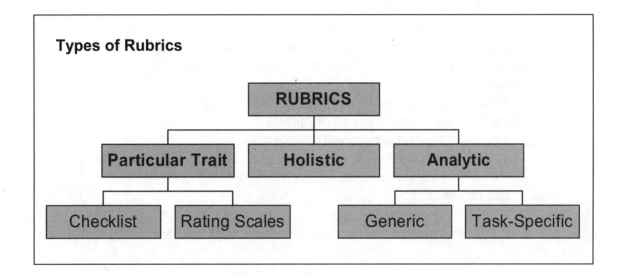

Types of Self-Assessment—Rubrics

Particular Trait Rubrics

Checklist:
- Discrete, observable behaviors
- Observer only watches to see if behavior occurred or not
- Extremely efficient
- Require simple judgments
- Used as diagnostic tools

Rating Scales:
- Assessing complex products
- Assigns numbers to certain levels or degrees of performance
- Continuum that indicates the frequency or quality of the behavior
- Requires more time than checklists

(For more information see Tombari & Borich, 1999)

Types of Self-Assessment—Rubrics

Holistic Rubrics

- Observer estimates the overall quality of the product, demonstration, or exhibit
- Assigns numerical value to that overall quality
- Gives an index of performance
- Requires only one judgment
- Cannot serve as diagnostic rubric since specific strengths and weaknesses are not noted

Types of Self-Assessment—Rubrics

Analytic Rubrics

Generic:
- May be broadly applied to several assignments in varying disciplines
- Useful because of time saved and broad use possible

Task-specific:
- Allows for analysis of specific learning outcomes
- Relevant to one content topic
- Can provide a framework for concepts to be learned and then assessed

Types of Self-Assessment—Rubrics

Developing Analytic Rubrics

- Measure your goals

Learning outcomes should match rating assessment
- Will you expect evidence of knowledge acquisition?
  - Design a rating scale that reflects this
- Do you wish to assess problem-solving strategies?
  - Rating scales should assess their use
- Will you be observing the processes learners show as they complete the task?
  - A checklist may need to be constructed

(For more information see Tombari & Borich, 1999)

Types of Self-Assessment—Rubrics

Developing Analytic Rubrics

- Select an appropriate scoring system
    - Particular trait rubrics
        - Checklists
        - Rating scales
    - Holistic rubrics
    - Analytic rubrics
        - Generic
        - Task specific

(Tombari & Borich, 1999)

Types of Self-Assessment—Rubrics

Developing Analytic Rubrics

- Identify the criteria to be evaluated
    - Type of criteria (varies per type of rubric)
        - Conceptual understanding
        - Systematic approach to task?
        - Is the answer correct?
        - Is the work presented neatly?
    - A successful approach:
        - Consider the task and imagine an excellent student's response to it!
    - Select the number and detail of criteria
        - All important aspects of performance should be found in the criteria
        - Each criteria should be specific, but not too detailed
    - Use subcriteria or elements when necessary and relevant

(For more information see Danielson & Abrutyn, 1997)

Types of Self-Assessment—Rubrics

Developing Analytic Rubrics

- Decide on the number of points for the rubric
    - Detail in distinctions
        - Larger numbers of points can provide specific feedback, but can be cumbersome
        - Limit rubrics to 4-6 points
    - Divide the line between acceptable and unacceptable performance
    - Provide general headings for different points

Types of Self-Assessment—Rubrics

Developing Analytic Rubrics

- Writing the descriptions of performance levels should include:
    - The language used
        - Serve to further define the criteria
        - Use positive rather than negative wording
    - All subcriteria or elements defined
    - Distance between points
        - Distance between points on a scale should be equal

(For more information see Danielson & Abrutyn, 1997)

Types of Authentic Assessment

Portfolios

- What is a portfolio? A collection of student work over a period of time
- Provides a rich array of what students know and can do
- Provides for individual or group accountability
- Can be single-subject or interdisciplinary

(For more information see Tombari & Borich, 1999)

Types of Authentic Assessment—Portfolios

Benefits of Portfolio Use

- Show a learner's ability to think and problem solve
- Tell about a learner's persistence and effort
- Show a learner's skill in self-monitoring and ability to be self-reflective
- Can alter the nature of classroom instruction
- Means to communicate academic achievement to parents and other teachers
- Supplement regular report card grades

(For more information see Tombari & Borich, 1999)

Types of Authentic Assessment—Portfolios

What Makes a Portfolio a Portfolio?

- Developing a portfolio offers the student an opportunity to learn about learning.
- The portfolio is something that is done *by* the student, not *to* the student.
- The portfolio is separate and different from the student's cumulative folder.
- The portfolio must convey explicitly or implicitly the student's activities.
- The portfolio may serve a different purpose during the year from the purpose it serves at the end.
- A portfolio may have multiple purposes, but these may not conflict.
- The portfolio should contain information that illustrates growth.
- Finally, many of the skills and techniques that are involved in producing effective portfolios do not happen by themselves.

Types of Authentic Assessment—Portfolios

Building a System for Portfolio Assessment

Step 1: Decide on the purpose
- Monitoring student progress
- Communicating what has been learned to parents
- Evaluating how well something was taught
- Showing off what has been accomplished
- Assigning a course grade

(For more information see Tombari & Borich, 1999)

Types of Authentic Assessment—Portfolios

Building a System for Portfolio Assessment

Step 2: Identify Cognitive Skills and Dispositions
- Knowledge organization
- Cognitive strategies
  - Analysis, interpretation, organizational revising
- Procedural skills
  - Editing, drawing, speaking
- Metacognition
  - Self-monitoring, self-reflection

Types of Authentic Assessment—Portfolios

Building a System for Portfolio Assessment

Step 3: Decide who will plan the portfolio
- Teacher
- Parent
- Students
- Ideal situation involves planning from all three!

Types of Authentic Assessment—Portfolios

Building a System for Portfolio Assessment

Step 4: Choose the products and number of samples
- Ownership
  - Involve parents and students in learning
- Portfolio's link with instruction
  - Connect portfolios and learning outcomes

Types of Authentic Assessment—Portfolios

Building a System for Portfolio Assessment

Step 5: Determine the scoring rubrics
- Type of rubric: checklist, rating scale, holistic, analytic
- Rubric for each entry in the portfolio
- Scoring criteria for the portfolio as a whole product

Types of Authentic Assessment—Portfolios

Building a System for Portfolio Assessment

Step 6: Aggregate all portfolio ratings
- Learners should receive a score for each draft and final product in the portfolio
- Decide how to aggregate scores
- Develop a procedure for combining all scores

Types of Authentic Assessment—Portfolios

Building a System for Portfolio Assessment

Step 7: Determine the logistics
- What are the timelines?
- How are products turned in and returned?
- Where are final products kept?
- Who has access to the portfolio?

Types of Authentic Assessment—Portfolios

Building a System for Portfolio Assessment

Step 8: Plan a final conference
- Plan to meet with individual students
- Include parents if at all possible
- Discuss the learner's development and academic achievements

References, Recommended Readings

Adams, D. C., & Salvaterra, M. E. (1997). Structural and teacher changes: Necessities for successful block schedule. *High School Journal, 81*(2), 98-105.

Adey, P., & Shayer, M. (1990). Accelerating the development of formal thinking in middle and high school students. *Journal of Research in Science Teaching, 27*(3), 267-285.

Adler, M. J. (1982). *The Paideia proposal: An educational manifesto.* New York: Macmillan.

America 2000: An education strategy. (1991, December). *Congressional Digest, 70*(12), 294-296.

Babcock, B. (2000). *Learning from experience: A collection of service-learning projects linking academic standards to curriculum.* Madison: Wisconsin Department of Public Instruction. (ERIC Document Reproduction Services No. ED444920)

Bailey, J. M., & Guskey, T. R. (2001). *Implementing student-led conferences.* Thousand Oaks, CA: Corwin.

Barr, B. (1994). Research on problem solving. *Elementary School Journal, 5* (3), 237-247.

Beauchamp, G. (1975). *Curriculum theory.* Wilmette, IL: Kagg.

Becker, W., & Englemann, S. (1971). *Teaching: A course in applied psychology.* Chicago: Science Research Associates.

Beyer, B. (1988). *Developing a thinking skills program.* Boston: Allyn & Bacon.

Blake, R. (1984). *Discovery versus expository instructional strategies and their implications for instruction of hearing-impaired post-secondary students.* New York: Author. (ERIC Document Reproduction Service No. ED248651)

Bloom, B. S. (Ed.). (1956). *Taxonomy of educational objectives: The classification of educational goals: Handbook I, cognitive domain.* New York: Longmans, Green.

Bohince, Judy. (1996). Blockbuster ideas: Activities for breaking up block periods. *Science Teacher, 63*(6), 20-24.

Boocock, S. S., & Schild, E. O. (1968). *Simulation games in learning.* Beverly Hills, CA: Sage.

Boyer, E. (1983*). High school: A report on secondary education in America.* New York: Harper & Row.

Boyer, M. R. (1993). Avoid the isolated road. *School Administrator, 50*(3), 20-21.

Brophy, J. (1996). Working with shy or withdrawn students. *ERIC Digest* (ERIC Identifier ED402070). Retrieved April 30, 2002, from www.ed.gov/databases/ERIC_Digests/ed402070.html

Bruner, J. S. (1966). *Toward a theory of instruction.* Cambridge, MA: Belknap Press of Harvard University.

Burke, D. L. (1997). Looping: Adding time, strengthening relationships. *ERIC Digest* (ERIC Identifier ED414098). Retrieved April 16, 2002, from www.ed.gov/databases/ERIC_Digests/ed414098.html

Butts, D., & Jones, H. (1966). Inquiry training and problem solving in elementary school children. *Journal of Research in Science Teaching, 4* (1), 12-24.

Canady, R. L., & Hopkins, H. J. (1997). Integrating the curriculum with parallel block scheduling. *Principal, 76*(4), 28-31.

Canady, R. L., & Rettig, M. D. (1995a). *Block scheduling: A catalyst for change in high schools.* Princeton, NJ: Eye on Education.

Canady, R. L., & Rettig, M. D. (1995b). The power of innovative scheduling. *Educational Leadership, 53*(3), 4-10

Carnegie Council on Adolescent Development. (1989). *Turning points: Preparing American youth for the 21st century.* New York: Carnegie Corporation.

Carroll, J. M. (1990). The Copernican plan: Restructuring the American high school. *Phi Delta Kappan, 71,* 358-365.

Carroll, J. M. (1994). Organizing time to support learning. *School Administrator, 51*(3), 26-28, 30-33.

Cawelti, G. (1994). *High school restructuring: A national study.* Arlington, VA: Educational Research Service.

Chesler, M. A., & Fox, R. S. (1966). *Role-playing methods in the classroom.* Chicago: Science Research Associates.

Clark, C., & Peterson, P. (1986). Teachers' thought processes. In M. Wittrock (Ed.), *Handbook of research on teaching* (pp. 225-296). New York: Macmillan.

Coalition of Essential Schools. (1999). The cycle of inquiry and action: Essential learning communities [Special issue]. *HORACE, 15*(4).

Collins, K. (1969). The importance of a strong confrontation in an inquiry model of teaching. *School Science and Mathematics, 69*(7), 615-617.

Cookson, P. W., Jr. (1995). Goals 2000: Framework for the new educational federalism. *Teachers College Record, 96*(3), 405.

Corley, E. (1997, October). *Teacher perceptions regarding block scheduling: Reactions to change.* Paper presented at the annual meeting of the Mid-Western Educational Research Association, Chicago.

Costa, A. (1985). *Developing minds: A resource book for teaching thinking.* Alexandria, VA: Association for Supervision and Curriculum Development.

Couch, R. (1993). Synectics and imagery: Developing creative thinking through images. In R. Braden, J. Clark Baca, & D. Beauchamp (Eds.), *Art, science, and visual literacy: Selected readings from the Annual Conference of the International Visual Literacy.* Blacksburg, VA: International Visual Literacy Association. (ERIC Document Reproduction Service No. ED363330)

Crosby, E. A. (1993). The at-risk decade. *Phi Delta Kappan, 74*(8), 598-604.

Dallman-Jones, A. (1994). *The expert educator.* Fond du Lac, WI: Three Blue Herons.

Danielson, C., & Abrutyn, L. (1997). *An introduction to using portfolios in the classroom.* Alexandria, VA: Association for Supervision and Curriculum Development.

Davidson, N. (1971). *The small group-discovery method of mathematics instruction as applied in calculus.* Madison: Wisconsin Research and Development Center for Cognitive Learning. (ERIC Document Reproduction Service No. ED162879)

Day, M. M., Ivanov, P., & Binkley, S. (1996). Tackling block scheduling: How to make the most of longer classes. *The Science Teacher, 63*(6), 25-27.

Dewey, J. (1910). *How we think.* Boston: Heath.

Dewey, J. (1938). *Experience and education.* New York: Macmillan.

DiBiase, W. J., & Queen, J. A. (1999). Middle school social studies on the block. *The Clearing House, 72*(6), 377-383.

Downs, R. B. (1975). *Heinrich Pestalozzi, father of modern pedagogy.* Boston: Twayne.

Doyle, D. P. (1991). America 2000. *Phi Delta Kappan, 73*(3), 184-192.

Dragositz, A. (1969). *Curriculum innovations and evaluation: Proceedings of the association for supervision and curriculum development pre-conference seminar.* Princeton, NJ: Princeton University Press.

Drew, N. (1987). *Learning the skills of peacemaking: An activity guide for elementary-age children on communicating, cooperating, resolving conflict.* Torrence, CA: Jalmar.

Dukes, D. D. (1978). *A study comparing measures of auditory discrimination to other measures relative to reading achievement.* Unpublished master's thesis, East Tennessee State University, Johnson City.

Dukes, R. L., & Seidner, C. J. (1978). *Learning with simulations and games.* Beverly Hills, CA: Sage.

Edwards, C. M. (1995). Virginia's 4 × 4 high schools: High school, college, and more. *NASSP Bulletin, 79*(571), 23-41.

Eggen, P. D., & Kauchak, D. P. (2001). *Strategies for teachers* (4th ed.). Boston: Allyn & Bacon.

Eisner, E. (1979). *The educational imagination: On the design and evaluation of school programs.* New York: Macmillan.

Elefant, E. (1980). Deaf children in an inquiry training program. *Volta Review, 82*(5), 271-279.

Engel, B. S. (1994). Portfolio assessment and the new paradigm: New instruments and new places. *Educational Forum, 59*(1), 22-27.

Ennis, R. H. (1993, Summer). Critical thinking assessment. *Theory Into Practice,* pp. 179-186.

Erikson, E. (1980). *Identity and the life cycle.* New York: Norton.

Farmer, R. F., Gould, M. W., Herring, R. L., Linn, F. J., & Theobold, M. A. (1995). *The middle school principal.* The Practicing Administrator's Leadership Series. Thousand Oaks, CA: Corwin.

Fields, E. (1977, January). *How to evaluate proposed curriculum changes.* Paper presented at the annual meeting of the National School Boards Association, Houston, TX.

Forsten, C., Grant, J., & Richardson, I. (2000). Multiage and looping: Borrowing from the past. *Principal, 78*(4), 15-16, 18.

Frasier, C. H. (1997, January). The development of an authentic assessment instrument: The scored discussion. *English Journal*, pp. 37-40.

Furness, P. (1976). *Role play in the elementary school: A handbook for teachers.* New York: Hart.

Gabel, D. L. (Ed.). (1994). *Handbook of research on science teaching and learning.* New York: Macmillan.

Gable, Robert A., & Manning, M. Lee. (1997). In the midst of reform: The changing structure and practice of middle school education. *Clearing House, 7*(1), 58-62.

Gardner, H. (1993). *Multiple intelligences: The theory in practice.* New York: Basic Books.

George, P. S., & Alexander, W. M. (1993). *The exemplary middle school* (2nd ed.). Fort Worth, TX: Harcourt Brace.

Gerking, J. L. (1995). Building on block schedules. *The Science Teacher, 62*, 23-27.

Gesell, A. L. (1971). *The first five years of life: A guide to the study of the preschool child.* London: Yale University Clinic of Child Development.

Gillies, R. M., & Ashman, A. F. (2000). The effects of cooperative learning on students with learning difficulties in the lower elementary school. *Journal of Special Education, 34*(1), 19-27.

Glickman, C. D., Gordon, S. P., & Ross-Gordon, J. M. (2001). *Supervision and instructional leadership: A developmental approach* (5th ed.). Needham Heights, MA: Allyn & Bacon.

Glynn, S. M. (1994). *Teaching science with analogies.* Athens: University of Georgia, National Reading Research Center.

Goals 2000: Educate America Act (1994), P.L. No. 103-227.

Goodlad, J. I. (1984). *A place called school: Prospects for the future.* New York: McGraw-Hill

Gordon, W. J. (1961). *Synectics.* New York: Harper & Row.

Green, J. A. (1969). *The educational ideas of Pestalozzi.* New York: Greenwood Press.

Guetzkow, H. (1995). Recollections about the inter-nation simulation (INS) and some derivatives of global modeling. *Simulation & Gaming, 26*, 453-470.

Gullo, D. (1992). *Developmentally appropriate teaching in early childhood: Curriculum, implementation, and evaluation.* Washington, DC: NEA Early Childhood Series.

Guidelines for appropriate curriculum content and assessment in programs serving children ages 3 through 8: A position statement of the National Association for the Education of Young Children and the National Association of Early Childhood Specialists in State Departments of Education. (1991). *Young Children, 46*, 21-38.

Gunter, M. A., Estes, T. M., & Schwab, J. (1990). *Instruction: A models approach.* Boston: Allyn & Bacon.

Guskey, T. R., & Bailey, J. M. (2001). *Developing grading and reporting systems for student learning.* Thousand Oaks, CA: Corwin.

Gutek, G. L. (1986). *Education in the United States: An historical perspective.* Englewood Cliffs, NJ: Prentice-Hall

Hackmann, D. G. (1995). Ten guidelines for implementing block scheduling. *Educational Leadership, 53*(3), 24-27.

Hansler, D. D. (1985). *Studies on the effectiveness of the cognition enhancement technique for teaching thinking skills* (Report No. CS-008-331). East Lansing, MI: National Center for Research on Teacher Learning. (ERIC Document Reproduction Service No. ED266432)

Hart, W. H. (2000). *A comparison of the use of instructional time in block scheduled and traditionally scheduled high school classrooms.* Doctoral dissertation, University of North Carolina at Charlotte.

Heitzman, A. J. (1983). Discipline and the use of punishment. *Education, 104,* 17-22.

Henderson, J. G., & Hawthorne, R. D. (2000). *Transformative curriculum leadership* (2nd ed.). Upper Saddle River, NJ: Prentice Hall.

Hermann, G. (1969). Learning by discovery: A critical review of studies. *Journal of Experimental Education, 38,* 59-71.

Hertz-Lazarowitz, R. (1990, April). *An integrative model of the classroom: The enhancement of cooperation in learning.* Paper presented at the annual meeting of the American Educational Research Association, Boston.

Hottenstein, D. S. (1998). *Intensive scheduling: Restructuring America's secondary schools through time management.* Thousand Oaks, CA: Corwin.

Huff, L. (1995, May). Flexible block scheduling: It works for us. *NASSP Bulletin, 79,* 19-22.

Huggins, P., Manion, D.W., & Shakarian, L. (1998). *Helping kids handle put-downs: Teaching assertion, use of humor and self-encouragement.* Longmont, CO: Sopris West.

Hunter, M. C. (1982). *Mastery teaching.* El Segundo, CA: TIP.

Institute for Educational Leadership. (2000). *Leadership for student learning: Reinventing the principalship.* Washington, DC: Author.

Ivany, G. (1969). The assessment of verbal inquiry in junior high school science. *Science Education, 53*(4), 287-293.

Jarrett, D. (1997). *Inquiry strategies for science and mathematics learning.* Portland, OR: Northwest Regional Educational Laboratory.

Jasparro, R. (1998, May). Applying systems thinking to curriculum evaluation. *NASSP Bulletin, 82,* 80-84.

Jensen, J. (1998). *Improving student achievement: Schools as a learning organization, a collection of articles.* Portland, OR: Portland Public Schools.

Johnson, D. W., & Johnson, R. T. (1992). Implementing cooperative learning. *Contemporary Education, 63*(3), 173-180.

Johnson, D. W., & Johnson, R. T. (1994). *Learning together and alone: Cooperative, competitive, and individualistic learning.* Boston: Allyn & Bacon.

Johnson, D. W., Johnson, R. T., & Holubec, E. J. (1993). *Circles of learning: Cooperation in the classroom* (4th ed.). Edina, MN: Interaction Book.

Johnston, J. H., & Johnston, L. L. (1993). Planning for the human response in middle grade reorganization. *School Administrator, 50*(3), 22-43.

Jones, H. (1966). The development of a test of scientific inquiry, using the tab format, and an analysis of its relationship to selected student behaviors (Report No. SE-002-034). East Lansing, MI: National Center for Research on Teacher Learning. (ERIC Document Reproduction Service No. ED013212)

Jones, K. (1980). *Simulations: A handbook for teachers.* New York: Nichols.

Jones, K. (1987). *Simulations: A handbook for teachers* (2nd ed.). New York: Nichols.

Jones, K. (1988). *Interactive learning events: A guide for facilitators.* New York: Nichols.

Joyce, B. (1978). Toward a theory of information processing in teaching. *Educational Research Quarterly, 3*(4), 66-77.

Joyce, B., & Calhoun, E. (1996). *Creating learning experiences: The role of instructional theory and research.* Alexandria, VA: Association for Supervision and Curriculum Development.

Joyce, B., & Weil, M. (1983). *Models of teaching.* Englewood Cliffs, NJ: Prentice Hall.

Joyce, B., Weil, M., & Calhoun, E. (2000). *Models of teaching* (6th ed.). Boston: Allyn & Bacon.

Kagan, S. (1992). *Cooperative learning.* San Juan Capistrano, CA: Kagan Cooperative Learning.

Kemmis, S. (1980). *Seven principles for program evaluation in curriculum development and innovation* (Report No. TM810286). Geelong Australia: Deakin University. (ERIC Document Reproduction Service Website No. ED202869)

Kennta, B. (1993). Moving with cautious velocity. *School Administrator, 50*(3), 17-19.

Khazzaka, J. P. (1997-1998, December-January). Comparing the merits of a seven-period day to those of a four-period day. *High School Journal,* 89-97.

Klesius, J., & Searls, E. (1990). A comparison of two methods of direct instruction of preservice teachers. *Journal of Teacher Education, 41*(4), 34-45.

Kolstad, R., & McFadden, A. (1998). Multiage classrooms: An age-old educational strategy revisited. *Journal of Instructional Psychology, 25*(1), 14-18.

Ladousse, G. P. (1987). *Role play.* New York: Oxford University Press.

Lasley, T., & Matczynski, T. (1997). *Strategies for teaching in a diverse environment.* Belmont, CA: Wadsworth.

Leslie, C., & Halpert, J. E. (1996, December 9). One class fits all. *Newsweek,* p. 71.

Lewis, A., & Smith, D. (1993, Summer). Defining higher order thinking. *Theory Into Practice,* pp. 40-48.

Lilley, I. M. (1967). *Friedrich Froebel: A selection from his writings.* Cambridge, UK: Cambridge University Press.

Lunenburg, F. C., & Irby, B. J. (2000). *High expectations: An action plan for implementing goals 2000.* Thousand Oaks, CA: Corwin.

Lyman, L., & Foyle, H. C. (1998). Facilitating collaboration in schools. *Teaching and Change, 5*(3-4), 312-339.

Maidment, R. (1973). Differentiated staffing. *NASSP Bulletin, 57*(369), 53-56.

Maidment, R., & Bronstein, R. H. (1973). *Simulation games: Design and implementation.* Columbus, OH: Merrill.

Marsh, C., & Willis, G. (1995). *Curriculum alternative approaches, ongoing issues.* Englewood Cliffs, NJ: Prentice Hall.

McBurney, D. H. (1995, February). The problem method of teaching research methods. *Teaching Psychology,* pp. 36-38.

McClure, P. (1998). *State policies to support middle school reform: A guide for policymakers.* New York: Carnegie Corporation, Council of Chief State Offices. (ERIC Document Reproduction Service No. ED441273)

McCormick, R., & James, M. (1983). *Curriculum evaluation in schools.* London, England: Croom Helm.

Merrell, H. J. (1998). Performance based tests improve student learning. *Kappa Delta Pi Record, 34*(4), 124-128.

Miller, B. (1997). Educating the "other" children. *American Demographics, 19,* 49-54.

Morine, H., & Morine, G. (1973). *Discovery: A challenge to teachers.* Englewood Cliffs, NJ: Prentice Hall.

Nadler, R. (1998). Failing grade. *National Review, 50*(10), 38-40.

Nation at risk, A. (1983). Retrieved May 3, 2002 from www.ed.gov/pubs/ NatAtRisk

Nelson, B., & Frayer, D. (1972). *Discovery learning versus expository learning: New insight into an old controversy.* Madison: Wisconsin Research and Development Center for Cognitive Learning. (ERIC Document Reproduction Service No. ED061532)

Neufeld, B. (1995). Improving principals' practice: The influence of professional development on principals' work in middle school reform efforts supported by the Edna McConnell Clark Foundation. Cambridge, MA: Education Matters. (ERIC Document Reproduction Service No. ED386521)

Newmann, F. M., Lopez, G., & Bryk, A. S. (1998). *The quality of intellectual work in Chicago schools: A baseline report.* Chicago. Consortium on Chicago School Research.

Ngeow, K. Y. (1998). *Enhancing student thinking through collaborative learning.* Bloomington: Indiana University, ERIC Clearinghouse on Reading, English, and Communication. (ERIC Document Reproduction Service No. ED42258698)

Noble, M. C. S., & Dawson, H. A. (1961). *Handbook on rural education: Factual data on rural education, its social and economic backgrounds.* Washington, DC: National Education Association of the United States, Department of Rural Education.

North Carolina Department of Public Instruction. (2000). *Standard course of study.* Raleigh, NC: Author.

Olson, L. (2000, January 19). New thinking on what makes a leader. *Education Week,* pp. 1, 4-15.

Olson, L. (2000, November 1). Principals try new styles as instructional leaders. *Education Week,* pp. 1, 15-19.

O'Neil, J. (1995). Finding time to learn. *Educational Leadership, 53*(3), 11-15.

Ornstein, A. C., & Hunkins, F. P. (1998). *Curriculum foundations, principles, and issues* (3rd ed.). Needham Heights, MA: Allyn & Bacon.

Ornstein, A. C., & Levine, D. U. (1989). *Foundations of American education* (4th ed.). Boston, MA: Houghton Mifflin.

Parsons, J., & Smith, D. (1993). *Valuing students: Rethinking evaluation.* Alberta, Canada. (ERIC Document Reproduction Service No. PS021745)

Perrone, V. (1992). Stop standardized testing in early grades. *Education Digest, 57*(5), 42-47.

Piaget, J. (1954). *The construction of reality in the child.* New York: Basic Books.

Piaget, J. (1969a). *The child's conception of time.* New York: Basic Books.

Piaget, J. (1969b). *The mechanisms of perception.* New York: Basic Books.

Piaget, J., & Inhelder, B. (1969). *The psychology of the child.* New York: Basic Books.

Picciotto, L. P. (1996). *Student-led parent conferences.* New York: Scholastic Professional Books.

Pike, K., & Salend, S. J. (1995, Fall). Authentic assessment strategies: Alternatives to norm-referenced testing. *Teaching Exceptional Children,* pp. 15-20.

Platten, M. (1991, March). *Teaching concepts and skills of thinking simultaneously.* Paper presented at the meeting of the annual conference of the National Art Education Association, Atlanta, GA.

Queen, J. A. (1999). *Curriculum practice in the elementary and middle school.* Upper Saddle River, NJ: Merrill.

Queen, J. A., (2000). Block scheduling revisited. *Phi Delta Kappan, 82*(3), 214-20, 221-22.

Queen, J. A. (2002). *Students' transitions from middle to high school: Improving achievement and creating a safer environment.* Larchmont, NY: Eye on Education.

Queen, J. A., Algozzine, R. F., & Eaddy, M. A. (1997, April). The road we traveled: Scheduling in the 4×4 block. *NASSP Bulletin, 81,* 88-99.

Queen, J. A., Algozzine, R. F., & Isenhour, K. G. (1999, January). First-year teachers and 4×4 block scheduling. *NASSP Bulletin, 83,* 100-103.

Queen, J. A., Burrell, J. R., & McManus, S. (2000). *Planning for instruction: A year-long guide.* Upper Saddle River, NJ: Prentice Hall.

Queen, J. A., & Gaskey, K. A. (1997). Steps for improving school climate in block scheduling. *Phi Delta Kappan, 79*(2), 158-161.

Queen, J. A., & Isenhour, K. G. (1998a, November). Building a climate of acceptance for block scheduling. *NASSP Bulletin, 82,* 95-104.

Queen, J. A., & Isenhour, K. G. (1998b). *The 4×4 block schedule.* Larchmont, NY: Eye on Education.

Randall, V. (1999, March-April). Cooperative learning: Abused and overused? *Gifted Child Today Magazine,* pp. 14-16.

Reinhartz, J., & Beach, D. M. (1997). *Teaching and learning in the elementary school: Focus on curriculum.* Upper Saddle River, NJ: Merrill.

Rettig, M., & Canady, R. (2000). *Scheduling strategies for middle schools.* Larchmont, NY: Eye on Education.

Rettig, M. D., & Canady, R. L. (1996). All around the block: The benefits and challenges of a non-traditional school schedule. *School Administrator, 53*(8), 8-14.

Romano, L. G., & Georgiady, N. P. (1993). *Building an effective middle school.* New York: McGraw-Hill.

Rosenshine, B. (1971). *Teaching behaviors and student achievement.* London: National Foundation for Educational Research.

Rosenshine, B. (1978). *Academic engaged time, content covered and direct instruction.* Paper presented at the annual meeting of the American Educational Research Association (ERIC Document Reproduction Service No. ED152776). Retrieved March 22, 2002, from www.education.ucsb.edu/~ed219b/Rosenshine.html

Rosenshine, B. (1985). Direct instruction. In T. Husen & T. N. Postlethwaite (Eds.), *International encyclopedia of education* (Vol. 3, pp. 1395-1400). Oxford, UK: Pergamon Press.

Rosenshine, B. (1995). Advances in research on instruction. *Journal of Educational Research, 88*(5), 262-268.

Routman, R. (1988). *Transitions: From literature to literacy.* Portsmouth, NH: Heinemann.

Routman, R. (1994). *Invitations: Changing as teachers and learners, K-12.* Portsmouth, NH: Heinemann.

Rural School and Community Trust & Harvard Documentation and Assessment Program (Eds.). (2001). *Assessing student work.* Retrieved May 6, 2002, from http://216.239.51.100/search?q=cache:Nl-yiWEeWPgC:www.ruralchallenge-policy.org/assess_guide.pdf+finkel+noble+high+school+maine&hl=en

Russell, J. F. (1997). Relationships between the implementation of middle-level program concepts and students' achievement. *Journal of Curriculum and Supervision, 12*(2), 169-185.

Saks, J. B. (1999). The middle school problem. *American School Board Journal, 186*(7), 32-33.

Sanders, J. R. (1992). *Evaluating school programs: An educator's guide.* Newbury Park, CA: Corwin.

Schlenker, R. M. (1986). *Planning training sessions that start, go, and end somewhere.* (ERIC Document Reproduction Service No. 276837)

Schroth, G., & Dixon, J. (1996). The effects of block scheduling on student performance. *International Journal of School Reform, 5*(4), 472-476.

Scieszka, J. (1999). *The true story of the 3 little pigs/by A. Wolfe.* New York: Viking.

Seitsinger, A. M., & Felner, R. D. (2000, April). *Whom and how is service learning implemented in middle level: A study of opportunity-to-learn conditions and practices.* Paper presented at the annual meeting of the American Education Research Association, New Orleans, LA. (ERIC Document Reproduction Service No. ED441741)

Shaftel, F., & Shaftel, G. (1967). *Role-playing for social values: Decision-making in the social studies.* Englewood Cliffs, NJ: Prentice Hall.

Sharan, S., & Sharan, Y. (1992). *Expanding cooperative learning through group investigation.* New York: Teachers College Press.

Shore, R. (1995). How one high school improved school climate. *Educational Leadership, 52*(5), 76-78.

Shortt, T. L., & Thayer, Y. V. (1998-1999). Block scheduling can enhance school climate. *Educational Leadership, 56*(4), 76-81.

Siefert, E. H., & Beck, J. J. (1994). Relationships between task time and learning giants in secondary schools. *Journal of Educational Research, 7,* 5-10.

Sigmon, C. (2001). Modifying four-blocks at the upper grades. Charleston, WV: Carson: Dellosa

Silver, H. F., Strong, R. W., & Hanson, J. R. (1988). *Teaching strategies library.* Alexandria, VA: Association for Supervision and Curriculum Development.

Sizer, T. R. (1984). *Horace's compromise: The dilemma of the American high school.* Boston: Houghton Mifflin.

Skrobarcek, S. A., Chang, H. M., Thompson, C., Johnson, J., Atteberry, R., Westbrook, R., & Manus, A. (1997, May). Collaboration for instructional improvement: Analyzing the academic impact of a block scheduling plan. *NASSP Bulletin, 81,* 104-111.

Slavin, R. E. (1983). *Cooperative learning.* New York: Longman.

Slavin, R. E. (1987). *Cooperative learning: Student teams.* Washington, DC: National Education Association, NEA Professional Library.

Slavin, R. E. (1995). *Cooperative learning: Theory, research, and practice* (2nd ed.). Boston: Allyn & Bacon.

Slavin, R. E. (1996). Cooperative learning in middle and secondary schools. *Clearing House, 69*(4), 200-204.

Slavin, R. E., Sharan, S., Kagan, S., Hertz-Lazarowitz, R., Webb, C., & Schmuck, R. (Eds.). (1985). *Learning to cooperate: Cooperating to learn.* New York: Plenum.

Stahl, R. J. (1994). The essential elements of cooperative learning in the classroom. *ERIC Digest* (ERIC Identifier ED370881). Retrieved May 1, 2002, from www.ed.gov/databases/ERIC_Digests/ed370881.html

Stratemeyer, F. (1947). *Developing curriculum for modern living.* New York: Columbia University Press.

Suchman, J. R. (1962). *Elementary school programs in scientific inquiry for gifted students* (Cooperative Research Project No. D-076). Urbana-Champaign: University of Illinois, Research Board of the University of Illinois.

Sudzina, M. R. (1993, February). *Dealing with diversity issues in the classroom: A case study approach.* Paper presented at the annual meeting of the Association of Teacher Educators, Los Angeles. (ERIC Document Reproduction Service No. ED354233)

Svinicki, M. (1998). A theoretical foundation for discovery learning. *Advances in Physiology Education, 20,* 4-7.

Thiagarajan, S., & Stolovitch, H. D. (1978). *Instructional simulation games.* Englewood Cliffs, NJ: Educational Technology Publications.

Tombari, M. L., & Borich, G. D. (1999). *Authentic assessment in the classroom: Applications and practice.* Upper Saddle River, NJ: Merrill.

Trump, J. L. (1959). *Images of the future.* Urbana, IL: National Association of Secondary Principals.

Tyler, R., Gagne, R., & Scriven, M. (1967). *Perspectives of curriculum evaluation.* Chicago: Rand McNally.

U.S. Department of Education. (1983). *A nation at-risk: The imperatives of educational reform*. National Commission on Excellence in Education. Washington, DC: Government Printing Office.

Van Ments, M. (1999). *The effective use of role-play: Practical techniques for improving learning*. London: Kogan Page.

Viadero, D. (1995). Against all odds. *Teacher Magazine, 6*(8) 20-22.

Weddington, D. (1973). *Needs assessment for continuous curriculum revision* (Report No. JC780486). North Carolina. (ERIC Document Reproduction Service No. ED158826)

Weil, M., & Joyce, B. (1978). *Information processing models of teaching: Expanding your teaching repertoire*. Englewood Cliffs, NJ: Prentice Hall.

Weil, M., Joyce, B., & Kluwin, B. (1978). *Personal models of teaching*. Englewood Cliffs, NJ: Prentice Hall.

Wiggins, G. (1993). Assessment: Authenticity, context, and validity. *Phi Delta Kappan, 75*(3), 200-208, 210-214.

Wilson, C. (1995, May). The 4x4 block system: A workable alternative. *NASSP Bulletin, 79*, 63-65.

Woodham-Smith, P. (1969). The origin of kindergarten. In E. M. Lawrence (Ed.), *Froebel and English education: Perspectives on the founder of kindergarten* (pp. 15-33). New York: Schocken.

Woods, G. S. (1998). *A study of self-concept as it relates to academic achievement and gender in third grade students*. Unpublished doctoral dissertation, Rowan University, Glassboro, NJ.

Zais, R. S. (1976). *Curriculum: Principles and foundations*. New York: Crowell.

Internet Resources

American Federation of Teachers: www.aft.org

Association for Supervision and Curriculum Development: www.ascd.org

Education Week on the Web: www.edweek.org

Educational Resources Information Center (ERIC): www.eric.ed.gov

Eisenhower National Clearinghouse: www.enc.org

International Society for Technology in Education: www.iste.org

Latest Middle Schools News and Views: www.middleweb.com

Middle School Teachers: www.westnet.com/~rickd/Teachers.html

National Association of Elementary School Principals: www.naesp.org

National Association of Secondary School Principals: www.nassp.org

North Carolina Department of Public Instruction: www.ncpublicschools.org

Ohio Middle School Association: www.ashland.edu/~omsa

Phi Delta Kappan International: www.pdkintl.org

Regional Technology in Education Consortium (RTEC): http://rtec.org

Search for education sites at http://Searchedu.com

U.S. Department of Education: www.ed.gov

Violence Among Middle and High School Students:
     www.ncjrs.org/txtfiles/166363.txt

Index